HOPE WITH GOD

And

A MOTHER'S LOVE

TJ Olander

HOPE WITH GOD

And

A MOTHER'S LOVE

Fiction Based on Actual Events

TJ Olander

BookLocker
Saint Petersburg, Florida

Copyright © 2020 TJ Olander

ISBN: 978-1-64718-714-9

All rights reserved. No part of this book may be reproduced or transmitted in any form or by any means, electronic or mechanical, including photocopying, recording, or by any information storage and retrieval systems, without permission in writing from the author, except for the inclusion of brief quotations in a review.

Published by BookLocker.com, Inc., St. Petersburg, Florida.

Printed on acid-free paper.

This is a work of fiction based on actual events. Places, names, characters, incidents, and dates are either products of the author's imagination or used in a fictitious manner. Any resemblance to actual events, locations, or persons, living or dead, is purely coincidental and not intended by the author. Though largely based on numerous journal entries, the author has taken artistic liberties for the sake of the narrative.

All scripture quotations, unless otherwise specified, are taken from the Holy Bible, New Living Translation, copyright @ 1996, 2004, 2015 by Tyndale House Foundation. Used by permission of Tyndale House Publishers, Inc., Carol Stream, Illinois 60188. All rights reserved.

BookLocker.com, Inc.
2020

First Edition

TJOLANDER.COM

To My Three Children:

May this book help you understand the reason for my overabundance
of protection as you were growing.
My intense love for each of you will never be extinguished.
Together, we have overcome many obstacles.
Always remember, you will not drown; you will not be burnt!
I am so proud of each of you.

A Special Thanks

Karen, thank you for your personal encouragement
throughout the writing of this book.
To my sister and brother-in-law, a special thank you for your honest
feedback and suggestions.
Sally, thank you for being my mentor along the way.
To my children, thank you for standing with me throughout this journey.
To my loving mother and father, thank you for all your
love and support throughout my life.

I could not have completed this without the
dedicated love and support from everyone.

Table of Contents

PROLOGUE 11
1. Naive 13
2. Deceived 24
3. Independence 64
4. The Test 80
5. Healing 102
6. Legal Entanglements 129
7. The Eye Of The Storm 157
8. The Nightmare 172
9. The Journey 193
10. Labyrinth 214
11. Breakthrough 237
12. 11:59 271
13. Complications 303
14. 11:59:59 312
EPILOGUE 322
ENDNOTES 331

PROLOGUE

My friends, if you think about it long enough, each of you have a story to tell. I silently held onto mine for 40 years. The painful memories presented in these pages were buried deep within the recesses of my mind. I was not sure I ever wanted them revealed. They could have easily been erased and no one would ever know, but God had a different idea.

A family member would occasionally suggest I write a book, but I would always brush off the suggestion. After helping my daughter with a class assignment, God started nudging me; the time had come. I found it impossible to purge the idea from my thoughts. Even though under God's guidance to proceed, I was hesitant. I knew, with the writing of this book, I would have to unbury emotions that were entwined within my soul from a dark period in my life. It was hard enough going through this the first time, let alone reliving it. But now, I had a much stronger relationship with my Heavenly Father to carry me through these difficult memories. I often wept as I wrote. One of my biggest discoveries during this process was that I needed to forgive myself from the guilt and shame I felt because of my perceived failure during this time in my life.

While the children were gone, I prayed, I cried, I begged, I pleaded. Yet, I persevered. "Weeping may last through the night, but joy comes in the morning." (Psalms 30:5) As I traveled through this nightmare, it seemed as though the night would never end, and morning was out of my grasp. Just like gold is refined and tested by heating and skimming off the worthless metals, I found myself in the fire on more than one occasion. Each time God was making me stronger by exposing my weaknesses and strengthening my faith. I knew only God could help me through this dark season by walking beside me. If I had been walking by sight, I would have given up my search for my children, but I was walking by faith. "For we walk by faith, not by sight." (2 Corinthians 5:7) Through times of doubt, God always pulled me back under His trusting wing. My hope remained with God.

My children had no idea what transpired. All they knew was their father took them when they were incredibly young, and it took a great deal of effort to locate them. They did not fully comprehend the gravity of the situation until reading this book. Now, as parents themselves, my children can easily understand the tenacity of a mother's love, how and why I fought with such perseverance.

This story is a message of hope. We must put all our faith in God and believe in Him for the answer. "You [Satan] intended to harm me, but God intended it all for good." (Genesis 50:20) God used my trial for my good and His glory. Hopefully, He will instill within you the same message of hope. Walk with me as I take you through my doubts and fears, sharing with you my testimony of hope with God and a mother's love and endurance.

1. Naive

~ A noun referring to the kind of inexperience that allows you to be tricked ~

My children, ages five and three, had been away two weeks for an out of state visit with their father. Those two weeks, without seeing smiling faces and hearing lighthearted giggles crept along excruciatingly slow, like pouring crystallized honey from a jar. Easter Sunday, 1982, was the day they were to return home. Tom and I arrived at the airport early to meet the children. With great anticipation we were sitting at the arrival gate when the incoming flight was announced. My heart was racing, and I jumped to my feet as the passengers disembarked. I craned my neck to get a glimpse of the next person to show their face in the doorway. Finally, I saw the flight attendant appear from the jetway. Not seeing additional passengers behind her, I approached her and asked, "By any chance are there two small children yet on board?"

"No, everyone is off. I was the last person to leave the plane," she replied.

Collapsing into Tom's arms, amid deep sobs, all I could say was, "Please, tell me it isn't so! Please, tell me it isn't so!"

The flight attendant saw my distress but all she could say was, "I'm sorry. I'm so deeply sorry."

For the next several months the same question kept running through my mind. "How did I get myself into this predicament?"

Inexperience was my middle name. Being deceived was my consequence.

I grew up in the 60's, when not every little girl was a Disney Princess and not everyone was awarded a trophy. My life was overly simple. I was raised on a small family farm in Nebraska, so our lifestyle was supposedly easy, but the work was hard. With an eighth-grade education, my dad was the sole breadwinner. We lived on a small farm, just outside a modest rural community. Dad farmed with two row equipment: plow, planter, disk, and corn picker. It was monotonous work, taking forever. However, he was always unyielding in accomplishing the repetition of going back and forth and back and forth in his fields.

Mom graduated from high school and upon graduation attended a business school in Omaha. This was her first experience being outside our small rural community. When Dad heard another man was interested in her, he made a quick trip to Omaha to persuade her to return home and marry him. The rest is history. Mom ruled over the hearth and home. With solid determination Mom was forced to live within a very tight budget. There simply was not enough money to go around. Times were tough. Cooking for a farmer, our meals were always delicious, large, and timely. We had one cow that supplied all the milk we could possibly drink. All the food Mom prepared was made from scratch. Mom learned to sew when she was in high school, so she was an excellent seamstress. All our clothes were homemade except our jeans and underwear. My older sister and I were always thrilled to wear a new dress at Christmas and Easter while our younger brother would sport a new shirt. We would boast of a new pair of shoes once a year, just before school started. You had to hope your feet did not grow exceptionally fast. Sometimes I would get my sister's hand-me-downs, not that I counted that as fair but being the middle child, it happened. Dad and Mom sheltered us from realizing how poor we were. We were happy children in our sheltered environment.

The summers were the best. Farmyards were open to unsupervised all-day play and exploration. One could lay in the lush green grass for hours watching the lily-white clouds dance across the sky and hear the wind whisper through the trees. It was so peaceful, the singing of the birds and sounds of the insects stirred your senses. We would stay outside all day, but a meal was never to be missed. When Mom called "Dinner's ready!" you would drop everything and run for the house. There was no air conditioning. Cars did not have seatbelts. Mom saved

Green Stamps. Dishes came in boxes of laundry detergent. Blue jeans were only worn by farmers. We watched *Leave It to Beaver*, *My Three Sons*, *Father Knows Best*, *Make Room for Daddy*, *I Love Lucy*, and *Ozzy and Harriette* on our small black and white tv with rabbit ears flying aluminum foil flags! These programs always portrayed happy families where the mother was in the kitchen and the father was always home at night.

Dad ruled. Mom was submissive. His decisions always stood. When Dad made up his mind to make a large purchase, such as a new piece of farm equipment or a new car, Mom would turn her back to us so we would not see her tears. She was trying to feed and clothe us with extremely limited means. The pressure she felt must have been enormous and exhausting.

Neither Dad nor Mom were fighters. My folks never argued, at least not within earshot of us kids. They were genuine, hard-working people trying to get ahead, or in our case, not to fall too far behind. Dad was non-confrontational to the bone. If he had a disagreement with someone, he would remain extremely quiet for days as he worked his way through the situation. He would never confront an issue head on. Mom never said anything bad about anyone. Meek is the only word to describe her. The most confrontational of us three kids was my older sister. She tended to push boundaries and argue her case. I took after my mom: meek, do not make waves, obey the rules, never question, just do as you are told. A rule was a rule and it was not to be tested. My younger brother was quiet until he turned sixteen. From then until graduation it was a rocky road for my parents. But, again, my Dad never confronted my brother regarding his behavior. Dad and Mom just prayed for his safety and that everything would eventually turn out for the best.

Back in the 60's flying was a luxury. Anyone who flew dressed up in their best Sunday clothes. The flight stewardesses, as they were called back then, were all beauties and they treated you like royalty. Only the very wealthy could afford to fly. At least, that was how we saw it. Seeing a plane on tv would elicit a daydream of becoming a stewardess someday, but never thought of it as a possibility to be achieved. The very thought of driving 20 miles to a neighboring city was inconceivable. A weekly trip was made into town to purchase the necessary groceries for our meals. Expert planning had to be a maternal instinct. If you ran out of an ingredient you could try to borrow from a neighbor, or you did without.

Unconcerned about safety, we walked to our friends' houses unaccompanied. We drank from a garden hose or a cup hanging from the well pump, played outside until well after dark, and made up games with sticks and balls. In the country your telephone was on a party line, meaning you shared a phone line with your nearest neighbors, thus limiting how long you could talk or even when you could talk. Every call outside your little area was long distance and would cost you much more. Therefore, long distance calls were never made. We were always surrounded by family or extended family, thus limiting conversational topics. This could be good or bad. Exposure to outside events, thoughts, and ideas was restricted because the sphere of our existence was small.

Through the sixth grade I attended a one room schoolhouse, located a quarter mile up the hill from our home. Everyone was expected to walk or ride your bike to school. There we were taught the three R's: Reading, Writing, and Arithmetic. During the 50's Nebraska experienced a teacher shortage. Those teachers lucky enough to have a bachelor's degree taught in the city. A bachelor's degree was not a requirement to teach in the country. Here, the only requirement was completing high school refresher courses and a willingness to teach kindergarten through sixth grade to around 20 total students. When it was time for each class to be taught, those students in that grade would gather around the teacher's desk. The rest of us sat quietly and worked on assignments or read.

Our daily drinking water came straight from a well and was ladled from a bucket that was filled each morning. Everyone drank from the same metal cup. The only access to the water was a dingy grey and rust covered, cast iron water pump located outside. The water was pumped by hand, usually by one of the older kids. During the winter it was not unusual for the pump to be encased in a blanket of ice or buried under a snowbank. Down the hill was the two-hole outhouse. You hoped you did not have to go there often, especially in the winter.

When the weather was nice, we would play softball after lunch and during recess. Everyone attending school got to play. It took all of us to make two teams.

I was the only person in my grade level, so my class time would get bypassed whenever the teacher ran behind schedule. Most of my work was completed independently. Though I had no competition I always tried my hardest, never giving up. Reading, to me, was never enjoyable so I tried to avoid it as much as possible. By the fifth grade I was a chunky tomboy with thick glasses. Talk about an awkward period. I did not care because I did not know any better. I was very sheltered. But I knew I was loved, and we had food on the table, which was all that mattered.

Church was a priority with my parents. Dad had been raised Baptist, so that was what the family became. The little country church, located just a quarter mile up the hill from our house, allowed us to stay right within the confines of our little community. Outside influences were extremely limited. Every Sunday the entire family attended Sunday school followed by the church service. Sunday night, as well as Wednesday night, was a time for the youth to be together. For the longest time, the kids attending this little country church were my only friends, as I spent the most time with them. Age did not matter. We played and mingled together.

Having a meek personality, I usually went along with any program handed to me. Early in the seventh grade going to Sunday school was anything but enjoyable. In fact, I would try everything to get out of going, but that was to no avail. I remember not being very cooperative with the Sunday school teacher, but one Sunday I gave her more grief than usual. Much to my surprise, who shows up at our door the following Monday, yep, the Sunday school teacher. Hoping not to be seen I ran to the back porch. It was not long before I heard my mother calling for me. Knowing I had to face the consequences, I sheepishly entered the kitchen and was told to sit down. Mom asked it if was true regarding my behavior. Hanging my head, I admitted it was. After an apology and a promise that it would not happen again, I was set free. This was about the only rebellious incident I can remember. If there were rules, I obeyed them. That was just who I was.

Upon entering seventh grade I got to ride the school bus into town. I was so excited to finally be around kids my own age. The first time I walked into the school I was overwhelmed with shock. My country school had 20 kids in seven grade levels. My seventh-grade class alone had over 200 students and this building contained both junior and senior high school grades. Kids were everywhere. They swarmed throughout the corridors like bees, yelling at friends in passing, laughing, teasing, pushing as they went. Each subject was in a different room. Each class had a different teacher. I had no friends. I felt like a lost soul, so small, so insignificant. I suffered nightmares about getting lost and being tardy to class. Pretending to be sick I would ask to go to the nurse's office, especially during Literature (another term for Reading). I was simply scared to death and overwhelmed. The classwork was hard, the assignments long, but I kept pushing forward. I was totally unprepared for this transition. The depth of the class material was like jumping ahead two grade levels. In hindsight, I wished my elementary teacher had made reading a priority. Since I was a slow reader, keeping up was a struggle.

To make matters worse, the school had a dress code. Girls were expected to wear dresses or skirts, even in the winter. Up to this point, the only time I wore a dress was to church. Now, I suffered the innuendos of being labeled a country girl. I felt my homemade clothes made me obtrusive. Monday mornings were filled with the girls showing off their new purchases from the weekend. "Did you get anything new?" they would ask. How could I reply to that? Was it a dig or a genuine question? I would just shake my head. I was just lucky enough to have a different outfit for each day of the week. Even my shoes were different from everyone else. All the girls had multiple pairs of shoes to match appropriate outfits. The ones I wore were my Sunday shoes, my best. My only other pair of shoes were old, tight, dirty shoes that could only be worn on the farm. Close friends were difficult for me to acquire during those first few years. Unless we shared several classes together, everyone was a passerby, going here, going there, but never stopping to visit. Since the only way home was the bus, I was not allowed to participate in after school activities.

Besides, there was always work that needed tending to when I got home.

I was baptized as a young teenager, but in our country church it was perceived more as a rite of passage for teenagers at a certain age rather than a life changing experience. In fact, I remember the preacher coming to our home one evening asking to talk with my parents. The pastor, along with my parents, went to the kitchen and sat around the table. Us three kids continued watching tv. Suddenly, I heard my dad.

"Mary, come out here please."

That was not a good sign! My mind raced trying to recall if I had been rude to my Sunday school teacher again. I wanted to run and hide but knew I was caught. I lumbered to the kitchen not knowing what my punishment would be.

"Sit down," my dad said as he pulled out a chair.

Oh, I knew there was no hope for me.

My dad started, "The pastor wants to talk with you."

My heart was racing with anxiety.

"Don't you think it's about time?" the pastor asked.

In my naivety I asked, "For what?"

"It's time for you to accept the Lord," he said very matter-of-factly.

"Okay," I said and that was it.

The pastor said a quick prayer and I was excused. "Whew, that was easy," I was relieved.

The semi-annual baptism was scheduled at the Baptist church in town in a couple weeks. I must have been the last holdout. Being oblivious to the true intent of the ceremony, I was baptized with my peers. At the time, it did not mean a thing, and did not for a long time. To me, church was a parent pleasing obligation. We did not have a choice. I really did not know what a personal relationship with God was supposed to feel like. We said a repetitive prayer at our evening meal but that was the depth of my religion.

Sitting Sunday after Sunday in church I would try to listen to the boring sermons, but my mind would always wonder. I would look over at my dad and he would be sleeping so I did not feel bad not paying attention. It seemed to me that the Baptist religion was a long set of thou shalt not rules. Thou shalt not dance. Thou shalt not wear makeup. Thou shalt not play cards. Thou shalt not ... everything, it seemed. It made one wonder if you were ever supposed to have fun. When it came to boys there was another long list of thou shalt nots. If, or when, I did anything against the rules I would usually get caught. Even when I thought about doing something, my personality convicted me immediately. I guess the thou shalt nots were deeply imbedded into my soul.

By the time I was in upper junior high I knew the ropes much better and melded with several friends. There were the traditional slumber parties, but the highlight of every week was the Friday night dance at the YMCA. After an early dinner, my folks would drive us into town where they would purchase their weekly groceries. Us kids headed for the "Y." The junior high kids were sequestered to the basement where the girls and boys stood on opposite sides of the room. The high school kids were upstairs, where their activity could be closely monitored. By 10:00 p.m. the dance was over, and I would find my parents patiently waiting for me outside the "Y" door so we could head straight home.

Intellectually I was average but I focused all my energy on good grades so I could be on the honor roll. Dating was non-existent for a couple reasons. Our farm was located eight miles from town. Parents discouraged their sons from making that trip twice an evening just for a movie or to share a pizza. There were no pizza shops in town, but there was a bar where kids could order a pizza, pick it up at the window in the back alley, and find a place to eat; which was usually in the car. Another reason I did not date was because when I started high school, I developed a weight issue. That was not conducive to attracting boys. All my friends had dates to the Junior Senior Prom in the spring of my junior year, but not me. I felt excluded from a particularly important event. That was an incredibly low point for me. Low self-esteem meandered throughout my brain. Socially I felt inept since dating had been infrequent at best. During the summer following my junior year, after this heartbreaking event, I decided if I ever wanted to fit in, dieting was my only option. Today one would call it an eating disorder. I simply quit eating until I got my weight within a manageable range. When I returned to school, it was much more enjoyable as everyone noticed a big difference. I received many compliments from my peers and I finally felt good about myself. Having friends and dates made me feel like I belonged, finally. It took until my senior year but, at last, I was having fun.

After seeing how hard my parents worked and scrimped to save every dime, as well as knowing my mom was stuck on the farm because she had no employable job skills, made me pursue the thought of a college education. My intent was to never live the same dependent life as my mother, without options. She was fortunate because Dad was a good man and he was good to her. If she had married someone that abused her, she would be stuck in that relationship because she would never be able to support herself and her children. I never wanted to be in that situation.

Craving an occupation where I would be able to care for myself, I started talking about college with my mom. That was the best way to ease into the topic with my father. With my high school counselor's assistance, I registered for only college curriculum classes. I knew convincing my dad would be an uphill battle. Since my father only had an eighth-grade education, anything beyond high school, to him, was not necessary. After all, he was doing okay. In his opinion, he did not believe it beneficial for any girl to attend college. "Girls are supposed to be secretaries, get married, and raise a family." End of discussion. That was not my aspiration. My sister had encountered this same argument. She complied, but she was also in a serious relationship throughout her senior year. Surprisingly, I stood up and challenged Dad's belief about an education. It probably helped that I had not dated anyone seriously, so Dad knew I would not be getting married anytime soon. We compromised a little; I took a typing class along with the college prep curriculum.

My first love was to be an architect, but that required five years of college. I made an appointment with the head of the architectural college at the neighboring university in Lincoln. Very emphatically I was told, "You would be our first female student and I can guarantee you failure as we would make it very difficult on you." That was all it took. I lacked the fortitude to fight that battle along with my father. I tucked my tail between my legs and headed home. But my pursuit for an education was relentless. My dad finally gave his blessing for an education if it was for a teacher or a nurse, but nothing more. Under those circumstances, I guess I was going to be a teacher. I wrote my essay and filled out the application to the University of Nebraska at Kearney. It was not long before I received my acceptance letter.

Now the hard part started. My folks were unable to provide any financial assistance, so I had to do whatever it took to make this work. I received scholarships, financial aid, and found a job where I worked every weekend. Between studying and work there was no time for dating. In a way I felt like I should not date. What would happen if I fell in love with someone before I graduated? My dad would say he was right about girls wasting their time and money getting an education. I had to prove him wrong. I could not fail. I had to succeed. In doing so, I denied myself the fun and friendships that were always within reach at the university because I was too busy working.

Late in my junior year I discovered a field I dearly loved: computers. That was before universities offered computer science degrees. Back then you were sent to IBM technical schools to learn a coding language and the rest was on the job training. Now I had a dilemma. To change from a teaching curriculum to a business curriculum would require an extra year of school. To put five years into my education, I could have pursued the architectural degree I desired. I knew, deep in my heart, I did not have a passion for teaching. Since computer technical training came once you were on the job, I decided to finish my teaching degree and take the rest of my electives in business. At least I would have a degree.

The clock was ticking. The final semester of my senior year I knew I needed to find a computer specialist job. If not, I would be faced signing a teaching contract for the next school year. During spring break, I embarked on my search. Bright and early Monday morning I dressed up, headed to Omaha, and spent the day filling out application forms. By mid-week I had received a few phone calls asking me to return to take an aptitude test. That was their only way to determine one's problem solving skills and logic abilities. Before the end of the week, I had secured a job with a large direct mail company for $750 a month! I was speechless being offered that amount of money. They told me no one had ever achieved such a high score on their test before and were eager for me to start work. My folks were proud of me. Dad had never made that amount of money in any given year. And as he said so often, "You're just a kid." What an accomplishment! What a relief! For the first time in my life I had confidence, I was ecstatic, and I was eager to get started. I knew this was the profession for me. I felt like my life was about to take shape.

2. Deceived

~ A verb referring to an action by a person causing another to believe something that is not true to gain some personal advantage ~

My job with the direct mail company was enjoyable. Even though the training was like drinking from a fire hose, I enjoyed every aspect of learning the business as well as the specialist skill set. Everyone was so helpful getting me settled in and making me feel comfortable. We were all about the same age. That is what made it fun as we teased each other throughout the day but worked hard. On Friday night we would walk across the street to the bar for drinks. We shared a lot of camaraderie within our department. After a few months, as I was walking to my desk, I heard one of the guys say,

"You know, two people working at this job could bring home a lot of money!"

I blew it off and did not think any more of it.

On several different occasions this same specialist, Donnie, asked me out, but I continued to decline all offers. At work I found him to be obnoxious: making disparaging remarks about other people, acting like he was superior to everyone else, and bragging about his accomplishments in all areas of his life. My friends finally convinced me I had nothing to lose.

By the end of August, I finally gave in and accepted an invitation for dinner. We went to a nice restaurant and I had a good time in an engaging conversation. Donnie did most of the talking but I found him to be much different away from the office, away from an audience. Our second date was close to my birthday, so when he arrived bearing roses and a box of candy, I was flabbergasted and thoroughly blown away. "This only happens in the movies," I thought. From this point forward, it was a fast courtship and I was very much in love. Much to my parents' disapproval, we were engaged by November and set the wedding for the spring of 1972.

Donnie was an only child. His parents waited nine years to have him and were both in their mid-30's at the time of his birth. Donnie was the apple of their eyes and his father could see no wrong in anything Donnie did. Both his mother and father were hard working, middle class individuals. Arlene was a stay-at-home mom and cared for the house, inside and out. As with most women during this time, Arlene was very dependent on her husband. For some unknown reason she had not learned to drive. His father made a decent wage as a plumber but died unexpectedly before Donnie graduated from high school. After his passing Arlene discovered he had no life insurance and left her with a heavy debt load. Living on their acreage soon became too difficult for Arlene to maintain.

Following Donnie's high school graduation, Arlene was forced to sell the acreage, move into town, and find employment. Widowhood was hard on Arlene, so Donnie continued living with his mother following the move. After moving into town Donnie acquired a job with a direct mail company as a machine operator. It was there he helped his mom obtain a job as a filing clerk. Since they worked for the same company, he was able to provide her transportation to her job. After a few years working as a digital machine operator, Donnie showed an interest in the specialist area. After taking an aptitude test they determined he had the logic skills required for the job, so he was promoted and trained.

Donnie's family did not belong to a traditional denominational church, but were part of a small religious sect that occasionally met in each other's homes. Francis was the shepherd of this little group, and they all looked up to him for spiritual advice. He and his wife, Cora, later moved to Texas. After the passing of Donnie's father, Francis ministered to Arlene, providing a spiritual sounding board, offering advice, and being a father figure to Donnie. I met most of the people in this religious group but did not understand what it was all about. It did not appear to me there was ever any religious teaching being performed, at least not at the point of my introduction. Anyone experiencing a problem called Francis for spiritual advice and prayer.

Throughout the planning of the wedding, I started questioning myself. I noticed character traits about Donnie that seemed unusual.

On several occasions Donnie's lack of respect for his mother became extremely uncomfortable. He refused to help with any of the household tasks, including mowing the lawn. He would become angry if a drop of mustard dripped to the outside of a sandwich that she had prepared for him. He would throw a fit if she had not ironed his favorite shirt that he thought he had to wear. Again, being so naive I thought, "There is no way he'll ever treat me that way. Right?" I should have seen the writing on the wall. But once again, I am not a quitter. After deciding, I followed it through to completion. My folks had put nonrefundable deposits down for the church, my dress, invitations, and flowers. The snowball was rolling downhill gathering momentum and increasing in size by the day. It seemed as if stopping this train was literally impossible.

The trickery started shortly after the marriage ceremony. Our honeymoon destination was Las Vegas. To catch the plane, Donnie cut the wedding reception short, causing more disappointment for my family.

He ordered, "You have to change your clothes now! We have to go!"

"Really? I haven't talked with most of the guests."

"It doesn't matter. They are not important. We are leaving, so hurry!"

Donnie was so eager to leave the church and be on our way, he could hardly tell my folks thank you or tell anyone goodbye. It was just rude and bizarre. I tried to put a positive spin on his behavior. "How charming," I thought, "he wants to be alone with his bride!" Donnie had changed into a suit, and I into a dress adorned with a lovely corsage. After we got onto the plane and into the air, we attracted a lot of attention once the stewardesses discovered we had just been married. Donnie flirted with all the attendants and received free drinks and food the entire trip. He was on cloud nine with all the recognition.

Upon our arrival into Las Vegas, we grabbed a cab and headed to our hotel. We checked into the room, the bellhop set our bags down, and Donnie tipped him. The door shut. My anticipation was mounting! Donnie spun on his heel with eyebrows furrowed, pointed his finger into my face, and ordered, "Take off that damn corsage. I don't want anyone to know we just got married." Then he proceeded to proclaim, "I'm going downstairs to gamble. You may choose to follow me if you want, but don't get too close."

I stood in shock, speechless. My mouth dropped open. What happened to the man I just married a few hours ago? He had never spoken to me in that tone before. But I had heard him speak to his mother with that demeaning, harsh tone. I wanted to take my bags and catch the first flight back to Nebraska, but I could not. Tears filled my eyes, but I knew better than to let him see me cry, as that would just make the situation worse. So, what was an obedient wife to do? I took off the corsage and followed him all night. In the back of my mind I knew I had just made the biggest mistake of my life, but it was too late.

Our Vegas honeymoon lasted six days. It became obvious, our expectations of the vacation were on opposite ends of the spectrum. I had anticipated lounging by the pool all day, enjoying the warm weather, and taking in a show after dinner. Donnie's intention was to sleep all day and cram as many activities as possible into the evening. Since this is a city without clocks, it was easy to stay up until daybreak. Therefore, our evenings started with a free show and dinner, followed by one of the larger shows we had made reservations to see. He would volunteer to get on stage every chance presented to him, flirt with all the waitresses, lust over attractive women, drink, and gamble until the sun came up. He had no interest in me or intimacy. In my naivety I thought that was what couples did on their honeymoon. Whenever I tried to initiate sex, I got shut down. He was perpetually too tired. Having nothing as a comparison I had to accept this as normal.

Donnie volunteered to be in charge of our finances and that was fine with me until I discovered the rules associated with his bookkeeping. Every two weeks I would hand him my paycheck. He, in turn, would give me $2.00. This "allowance" was to last two weeks, until the next paycheck. In his eyes this generous amount was sufficient to purchase a ten-cent cup of coffee twice a day during my breaks. This just did not add up. I earned $345 every two weeks, yet I was given $2 in return. My name was on the checking account, but I had no checks and no credit card. I had no access to money. If I needed something, I had to ask Donnie's permission. Heaven forbid I walk into the nearest bank branch, provide my identification, and ask for cash. It was not worth incurring his wrath. I did not have it within me to confront him, for that was not my nature. Between my upbringing and my meek personality, I did not know how to fight or stand up for my beliefs. I was his wife and I was expected to just do as I was told.

It was not long after this that Donnie lost all interest in intimacy. It had been a month since we had sex. My goodness, we were still newlyweds! My advances were squelched due to a tv sporting event or exhaustion. Rejection flowed throughout my entire being. He made me feel ugly and repulsive. I vowed to never approach him again. That was the only way to protect my broken heart.

When I started working, I owned a car, but once we were married Donnie found it an annoyance having an extra vehicle in the parking lot, so he sold it. That left us with one car, his, which I was not allowed to drive. Since we worked for the same company, getting back and forth to work was not an issue. Occasionally I would get called back into work after hours to fix a problem. Rather than let me drive into work, he would take me in, return home, and wait for my call when I was finished, no matter what time of the night. Every errand we ran, we ran together. Every item I put into the grocery cart was monitored. All purchases had to be justified.

On the rare occasion that we would be around other couples I became his personal source of jokes, a human punching bag. His favorite past-time was making fun of me. It was obvious he had no respect for me as a person. I was only a financial resource, a maid, and his personal prostitute when he became interested.

Some of my college friends were in town so I invited them to our apartment for the evening. It had been quite some time since we had seen each other, so I was extremely eager to catch up. From the moment they arrived, Donnie controlled the show. He did not even know these women but that did not stop him. He talked nonstop. He belittled me and my family so horribly my friends became uncomfortable and excused themselves early. His actions humiliated and embarrassed me to the point I never wanted to face my friends again. I felt helpless and hopeless. I had no voice. I wanted to hide under a rock. His control was seeping deep into my soul and taking over my thoughts. I blamed myself for not being a good enough wife.

Everyday Donnie's noose tightened more around my throat. It became hard to breathe. His control was overwhelming. The mental anguish was incessant. Every morsel of food I ate made me nauseous. Insomnia filled the nights. Weight was no longer an issue. My clothes hung from my torso like a scarecrow. I knew that voicing an opinion would only invite his terror. If something did not change, I perceived a nervous breakdown was imminent. There was not even a battle to pick anymore. I had lost them all. Here I was a college graduate, successful at my job, but Donnie had me mentally and emotionally beaten to a pulp (today this is termed domestic violence). Somehow, I needed to sort this out.

Because of my upbringing, divorce was not an option. There had never been a divorce in our family and I really did not relish the thought of being first. Besides, I am not a quitter. My nature is to dig deeper and keep going. The decision to marry Donnie was mine and mine alone, so it was up to me to make the marriage work. In my simplistic mind total submission was the only answer. No friends, no writing letters, no talking on the phone. Do exactly as you are told. Try to keep your husband happy. Personal compliments and praise would have to come from my job for nothing could be expected from Donnie. He did not view me as an equal. I was his rug.

The motivating factor for getting a college degree in the first place was so I would never feel stuck in a relationship. Well, here I was in the same position as my mother, only worse. My father loved my mother. He looked upon her with great admiration. He would never dream of abusing her in any way. I was shunned by Donnie and looked upon with disdain. Mental and emotional abuse occurred daily. Desperation set in.

With my health at risk, I was forced to dig deep. Without any friends, I was unable to share my burden with anyone. Donnie had me backed into a corner: fight or die. Since it is not in my nature to fight that really was not an option, but I did not want to die. Lying awake at night I remembered the day of my baptism and how lackadaisical I entered that covenant relationship with God. In desperation I tried to remember bible verses I had been taught. All I could remember was the Lord's Prayer and portions of the 23rd Psalm. How pathetic! What a disappointment I must be to God. I began to pray. I had ignored Him all these years. Was He going to take His turn and ignore me now? I hoped not. I laid my life before Him and begged for His forgiveness. I had no scriptures I could reference and lacked eloquent words. I laid myself at His feet, begging for His help. Little did I realize God had been waiting at the door for me all these years, but it was my responsibility to open the door, inviting Him to come into my life. I wept silently; Heaven forbid if I disturbed Donnie. I knew I had to hide my desire to have a relationship with God. Donnie would only criticize my commitment. This was just so wrong, on so many different levels. I should not have to hide my faith and belief in Jesus from my husband, but I did. My walk became a very personal, quiet dialog with God. No one knew but God and me.

It did not take long before I began to feel some peace. Just like the poem "Footprints in The Sand" when the Lord replied, "My precious, precious child, I love you and I would never leave you. During your times of trial and suffering, when you see only one set of footprints, it was then that I carried you."[i] During this time of healing I was being carried by my Lord because I lacked the strength to move forward on my own. I prayed, "Thank you, Jesus, you are my strength and source of safety. My trust is in you." Slowly my health improved. I was able to eat again. Sleep returned to me. I gained a few pounds. My confidence returned. God placed a Teflon coating around me to protect me from Donnie's insinuations. All I could say in my prayers was "Thank you, God, for hearing my cries, rescuing me, and giving me hope again."

After a year, we were able to buy our first home. Overwhelmed with excitement I could not wait to move out of the downtown apartment. Being a farm girl at heart, apartment living felt so confining. Donnie's first, and only priority once the truck was unloaded, was to set up the tv. Unpacking and setting up the house was my responsibility, and what a chore it was. Painting, making curtains, landscaping, mowing, washing the car in addition to the normal household tasks of cleaning and cooking were exhausting. Donnie was too busy watching sports to be bothered with work. If I hinted about needing help his answer was, "I work Monday through Friday." I found it easier to do it myself rather than risk incurring his wrath.

Arlene was barely making ends meet. Loneliness was weighing heavy upon her. Donnie rarely called her to chat. Neither did he volunteer to help with those extra chores required with home ownership. Expenses were increasing and she did not know where to turn. Deep down she knew her son would not help. Her friends from Texas, Francis and Cora, suggested she sell her home and move in with them. Financially she did not have a choice; reluctantly, she took them up on their offer. Once the house sold, she stripped herself of most of her household items in preparation for the move. Here was a lady living a good middle-class life and in a matter of a few years lost everything. When all was settled, she had $13,000, which she gave to Donnie with the instructions that it was to be used for her burial. In my heart I knew this was a bad idea, but Donnie was all she had left. Once she moved, we had no family or friends left in town.

Christmas, Thanksgiving, and Easter traditions on the farm were always a joyous time for the extended families to get together. All the families gathered for a fun filled, memorable occasion where aunts, uncles, and cousins met for mouthwatering food and catching up on each other's latest escapades. After we were married, Donnie refused to attend the family gatherings, which meant I was not allowed to either. "Christmas is only for immediate family," he would say. He told me time and time again, "Family isn't necessary." I could only imagine what my family thought: now that I lived in the big city was I too good for them? This was far from the truth. Since phone calls or letters were not permitted it simply appeared as though I vanished. My heart ached not being able to join them, but I had to live with Donnie, and making my home situation worse was not an option. Once again, I had to pick my battles.

As with most young females in their 20's, my biological clock was ticking. I longed to start a family. My naive mind thought a child would bring us closer. When I broached the subject Donnie said very emphatically, "No, I hate kids and don't ever want one around." He was so vehement about it; I suppressed my feelings. Another battle I could not win. Extremely dejected I stuffed my emotions and feelings into the recesses of my mind. Naturally, suppressing emotions that deep, causes something else to give. Just like trying to stuff a balloon. Poking it one way causes a bulge to come out another direction. Stuffing my emotions caused my nerves to flare up. Again, I found myself in the pressure cooker. Eating and sleeping became an issue. My weight dropped like melted butter. My life was not anything like I had imagined it to be.

Here I was again, at another fork in the road. What a bumpy, short ride it had been since the last major decision point. The marriage was only two years old. How did I really feel about this marriage? It had been so long since I thought about my feelings it was difficult unearthing them. Was I going to allow Donnie to destroy me? Constantly living under these circumstances was excruciating. I knew the Bible talked of trials, especially after giving your life over to God, but this was becoming a matter of life or death. Was this going to be my life, "Till death do us part?" At this rate it would be sooner rather than later. I knew my treatment from Donnie was not of God, for the Bible says a man is to love his wife as he loves himself. I also knew God did not approve of divorce, but since I had a good job, providing me with a good salary, it was becoming a consideration. I was facing a dilemma, so I asked God for a clear sign. This time, God was providing me with discernment and additional strength, thus enabling me to contemplate alternatives; I had peace knowing God was directing my decision.

One weekend, while visiting my parents, Mom asked if I was okay.

"No," I exclaimed, "I'm thinking of filing for divorce."

"Oh, you don't want to do that. Give it a little more time and it will work out. No marriage is easy. There are always ups and downs."

Divorce was never an option for her and Dad as it took both to survive the harsh reality of farm life. No one was aware of the daily emotional and mental abuse I faced. Since no one in our family had ever been divorced I knew Mom would dread the imminent humiliation with such a drastic decision. Was this my sign? I carefully weighed her advice and submitted my situation to God in prayer, I felt He was telling me the time was not right for a divorce. I prayed, "Thank you, God, for your answer. Now, heal my body, give me strength and courage every day, and grant me peace."

After resigning myself to the fact I would never have a baby I focused all my energy into my career. I found a new job in the insurance industry and immersed myself into learning a new business. After only two years of working I was making as much as Donnie. He always said he did not care how much money I made if I gave him my paycheck. Because of his superiority complex, I knew deep down this irritated him, but his greed of money outweighed his feelings of inferiority. Besides, he had me exactly where he wanted me, which was under his thumb.

The new job created a situation Donnie did not want to face but there was no choice. Since we no longer worked for the same company, we needed another car. With my new job, we were not even on the same side of town, so carpooling was out of the question. He found a cheap used car that he claimed was good enough for me. The car was old, but it provided me a little taste of freedom. It felt exhilarating!

Even though we both worked with people our own ages we did not have friends. Those working with Donnie did not want to socialize with him outside of work. In this profession there were very few female specialists, so I had to be incredibly careful with the relationships I formed with my peers.

Donnie came home one evening talking about a new co-worker, Larry, that had just moved from Missouri. He had asked them over for dinner. "Great," I said. Maybe this is what our marriage needed, friends to share our weekends with. Larry and Barb were a delightful couple. They did not have children either, so we would get together a couple times a month to play cards. Once we got to know them better it did not take Donnie long before he dominated every conversation and voiced his opinion about everything. Of course, it was expected they would accept his viewpoint at the end of each of his tirades.

If it was not the conversation, it was the card game. His temper flared into an emotional outburst when he did not win. Cards would be tossed into the air and scattered across the floor. It did not take many months before Larry and Barb found excuses and declined our invitations. We were never invited back to their home. Donnie destroyed the friendship. Disappointment filled me because Barb and I had become close friends, allowing me to release some emotional pressure.

After this experience we never socialized again. Because of my quiet side, I shouldered the blame for losing friends.

"You are so pathetic to be around," he jabbed. "No wonder we don't have any friends, you never say a word the entire time."

My mind was screaming, "It's because you never give me a chance to open my mouth," but I kept those thoughts to myself.

Just have me shoulder another brick upon my back. Everything was my fault, always was, and always would be.

My grandmother died and the funeral was scheduled for the weekend. All the family was coming home by the end of the week. It was particularly important for me to show my respect and be with the family. Donnie and I only lived an hour away. Donnie had no desire to go and denied me permission to make the trip home without him. He insisted we would only attend the funeral. We arrived just minutes before the service commenced and left as soon as the benediction was given. There was no opportunity to mingle with family. It had been several years since I had seen many of my cousins. It did not matter. Again, I had this feeling of having to cut off all family ties because of my husband's selfishness. A choice had to be made regarding our marriage. I prayed. Again, I stayed. I felt somehow this was all my fault, so my prayers changed asking God to make me a better wife. In hopes of making this better, I submitted even more.

Intimacy was never a priority with Donnie. After having my advances shut down so often in the past, I still refused to initiate any sexual desire. For us, having sex once a month was considerable. Not taking the chance of ever getting pregnant I tried taking birth control pills, but I experienced too many side effects. Then I was forced to use alternative birth control devices. Much to my horror, I found myself pregnant in 1975. Knowing Donnie's disgust for children I was petrified to tell him. Not being able to predict his response to the announcement I was going to maintain my distance from him just in case he threw something. Much to my surprise he calmly accepted the news. In fact, this gave him an opportunity to tout his masculinity, and he did every chance he had.

Outside of being tired, the pregnancy itself did not present many problems. As the pregnancy progressed, my anxiety increased due to Donnie's emotional and mental pressure on me. It seemed he expected more from me than before. Now that I was pregnant and showing he found the sight of me revolting and started distancing himself even further. In the last trimester, I again developed digestive issues. Subsequently, my iron count dropped. By the end of each week, just getting out of bed was an undertaking. I kept going. I had to. Throughout the entire pregnancy I only gained 9 pounds, which meant I was losing weight the entire time.

Our son, Alex, was born in 1976. I was elated with joy. Since it was a boy, Donnie seemed excited. "Now I have a little man just like me," he would say. Every time he would repeat this I would pray under my breath, "Oh dear God, I certainly hope not." I remained in the hospital several days. Each of Donnie's visits were filled with him flirting and carrying on with the nurses. Before being discharged he bought flowers for the nursing staff. I never received as much as a kind word. I was only an object.

Donnie was very much hands off when it came to taking care of Alex. In his eyes, changing a diaper was disgusting, so therefore, never done. "I have to get up in the morning so keep the kid quiet," he would say as he proceeded to bed each night. Every morning he would say, "I can't feed him now, I'll get my clothes dirty." The excuses were endless. But, have a camera ready and Donnie would immediately jump into the picture as if Alex were his best buddy and he was "Father of the Year."

During this period, cereal was offered to babies by the time they were four weeks old. Donnie wanted to be the first to feed his son. The day came when we were going to give it a try. Rather than accepting the cereal Alex started fussing, for he wanted a bottle. Donnie grew impatient. I could see the frustration growing in Donnie's face as his brow's furrowed and his eyes squinted. It was not long before the bowl of cereal was hurled into the sink. Donnie yanked Alex up from the infant seat and spanked him very hard. I could not believe what I was seeing. My heart was broken. I thought I would be sick. Fearing I would be next, I did not say a word. I snatched Alex from Donnie's arms and removed him and me from the room. From that point forward Donnie spent less and less time with Alex. Donnie was always very proud to say he spanked his kid when he was four weeks old.

I had every intention of resuming my job following my maternity leave. I enjoyed the challenge my job presented and was eager to return. The first part of June Donnie became very discouraged with his job after not getting the raise he thought he deserved. Out of the blue he declared, "I'm going to get a headhunter to find a job for me in another state. I am tired of Nebraska. There are no opportunities here!" He was serious. Omaha had plenty of opportunities but, no, he had already decided he was too good to stay in Nebraska. At the end of five weeks leave, I reluctantly wrote a letter of resignation from my position. It was not fair for me to return to my job only to have to quit once Donnie secured other employment.

It did not take long before job inquiries started rolling in. Donnie enjoyed the phone interviews and an occasional trip for an on-site interview. Finally, he was offered and accepted a job with an insurance company at Columbia, Missouri. This was a much smaller town and a much smaller company. He technically was not bettering himself, for the position and salary resulted in a lateral move. Donnie left for Missouri the end of July. We immediately put the house on the market. I stayed behind waiting for the house to sell and to ultimately get everything packed in preparation for the move.

The first couple weekends Donnie drove home to be with us. It was only a four-hour drive. After the first two weekends he did not bother to come home again.

He whined, "I'm just too tired by Friday and it's too far to drive."

"Really?" I questioned. "Having a new baby, with no help, is not tiring?" I kept those thoughts to myself.

"I have so much to learn and I'm exhausted all the time. Besides, the only time I can look for houses is on the weekend," he complained. Not knowing the Columbia housing market, I believed him.

By the end of August our home sold. Now Donnie was forced to find a place for us to live. Since there was not enough time now to purchase a house, we decided it best to rent a home until we knew more about the area. It was amazing how fast this could be accomplished when not given any room to play. Now, it was up to me to get boxes and pack up our belongings. This was not easy with a newborn, but I had no choice. At least Donnie's workplace would be moving our household goods; that was a blessing.

Donnie did not bother to come home on the weekends to help pack. His excuse was that he was just too busy. His employer did give him the week off prior to the move to finalize the paperwork. Donnie came home and the first thing he did was place an ad in the paper for my car. It was sold within the week. I hated being without transportation but until circumstances changed, I guess I could do without. We moved to Missouri the end of October with a five-month-old. Leaving my family was hard but, by this time, I hardly saw them anyway.

Donnie would go to work early and come home very late. I did not think much of it since it was a new job and I presumed he was trying to make a good impression. The week before Christmas Donnie came home in the middle of the afternoon. I heard doors being slammed as he walked into the house from the garage. In his arms he carried a box which he tossed onto the kitchen table.

"What's that?" I asked.

As he stormed past, he mumbled, "I've been fired."

I could not believe my ears. Surely it was a joke! Let me ask again.

"What did you say?"

He turned abruptly with nostrils flaring and yelled, "You heard me the first time!"

I just stood there in shock.

"Now what?" I asked.

"That's a fucking stupid question! I do not have a job. That's what! They paid me through the end of the year and told me not to come back."

"How could that be?" I questioned. "Only five months, you haven't had time to learn the company procedures."

He bellowed, "I don't know why! They did not say. Obviously, they don't like me." With that, he stormed out of the room.

Things did not add up. No one gets fired out of the blue without an incredibly good reason.

After Donnie settled down, he called Texas, asking to speak with Francis. I positioned myself so I could hear the conversation but remained out of Donnie's sight, and finally discovered the reason for his firing. He had been openly making passes at the women in the office. The name of one gal, in particular, frequently came up in his conversations at home. I figured it was a co-worker. No, it was someone in a different department. Why would he do this and jeopardize his career? This was a small, family owned company. Personnel would be aware of every complaint and rumor. From my perspective, his firing came out of left field but having worked in the corporate world, I was sure he had been given plenty of warnings. Now his reasoning for not coming home on the weekends, while I was still in Omaha, made perfect sense. He was having an affair.

Now what do we do? There was a deep cavern in our relationship before this surfaced. He had completely lost interest in any intimacy with me since the pregnancy. Then there was his reluctance to come home on the weekends. He knew I could take care of everything at home, so his focus was on himself and having fun. Just like the good old days. Was I just to accept this behavior? It still made no sense to me. Could God mend a relationship that was so badly broken to begin with? Was this Donnie's revenge of getting back at me for getting pregnant? Was he revolting because I was not bringing home money? My head was swimming trying to make sense of everything. I was sure, in some way, this would end up being my fault.

Donnie did not seem overly worried about the situation. We had money in savings after selling our home, so we would be okay for a while but emptying our savings account was not a wise plan. Not having health insurance with a baby made me nervous. Donnie filed for unemployment right away. He never went to a single job interview but filled out the paperwork religiously as though he had. In his eyes, receiving free money was great! He could sleep in late every morning. "Don't worry about it," he told me, "I'll start looking for work when the free money runs out." His superiority complex was reigning high even in the shadow of being fired.

When it came to Alex, Donnie lacked patience to begin with, but he grew more intolerant now that he was home all day. Banging on toys made Donnie irritated, especially if he could not hear the tv. In the mornings I would make sure the house remained quiet so Donnie could sleep. Alex's crying and whimpering were not tolerated. "Get him out of here," he would scream. "Do you want a spanking?" he would yell. I would immediately remove Alex from the room.

When spring arrived, Donnie spent a lot of time on walks. He would stop and carry on lengthy conversations with every neighborhood female he encountered. I tried to brush it off as him trying to be friendly, but it appeared a little too friendly in a couple situations. Was he on the prowl again? It was for sure there was no intimacy going on between us.

Occasionally, Donnie would glance at the local want ads. He always claimed there was nothing challenging enough for him. One day, as I was reading the ads, I saw an opportunity with a manufacturing company for an analyst position, so I updated my resume and sent it in. Within a few days I was called in for an interview. The interview was very strange. They did not ask me a single question regarding my experience. In fact, I hardly talked. They ended up offering me a management job for the same salary Donnie was making when he was fired. I had no management experience and having lived the past five years under Donnie's thumb, I lacked confidence to manage even myself. I prayed for guidance. "Make this noticeably clear, God. This would solve our problems right now, but I am not sure I can handle the stress of this job as well as the stress at home. I need direction. Are you laying this job before me for our benefit or is this a token female management position where I will be used? Please make this clear."

All sorts of thoughts roamed through my head. I realized I could take the job, but I knew Donnie would seize the opportunity and never work again. He would love to have me support him, plus do all the work around the house. It was obvious he was enjoying his time off too much. Another concern was that I did not trust Donnie being around the neighborhood women all day. Having no one home would be an open invitation for Donnie to entertain. My paramount concern though was Alex's care. Donnie's temperament was not conducive to being a caregiver. I just knew I would find a beaten child when I would return home, and professional childcare was not an option. I just did not have a good feeling in my soul. I made the call and declined the job.

The next time we talked with Francis we told him about my interview and explained I had turned the offer down. With that, he became furious with me.

"Don't you realize God sent that job your way? God laid this job at your feet. It was a gift. How could you turn it down?" He was very emphatic I was outside of God's will for not accepting His gift.

"I prayed about it and felt it best for everyone concerned to turn it down," trying to explain my actions.

"Well, you're wrong! You are very wrong! Now you're going to suffer more for not doing God's will."

Francis kept reiterating this over and over.

Oh great, all I needed was to have more guilt heaped upon me. Were we going to be like Moses and wonder around in the wilderness for 40 years for not obeying God? What I found interesting was that Francis was never upset with Donnie for getting us into this situation in the first place. No, Francis was only upset with me. I did not understand it.

Our resources were being depleted. Donnie couldn't find another job within the area, especially after being fired from a job that only lasted a few months. He refused to look for part time employment. Once the unemployment benefits were consumed, he finally broke down and hired a headhunter. The man was very frank with Donnie.

"This won't be easy since your last job only lasted five months. You will not find another job in the immediate area because the town is too small. Are you okay if I send your resume to other states?"

"Sure," Donnie said. "It was a mistake coming here in the first place. See what you can do."

With that the headhunter sent Donnie's resume all around the country.

Finally, Donnie received a call from the city offices in Redwood City, California (a suburb of San Francisco). At our expense, Donnie flew to California for an interview and was offered the job. The company would not pay our moving expenses, so we had to lighten our load. We sold as much furniture as possible, keeping only the basics. In May 1977, we packed up our belongings into a U-Haul truck and started our "U-Haul Adventure" driving across country. Donnie drove the truck. We had elicited the help from Francis to ride in the car with me. Having a twelve-month-old toddler made progress slow.

Once we arrived in California Francis immediately flew back home to Texas. Our next challenge was finding a place to live. We stayed in a motel and hoped the truck would not get broken into during the night! We finally found a small duplex in Saratoga. The development had duplexes all around the perimeter so there were plenty of neighbors and walking paths. It was a long drive for Donnie each day but the housing areas for several miles around Redwood City appeared undesirable.

Donnie started his job in June and I set up house. With his job so far away, we decided to purchase another car. This was not an expense we could afford, but I needed transportation to get to doctor visits and run quick errands. It was not long before Donnie's hours got longer and longer. Many nights he would not get home in time to see Alex before his bedtime. In fact, he would get home about the time I was going to bed. My days were exceptionally long as I knew no one. I would take Alex on walks, but people tended to stay to themselves. They certainly were not as friendly as Midwesterners. In conversations with Donnie, I picked up on a recurring name he kept bringing up, Linda. "Again?" was my thought. It was July. He had only been working a few weeks. I prayed, "Do I really have to endure this again, God? Please say, 'No!'"

One evening Donnie came home and announced he had invited Linda and her husband for dinner. I agreed. What was I to do? He had already asked them. The day arrived. Donnie was inexplicably nervous. As the time approached for their arrival, he paced nonstop around the living room. Donnie's face beamed with delight when he saw their car pull in. As soon as I saw Donnie and Linda look at each other it was obvious to me, this was more than just a working friendship. The sparks flew between them. I could not discern what her husband thought, but I was extremely uncomfortable. Donnie directed the entire conversation between himself and Linda. Any comments about or to me were disparaging in nature, providing a laugh for everyone. My heart was crushed.

On the weekends we would make trips to the beach. It was not the closest beach to us. It was the beach close to Linda's home. He would drive relentlessly around the block, hoping for a glimpse. We would finally stop near the vicinity of her home, where I would lay out a blanket and toys so Alex could play in the sand. Donnie would walk the beach, hoping to lay eyes on her. This was our weekend routine.

After some time, I could not contain myself any longer. My nerves were on fire, and I needed to get this off my chest. I boldly walked into the living room one Sunday, interrupting his sports event.

"What's going on between you and Linda?" There, I had blurted it out.

In a demeaning tone he declared, "Don't get so excited! Everything is okay because I'm doing God's will."

"Really?" I said sarcastically. "I don't get it?" I questioned.

"Just call Francis, he'll tell you I'm right. Besides, it says so in the Bible!" About this time, he was getting extremely cocky.

"I don't think I've read that having an affair with a married woman is acceptable in God's eyes."

"It sure is," he shouted back. "You're so stupid. You do not know anything. It says that what God has joined together let no man come between."

"I agree that passage is in the Bible (Matthew 19:6) but that scripture is used in wedding ceremonies," I countered.

"Yeah, but it applies to anyone. If I am attracted to someone, that's God telling me He wants me to be with them. So, you have to accept it as God's will."

He was dead serious!

I, on the other hand, stood in disbelief.

But what was I to do? Here I was in California with a fourteen-month-old toddler, no money, no job, no friends, and no way out. Further from my family than I had been my entire lifetime. Once again, the feelings of hopelessness set in. All I could do was fall on my knees and cry out to the Lord once more. I prayed, "Please, God, make a way, for I see no way. I am so sorry for my shortcomings against you. I need your strength, wisdom, and peace." I tried to rationalize it as Donnie's attempt to regain his self-confidence after being fired. He had not been looking to me for encouragement. We barely talked for he was never home.

Donnie's answer to every situation, when I would come to the end of my rope, was to put me on a plane to visit Francis, Cora, and his mother. "You're getting too worked up. They'll calm you down," he'd advocate. Before I knew it, Donnie would make the reservations and I would be on my way to Austin.

This time the visit was different, I did not receive much encouragement. In fact, it was quite the opposite.

"You know, if you'd taken that job God offered you in Columbia, you wouldn't be in this predicament," Francis preached.

"I fail to see where this is my fault," I sprang back.

He explained, "You are outside God's will, so you are on your own right now."

"I just don't understand. What about Donnie?" I asked.

"This isn't about Donnie. You are the one that turned down the job. You are the one God is dealing with. You must deal with your punishment."

"Punishment?" I thought. To the best of my knowledge, God does not dole out punishments. Besides, your spouse having an affair is not a punishment God would inflict on anyone.

Feeling only exasperation, I could see talking about this any further was not going to help. I did not understand any part of this. Did Francis have the same convictions as Donnie regarding affairs? Was Donnie taught this? Was our marriage one of these affairs taken to a higher level? I do remember Donnie being extremely anxious for me to meet Francis, Cora, and some of the other members of their religious family. Did I have to meet their approval? I had no idea. This was way beyond my thought process. I was beginning to question Donnie's real motivation for marrying me. Did God direct him? Did Francis direct him? Was it simply his greed to double his income? I prayed, "I'm sorry, Father, this doesn't make sense. I do not understand. Please enlighten me, somehow."

I did not want to be in Texas, but I did not want to be home either. The pieces of the puzzle just did not fit together. By being in Texas I had help with Alex during the day. But, in the evenings Francis was putting pressure on me that made me feel uncomfortable. He was getting a little too close and I did not accept it.

The affair between Donnie and Linda lasted all winter and seemed to taper off in the spring. I had weathered this storm, with the grace of God, but was concerned with what lie ahead. "Don't ask!" I told myself.

I discovered I was one of those individuals who could get pregnant without much effort. Donnie still had no interest in me, so our occasional intimacy was just that, occasional. The end of April 1978 I found myself pregnant, despite the fact I had an IUD in place. I started hemorrhaging, bad. I knew something was terribly wrong. Fortunately, Donnie's mother happened to be visiting us at the time so was able to care for Alex. I tried calling Donnie.

"Hey, I need you to come home. I'm bleeding badly and need to get to a doctor."

"Then go!" he muttered. "Why are you bothering me? You've got a car."

"I'm not able to drive, it's that bad."

I could tell he was getting annoyed by his breathing, "I can't come home right now!"

"Please," I begged.

"No, figure it out," he railed.

"Okay, I guess I will."

I had a car, but Arlene could not drive, and I physically was unable. I contacted the only neighbor I knew, explaining the situation. She agreed to take me to my doctor. Once the doctor saw me, he immediately admitted me into the hospital. Thankfully, my neighbor stayed with me until I was assigned a room and settled in.

"Thank you so much for helping me today. I appreciate it more than you can imagine."

"It has not been a problem, Mary. Is there anything else I can do for you?"

"Would you mind going over to the apartment and give Arlene the news along with the phone number of the room and a message for Donnie to call as soon as he gets home?"

"I can do that. Are you sure you're going to be okay?" she said sympathetically.

"I am sure. I'll be fine. Thank you!"

Donnie called when he got home but it was very late.

"Would you mind bringing me a few things?"

"It's too late. I don't want to come," he whined.

"Just please!" Guess I whined also.

He did come to the hospital, staying just long enough to drop off my things.

"They have scheduled the D&C for 10:00 in the morning."

"So?" he snapped.

"Aren't you planning to be here?"

"No! I cannot. I have too much to do. I can't get off work."

"Really?" I thought but did not question his motive. That was the way it was going to be.

He did not bother to call or visit the hospital the day of the procedure. I was there, alone. The third day he did manage to call to see what time I would be dismissed. At least he did show up to take me home.

Depression hit me hard after the miscarriage. I was smart enough to understand a pregnancy could not be viable with an IUD in place. The miscarriage itself was not the issue. I felt as if the bottom dropped out of me. Nothing could explain it. Maybe it did not need explained. Our marriage was a farce. Pregnancy should be a sign of joy, harmony, and intimate times. That was not my case. I felt used and unloved: Donnie's personal prostitute.

Mother's Day came. Depression lingered, like some sea monster had jumped on my back and wrapped tentacles around me. I could not break free. Donnie marched into the bedroom, eyebrows furrowed, finger pointed, threw back the covers from the bed, and ordered, "Get your ass out of that damn bed and get dressed. It's Mother's Day and we're taking my mom out for dinner." All I could do was keep praying, "God, please make a way for I feel so hopeless." I did as I was ordered: got dressed and went for lunch, never speaking a word. Just present.

The day finally arrived for my appointment to have another IUD inserted. It had been at least eight weeks, maybe longer since the D&C because of the doctor's scheduling conflicts and my inability to find a sitter.

"That won't be a problem," I told the receptionist very confidently when I made the appointment. "Just work me in, six weeks or three months, not an issue."

The gap of time did not concern me since we had sex so infrequently and my menstrual cycle had not even started.

At my appointment, the doctor examined me and said,

"It's too late, you're pregnant!"

I gasped, "What? How can that be?"
I know that had to sound pretty dimwitted. We had sex once. Was this a joke? Silently I prayed, "Lord, please, this can't be true!"

The doctor looked at me and smirked, "No, you are definitely pregnant, so we'll just start with a new set of questions."

I was not amused. The baby was due in late spring. How unbelievable!

Initially, Donnie lacked all emotion regarding the news. Since he rarely cared what Alex and I did anyhow, his reaction did not surprise me. Once he had a few hours to think about it, his fury was unleashed. I heard the pounding of his steps as he marched down the hall.

"How could you let this happen?" he yelled, "Why did you wait so long to get into the doctor? You are so dumb. You know you should have used protection. It's not up to me to know these things."

These questions did not deserve a response, but he was expecting one. He kept pressuring me and finally, I blew.

"Don't put all the blame on me. I didn't do this by myself, you know!" I blurted out. I let that slip out without thinking through the consequences. I thought, "Oh, I hope he doesn't hit me for making that comment." That was one of the few times I ever came back at him.

"You just have to be one of the dumbest females I know!"

I got up from my chair and walked away, for this conversation was going nowhere.

This pregnancy was different from my first. For the first three months my morning sickness came like clockwork, right after our evening meal. Donnie would get furious at me.

"What's your problem?" he'd snap, "Don't you know you're wasting good food? Just stop eating. This is costing me money!"

I wanted to tell him it was not fun for me either but knew it would not help. Lacking the energy to fight, I would go back into the kitchen and clean up from dinner.

Donnie lost all patience with Alex. He expected Alex to immediately obey his every command. When Alex deviated from that expectation a severe spanking awaited him. Since Alex was still in diapers Donnie felt hand spankings were not effective so he resorted to a breadboard. Everyone knows a two-year-old only explores and does not conform to any expectations. Alex grew more nervous by the day. He would be fine with me during the day but would whimper and get clingy upon Donnie's arrival home from work. Feeding Alex before Donnie got home was the only way I could encourage him to eat, even his favorite foods. The weekends were the worse. Donnie only tormented and teased Alex to the point of tears. Then Donnie would get mad and explode at both of us. "Get him out of here! He is a waste of my time! I've got better things to do than try to play with that crying brat." There was nothing Alex or I could do to make this man happy.

The first part of December 1978 Donnie came home early from work. My first inclination was that he had gotten ill and just came home rather than waiting until the end of the day.

"Are you ok?" I questioned as he came through the door.
His head was down as he trudged into the house, tossing his briefcase onto the floor.

"No, not exactly," he bemoaned.

"Are you sick?" Still, no response. "Ok, what's up?" I demanded. With a scornful look on his face he explained, "My boss called me into his office and gave me the option to quit or be fired. So, I quit."

He did not seem overly surprised regarding the news.

"Please Dear Jesus," I said under my breath, "I wonder what he could have done now?"

An explanation was never uttered from his lips, I could only surmise. He had been at this job eighteen months. I tried to look at this in a positive manner. At least they had given him the courtesy of quitting rather than being fired, because he could not afford to explain two firings on his resume. On the flip side, here we were again: no job, no insurance, a two-and-a-half-year-old, I'm six months pregnant, and since he had technically quit there would be no unemployment benefits.

"Dear God, I don't even know how to pray anymore," I said to God privately. "Is this my punishment for not taking that job back in Columbia?" Guilt grew deeper. I felt this was all my fault.

Thinking things could not get worse, they did. Francis called the end of the month to say he had received a message from God that San Francisco was going to experience a huge earthquake and drop into the ocean. Francis even gave Donnie the exact date. He advised us to pack up and be prepared to leave before the "date of destruction."

"What? How does he know this?" I quizzed. "They talk about earthquakes every day in San Francisco. He's not a scientist, besides, he lives in Texas." I was having difficulty following the logistics of this story.

"Don't ask, just do as you're told!" Donnie shouted. His eyes were burning with determination. He headed for the garage to start prepping.

"Wait! How can we be sure of this?" I queried, trying to get him to slow down.

Spinning abruptly on his heel he pointed his finger at me and said, "Francis said it, so it must be so! I advise you to get started. We have a lot of work to do in a short period of time!" Donnie asserted and left the room.

I stood in the middle of the room in disbelief. This was the craziest thing I had ever heard! Since I did not have a choice I went into the kitchen and started organizing.

Donnie immediately gathered boxes for me to start packing. He sold my car within the week. Being an opportunist, Donnie went to every major department store applying for credit. Once approved, he would use the new credit card to purchase whatever he wanted. Up to the limit! It was a Christmas holiday for him. This was not just one department store, it was several. He even took out a couple personal loans from banks. He craved "free money and free stuff." He beamed with delight as he would bring home his purchases.

"What are you doing?" I would question.

"It's free! Once San Francisco drops in the ocean, they cannot track us," he was giddy with delight.

Timidly I asked, "What do you mean us?"

"This credit is in your name also."

"Oh, dear God," I prayed under my breath, "this man is sick! What can I do now? He is out of control. This cannot be Your will, God. This can't be so!"

While Donnie was employed in California, he joined a group that met monthly for dinner, had a guest speaker, shared information, and socialized. Since Donnie enjoyed handling money, he had been elected treasurer of this organization. Given his warped thinking, he thought it would be a shame for that money to go into the ocean. So, the day before we were to leave, he withdrew all the money from the organization's account but did not tell a soul.

Donnie, once again, asked Francis to help us move. Francis flew into San Francisco a few days before the "date of destruction." The day before the desecration was to take place, we put the final things into the truck and headed out. Once again, Donnie drove the U-Haul and I drove the car with Francis and Alex. The guys wanted to get as far as Reno the first day, thinking we would be far enough away from the impending disaster. Waking up the next morning, Donnie anxiously turned on the news. Guess what? No earthquake! I prayed silently, "Lord, what a mess we are in. Are you able to help us?"

Donnie became extremely nervous and would not tell us what troubled him. Francis finally got him to confess what he had done regarding "stealing" the money from the organization. Donnie had no choice but to return to San Francisco and deposit the money back into the account. Francis, Alex, and I stayed in the motel all day.

While we waited, I asked Francis, "Okay, so what happened? You said God told you there was going to be an earthquake. But it didn't happen. Can you explain that?"

"I guess God changed His mind. Maybe God saw what you and Donnie did and decided you needed to pay for your greediness."

My blood pressure was rising. "Wait a minute here! You're lumping me in with what Donnie did?" I asked.

Very confidently he said, "Yes, you're a part of it also!"

My button had been pushed! "You, of all people, should know that Donnie does whatever Donnie wants to do, regardless of my beliefs." I could not hold the next question back. "Don't you feel somewhat responsible for telling Donnie about the earthquake in the first place and insisting we move?"

"No, obviously, God changed His mind."

I could see this conversation was going nowhere.

Donnie returned late that evening. He had returned the money, but my mind had been racing all day. How is this going to look? Will they press charges against him? How can you withdraw an organization's funds one day and deposit them back the next? Shouldn't there be two signatures on the account? Did he forge someone's signature? All the credit cards! The loans! He does not have a job! I am pregnant! There were no answers. This had turned into an outrageous nightmare that was going to take on a life of its' own.

Here we were in Reno and we had nowhere to go. We could not go back to California. We had moved out without notifying our landlord. Everything about this was so wrong. My personality of wanting to please and go by the rules was being tested to the limit. Donnie was breaking rules left and right but still, Francis found no wrong in Donnie directly. Francis felt no responsibility for telling us to leave California in the first place. Was I the only one feeling blame or guilt or both at this point?

Francis and Cora opened up their home to us. Since Arlene had moved in with them, their house was already full but they managed to make room for us as well. All our belongings fit into their garage. They had one extra bedroom. Donnie didn't care about finding a job, which caused Francis and Cora additional frustration because Donnie was not contributing anything towards their monthly expenses.

I found a doctor for the remainder of the pregnancy. Since Donnie had nothing better to do he did go to most of the doctor visits with me, but not out of concern regarding the pregnancy or me, he just wanted to flirt with one of the nurses he found attractive.

The end of March I went into labor. Donnie did not help me get through Alex's delivery so I knew I would not get help this time either. We had a beautiful little girl and we named her Jennifer. The doctor must have felt sorry for me. After Jennifer's delivery the doctor stood by my side and held my hand while Donnie cracked jokes, made disparaging comments about me, and flirted with the nurses.

Donnie finally started looking for work after Jennifer's birth. It was not an easy process to procure a job with his gaps of employment, but in May 1979 he was offered a job working with a large computer hardware company in San Antonio. He was to work as a technical advisor within the sales department. Rather than being thankful for the job, all he did was complain that they did not offer him enough money. Donnie's ego was untouchable. He failed to see what a chance this company was taking by hiring him. Not only had he been fired twice, but Donnie had no experience as a technical advisor. Or maybe he lied on the employment form. Anything was possible. Francis finally convinced him he'd better be happy and take the job, which he finally did.

Once Donnie started working, he found a home for us to rent. Finally, after six months living with Francis, Cora, and Arlene, we would be on our own again. I could not wait. I knew the children were getting on everyone's nerves. Jennifer was a fussy baby. Moving with two small children was not easy, especially having no help. Like always, once the truck was emptied and the tv set up, Donnie's responsibilities were over. I asked Donnie to feed Jennifer once and all she did was cry. "Come get your kid," he yelled. Never again did he have anything to do with her.

At least Donnie's salary was enough that we could afford another car. With two children now, I needed transportation to get around. It seemed there were always doctor visits and grocery runs. A car provided me with a little independence again. It felt good!

In July Donnie was sent on his first business trip to Phoenix. As soon as he returned home, I knew something had transpired. His face was drawn, his skin ashen, exhaustion filled his bones, darkened circles under his eyes… he sat in a stupor. I asked him if he was okay and all he did was grunt. I inquired again and he finally told me he had been up all night the last two nights and attended classes during the day. "Really?" I thought. I could not believe he would be drinking all night for that was not his nature. My antennas were raised and the signals I received were telling me what had really transpired. I decided to wait to see how this played out before I confronted him.

I overheard him brag to our neighbor he had met a "lady friend" while in Arizona. Up to this point he had made no mention of meeting anyone to me. Sure enough, within the week we started receiving phone calls from a woman asking to speak with Donnie. Initially, the calls were weekly. Then they became more frequent. Donnie made daily calls after I would go to bed. Déjà vu! It had happened again. But this one was different from all the others. This romance was intense. Rather than ignore the situation, I finally confronted him.

"What's going on?" I questioned.

Trying to avoid making eye contact he answered, "Not much."

With more force I asked again, "Yes there is. Tell me what's going on."

He looked at me with this angelic look on his face and said, "I've found my angel. God sent her to me. We're meant to be together."

That set me back on my heels. I was not expecting all that to voluntarily come spewing from his mouth.

"What's her name?" I asked trying to remain calm. I needed to be able to put a name to this intruder.

Beaming with delight and with great confidence he said, "Patricia. She lives in Phoenix and has five children. I just know that God sent her to me."

I could not believe it. He was talking to me like I was a friend rather than his wife! Did he expect me to say, "Congratulations, I'm happy for you!" He was having another affair. Was I supposed to say, "Have fun, enjoy yourselves, I'll be here when it's over?" He obviously had no feelings for me. And no respect for our marriage.

Everything was blatantly in the open after that. Donnie and Patricia didn't care if I was in the house or what time of the day it was. No calls were being hidden. I could not afford clothes for Jennifer, but he could justify spending $60 for stereo tapes containing their favorite songs. Whenever he was in the house he was playing "their songs." I knew his priorities were not with us. I could feel the end of our marriage was drawing nigh. I just did not know how God was going to work it out. The logistics were harder, for now I had two small children to support. I left this mess in God's hands to solve, because I could not deal with this any longer.

Donnie's frustration of "being married to the wrong girl" became more evident by the day. He was extremely intolerant of Alex and me, while totally ignoring Jennifer. Alex's spankings with the breadboard were getting more severe and frequent, and over the most insignificant events. The only way Alex would eat was for me to feed him before Donnie got home, although that was not a problem because Donnie would call about dinner time saying he was working late at the office. Really? Every night? Even Friday? I questioned the frequency of his late nights. One Thursday night I put the kids in the car and drove to the office. His car was not at the office; it was parked across the street at one of the bars. It was obvious, he just did not want to be home.

It was apparent to me that in Donnie's eyes, our marriage was over, but I knew it would be up to me to orchestrate the conclusion. For that, I would have to rely on God for the answer. My personality was such that I like to know how to do something before I act, rather than act and ask forgiveness later, so I was not about to do anything hastily. From experience I would have called Francis and he would provide spiritual advice. This time I was not calling Francis. I knew I would get the same story about letting this work itself out over time. No, this affair was totally different from the others. I had enough faith to know God would provide the sign I needed to set the wheels into motion.

And the answer came quickly. When Donnie got home from work the following night, he was more irritable than normal. I was fixing dinner and, in haste, had left a knife handle too close to the edge of the countertop. With his toddler curiosity, Alex reached for it. Donnie grabbed him by the arm, yanked him straight up by his outstretched arm, and relentlessly spanked him while his little body was swinging back and forth like a pendulum. Alex was hysterical. Fortunately, Alex's arm did not dislocate when Donnie grabbed him. I took Alex from Donnie's arm, we left the kitchen, and I hugged Alex. I knew I had been given the sign. It was time to get out before Donnie physically harmed one or both of us.

The first of the week I set the wheels into motion. I had not made a collect call to my parents since my college days, but this was an emergency. As quickly and briefly as I could, I explained I had to get the kids and myself away from Donnie. They were shocked. As far as they knew our marriage was fine. I told them I had no choice, I had to leave. I asked if I could come home for a while. They advised me to see an attorney first to make sure Donnie could not have me arrested for taking the children out of state without his approval. Thankfully, they thought of this because getting arrested was the furthest thing from my mind. They promised to call the following day to make sure I was okay.

Find an attorney. Reality was setting in. I knew on my wedding night I had made a big mistake. Now, six years later with two small children and a lot of heartache, it was time to pick up the pieces and move forward. I had no idea where to start. San Antonio was so large and we were new to the area. I reached out to my neighbor. After visiting with her and explaining the situation she made some inquiries and found a recommendation for me. I made the appointment for the free consultation. She volunteered to watch the children for me while I went to find out about the process.

I had to drive into downtown San Antonio to Sam's office. That unnerved me but I made it! I explained the circumstances to Sam while he took notes. He, in turn, explained the Texas Divorce Laws to me along with what I could expect. Before my time was over, he asked if I had any questions. I sure did.

"I really need to get away and think everything through," I explained to him. "I want to take my children and visit my parents in Nebraska, but I need to know if I can take the children out of state?"

He advised, "It's perfectly within your right to visit your parents. This is not an abandonment or a kidnapping. It's a visit."

"Great," I responded.

I needed some space from Donnie. I thanked him for his time and said I would get back to him once I decided to proceed.

I knew talking to Donnie about a trip home would be met with a lot of resentment, he would never consent. Rather, he would encourage me to drive to Austin and spend time with Francis and his mother, so they could settle me down. In my eyes, leaving was my only escape. Mom agreed to fly into San Antonio and help me drive home with the children. The night before she was to arrive, I sat and wrote a letter to Donnie explaining where I was going and why I was leaving. The entire time I was writing, he was deeply engrossed on the telephone, laughing, and talking with Patricia. He had no interest in what I was doing. Here we were, sitting in the same room, he talking to his girlfriend and I was writing a goodbye letter.

The day for departure arrived. Once Donnie left for work, I packed the suitcases and placed the letter on the kitchen table where he would see it when he entered from the garage. My neighbor picked up Mom from the airport and delivered her to the house. I did not give Mom much time to recover from the plane ride. Within an hour I had the car packed and we were on our way out of town.

Donnie called my father that evening.

"Is Mary there?"

"No," Dad replied calmly.

Donnie grew more demanding. "Do you know where she is?"

My father really didn't know the exact location so said, "I don't know. All I know is that she and the kids should arrive tomorrow."

"Okay, I'll call tomorrow night." Donnie was satisfied with that and hung up.

We arrived home the following day. Being home felt good. Just as we were sitting down for dinner the phone rings. Dad answered and he immediately handed the phone to me.

In a very demeaning manner Donnie asked, "What do you think you're doing?"

"I explained everything in the letter. I needed to get away for a couple weeks and think things through." I remained calm as I was not going to let him talk me into anything.

Just as I suspected his first response was, "Why didn't you just drive over to Austin and talk with Francis?"

"I wanted to come home," I replied, "I knew you wouldn't allow me to come home."

He suggested, "Then I'll fly to Nebraska this weekend and we can talk things over."

I knew his controlling personality would drag us back to Texas with him if that were to happen. There would be no reasoning with him if he came to Nebraska.

"Please, just give me a couple weeks," I pleaded. "That's all I'm asking for."

"Okay," he said very snidely. "Have it your way!" And he abruptly ended the conversation.

What did he mean by that? I was not about to second guess him. After that initial phone call, I never heard from him again.

Home provided a breath of fresh air. I needed time to decompress from his mind control and slowly reflect on the past several years, without Donnie's constant abuse keeping me on edge. Up to this point I had not told anyone what was going on within our marriage. Reopening the wounds, I explained everything to my parents. It was amazing how much clearer the situation looked when I was able to verbalize it.

My parents were not happy I was on the brink of divorce and struggled to understanding what I had been through. They loved and respected each other, so found it hard to believe someone could treat their spouse and children the way we had been treated by Donnie. No matter how old you get, no one wants to see their child hurt. My dad remembered a time during a visit with us in California, where he experienced Donnie's quick, violent temper firsthand. He and Donnie went to the clubhouse to play a game of pool. Donnie thought he was going to easily whip this old farmer. It did not quite turn out that way, for Dad beat him hands down. Donnie became so angry he pounded a new, very expensive pool cue over the table, breaking it into several pieces. This experience helped my folks understand, firsthand, Donnie's capabilities.

My parents recommended I talk with their country pastor so I could understand where the church stood concerning divorce. I already knew divorce was not an accepted solution, but I did as they suggested. It turned out to be quite the conversation. The pastor knew why I was coming, and he wasted no time getting to the point.

"According to the beliefs of the Baptist Church, divorce is a forgivable sin, under certain conditions, but on the whole the church does not sanction divorce. You understand that don't you?"

Here we go, "Yes, I realize that, but I can't continue living with the mental and emotional abuse."

"But abuse is not a valid reason within the church for getting a divorce."

"Okay, if that is what you say, but he has had multiple affairs besides the abuse."

His eyes glared into mine and he said, "Are you sure about that?"

"Oh, yes!" I said quite confidently.

With his eyes piercing into me he asked, "Have you remained faithful?"

Without hesitation I said, "Yes, I have."

"Then, the church would recognize his infidelity as being a reason to acknowledge the divorce. The first thing you two must do is submit to counseling. Have you thought about that?"

Digging my heels in I said, "No, I've come to the end of my rope. I cannot see Donnie ever changing his ways. Besides, he'd never be honest regarding his behavior."

Now I could feel the pastor's eyes staring holes through me, "Are you sure about that?"

"Believe me, I've lived with this man six years, I know what he will and won't do."

Calmly he replied, "Well, you need to ask for forgiveness because God could heal this marriage."

By this time, I was ready to walk out. Was he really trying to make this out to be my fault?

Very honesty I asked, "Are you implying I ask for God's forgiveness or Donnie's forgiveness?"

"Both, because if you proceed with the divorce you are breaking your covenant vows you made before God at your wedding ceremony."

"But Donnie's actions are all justified as being religious. How do you explain that one?"

Matter-of-factly he said, "I can't determine that without talking with him."

What? Whose side was he on? At this point I did not care how the preacher was looking at this, it was plain infidelity as well as abuse and I had enough! Obviously, abuse was something the pastor believed should be tolerated. With that, I thanked him for his time and excused myself.

When I left the church, I was terribly upset. I had gone to the pastor seeking encouragement but left feeling condemned. I knew Donnie would not go along with counseling because, in his eyes, God had sent this angel to him. Besides, Francis would be the only counselor Donnie would ever listen to, and Francis found no fault in Donnie's behavior. All I knew was that I could not continue living with Donnie without jeopardizing the health and safety of my children and myself. It was that simple. I just kept praying, "With your help, Lord, I can do this."

Every day I felt a little stronger. The children were incredibly happy. God was answering my prayers for I needed physical and emotional healing to face the imminent nightmare. My decision was made.

While still in Nebraska, I made the phone call to Sam, setting the wheels in motion. The plan was to schedule the return trip to San Antonio around the initial appointment. First step was to initiate the paperwork and pay the retainer. Fortunately, my folks lent me money for the retainer because I did not have access to the checkbook. Mom made the return trip to Texas with the kids and me and volunteered to stay until Donnie had been served the divorce papers.

My appointment with Sam was scheduled the day after we returned to Texas. The first step was simple for Sam had all the papers ready for my signature. At this juncture it was easy, sign the Service Order for Donnie to be served notice and pay. Sam assured me Donnie would be served in three to four days.

Sam called me the day before Donnie was to be served. I had no idea what Donnie's reaction was going to be, so I asked my aunt and uncle, who lived in San Antonio, to spend the afternoon with us. I could picture Donnie being relieved but, on the other hand, I could see him irate. Surprisingly, he took the news rather calmly. The day he was served I overheard his conversation with Patricia that evening.

"She made this easy for us. Now I don't have to look like the bad guy and make the decision. She told me I had to move out. She makes me so angry I cannot hold it back much longer. It's a good thing her mother is staying here, or I would have punched her tonight. It's too bad she just doesn't die so we could have everything."

He was dead serious!

Up to this point he had not physically abused me; it was all mental and emotional. Now did I have to fear for my safety as well? I prayed, "God, keep the children and me safe through this. Surround us with Your protection."

Once again, Donnie proved to me he was out of control. The neighbor up the street had a fourteen-year-old daughter that occasionally babysat for us. She enjoyed the kids and would come down periodically to play with them. One afternoon she knocked on the door. Donnie happened to be home. He started teasing her and she took off running for home. He chased her up the street, grabbed her in front of her house, gave her a big hug, and tried to kiss her. Her mother witnessed it, as did I. Immediately the phone rang.

Her mother, on the other end, was screaming, "What the hell does your husband think he is doing to my daughter? I'm going to call the authorities!"

"Please don't! I am so sorry. We are getting a divorce and will be moving soon." I begged her not to call the police.

When Donnie got home, I asked him what he thought he was doing. His comment was "Old enough to bleed, old enough to breed." I knew, without a doubt, I was doing the right thing by leaving, if only for my daughter's sake.

Donnie found an apartment and moved fairly quickly. He became furious when he discovered I had changed the locks. I was not about to take a chance on him coming back into the house at night and harming us. I had to have peace. He could not figure out what he had done to deserve such treatment. Oh, he really did not want to get me started.

On the weekends, Donnie would come to the house to sort through our things. Splitting the furniture was an easy task. I did not want much: just a bed, a single couch, and all the kid's things. Like our previous moves, he was reluctant to pack. To keep the ball rolling, he would make piles on the weekend, I would pack them up during the week, and he would take the boxes to his apartment the following weekend.

Every weekend Donnie became more agitated. Alex would cry hysterically when Donnie got close to him. From Alex's perspective he did not know if he was going to be played with, teased, or spanked. Eventually, Donnie just ignored him. Alex did not seem to miss his dad and never asked for him. In fact, with Donnie out of the house Alex began to settle down. He ate better and did not have recurring nightmares.

In addition to the divorce I needed to find a job. My desire was to move back to Nebraska where I would have family close to help with the children, for the kids were only three and eight months old. Before I could proceed, I needed Donnie's permission to remove the children from the state. This might have been a stumbling block, but it was a nonissue for him. He did not care where we went; his only concern was Patricia.

Before getting serious about job hunting, I needed an outfit for the task. Donnie continued to hold the purse strings. I asked him for money to purchase a dress.

His response was an emphatic, "No. It's not a required expense."

"But, if I don't have a decent outfit, I'll never get a job," trying to justify my request.

"Sorry, it's not food or shelter. I'm not giving it to you," he declared.

I had no choice but to explain my dilemma to Arlene. She could not believe her son's behavior. Finally, Francis and Cora took me shopping and paid for a dress.

Next step was updating my resume and responding to want ads. I sent my resume to five businesses. All five requested an interview. One company was willing to pay my airfare. Wonderful! All I needed to do was purchase a ticket for Alex and I would hold Jennifer on my lap. My folks, once again, lent me money to buy Alex's airline ticket. So, my intent was to fly home over Thanksgiving, schedule all the interviews in a few days, and get to see family as a bonus.

I had not worked for three years, so I was extremely nervous about starting over. Desperation is a motivating mechanism though. I had to have a job, or I could not leave Texas. I knew I might be a little rusty, but I could perform the job again. Just like riding a bike, you never forget. I prayed, "God please lead me to the company where You want me to be."

From the five interviews I received four job offers. I could not believe it! God was opening a way for me. He had answered my prayers. My confidence was returning. I knew I had to talk with Donnie one more time to make sure he still approved of us leaving the state. Once again, it was not an issue because he just wanted out of the marriage. I accepted one of the jobs and started preparing for the move. They wanted me to start mid-December, so I had a lot to accomplish in a short time frame.

Donnie wanted Alex to spend a night with him before we left. I thought it would be a good idea. Prior to Donnie's arrival I talked to Alex about what to expect. Alex picked out his favorite toys to take with him to play and share with his Dad. Fortunately, there was no hesitation on Alex's part regarding going with Donnie. They had not been gone an hour before I received a call.

"All Alex is doing is crying and wants to come home," Donnie complained.

I asked, "Are you playing with Alex?"

"No, I've been watching tv," he grumbled.

"You need to spend time with Alex. I sent toys so you could play with him," I explained.

"Okay, I'll try again." He sounded reluctant, but willing to try.

Another hour passed. Donnie called to say he was bringing Alex home. It was dark so I turned on the porch light. When the doorbell rang, I opened the door to find Alex, by himself, at the front door with his little sack. Donnie was standing by his car.

"Don't you want to come in to patch things up?" I asked.

"No!" he shouted. "Who needs that damn kid anyway."

I took Alex inside, gave him big hugs and kisses, a bowl of ice cream, and played with him. He settled down before going to bed. My heart was crushed. I had a hard time believing anyone could say that about their own child.

Donnie shared the same attorney as myself. That way he did not incur attorney fees. We had decided how the furniture would be split, the amount for child support, and he agreed to take on all the debt. Since Donnie gave his approval for us to live in Nebraska, that was written into the Separation Agreement. Specific visitation arrangements were not clearly defined as Donnie promised we would be able to agree on specific dates, and since the children were so young, we knew the arrangements would evolve over time. He also agreed to start paying child support in January, although he insisted upon paying me directly rather than having payments go through the courts. Since my children were going with me, and my new job had excellent benefits, we decided I would carry the health insurance. Donnie signed the Separation Agreement the day before we left Texas.

My father flew into Texas to help drive the kids and me back to Nebraska. My new employer was moving my household goods, so I did not have to be concerned about that. Dad arrived the same day as the movers. It did not take the movers long to load my share of the household items. Donnie was also at the house while the movers were working. Once they were finished, I handed Donnie the house key. It did not seem to bother him that we were leaving, and I could not wait to get on the road.

It appeared this was going to be simple. Until I was tricked again.

3. Independence

*~ A noun referring to having to do things alone,
standing on your own two feet ~*

December of 1979, life's new chapter for me! The divorce was not final, but all the paperwork had been signed. Now it was a matter of waiting for the court date and the final order. I had forgotten what Nebraska was like in December: ceaseless days of grey skies, winds piercing your soul and robbing your breath, wheels spinning on ice, snow heaped everywhere swelling daily like yeasted bread, batteries challenged, itchy dry skin, burning chapped lips, layers upon layers of clothing.

I wasted no time and jumped right into the work environment. The only way to start a flow of income was to start working. We stayed with my folks while I found a place to live as well as a babysitter for the kids. After paying the deposit and first month's rent on a duplex, I had $200 to my name. That was cutting it incredibly close, but God had supplied my needs. The moving company had unloaded my belongings, so each night after work, I would stop at the duplex to unpack a few things before heading to my folks and the children. I felt it was important to have a few items settled before the kids and I moved into our home.

A co-worker recommended a sitter to me. After going to her home for an interview I discovered she had a boy Alex's age. Meg was willing to take my children and I felt good about the environment. I explained it might be a rocky start since we were adjusting to a lot of new situations and I had been home with Alex since birth, but she was confident it would be fine.

One of my first tasks was to locate a thrift store, where I purchased an outfit for each day of the week. Thankfully, my mother passed along her sewing skills so I knew I could purchase material and make clothes once I had a little monetary cushion. Christmas was coming.

Fortunately, my children were young for I bought used toys, cleaned them up, wrapped them, and put a big bow on top. The children were elated with anything. I knew I was going to be okay. "Thank you, God, for getting me out of that toxic environment."

Leave it to a child to hit you between the eyes with a dose of reality. I had not realized how much Donnie had traumatized Alex and myself. For Christmas I gave Alex a puzzle, which he put together with ease.

"You are so smart," I exclaimed.

He looked at me and asked, "What's that Mommy?"

Oh my! We had a long road of recovery.

The big day arrived when I left the cocoon of my parents' home and moved to the duplex. I had sole care of my beautiful children, which was nothing new. When you throw a new job on top of being a single parent it seemed daunting at first. Fear occasionally overtook my psyche; despite the fact I knew God was watching over me. There was just so much to do and learn. In addition to the job, I had to learn how to overcome Donnie's mental and emotional abuse that had been thrown upon me for so long. My confidence had been stripped to the bone. From the deep hole I found myself, I could see daylight when looking up but there was darkness all around me. Climbing out of this hole would be a daily struggle, but I knew with God's help I could make it. He was my sole source of strength.

The last seven years had been so difficult, but God had answered my prayers. I could not see a way out for such a long time, then God made the way. He also provided a perfect job for me, a babysitter for my children, and a roof over our heads. I even received a paycheck by the end of December which allowed me to make January's rent payment. God was good! My needs continued to be met.

Donnie called about every three weeks with the anticipation of talking with Alex. Most of the time Alex refused to come to the phone. I knew I would eventually get blamed for this refusal to talk so I tried everything I could think of to entice Alex, but I could not make him say anything to his father. Thankfully, Donnie was not insisting Alex spend a certain amount of time with him on each call. It had to be disappointing, but I do not know what Donnie expected from a three-year-old.

This winter seemed particularly brutal. This might have been because I had to have the kids up and out the door early. My duplex had a long driveway. When it snowed, which seemed nonstop, I would tuck the kids into bed, make sure they were sound asleep, bundle myself up, and go out to shovel. Waiting until morning was not an option, for on any normal day our mornings were chaotic. Being out in the evening was rather tranquil. By then the storm had usually passed and the winds calmed. Snow laid glistening off the streetlight, no tracks, no noise, sheer beauty. On a cloudless night, with the moon shining, the snow twinkled like diamonds under a bright light. There was plenty of beauty to be appreciated during these moments.

As soon as I was settled, I found a church to attend. It was time for Alex to start hearing the Bible stories from the Sunday school teachers. I found a church where I met some wonderful people. After going a few Sundays, I discovered the HR manager from work attended this church, as well as my neighbor just two doors down. My friends personally introduced me to the pastor and his wife. Everything felt right, like I belonged. Several knew I was a single mother and volunteered to help whenever I needed assistance.

Most of those first months the kids were sick. They had so much to adapt to: new daycare, new nursery school, new environment, having to get out each morning. Alex had recurring ear infections and required surgery for tubes. I was so thankful my job had good health benefits. As per the Separation Agreement, my insurance was primary, Donnie's insurance was secondary, and we were to split the outstanding balance after all insurance payments. Of course, it was my responsibility to pay the outstanding balances and all prescriptions, so Donnie would owe me directly for his portion of the expense. Because his insurance was affected, I felt, as a parent, he needed to be informed whenever anything major went on with the children. I know I would want to know if I was not the custodial parent.

Jennifer was admitted to the hospital in March with pneumonia. All I could do was pray, "Dear God, now what am I to do? I need to be three places at once: with her, at work, and with Alex." I had not worked long enough to accumulate sick leave and not getting paid was out of the question. My dear mother volunteered to sit at the hospital each day to tend to Jennifer's needs and Meg was willing to keep Alex a few extra hours each day. After work I would run to the hospital, Mom would leave, and I would stay until Alex's bedtime. Each night, after telling Jennifer goodnight, I would hurry out the door. Jennifer's bloodcurdling cries ripped at my heart as I ran down the hall. Her sobs reverberated in my ears as the elevator doors closed. I was helpless to do anything about the situation. It was just a terribly long six days.

On the day she was admitted I knew I needed to inform Donnie, so I gave him a call.

"Hey, I just wanted to let you know Jennifer is in the hospital."

"What's her problem?"

I explained, "She had a cold that turned into pneumonia."

Very harshly he asked, "Okay, so what? Am I supposed to do something?"

"There's nothing you can do. I just thought I should let you know."

He blurted, "I really don't care. That is for you to take care of. I have enough going on here. I don't have time to care about what happens to you guys."

Apologetically I said, "Okay, sorry to have bothered you."

After hanging up I could not believe a father could be that detached and apathetic.

The divorce was final in late spring 1980. Even though I had eagerly awaited the arrival of this day, it left me depressed. Everything felt so…terminal…as though an entire period of my life was wiped away with the stroke of a pen. At one point I thought being married would make me feel whole. After all, two people are better than one. Right? Having a partner to share life with would make things easier. Right? This must have been the fairy tale story we were spoon fed since high school. I saw myself as a failure. What should I, or could I, have done different to save this marriage? I had no answer to that question, so I took it before the Lord. God helped me realize I had done everything possible. The divorce was not my fault. God was not blaming me, so I needed to quit blaming myself. I was God's daughter and knew God loved me for who I was.

A byproduct of this failed marriage left me a broken individual. Donnie had made sure of that. His mind control was seared deep within me, like branding an animal so you know to whom it belongs. Even thinking about some of those years provoked a sense of fear. I felt a "hook" remained deep within me. This was Donnie's grip on me that would not let go. Even though the divorce was over, I realized I would never totally be separated from Donnie; for a spirit of cooperation would be required in the sharing of visits with the children for many years to come.

Much to my surprise, Sam, phoned to inform me he had been to court and the divorce was officially over.

"You're never going to believe this," he chuckled, hardly able to contain himself. "Donnie showed up at the divorce hearing. He was unaccompanied: no attorney, no papers, nothing."

(Sam was representing me as the petitioner. I did not have to appear due to the distance involved. Donnie, as the respondent, had not retained counsel but was not required to attend the hearing.)

Sam went on to explain, "This was certainly a new experience for me," he said laughingly. "Donnie needed the divorce case number to apply for his marriage license. Donnie couldn't wait for all the documents to get registered here in Bexar County because he and his fiancée are getting married in two days! Since he lives in Devine the marriage license requirements are in Medina County."

Sam was laughing hysterically.

Their marriage did not surprise me because Arlene had told me Donnie and Patricia had been living together since January. The haste of it did. He could hardly wait for the ink to dry on the final decree before starting his new life. The kids and I had been discarded like an empty milk carton. Reality hit. Yes, I did want the divorce and proceeded with the filing, but the final signing still left me with an empty feeling.

I could count on Arlene calling every week. The calls were short, but she always asked to speak with Alex. Every so often, Arlene would visit her friends in Omaha and ask to spend a couple nights with us. I carried no animosity towards her, I felt sorry for her. The visits always went well. The kids adored playing with her, and I enjoyed having a helping hand around the house. She would never mention Donnie and neither did I.

Since life had settled into a routine I decided to see if I could locate my friend, Barb, in Omaha. The last time I had talked with her would have been five years ago when Donnie got so angry losing a card game that he threw the cards all over the floor. Much to my surprise, she worked at the same job and was extremely happy to hear from me.

"Mary, I can't believe it's you! I didn't think I'd ever hear from you again," she exclaimed with delight.

We were both giddy over finding each other again after all these years.

"What are you doing these days?" Barb asked.

"I'm divorced with two children, three and one, and we live in Lincoln."

"Well, I'm not at all surprised you're divorced. Donnie was something else!" she uttered. "Larry and I are divorced as well."

"I'm sorry to hear that."

"Well, as you know, those things happen. Hey, when can we get together? We need to catch up."

"Since I have the two kids can you come to Lincoln?"

"That won't be a problem. I can't wait to see you," she exclaimed.

We agreed on a date and eagerly awaited the reunion. Most often she would come to Lincoln to visit. She loved spending time with the kids. Every so often, we would venture to Omaha and visit her. It felt good having a friend to share life with.

Now that the divorce was final, and Donnie and Patricia were married, I wondered when things would change. I do not know if you call it intuition or God preparing me, but Donnie had been exceptionally cooperative these first five months. One's personality does not go from controlling to cooperative in a few months. I started bracing myself.

May turned out to be a tumultuous month for us. The first week of May Donnie called to speak with me.

"I just want to tell you I'm coming to pick up the kids in June and I'm bringing them back to Texas for a two-week visit," he dictated his request.

Oh boy, I thought, the fun is about to begin.

I bantered back, "The decree states visitation is to be agreed upon and I certainly don't agree with this. You've selected dates and we haven't even discussed it."

He wasted no time firing back at me, "I guess we just did. Consider it done! I'm coming to get them." He was very dictatorial. Just like old times.

"I feel the kids are too young to be gone that long. Especially Jennifer, she's only fourteen months old!" I interjected.

"They'll be fine. Patricia and the kids are eager to meet them. Besides, Patricia is quite capable of caring for Jennifer if that is your problem. She has raised five kids, you know! Don't you think she can care for a one-year-old?" he said very sarcastically. "It's been a long time since I've seen the kids and know it's my right to have them." He was becoming harsh and agitated.

I snapped back, "I agree with the last part of that statement, but the time of the visit must be agreed upon between us. Besides, I do not appreciate you telling me what you are going to do. I have a say in this decision also." I am not sure where that little bit of courage came from, but I had said it and he did not like it.

He snapped, "I told you… I am coming to pick them up in June. I'll let you know the exact dates."

With that declaration, he hung up. He had announced his intention and it was final. His mind was made up. We had been away from him for five months, yet he continued to control my life. His abusive hook was buried deep within me. All he had to do was tug on it ever so slightly and he knew that was all it took. He was very calculated; he knew exactly how and what to say to me since he knew I was not a fighter.

When Donnie and I were agreeing on the terms of the Separation Agreement Donnie did not want specific visitation dates spelled out. Donnie reassured Sam that he and I would have no problems agreeing on visitation dates. The decree did state the kids could visit their father if Donnie came to Nebraska to pick them up and return them at the end of the visit. There were no but's, if's, or what if's written into the agreement. It was clear. At this point I had no options. I would have to comply to a visit. I had signed the agreement just as he had. But my objection was the length of the visit because the kids were SO young. I waited a few days before reluctantly giving him a call.

"After giving this more thought I guess you can have the kids a week," I cowered because I knew what his response would be.

"No! I expect to have the kids the full two weeks. If I'm going to the expense to fly to Nebraska to get them and then fly them back, I want to make the most of it." He was very insistent.

After bantering back and forth I reluctantly agreed. In all honesty, I could understand his point. He had to pay for two round trip tickets for himself as well as one for Alex. Jennifer was young enough to fly free.

I needed to reach out to someone for help, so I called my pastor and shared the details of the upcoming visit and our need for additional prayer. My gut was telling me this was going to be a challenge.

Just two days later, when I picked up the kids from the sitter, I could see Jennifer's breathing was labored. As the night progressed, it became worse, so I took her to the Emergency Room. She was, once again, diagnosed with pneumonia. They gave me the option to admit her immediately or give it another twelve hours at home. I chose to take her home. The doctor gave her a shot and sent us on our way. All night I held her close to my chest and prayed. Each breath was labored. At some point I fell asleep, but when I awoke, she was a little better. God was touching her. He answered my prayers! "Thank you, Jesus."

Since Donnie's insurance would be called upon for a secondary payment, I felt I should call Donnie and inform him of the situation. He did not seem overly concerned. Later that afternoon Alex fell going up the outside steps. We returned to the Emergency Room where seven stitches were required in his chin. The ER staff recognized me and said, "You again?" I'm sure I am not the only parent they had seen two days in a row! I only smiled at them as I had laryngitis so bad nothing came out above a whisper. I needed this first year to be over and it had only been five months. Again, I called Donnie and told him about Alex's little mishap.

"What's the matter? Aren't you capable of taking care of the kids? What are you doing to those kids?" He was not joking. He was getting angry and belligerent.

"We are fine. I'm just calling to inform you of what happened. You will see it on your insurance anyhow. It was just an accident."

Not wanting this conversation escalating into a full-blown condemnation, I got off the phone quickly. I did not want to hear what an incompetent mother I was.

While staying home a few days with Jennifer, I contacted two local attorneys to get their opinion regarding the children's visit to Texas. Neither one thought I should send Jennifer due to her age and illnesses, but neither was willing to make a commitment. When I took Jennifer back to the doctor, we discussed the upcoming visit. The doctor said we would have to wait until closer to the date, but he would not hesitate to say she could not fly if her difficulties persisted. At this point he did not know what had caused her two bouts of pneumonia, whether it was a cold, an allergy, or asthma. He just wanted me to keep a close eye on her.

The next day I was leaving on a business trip. My mother was coming to care for the children during the evenings, but she would take them to the sitter each morning. This was a road trip and I would be driving myself. As I left, the clouds were low and grey, driving in and out of showers. During the first three hours there was a small hole in the clouds ahead of me that did not appear to move. Behind the hole I could see cobalt blue sky. The sun was not visible, but the rays of the sun streamed through the hole creating golden pillars on the ground ahead of me. I felt as though I had a direct pathway to Heaven. For the first three hours I talked continually with God, feeling His presence all the way, and sensing He was proud of me. I relinquished myself and the children back to God. I realized they were not my children, they belonged to God, and I needed His constant help and protection moving forward.

I should have realized that after such a complete surrender to God, Satan would be ready to test my strength and resiliency. In my absence, the sitter had to take Jennifer to the Emergency Room. They determined she had an asthma attack. She was okay but was still experiencing problems when I returned home.

As I looked through the mail, I noticed a note my mother had written. Donnie had called while I was gone and gave her the flight arrangements for the upcoming visit.

Donnie's arrival: June 18, American flight 314 at 3:55 p.m.

Donnie's departure (with children): June 18, American flight 441 at 7:23 p.m.

Donnie's arrival (with the children): July 7, American flight 630 at 1:42 p.m.

Donnie's departure: July 7 at 2:11 p.m.

I did a double take. Something was not right. I grabbed the calendar to examine the dates. Rather than the initial fourteen days I had reluctantly agreed to, he had now extended the visit to nineteen days.

Anger swelled within me. I was ready to explode! How dare he extend the visit without any discussion. I knew this was once again an extension of his control. He knew all the buttons to push. I decided I needed to confront him.

"What's this visitation schedule? I didn't agree to the extension," I exclaimed.

"I have a business trip I'm working around, so the earliest I can pick them up is the 18th. Since it was so close to the holiday, I knew you would not mind if I included the week of the 4th. Besides, it will only be a couple extra days," he said with complete arrogance.

I continued to press the issue regarding the fact that was not our agreement. Of course, it only escalated the situation. Then, he hurled a bomb at me.

With evil in his voice he said, "I know just what I need to do to take those kids from you and I'll do it if you push me!"

I recognized all too well, the tone of his voice. He was not kidding. What did that mean? Was that a threat?

"I'm also turning over half the debts from the divorce to you because it wasn't clearly stated in the decree," he declared emphatically. "Get ready!" he yelled and hung up.

How could he do that? It was stated explicitly in the Temporary Orders that he was responsible for the $20,000 debt we had at the time of the divorce. Once again, panic set in. Could he take my children from me? Could he turn over the debt to me?

I called the same two local attorneys to discuss my situation. Both agreed; I should not allow the children to go since I had not agreed on the dates and Jennifer was too young to be gone that long. On the other hand, this was the first visit following the divorce. They both doubted that I would be successful stopping the visit entirely. Of course, neither attorney would commit to helping me further without a retainer. At this point I had no money for legal battles. Donnie was counting on that.

True, this was the first visit following the divorce. Technically, I had no grounds to say the children could not visit their father. The entire conflict came down to how many days would the children be gone. It was an accepted conclusion they were going. Otherwise, I would be held in contempt of court and I was not about to go down that rabbit hole. If we were to go to court over this, a judge would be very irritated and tell both of us to grow up and get along for the sake of the children. And that would be a true statement. After a week of internal turmoil, I rationalized my bitterness towards Donnie should not stand in the way, so once again, I cowered under his control. I really did not see a viable option.

May finally came to an end but I dreaded turning the calendar over to face June.

The thoughts going through my mind were conflicting. Why was I so deeply troubled regarding the upcoming visit? I was receiving advice from all directions. Everyone had an opinion, whether I asked for it or not. Some of my friends wanted me to fight. Others suggested I take advantage of the break and take a trip. I was so confused. At this point in my life I did not have a very deep relationship with God, and I was facing my giant head on. In my heart, I honestly did not want Donnie to ever see the kids again. Deep down I wanted to hurt him for what he had done to me. On the other hand, if God really intended for the children to be with their father that long, I did not want to stand in God's way. I knew God's will would be done regardless of what I did or did not do. I also knew Satan was out to destroy me. I remembered, all too well, the many times Satan had his grip on my life during my marriage, almost to the point of a complete breakdown. Deep down I was scared, for I had experienced Donnie's relentless control; I knew he could not be trusted.

Once again, I needed a sounding board, so I invited Pastor John, and his wife, Sherri, to my house. They suggested a little cooperation might be what Donnie needed to make the visit go smoothly. As they mentioned, if things worked out well with this initial visit, I would have more confidence for subsequent visits. After talking more, I admitted my bitterness. The pastor walked me through the steps of unwinding all the hurt I harbored. I was up most of the night talking with God, admitting to Him my feelings of resentment, and pleading for His forgiveness.

As I was driving home from work one night it really hit me how it must hurt God when He must chastise us. I certainly did not like correcting my children. Was God correcting me for my feelings of resentment towards Donnie. Was I still being punished for not taking the job in Columbia? Everything for the past eight years had always been my fault, so it was hard for me to rise above the guilt.

I was extremely confused by the change in Donnie's attitude. From the time of Alex's birth through last December, Donnie did not want a thing to do with either of the children. They were nothing but a thorn in his side. Even once we moved, he did not attempt to stay close. And now, he was yearning to see them? This did not make sense to me. Doubting that he really had the children's interest at heart there had to be something else going on. If he had cared about the children, he would realize two and a half weeks is excessive for children that age to be away from home. I just knew within me I could not be the stumbling block. With that decided, I was not going to fight Donnie on this any longer. He could have the children for the nineteen days. If I were in his shoes I would want to spend as much time as possible with the children also, for he had not seen them since December.

My soul truly felt forgiveness for my bitterness and resentment. Peace now filled my soul concerning the visit. My facial expression was relaxed rather than worried. Positive encouragement and energy were all around me. Since I had turned my burdens over to God, I felt good. It was out of my hands. I felt relieved.

That night as I looked through the mail, I saw a letter from Donnie. It was the first of the month, so I expected the child support check. Indeed, it was, with the following note: "Sorry. With the upcoming trip funds are a little short this month. I hope you understand." The check was for half the amount. Before I called Donnie to get an explanation I prayed, "Lord, help me to just breathe, slow to anger, and continue to do the right thing." I called and Donnie answered.

"I received your note and the check today. What's going on?" I asked.

"Oh, getting the kids back and forth to Texas is going to be expensive, let alone the extra expense while they are here," he was very matter of fact.

Assertively I asked, "Do you stop paying rent when you go on vacation?" God had to put those words in my mouth because I usually do not think that fast.

By this time, he was irritated, "That's different. I know you'll understand." He hung up with no further explanation.

Understand? Is this a free pass? Payment of child support was going to be hard for Donnie. His consistency of paying bills was not the best, especially if something better came along that he wanted. I had received full support checks for five months. I trusted this would be a onetime event. He knew "I'd understand." Again, nothing but control. And what was I to do about this? He knew there was not one thing I could do.

After talking with both local attorneys I knew I had to decide which one to use for my counsel. Both attorneys came with strong recommendations. Finally, I decided on the older, more experienced, family law attorney in Lincoln. I made an appointment with Carl to discuss the situation.

He became perturbed with me almost immediately. "You don't need a lawyer if all you're going to do is comply with Donnie's wishes!"

At least he impressed me as being scrappy.

"It's not that I want to comply, but I really don't believe I have a choice. My question was more along the lines that he demanded two weeks and then extended the time to nineteen days. On top of that, he only sent half the child support money this month, saying the transportation expenses for the kids was going to be expensive."

"Then you have every reason to deny the visit until all the support money is received," he explained. "Besides, if you didn't agree with the nineteen days, you have every reason to fight that as well."

"But this is the first visit since the divorce became official. You tell me how any judge is going to react to this?" I asked.

"Well, you have a point there. He'd probably slap Donnie on the hand for not paying the full support payment and he'd tell you that five additional days is not excessive since Donnie hasn't seen the kids in six months."

"Okay, then, I think you've answered my question!" At that, I left.

Upon getting home I received a call from Donnie. He wanted to talk with Alex, but I could not get Alex to come to the phone. That set Donnie off and he became very belligerent towards me. Through it all, I remained calm. There was nothing I could do about Alex's refusal to come to the phone, but I was not going to fight back. I just listened to Donnie rant until it was over.

I had been so consumed preparing myself for the visit I had not mentioned it to Alex. This was not going to be easy, but I had to get him ready. As I anticipated, he did not want to go. Through his tears he threw his arms around my neck and said, "Don't make me go, Mommy. Please, don't make me go." My heart was heavy. So sad! I anticipated his physical reaction to the news: extreme nervousness, picked his fingernails, cried easily, and was extremely hard to reason with. Since we had no choice, I continued to talk it up. I spun this every way imaginable. He did not care there would be other kids at the house to play with. When Donnie called to talk with Alex he refused, once again, to come to the phone. This made Donnie even more hostile than the previous call. All I did was listen to another tirade until he calmed down. He did not realize how hard I was working in the background to make this visit successful for all of them.

Five days before the trip, Alex woke up sick. I took him to the doctor only to discover his tubes had already fallen out and he had another ear infection. The doctor was concerned whether he would be able to fly. He wanted to see both kids again before they left. Of course, I needed to make Donnie aware of the situation, just in case medically the kids had an issue. His reaction was not pleasant, but it was as I expected.

"What are you doing, trying to make those kids sick?" he asked in an accusatory tone!
Exasperation filled my body. How dare he accuse me of making my children sick!

"No one tries to make their kids sick. I have another appointment with both kids the day before they leave. I'm sure Alex's ear will be better, but I'll be sending him with medication."

Donnie was not happy.

At the recheck the doctor said Alex's ear was better but there was still fluid. All the doctor would say was that the altitude could cause Alex's ear to plug and he would be extremely uncomfortable for several days, but the ear was not bad enough to say Alex could not fly. He checked Jennifer and said her lungs were much better. So, it looked like both kids were cleared for takeoff.

The dreaded day arrived, June 18. The children and I went to the airport alone. Donnie's flight came in around 4:00 p.m. but we did not arrive until 6:00. This gave the kids a little time to get reacquainted before the return flight at 7:30. Alex remembered his dad but was very shy and withdrawn. Jennifer was fourteen months old, so Donnie was a complete stranger to her. During our conversation I suggested I would not call for the first few days because I knew Alex would be homesick and hearing my voice would only make the situation worse. Donnie jumped at that suggestion. He shared that his mother was staying with them the entire visit because she wanted to spend time with the kids as well. That brought some comfort to me knowing grandma would be there.

The moment came when I had to turn the children over to Donnie. Very matter-of-fact Donnie took Alex's hand, scooped up Jennifer, and headed down the jetway. Donnie was in such a hurry, he didn't give me a chance to kiss them goodbye. Jennifer was screaming and Alex kept turning around. I could see tears rolling down his face, his eyes questioning why this was happening to him. My heart was about to explode from my chest. My legs felt like Jell-O. I stayed at the window until the plane pulled away towards the runway. As I turned to head back up the concourse, I could sense the stares as I sobbed all the way through the airport. Tears would not stop flowing. Being face to face with Donnie opened a floodgate of emotions. My soul was deeply troubled.

4. The Test

*~ A noun referring to an event or situation that
reveals the reliability of someone ~*

Before I could leave the airport, I had to sit in my car until I got hold of myself. My mind was numb. Next thing I knew I pulled my car into the garage, but I had no recollection of driving home. That haunting look in Alex's eyes and Jennifer's screams filled my senses, as they must have felt I was abandoning them. Apprehension overtook me as I opened the door to the duplex. Scanning the room, I spotted Alex's little car and Jennifer's little musical radio. Butterflies flew around my stomach. The kids had spent nights away from me before without any problems. In fact, I looked forward to a night or two of freedom. But this was different. I knew Donnie and that was the problem. I walked into the living room, turned on some music, and started talking with God. Because my protective motherly instincts were in overdrive, the answer was obvious, completely surrender my children over to God and allow Him to protect them throughout this visit, for the children needed protection.

Sleep was nowhere to be found that night. Thursday morning, I managed to drag myself out of bed. When I looked at myself in the mirror you would have thought I had been in a fight. My eyes were swollen and bloodshot. I had to get to work regardless of how I looked. Since many of my co-workers were aware of Donnie's shenanigans with setting the visitation schedule, I knew there would be questions regarding how the transition went. I filled myself with positivity and attempted to put the best possible spin on a bad situation. I did not want them to know the true emptiness I felt and the guilt I harbored by putting my children in harm's way.

My smile may have been plastered on my face but that foreboding feeling never left the pit of my stomach. I knew this man all too well. My instincts could sense the longing of my children to be home. I just kept telling myself, "Grandma is there, and she'll love and protect them even if no one else will."

I knew I was incapable of going back to the duplex after work, so I went to visit my folks to get some much-needed support.

"You have to give him a chance to prove he can fulfill his end of the bargain," they reasoned.

"I know, but we are talking about children here, not objects."

I knew what they said was right. Donnie did have to prove himself.

"What can he do to them in two and a half weeks?" Mom asked.

I did not want my mind to go there, but that was exactly where my mind was and why I was so troubled. Since I had lived with this man for seven years, I knew, beyond a shadow of a doubt, what he could do. I had turned over a three-year-old and a fourteen-month-old into his web of power and control. I was also all too familiar with his temper and his inability to control it around children. Having experienced him spanking Alex from the time he was four weeks old, I realized there was the strong possibility he would do the same to Jennifer. Yes, I was genuinely concerned about what he could do to them in two and a half weeks. I was fearful for my children's well-being.

But, looking at this from the outside, I knew my distress would appear as though I was the unstable female that couldn't stand to be away from her children and wanted to deny Donnie a chance to visit his kids. No one, not even his mother, knew the real Donnie and no one would understand this man never plays by the rules. I had not shared with anyone his conversation with me where he threatened to take the children away from me. I knew that threat would be held over my head at every turn. My instincts were sending up warning signals like a fireworks display, and that troubled my soul. The problem was no one understood.

I knew what my parents said was right. After all, he was their father and perhaps my instincts were wrong.

Mom continued, "Arlene will be there, so try to relax and find something to help pass your time these next few weeks."

That was good advice. I needed a project to occupy my evenings and weekends, so I stopped at the fabric store on the way home and purchased material for a suit. That would keep me busy.

On Saturday I could not wait to call Donnie to see how the kids were doing. As I had promised on Wednesday, when he picked them up, I had waited three days, allowing the kids to settle in a bit. As I dialed the number my heart was racing, I was anxiously waiting to hear Alex's voice to assure me all was well. Donnie answered the phone.

"How is it going?" I asked.

"Oh, it couldn't be better," he was so bubbly. "The kids are all getting along so well. Alex loves having someone to play with," he expounded.

"That's good to hear," I said. "I take it his ears are doing ok?"

"Oh, yes, he hasn't complained once," Donnie sounded so proud.

I asked, "Could I please talk with Alex?"

"No," Donnie replied emphatically, "he's busy playing with the kids and I'm not going to interrupt him."

Silence. Just take a deep breath, Mary.

"How's Jennifer?" I inquired.

"She's fine. Thanks for calling."

With that, he hung up.

Tears filled my eyes. Just as I had presumed, Donnie was, once again, in control. He had control of the children and he was controlling me. As the old saying goes, "Possession is nine-tenths of the law." Ownership is easier to maintain if you have possession of something, or in this case, someone. "Lord, please keep those kids safe," I prayed. The knot in the pit of my stomach tightened like a boa constrictor around its prey. If I could have done something I would have, but I was helpless. I had to ride this train to the end of the line.

When I was in the office my days were fully occupied, but my evenings were excruciatingly long. I would stay at the office to avoid going home to an empty house. Yes, the house was lonely without the children's laughter, but this was different. It was the feeling in the pit of my stomach knowing Donnie's capabilities. After the futile attempt to speak with Alex on Saturday, I fought the urge to call again until the following Wednesday. Any earlier attempt would be wasted because I knew Donnie would not allow me to talk with the children. Seven days had passed since they left. I felt sure Alex had to be wondering why he had not heard my voice, for I had promised him I would call while he was gone. Anxiety started setting in as I dialed the phone, for I know what happens when this man is in control. Several rings, no answer. After an hour I tried again, this time the oldest girl answered.

"Hi," I said, "I'm Mary, Alex's and Jennifer's mom. Is Donnie there?"

"No, he, Mom, and Jennifer went to San Antonio."

"Okay, could I talk with Alex?"

"No, he's busy."

Obviously, she had been instructed in what to say.

"Okay, can I talk with Arlene?"

"No, she isn't here," she said.

"What time will Donnie be home?" I asked.

"I don't know," she replied

"When will Arlene be back?"

"Oh, she went home," she volunteered.

I was trying with everything within me to remain calm.

"All right, I'll try again later this afternoon."

Breathe, Mary, just breathe.

"Okay."

Before I could say another word, she hung up.

The gut-wrenching knot returned in my stomach. Several things were wrong here: a thirteen-year-old was in charge of five younger kids (Alex being the youngest), Arlene (who was supposed to be there the entire visit) had returned home, the thirteen-year-old had no idea what time her parents would return. My antennae were up and the signals I was receiving were not good. Another attempt to make contact was made later in the day. The oldest girl answered again but said they still were not home. Since I was incurring a long distance charge every time I called, I had to let it go. There was no other way to contact Donnie except the house phone. (Remember, in the 1980s we did not have cell phones. Every call was made via a landline.)

All I could do was toss and turn all night; no sleep was to be had. My intuition alarm was blaring full blast with no way to shut it down. I kept telling myself I needed to keep busy. The visit was not halfway over yet, so I needed to calm down. In my mind, because of the age of the children, there should be a spirit of cooperation coming from Donnie, not roadblocks. On Thursday, during lunch, I tried calling again, Donnie answered.

"How is everything?" I asked.

"Couldn't be better," he said joyfully.

Donnie kept talking unnecessary chitchat. Each time I asked to talk with Alex he would change the subject. On the third attempt to request talking with Alex his response changed.

"Oh, I'm so sorry, Patricia just left with all the kids. We had friends come down from Austin and Patricia had planned an afternoon with everyone away from the house."

"Really?" I questioned.

"Yes, it's a shame but I wanted to talk to you about a few things anyway. Alex got another bad ear infection, so we had to take him to the doctor. Jennifer was having problems breathing so we took her to an asthma clinic. Both kids are scheduled for complete physicals next week and we are getting Alex's eyes checked," he babbled.

"Is all that necessary?" I questioned. "All of their doctor visits were current before they left. I sent Alex's medicine with you. He should have just finished that a few days ago. I don't understand how he got another ear infection so soon."

"Oh, we just want to make sure they are okay. I've got a lot to do while the tribe is gone so take care," and he hung up the phone.

This was all sounding very peculiar. He knew I kept up with the kid's health. Besides, both kids were healthy when they left. The more I thought about it, the more troubled I became. My inner self was screaming. "Was I just overreacting?" I asked myself. No, I knew this man all too well. Again, I knew no one would understand.

Saturday morning rolled around after another troubled night's sleep. Now my children had been gone ten days. I could not anticipate what the weekend would bring. I decided to call Arlene, trusting she could provide enough insight so peace would return to my soul.

"Oh Mary!" she exclaimed. "I'm so glad you called."

"What's going on? Are the kids okay?" I was filled with questions.

"I couldn't take it any longer. I was there Wednesday when Donnie came in with the kids. I felt sorry for them because Patricia and her kids just mauled them. Both kids were scared to death. Donnie and Patricia made me feel so uncomfortable that I had to call Francis to come pick me up on Tuesday. Patricia was enraged with jealousy. She wouldn't even let me pick Jennifer up. If she caught me with Jennifer in my arms, she'd grab her away and go into another room. It was impossible to play with Alex because all the kids kept him away from me. One day, when I was by their bedroom, I overheard Patricia call several attorneys trying to find one who would start proceedings to take the children away from you. That really bothered me. They set up all kinds of doctor appointments for both kids. The house was so filthy I couldn't stand it. Seven kids, five dogs, and four cats made it impossible to keep up. By the time I left both kids were filthy. I asked if I could take the kids to Austin with me for a few days, but both Donnie and Patricia emphatically said no."

Arlene was beside herself. I tried to remain calm, but I was not doing a particularly good job of it. I found myself trembling as she continued.

"When Francis came to pick me up, Patricia asked his advice on starting proceedings to take the kids from you. He advised them to wait. I do not know what to tell you. I don't feel comfortable around Patricia at all. I don't trust her."

"I don't know what to say." I was in shock. "I don't know why they want to take my children from me. I am a good mother and can provide for them. It just does not make sense. If you hear anything, will you please call me? Donnie won't allow me to speak with Alex. The kids have been gone ten days now and I have not spoken with them. I'm overly concerned."

"Sure, I'll let you know for I'm concerned as well," she said, and we ended our conversation.

Collapsing into a chair I felt like a rag doll. All the energy had drained from my body. Where was I to turn? I prayed, "Lord, you are my only hope here. Please do something positive for us and please protect those babies." Some things still did not add up. If Arlene was so upset about Donnie and Patricia wanting to take the kids from me, why didn't she talk to her son about that. It did not sound like Francis or Arlene were even trying to dissuade Donnie from pursuing this course of action. She also could have called me when she first got home to let me know what was going on. I did not fully understand, but I also knew this was her only son and she did not want to betray him.

Just six months earlier Donnie had cast these kids aside like moldy bread. He could not stand to be around them and now he wanted to take them from me? He was attempting to make the kids' health an issue to prove my incompetence. Donnie knew I took good care of the children. The kids may have had a rough winter, but they had so many adjustments to make. Yes, there was a slight possibility Alex's ear could have become infected again or the flight to Texas exacerbated the situation, but that does not make me unfit. Jennifer's breathing problems could easily be explained if the house was as dirty as Arlene described, along with all those pets. Nothing made sense. What would make him think the children were better off with him rather than me, other than to hurt me? My mind was reeling. In the long run all I knew was that I was in trouble.

The first thing Monday morning I placed a call to both attorneys, Carl and Sam. Neither one provided very encouraging news. At least they both agreed, I would have to wait until July 7 before anything could be discussed. This was technically his time to have the kids. Great, another seven days to go.

Since both attorneys agreed it was Donnie's time with the kids, I had to accept the terms Donnie was dictating. They had been gone almost two weeks and I had not been allowed to speak with them. Control! Unrelenting control! Donnie was controlling the children and me. We were his puppets and he the puppeteer.

Even though Donnie kept me from speaking with Alex I continued to be persistent. I called again on Wednesday in hopes of talking to Alex. By now my children had been gone two weeks. Donnie answered. He wasted no time jumping right into his agenda.

"Things are going terrific here! I do have some news for you though," he said.

Tentatively I asked, "What's that?"

"We've had both kids to the doctor and he's not happy with either one. He's concerned about Jennifer's weight, and Alex's ear infection is worse, so a follow-up appointment has been scheduled for July 9."

"No!" I interrupted him. "I expect the children home on the 7th. That was our agreement. If Alex is not able to fly, then you can drive the children back."

"Oh, I can't do that," Donnie whined, "I don't have that much vacation time since I've taken several days of vacation while the kids have been here with me."

"I expect them on the 7th!" I was very explicit.

"We'll see," he said very cocky. "I'll call you on the 6th."

With that he hung up. My boat was going downstream and I did not have a paddle. I was about to plummet over the falls and into the rocks below. There was no reasoning with this man. All I could do was painfully wait.

On the 6th I woke up earlier than normal. My anxiety level was high before I ever stepped out of bed. Donnie said he would call on the 6th with the arrangements regarding the kids return. I knew he would wait until the end of the day to call but I was nervous regarding this commitment. I needed to get away from my own internal conflict, so I visited my folks following church. Home, at the farm, always brought a sense of calm, and my folks provided some much-needed relief to my pressure cooker. Throughout the day, whenever the opportunity was available, I spoke nonstop to the Lord. It had been a horrendous eighteen days but the day for return was at hand. God had provided me with strength to ride out this visit. From the outside, it appeared as though a loving father was enjoying a visit with his children and I was an unreasonable mother who could not let her children go, even for a short visit. Only God and I understood Donnie's capabilities. His behavior and domination could not be easily explained to anyone. My anxiety level was building for tomorrow. Waiting from late afternoon and into the evening for the elusive phone call was torturous. The minutes slowly slipped away like a slow dripping faucet, and by 11 p.m. I gave up waiting. Donnie never intended to call.

July 7 finally arrived. Excitement filled my bones! From Donnie's original itinerary, the children were to arrive around 1:45 p.m. The pastor's wife, Sherri, volunteered to drive me to Omaha so I could love on my children all the way home. I went into work early since I would only be working half the day. By mid-morning I called Texas to verify the flight schedule. Patricia answered.

"Is Donnie there?" I asked.

"No, he's already gone to work," she sounded so bubbly.

Work? He was supposed to be getting the kids ready to come home.

"May I speak with Alex?"

"Sure," she never hesitated a bit.

This was the first time I had been allowed to talk with Alex since he had left. I could tell she was listening on one of the extensions.

"Hi Buddy!" I said cheerfully, "How are you doing?"

"My daddy is having breakfast."

Huh? I heard Patricia laugh.

"Me and Jennifer aren't coming back." I caught that loud and clear.

I asked him to repeat that just in case I misunderstood. He said the same thing again.

"I love you and miss you very much, Son. Can I talk with Patricia again?"

She laughed after Alex hung up. I was fuming. I told her I wanted Donnie to call me immediately. Alex got back on the phone.

"I've gotten some new toys and I'm going to move into a big, new house with Daddy and Mommy."

"Is that so? I bet you are excited. I love you, Alex."

I could not believe my ears. Again, Patricia laughed. I could hear Alex ask if anyone else wanted to talk to Mary before he hung up the phone. Since I was unable confirm Donnie's whereabouts, I asked Patricia point blank.

"Are the kids flying home today?"

"I don't think so," she said very matter-of-factly. "We have follow-up doctor appointments for the kids on Wednesday. Donnie should be in the office by 9:30 so call him there."

At 9:30 I called Donnie at work. He was not there. I called the house. Patricia said he should be at work. Getting nowhere, my frustration level peaked, I felt like I was going to explode. I had to leave work. More phone calls had to be made, but most of all, I needed the freedom to scream.

Sherri arrived by 11:00. As soon as she stepped in the door I broke down.

"They're not coming home," was all I could blurt out.
She grabbed me and held me tight while I sobbed on her shoulder.

"That can't be!" she exclaimed.

We stood there wrapped in each other's arms for the longest time as she consoled me. I shared with her the phone conversation I had with Alex a few hours earlier, and that it would be a waste of time making the trip to Omaha.

"Have you checked the flights?" she asked.

"Only a law officer or attorney would be able to find out if Donnie is actually on that flight," I explained.

She called her husband to explain the situation. Pastor John knew someone in the Lincoln police station and was sure he would be able to find something out for us. Waiting was excruciating. The phone rang, I let Sherri answer. Just watching the expression on her face, I could see the news was not good. After she hung up, she shared the conversation. The local detective called the Omaha airport authorities who confirmed the tickets had been cancelled some time ago. Donnie never intended to return the children. My children were not coming home.

Once Sherri left, I fell apart, sobbing uncontrollably. The internal war that had been raging within me since the kid's departure had culminated. I succumbed to the giant.

Since my world had just fallen apart, I did not know where to turn. The first person I thought to call was my mother. As soon as I heard her voice I fell apart.

"Mary, what's wrong?" she asked.

Between sobs I managed to explain the situation.

"What are you going to do?"

"I have no idea right now. I have to think but I can't," I said.

"I'm so sorry," was all she could get out before she started crying. Neither one of us could talk. We both felt helpless.

"I've got to go," I said, "I can't talk."
With that I hung up.

Since I was unable to think straight, I called Barb for advice. She could not comprehend Donnie's actions.

"Mary, pull yourself together and go back to the office. You can't sit in that house," she demanded.

"And how do you expect me to go back to the office in this condition?" I cried back at her.

"Pull it together and go back. I'll come down as soon as I get off work," she was very insistent.

"I don't know if I can," I blubbered.

Forcefully she said, "You CAN, and you WILL!"

She was not accepting any other answer. In my current state of mind, all I could do was agree. I prayed, "God, just tell me what to do for my mind is not functioning."

It took me awhile to gain control. In a daze I drove back to work. Everyone in my department knew I had taken the afternoon off to pick up the children. They were surprised to see me walk back into the office, but no one asked a question. They knew something had gone terribly wrong. Their stares penetrated my core as I walked back to my cubical.

After work Barb arrived and tried to be upbeat. We hugged, we cried. I felt so helpless and hopeless at this point.

"Fix your makeup," she ordered lovingly. "We're going out."

"I'm really not up for that," I muttered.

There was no arguing with her. Barb's intent that night was to help me get my mind off the situation for a few hours. She knew the days ahead would be filled with chaos.

She drove us to a bar on the far side of town. My presumption was that Barb and I would have a couple drinks and talk for a few hours. Little did I know, she had arranged for a male friend of hers from

Omaha to join us. Chitchatting with strangers was not what I particularly wanted to do, but I did as best I could. The two of them visited quite a while before another gentleman, Tom Dietrich, walked up and joined us. Barb had not told me that she had given her friend an assignment; find a single local bachelor to join us. After a bit, Barb and her friend decided they needed to head back to Omaha since this was a weeknight. Naturally, Barb's friend asked Tom if he would make sure I got home.

"Not a problem," Tom agreed.

Since Tom and I had hardly talked to each other, he made a recommendation.

"Let's have one more drink and I'll take you home."

I agreed.

We made our way around the initial interview questions. He was a man of his word. After finishing our drink, we left.

Tom followed my directions to the duplex, parked in front of the garage, got out of the car, and walked around to open my door. As soon as I stepped out of the car the tornado sirens started blaring. In Nebraska one never ignores tornado sirens.

"You'd better come in until this storm passes," I suggested.

We headed for the basement. His eyes scanned the room as we stepped down each stair.

"I see you have kids," he said.

"Yes, I do. I have two, a boy and a girl," I responded.

"Aren't you going to bring them downstairs to safety?" he asked.

His question impressed me. That was extremely thoughtful of him. Telling the truth was the only way around his question. Here we go. I invited him to sit down at the children's table and I shared the story as to why they were not with me. As I told him the story, he had a puzzled, yet sympathetic expression on his face. He could not believe anyone would do something like that. The sirens finally stopped, and we went upstairs. He asked for my phone number, and he left. Tom had to be overwhelmed from the information he had just heard. If it were me, I would have run in the opposite direction.

The following morning, while attempting to work, the phone rang. It was Donnie.

"How are you?"

He was extremely cheerful.

"You were supposed to return the children yesterday. What's up?" I was not cheerful.

"I have to take Alex back to the doctor tomorrow for a recheck of his ears," he said. "I told you that."

"You had plenty of opportunity to get the recheck completed. Our arrangement was for you to return the kids on the 7th," I bellowed. I knew everyone sitting around me heard this entire conversation.

"I just wanted you to know. I'll call you tomorrow after I take Alex to the doctor," he said very matter-of-factly, and hung up before I could utter another word.

Exasperated, I called Sam in Texas. Earlier he had said we would have to wait until the 7th, to see if Donnie returned the children before anything could be done. Well, here we were, Tuesday the 8th. I gave him all the information.

"Thanks," he said very businesslike, "I'll personally call Donnie and see what's going on. Oh, I advise you to never make another verbal agreement with Donnie. Obviously, you two have problems understanding verbal commitments."

Did he just put the blame equally on both of us? Put off by that comment, I sat in silence before I opened my mouth to say another word. It was all I could do to say thank you and get off the phone before I said something I would regret.

The day moved at a snail's pace and I did not hear from anyone. My co-workers gave me space. No one put extra burdens on me. No one asked questions. No one talked to me.

Wednesday came, July 9, the day I was to receive two phone calls: one from Donnie and another from my attorney. By late afternoon I had not heard from either of them. I decided to call my attorney first.

"Oh, I'm so sorry, Sam is busy and unable to talk at this time," his secretary told me.

"Are you able to tell me anything? Sam was to call Donnie regarding returning my children," I asked.

"Oh yes, Sam did call Donnie and advised Donnie to return the kids back to you. Donnie gave him the name of his attorney and the doctor where he'd taken the children. Donnie told Sam to call them. I'm sorry but that is all I know," she said.

"Would you please ask Sam to call me before he leaves for the day?" I begged.

"I'll relay the message," she said cheerfully.

As I should have expected, I did not receive a call back.

After waiting yet another day, I lacked the patience for Sam to return my call, so I called his office again. I needed to get hold of him. To me, this was becoming an emergency. My children were not home. Donnie had violated his own agreement. We were talking about the lives of two small innocent children.

"Hello, Sam, I'm sorry to bother you but what is going on with my children?" I inquired calmly.

"Mary, please, don't get so upset! Donnie hasn't done anything, yet. Donnie told me some judge advised him the 19th wouldn't be too unreasonable for him to keep the children. He also told me he was concerned for the kid's welfare and health. He's had Alex to a doctor who claimed Alex did have an ear infection and shouldn't fly," he explained nonchalantly.

"What's wrong with Donnie putting the children in a car and driving them back?" I asked. I thought that to be a reasonable question.

"Oh, that would be unreasonable to ask. Donnie told me it would take him a week to make the trip," he insisted.

I could not believe he just said that. Hadn't he bothered to look up how far it was between Devine, Texas and Lincoln, Nebraska? Last I knew it was roughly 900 miles. That is not a three and a half day journey each way. At this point, I was not sure if Sam was working for Donnie or me. I did know Donnie's lies could be extremely persuasive and his delivery exceptionally smooth. Before finishing our conversation, Sam had one last piece of advice that made my blood boil.

"Just grow up and stop worrying about things."

"Thank you, Sam. I'm sorry to have bothered you today."

It was obvious Sam had more important things to do than to see that two children were returned to their mother. Anger was boiling up inside me to the point I could have fired him on the spot, but I needed him. I was not living in San Antonio, so it made it difficult to change attorneys. I just wish Sam would believe me and realize Donnie was a habitual liar. But, realistically, no one understood Donnie's capabilities but me.

By this time, all my buttons had been pushed. I was furious! I had been pushed into a corner and I was ready to come out fighting. I placed a call to my local attorney, fully intending to leave a message. Surprisingly, Carl was in the office and answered the phone. I explained what had transpired.

"There really isn't anything that can be done. There is no legal recourse to make Donnie return the children. Why don't you drive down this weekend and pick up the kids yourself?"

"Thank you for the advice," I said and hung up.

I really did not get it. It was okay for me to drive to Texas to pick up the children but not okay for Donnie to drive to Nebraska to return them. I knew beyond a shadow of a doubt, that if I made the trip to Texas to pick up the children, without legal intervention, Donnie would not allow me into the house nor would he turn the children over to me. If I were to step foot on his property, he would either have me arrested or shoot me, so that option was not worth pursuing. I concluded that no one cared that the children were not returned to me because they were with their father. But Donnie was a master manipulator, and no one could see that. I was alone, dejected, frustrated, in despair, and drained!

Up to this point I had tried to do everything right. I allowed the children to visit their father even though he extended the visitation period without agreement. I tried to be thoughtful and allow Donnie space with the children by not making daily phone calls of inquiry. We had a verbal agreement, and, in my eyes, it was as good as a written contract. But Donnie was not concerned about any agreement. He was in control, alienating the children against me by not allowing me any contact with them, and now, had extended the visit for a third time.

Topping the morning off, Donnie called late.

"Hey, just want to tell you we had Alex to the doctor yesterday and he has been given the okay to fly. But, before you say anything, I want to keep the kids until next weekend."

"No," I said emphatically. "You've already had them longer than our agreement. I want them home."

"Well, your home life can't be particularly good because whenever I mention going home to Alex, he gets terribly upset. He wants to stay here," Donnie said in a very accusatory tone.

Rather than argue, I said each word slowly and deliberately,

"Just bring them home. I want them home now!"

This time I hung up first.

My heart ached as I thought about the children. Alex did not want to go to Texas in the first place. Now, three weeks later, he does not want to come home. He had to be so confused. But last I knew, three-year-old children do not get to choose where they want to live. By this time Alex had to think I had deserted him. There were no options. Without legal help, I was boxed in.

One more phone call. This time it was to Donnie's mother.

"Hello, Mary. How are you doing?"

"Truthfully, Not good. I don't understand why Donnie doesn't bring the children home," I said pathetically.

"If need be," she said, "I'm ready to testify on your behalf that the children belong with you."

"Thank you," I said humbly, thinking maybe she understands.

"Donnie and Patricia called yesterday for prayer with Francis. They are still thinking of starting proceedings to take the kids from you."

All the blood drained from me. I felt like a deflating balloon.

"Thank you, Arlene. I do not know what to say. I cannot believe they are doing this to me. Patricia is a mother of five. She must know what this would feel like if she were in my shoes. Is it a matter that she wants two blond haired, blue eyed children?" I said grasping for answers.

"I don't know what she's thinking but she doesn't give me a good feeling," she said.

"Thank you. Please let me know if anything else comes up," I pleaded.

I knew I was a good mother. Where did I go wrong? There was no legal option but to send the children on this initial visit. I would have been held in contempt if I had not sent them. Now there was no legal recourse for Donnie to return them. It made no sense to me.

Sandwiched between the cracks of this storm swirling around me, Tom called and asked me out. Funny, I really did not think I would hear from him again. I could not have made that great of an impression the first night. Maybe he was simply curious to see if I was crazy. It really was not in me to go out, but I knew I could not sit home. Perhaps a little distraction would do me good, so I agreed. We went to a movie and out for drinks afterwards. It turned out to be a good choice because I could focus on the movie and forget my troubles.

Sunday, after church, I spent some time with Pastor John and Sherri. The pastor was a little concerned regarding Sam's cavalier attitude regarding the situation. Pastor John agreed that family law would not be simple, but a little compassion should not be too much to ask. From there I went to visit my folks for they needed to be made aware of the latest developments. They could not believe Donnie would attempt to take my children from me.

"Well, he is thinking rather seriously of doing it," I said.

"Is there anything we can do?" they asked.

"No, I'm not sure there's anything anyone can do. I am not even sure I have any influence. The laws are not written to protect children or the custodial parent."

Eventually, I had to make the painful trip back to the duplex and prepare, emotionally, for another week.

On Monday Pastor John placed a call to Sam only to find out he was going to be out of the office until mid-week. Lovely! Time was marching on with no progress being made. Divert, deceive, stall, lie, outwit, manipulate, Donnie's tactics, all while wasting time. These were Donnie's original intentions all along.

Later in the week, Pastor John finally got hold of Sam.

"Hello, Sam, this is Pastor John Palmer calling. I'm Mary's pastor and I'm calling to share with you my concern regarding the children not being returned from Donnie."

"Oh, yes," Sam said. "I did put a call into Donnie's attorney, but he hasn't returned my call."

"Is there any way you could call Donnie to make the arrangements for the return? Especially, since you advised Mary not to make any more verbal agreements with Donnie. Perhaps if you make the arrangement for the return, Donnie will be more apt to commit to the terms." Pastor John was pleading.

"I can do that," Sam agreed, "I'll get right on that."

"One more thing," Pastor John said. "If Donnie refuses to return the children, is there any way you can plead with the court for their return?"

"Yes, I can," said Sam, "but there is no need to do that for another week or so."

"Okay, but it is a possibility?" Pastor John questioned.

"Yes, it is, but let's see what pressure I can lend to the situation first," Sam recommended.

"Thank you for trying, Sam," Pastor John acknowledged and hung up.

Another couple of days passed. Still no word. I buried myself in my work. Compartmentalize. At home and on the weekends I was a wreck, but at work I was able to function. Escape! It worked. Otherwise, I would have lost my mind by now.

Late in the afternoon Thursday, the 17th, I received a call. On the other end was Sam and he was furious.

"I've never seen a more ridiculous situation in my life!" he screamed. "I contacted Donnie's attorney and he claimed he was not representing Donnie. In fact, he had never heard of Donnie. Then I called Donnie at work and he refused to talk with me. Next, I called the house and talked with Donnie's wife. She said they had been waiting all week for you to call and let them know the day you wanted them to bring the kids home. They were willing but it seemed like you were totally unconcerned and did not care when or if you get them back. She claimed you hadn't even tried to talk with Alex since he'd been there."

Breathe, Mary, just breathe!

"Sam, that is not the case," I cried out. "She is lying to you. I have been trying to get those kids back since the 7th!"

"Well, you'd better call and tell them when you expect the kids to be returned," he ordered.

"But you didn't want me making another verbal agreement with Donnie," I responded emphatically.

"**Just do it!**" he ordered.

"Okay, I'll try."

Dread filled me as I dialed the phone number for Donnie's house. Of course, Patricia had to answer.

"Oh, Donnie isn't home from work yet," she cheerfully responded.

Very matter-of-factly I stated, "Okay, please give Donnie a message for me."

"Sure," she said every so sweetly. "I'm ready, go ahead."

"I expect the kids to be returned Saturday, the 19th! That's it! There will be no negotiating. Saturday is the date." The message was noticeably clear.

"I'll give him the message. Do you want to talk with Alex?" she asked.

What? I've only been allowed to talk with him once the entire time that he has been gone and that was July 7 and now you are volunteering? Oh, she was so evil!

"Of course," I exclaimed. "I'd love to talk with him!"

"I'm having so much fun. Daddy took me swimming yesterday and let me get my hair wet," he said.

He sounded excited. That much was encouraging, but Donnie knew with Alex's history of ear infections, swimming was taking a risk of another infection. Maybe that was his intention.

"I'm so happy you are having fun, Alex. Mommy loves you."

"Okay," and he hung up.

Before I went to bed the phone rang. Donnie started chewing on me immediately.

"Patricia gave me your message. How dare you talk to her that way! You are being unreasonable and disrespectful! I cannot believe you just call up and demand the kids be returned Saturday when this is Thursday. We have had plans for this Saturday for a long time and I am not about to cancel them. If you're so eager to get them back why don't you fly out here and pick them up?"

Here we go.

"No, the decree states it's your responsibility to pick up the kids and return them on the agreed upon dates, and that date was July 7! Just go ahead and make the reservations for Saturday." I was trying to be assertive. Scared, but assertive.

He continued the bashing. Finally, I interrupted,

"I will call you in the morning to find out the flight schedule. Thanks. We'll talk in the morning."

With that I hung up.

Friday, I waited until mid-morning before I called. Donnie was home and answered.

"Can you tell me what flight you're coming in on tomorrow?" I asked.

"Well, I've made tentative reservations tomorrow, flight 678 arriving at 6:52 p.m.," he said grudgingly.

I knew this was a valid flight because I had checked all of them myself.

"That will be fine," I said. "I expect to see the children then. I'll be at the airport to meet you."

He was not happy about this situation. There was a long pause. The silence was deafening. I was not going to wait for him to suggest another alternative.

"See you tomorrow," I said. This time, I hung up.

An hour passed and the phone rang again. It was Donnie.

"I've been talking with Alex and he doesn't want to come back. He is really upset. I have this great idea. How 'bout you let me keep Alex all summer and I'll bring Jennifer back." Before I could even open my mouth, he continued, "Why don't you think about it and maybe God will show you the right thing to do here."

Right thing to do? Who has not done the right thing all along here? How could he think it was God's will to keep the children a month? Throughout our entire marriage he was always justifying his actions according to "God's will." My relationship with God may not be super deep but I know enough that it was not God's will for Donnie to keep the children from me.

"I've thought about it. I expect both of the children to be at the airport tomorrow night!"

I put it exceptionally clear to him. That was the way the conversation ended as I hung up abruptly.

How confident did I feel? Not! It was like trying to retain a water level in a bucket riddled with holes. There was no confirmation from Donnie that I would see him tomorrow. He had several hours to come up with another excuse. There was nothing in place to make him return the children. Again, this was a verbal agreement between the two of us.

On top of everything else going on, Tom wanted to go out Saturday night. Up to this point I had kept my personal situation away from him. With the kids' return, things would be different. I explained my children were coming home so we would have to go out another time. Whether he understood or not, did not matter. I was incapable of juggling Donnie, my children, and a new relationship all at the same time.

Time seemed to stand still all-day Saturday. I fully expected the phone to ring with Donnie bearing the news that they would not be coming home. Much to my surprise, the phone never rang all day. Pastor John and Sherri volunteered to take me to the airport. They realized I needed mental support as well as allowing me freedom with the children IF they were returned. We arrived at the airport in plenty of time. My blood pressure had to be through the roof as my anxiety level was skyrocketing. I had no idea who was going to show up: maybe no one, maybe just Jennifer, or maybe both kids.

The plane taxied to the jetway. My heart was pounding like a sledgehammer against my chest. The passengers began to disembark. The first one I saw walking up the ramp was Donnie. I did not realize I had been holding my breath. I finally exhaled. Relief overwhelmed me. Right behind Donnie was Patricia, holding Jennifer. The kids were back! "Hallelujah! Thank you, God!"

The kid's reaction to seeing me was exactly opposite of what I expected. Taking Jennifer from Patricia's arms, Jennifer wrapped her arms around my neck and snuggled her face into my neck. As I was hugging Jennifer, Patricia informed me,

"I just want to tell you we weaned Jennifer from her pacifier right after she arrived. She didn't need it any longer. She was much too old for it."

In my mind I was shaking my head. That would be the worst time to attempt to wean a child from their pacifier. Alex refused to look at me. He was nervous and seemed frightened. He hung onto my leg but would not talk or smile. Donnie handed over the kids things, Donnie and Patricia said goodbye to Alex, Pastor John exchanged some pleasantries, and we headed up the concourse. I refused to say thank you or goodbye. I was in no mood for charades. I just wanted away from there, as far away from them and the situation as possible.

The ride home was extremely quiet. Alex would not respond to questions. Jennifer would not release the clutch around my neck. She would lean back, look at me, and clutch my neck again. She seemed to be figuring out if it was really me. One thing I did notice, there were no smiles on their dear faces. No matter what I did or what I said, they would not smile.

My mind was disturbed. Alex was not acting normal. What had he been told? His eyes looked blank. Had they been mistreated? Why were they unable to smile? What had these people done to my dear happy children?

One thing was obvious. A verbal, mutually agreed upon fourteen-day visit, had turned into a thirty-one-day nightmare! Donnie had failed the first test.

5. Healing

*~ A noun referring to the process of making or
becoming sound or healthy again ~*

Pastor John and Sherri helped me get the kids, bags, and suitcase into the house. I thanked them profusely for taking their time to make the trip with me. They excused themselves quickly as they could see we needed some time together.

The children just stood in the living room like little soldiers staring at me with blank eyes. They did not seem excited to see me, to be home, to play with their toys, or look around, nothing, they just stood there. I prayed, "Oh Dear Lord, what has happened to them?" I might as well have picked two random kids up off the street.

For the sake of the kids, I needed to be upbeat, regardless of how I felt.

"Mommy is so glad you're home!"

I got down on my knees and gave them big hugs and kisses. Nothing, no response, no hug back, blank stares, silence.

"Okay, let's get your things to your rooms and we'll find something fun to eat."

"I'm not hungry," Alex said lifelessly.

"Let's go downstairs then and play until you are ready for something. Just let me know when you get hungry. I have all your favorite foods. Maybe we can have some ice cream later," I offered.

They needed a distraction to get their minds occupied.

"First, we need to change Jennifer's diaper," I said. "Alex, can you help Mommy?"

I put Jennifer on the changing table and removed her wet diaper. I was shocked at what I saw. Her little bottom had feces everywhere, all around and inside her vaginal area as well as between both legs. She had not soiled her diaper; she just had not been cleaned. Her little bottom looked like a piece of raw meat, fiery red! My heart went out to her for this had to be painful. She just laid there, motionless. Attempting to get Alex involved, I asked him to hand me things, which he did. I cleaned her up and lathered her in paste.

We played until close to bedtime. I did not attempt to bathe them as I was not about to push too hard, too fast. While I was getting Alex ready for bed, I noticed he was not wearing underwear.

"Where's your underwear, Alex?"

"I don't know. I couldn't find anything clean."

"That's okay, I have more here in your drawer," I said putting him at ease.

Getting him into his pajamas I noticed his little legs were covered with bruises and scratches. His feet were extremely filthy, so I got a washcloth and wiped them clean. I saw a cut on the bottom on his foot.

"What happened to your foot?" I inquired as I washed it.

"I stepped on a piece of glass."

"I bet that hurt! Let me get that really clean then I'll put some medicine and a Band-Aid on it for tonight," I said as I cleaned the wound. It looked infected.

The physical condition of these kids was something I would expect from people living in the back woods.

Getting back into our routine was important. After getting the children ready for bed, they ate their ice cream while I read their favorite stories. I explained to Alex I was putting Jennifer to bed first, so I made sure he had toys to play with while I put her into her crib. He just sat silently, staring straight ahead, not picking up a single toy.

Since Patricia told me Jennifer had been weaned from her pacifier, I gave her big kisses and hugs, put her into her crib, patted her back awhile, told her I loved her, and walked away. That was her routine prior to the visit. She started crying immediately. I understood this was a transition day, so I stayed with her, patting her back a little longer before walking away. Again, she started crying. This time I decided to give it a little while and see if she would stop crying. I stepped out of the room. She kept sobbing, inconsolable sobs. Then her cry turned to one of fear. I scrambled to find another pacifier, I picked her up, gave her the pacifier, rocked her awhile, and laid her down. This time she was content, exhausted, and went to sleep.

Next was Alex's turn. He asked to sleep with me, so I agreed. It had been a tumultuous day for all of us. Again, his routine was that we would talk a while, I'd rub his back, give him a kiss, we would tell each other "Good night, I love you," and I would walk away. He did not want to talk but was content with me rubbing his back. I gave him a kiss, but he made no motion to give me one back.

"Good night, Alex, Mommy loves you." I received no response back.

I pulled the door about three quarters of the way shut and he became frantic and let out a panicked cry.

"No! No! Don't," he yelled.

"What's wrong, Alex?" I asked.

"Please don't close the door," he begged.

"Okay. I won't. I will leave it open for you. I'll just be out here on the couch if you need me," I said.

It was not long, I heard him crying, so went to check on him. He grabbed me around my neck.

"I want to go back to Daddy," he cried.

My heart broke into a thousand pieces. Laying him back down I knelt by his side so we could talk.

"You're back with Mommy now," I tried to explain. "This is your home. You and Jennifer belong here with Mommy. You were just visiting Daddy."

He did not want to talk. He just cried. I stayed by his side with my hand rubbing his back, he could not relax. Finally, about 45 minutes later, his eyes became heavy enough that he fell asleep.

Once he was sleeping, I emptied the suitcase. What clothing was returned was filthy or ruined. My intention was to have all the laundry caught up before morning so I could focus all my attention on the children. In the bottom of the suitcase was a letter from Donnie. My fingers started trembling as I opened the envelope. After the encounter this evening, I was not sure I wanted to read it, but knew I had no choice. Before I even started reading, I felt tremors throughout my body. I sat down, slowly unfolded the pages and started reading.

Dear Mary,

I am writing this to get you to stop and absorb an important situation. I hold NO ill will, bitterness, or hatred towards you! I have something important to communicate to you so I am trusting that you will read this with an open mind.

It grieves me deeply to have to part with the children today. I cry many tears thinking of it, especially the way Alex reacts to leaving. The glassy stare that comes across his face is heartbreaking, he takes off by himself and begins to cry. He begs to stay. I have never seen him like this.

I do believe I know what his thoughts are, and I believe you do also if you stop to think about it. I have never questioned your ability as a mother! However, I present to you, for your consideration, the situation and ask you to think on it in depth. Currently you have a job that demands much of your time. Each day the children are shuffled off to a babysitter. On business trips this may be Grandma's, a relative, or a friend. This shuffling around of the children cannot be good. The demands of your job do not allow you to spend time with the children. It is not possible for anyone to be both a mother and father in a single parent role as has been proven and acknowledged by experts.

I have watched or observed, as has Patricia, Alex's and Jennifer's behavior since they arrived. They are happy and at peace here. I believe a great deal of this is attributed to the very harmonious family element that we have. Different from babysitters or other caretakers, Patricia's nor my job demand the same effort as yours. One of us is almost always covering the family if the other is out. It remains a stable family environment very much needed, especially by children.

Their health has greatly improved here, especially Jennifer's. She has experienced everything the others have done, within her limits, without any adverse effects or reactions. In addition, she has had no allergy or asthma problems. Jennifer is definitely talking more and with more clarity than upon her arrival.

Again, I reiterate this is not a reflection upon you, but upon the environment that exists there. I therefore submit to you for your <u>extreme</u> meditation that you allow the children to come stay with us. If *you love OUR children, you will evaluate what I have said with an open and honest reflection upon it.*

I know this will probably not go over well at this point, it probably would not with me either. However, I am asking only that you take a good look at the situation and scrutinize your own true feelings as to whether the situation is in Alex's and Jennifer's best interests. Make this consideration on your LOVE for Alex and Jennifer and their well-being not out of bitterness toward me. I do not wish to use the children as pawns in a game between us. I wish only God's best for you as well as Alex and Jennifer.

Please see what your conclusions are after having digested all things in a truly open-minded manner, free of ANY prejudices. Remembering ONLY that it is Alex's and Jennifer's best interests that we have as a common goal.

It is Patricia's and my desire to help Alex and Jennifer as well as you in any way we can. We are as close as the phone, use it if you need or desire. Don't let pride stand in the way. It has no place in God's midst. We send you God's love as well as ours.

Sincerely, Donnie

You may wish to read Ecclesiastes chapter 7 verse 7 - 14 and chapter 3 verse 1 - 12.

Donnie was right about one thing, I did not accept his proposal well. In fact, it made me extremely angry. He had never been close to the kids throughout our marriage, and so willfully discarded them seven months ago. Even up to two months ago, he did not want one thing to do with them. Now, you would presume I am the unfit parent, for his love and concern for the children's well-being transcends anything I can give them. Obviously, this was Donnie's best spin on why I should turn the kids over to his care. Based on what I had heard from Arlene regarding the living conditions at Donnie's house, he was painting a rosy picture.

Once I got over my little fit of anger, I fetched my Bible to see what scripture Donnie referenced, Ecclesiastes 7:7-14. I read and reread these words a dozen times. "Lord, I don't understand this." Truthfully, this passage made no sense to me. I did not understand how this fit into his proposition as to why he thought the children would be better off with him. The only part I understood was the last sentence of verse 14, "Nothing is certain in this life."

After the unsuccessful attempt to decipher the first passage I looked up Ecclesiastes 3:1-12. This was much easier to understand for I had heard it many times in sermons. "For everything there is a season...".

In this Bible reference I presumed Donnie thought it was his "time" to care for the kids. Donnie seemed to be living in some fantasy world or I was drastically missing something. Since I did not understand his point, I decided to not waste my time on interpretation.

These kids were SO happy before they left. After moving to Nebraska and away from Donnie's daily mental and emotional abuse it had taken me six months to rebuild Alex's security. Many nights I would lay awake wondering whether I was doing right by my children. Many mornings on the drive to work I would plead to God, with tears in my eyes, asking the Lord to give me peace of mind to see His way and show me what to do next. Everything I did was based on their well-being. And this was all destroyed by Donnie in four weeks. After the divorce Alex loved me and remembered the abuse from his father. Since this visit, I had become the bad person in Alex's eyes. This time I was fighting against myself. He had been totally brainwashed.

Morning came after getting only a couple hours sleep. I HAD to put on the cheerful face! The kids were still very despondent. "This was just going to take some time," I kept telling myself. At church Alex would not go to Sunday school. In fact, he would not let me out of his sight. No problem, he could just sit with me for I was not going to press him to do anything right now. After church I decided the best thing for us was to visit Grandma and Grandpa. Assimilating the children back into this environment was a priority. My folks were ecstatic to hear we were coming. My parents doted on the kids from the moment we arrived. Mom had arranged for the other cousins to come to the house also. All the other kids played together while Alex stayed around the perimeter, observing. I felt it was imperative for my kids to remember the fun they had playing with their cousins. It was important to be with our family. Getting the children to smile was a chore. Grandpa played with Jennifer and got her to smile and giggle a bit. One could see that Alex was burdened with something, but periodically he would forget and just be himself. "I'll take any little tidbit of normalcy at this point," I thought to myself.

After we got home from my parents, I called Arlene to let her know the kids were back.

"Oh good," she said, "I can finally relax."

"What do you mean by that?" I asked.

"Both kids were terribly upset when they arrived at Donnie's house. Patricia took Jennifer's pacifier away immediately and you could hear her cry herself to sleep each night, for hours. Alex wanted to sleep with his dad, so Donnie let Alex sleep with him and Patricia until the third night when Patricia kicked Alex out. I listened to Alex cry himself to sleep every night I was there. Patricia thought Jennifer was behind in her speech development so whenever she would point at something, they made her say the word before they gave it to her. This even included a drink of water. It broke my heart. After experiencing this I had to leave because I couldn't stand it any longer. I couldn't stand hearing the kids cry like that."

She seemed eager to get this off her chest now that the children were home.

I explained to her, "The children are having a few adjustment issues now that they have returned but I know they will be fine. A month is a long time to be away from home."

After talking with Arlene, the phone rang again. This time it was Donnie. He was not interested in talking with me, he only wanted to talk with Alex. In my mind I was thinking it is okay for him to call right away but I was only allowed to talk with Alex twice during the entire month and those conversations were towards the end. Of course, that was only after the brainwashing had occurred. This did not seem fair, but I knew if I did not allow Donnie to talk with Alex, I would incur the wrath of the monster. I gave the phone to Alex while listening on the extension. Donnie allowed all the kids to have a turn talking with Alex. Once Donnie got back on the line he said, "I can come back tomorrow and pick you up if you want, Alex."

"Okay, Daddy!"

I interrupted the phone call with that comment.

"I think that is enough for tonight. Say goodbye, Alex." He did and we hung up the phone.

Throughout the day I had seen Alex make a little progress, but that flew out the window with this phone call. Now he slid back to the blank far away stare and uncooperative spirit. Getting Alex to sleep was another laborious task. He would not tell me what he was feeling or thinking, he was just uncomfortable closing his eyes and fought sleep.

Going back to work, with my children in this condition, was out of the question. My boss always arrived early at work, so I called and explained a little what was going on. I asked if I could have the day to be with the children. He understood and I thanked him. Alex even woke up agitated.

"Today I'm going back to my Daddy!" He was confident and excited.

"I'm sorry, Son, but you are not going back to your Daddy. You are home with Mommy now. You can visit Daddy another time."

With that, he ran back to the bedroom crying. I called my folks and asked what their plans were for the day. They did not have anything scheduled, so I asked if I could come over. I needed their help.

Once again, Grandma and Grandpa doted on the children. This time it was just us, so the kids received special treatment. As the day progressed, I could see Alex coming around, ever so slightly. It appeared he was slowly remembering that home was not as bad as he had been told. Jennifer seemed pretty good as long as she had her pacifier. Her cheerful smile was returning little by little. Since I had no choice but to return to work the following day, we stopped by the sitters on the way home. The kids needed another reintroduction to a familiar setting. Meg and the other kids were happy to see Alex and Jennifer. It was as if Alex had totally forgotten his friends. I did not understand this. He would not play or talk to anyone. He just stayed by my side, hugging my leg, and asked to go home.

I knew the children's return to Meg was not going to be an easy transition, so I called the pastor's wife to see if she would watch my children for one day. When I explained that Alex was still very distant and needed another day of one-on-one attention before going back to the regular sitter's, she was more than happy to assist. Sherri would keep a close eye on both children, and that made my return to work more tolerable.

After dinner, the phone rang. It was Donnie wanting to talk with Alex. "Again?" My brain was shouting. I knew, all too well, the rage Donnie would fling my way if I denied the call. "Oh, Lord, I hope this is a better phone call than yesterday," I prayed as I handed Alex the phone. Again, I listened because I was going to interrupt Donnie if I felt he was saying anything inappropriate.

"We all miss you so much. We can't wait to see you again real soon. We are having so much fun. All the kids say hi."

"Okay, Daddy," and he walked away from the phone.

That was an encouraging sign, he did not want to keep talking. Donnie was not pleased that Alex did not want to spend more time on the phone, but that was as much time as Alex was willing to give him. There was nothing I could or wanted to do about the situation.

Outside of wanting to be held a lot, Jennifer seemed to be adjusting easier. She was eating well, played independently, and snuggled right down when I put her to bed, providing she had her pacifier. Her contagious laugh was returning. Alex, on the other hand, was not eating, would bite his nails, picked at his fingers, and cried easily. He would attempt playing with his toys but would soon drift off in a distant stare. He still would not sleep in his own bed. That was okay, for at this point he needed comfort. As I put him into my bed, I explained to him I was returning to work the next day. Rather than settle in, he was fearful and would not close his eyes. Whenever I tried leaving the room, he started crying.

"You won't leave me when I go to sleep, will you?" he finally asked.

Leave him? What had he been told? Anger filled me. How could anyone do this to a four-year-old child?

"No, Honey, I'll NEVER leave you! I'll ALWAYS be here." I stayed with him until he fell asleep.

To spend a little time with the children before taking them to Sherri's house, I awoke early to be completely ready when the kids awoke. Suddenly, I heard Alex screaming, so I ran into the bedroom.

"Mommy, Mommy, where are you?" he was sobbing uncontrollably.

"I'm right here, Alex."

"I thought you left me!" he exclaimed.

I grabbed him, held him close, and reinforced what I had told him the night before.

"Mommy will NEVER leave you. I will ALWAYS be here for you. You can count on that!"

"Lord, this child is so tormented. Please calm his mind and let peace return to him. After all, he is a mere child." I prayed as I held him.

Sherri was very cheerful as I dropped off the children, so I knew this transition would progress smoothly. Alex started whimpering but Pastor John had not left for work yet, so he came over to Alex to help get him interested in their toys. "Thank you, Lord, for these wonderful friends!"

Everyone in my department said how happy they were that the children were finally back. From all the well-wishes it was obvious the children's absence impacted several of my co-workers. Even though I had a lot of work to catch up on, I had difficulty keeping my mind focused. My children may have been home, but they were not home. Things were not as they were before the visit. I kept praying, "Please, Lord, keep your loving hand on Alex and restore him to me and clear his little mind."

If Donnie could have accepted this as just a two-week visit and not an indoctrination for permanent residence, how simple life would be. A man that never wanted kids, never showed them love or attention, now is caring for five children, and wants me to surrender our children over to him and his "family" environment. "I'm sorry, Lord, this just doesn't make sense. I have done nothing to make him think I am incapable of caring for the children. Besides, I can financially support two children better than he can support seven! Lord, please help me make sense out of this," I prayed.

Eager to see the kids, I rushed over to the pastor's home to pick them up after work. Sherri said both kids had an exceptionally good day. That was certainly a relief since I was not sure what to expect. As we were driving home Alex blurts out,

"I'm going back to live with my Daddy when I go to school."

"Oh, Alex, your teacher, Lori, would miss you so much if you didn't go back to school with her. I'd miss you also," I said.

He started sobbing. He remained so distant. When it came to his father, I was afraid to say anything. I tried talking with him when we got home but he ignored me. Where had that comment come from? Oh, I knew, but I did not want to believe it. Once again, you do not do this sort of thing to preschoolers.

After dinner, the phone rang. Naturally, it was Donnie wanting to talk with Alex. Jennifer needed help so I gave Alex the phone. It was not a long conversation but, because of Jennifer, I was unable to listen. Alex was very despondent the remainder of the evening, until bedtime, and then the fear returned to his eyes.

"You won't leave me if I close my eyes, will you?" he asked.

"I will NEVER leave you, Alex, I promise!"

After finally getting him settled into bed I went to the living room. Soon, I heard his screams, "Mommy, Mommy, where are you?"

I ran into the bedroom, took him into my arms, held him close to me, and continued reinforcing to him, "Mommy will NEVER leave you! I'll NEVER leave you, Alex!"

Morning rolled around and it was time for the kids to go back to Meg. Knowing the situation, Meg assured me she had special activities planned to help them. I was a little anxious regarding their first day back, but Meg said they did fine. What a relief! But, when we got home, Alex would not eat dinner. All he did was stare into space. I kept a running dialog with him; hoping at least one comment would break through, but there was nothing.

Right after dinner the phone rang. It was Donnie. This time I did not allow Donnie to talk with Alex. The children had been home four days and he had called three times. Alex did not need this. I did not need this. Donnie was not happy, but neither was I. Tit-for-tat was not my motive, but Alex needed time to decompress following Donnie's mind controlling tactics. If Donnie talked to him daily, these ugly thoughts would never leave. But those were Donnie's intentions, no peace, constant fear. I know, I lived it myself. Mind control.

I knew Donnie would try calling again, so I took the children outside. While Alex was swinging, he finally opened with his first comment regarding the visit.

"Do you know, Mommy, that the kids would pinch Jennifer and make her cry?"

I knew hearing some of these things was going to tear me up inside but at least he was talking! I had to remain strong and just listen.

"No, Alex, I didn't know that. That is very naughty for anyone to do," I said calmly.

"I know, but Carlos would trip me, hit me, and pinch me too! Daddy and Mommy have a wooden paddle they hit with."

" Did they hit you with the paddle?" I asked.

"No, just the other kids."

"Thank you, Lord, for that," I prayed. Alex had to be petrified he would be next. Alex never gave me a reason to spank him, ever! His disposition was always very cooperative.

He continued, "Mommy always closed the bedroom door every night and wouldn't let me come out."

"Alex, I'm so sorry. That had to make you feel scared. We do not do that here. I will NEVER force you to stay in a dark room," I said. My intent was not to criticize their actions, but rather reinforce our positive environment.

So that explains why he gets frantic at bedtime when I start closing the door. Later in the evening, as Alex and I were sitting together, he started talking again.

"You know I'm going back to live with Daddy and Mommy when school starts and move into their new house with all the toys that I left at Daddy's house."

So, this must have been the conversation with Donnie the night before when I was not able to listen.

"Alex, please, try to understand. You had a visit with your Daddy. This is your home and you are lucky to have toys both places. I am your Mommy. Patricia is not your Mommy. She is Carlos's Mommy. Patricia lives with Daddy."

This was a lot for a four-year-old to understand. Here I am telling him just the opposite of what he had been ingrained with during the past month.

Thursday morning was a disaster. Alex woke up screaming for me again but continued to put up a real fuss. He did not want to eat breakfast, get ready, or go to the sitter. He screamed when I left him with Meg. I could hear him all the way to the car. Naturally, I cried all the way to work. "Lord, what did this man do to this innocent child?" I put a call into the pediatrician. After explaining what was going on, he recommended I plan something special with Alex every day and just talk with him.

"It's very important that you get a line of communication established with him once again," he explained.

"I've been trying but he's very despondent. He won't respond to me," I said.

"You have to keep trying. You have to gain his confidence again."

"Okay, I'll keep trying. Thank you for your help," I said graciously.

After work Thursday, Barb came down from Omaha. She was eager to see the kids. Barb noticed the difference in Alex right away.

"I can't believe it. When you first came to Nebraska, he was hyper and nervous. You had gotten him past that. He was so happy before he left and now, he is right back where he was. Maybe a little worse because he just stares off into space."

"Oh, trust me, I know. It's been a nightmare for the past five days."

I knew Donnie would call. Sure enough, right after dinner, like clockwork. Barb answered the phone. She would not allow Donnie to talk with Alex. This made two consecutive nights that communication had been denied. If Alex was going to heal, I had to limit the phone conversations, or at least limit what Donnie said to him. I knew Donnie would be furious with me and I already anticipated what he would say. He was an expert instilling fear deep into one's soul. I grew apprehensive and jittery knowing he would be coming for me.

Arlene called later in the evening to see how the kids were doing. I confessed it was a struggle, but everything would be okay. I explained to her what Alex had said regarding the hitting and pinching.

"That doesn't surprise me. Many times, those kids were left totally unsupervised and Alex and Jennifer were forced to fend and defend themselves."

"That's funny," I said. "I was told there is an adult in their home at all times. Donnie and Patricia are never both away from the house."

I believed Arlene, not Donnie.

She continued, "Donnie and Patricia called the other night to talk with Francis. I understand they have a nursery school lined up for Alex when school starts but hadn't figured out what to do with Jennifer."

So, it was obvious they were confident the children would be with them when school started.

Thanking her for the call, I sank into the couch. Wonderful! They were proceeding with plans as though this was a done deal. Donnie's plan was to keep Alex upset to the point I would turn Alex over to him. I immediately turned to God, "Thank you for letting me see this, opening my eyes to Donnie's intentions."

Just as I was ready to walk out the door Friday morning the phone rang. I knew, without a doubt, who it was and questioned whether to answer it or not. Donnie hadn't talked with Alex for the past two nights so I knew he'd be furious. If I did not face the music this morning, I would be forced to face it tonight. I cowered and answered.

"Let me talk with Alex," Donnie demanded.

God gave me strength from somewhere deep with my response.

"I'll let you talk with him if you watch what you say."

"I have a right to talk to him anytime I want, and I can say anything I want," he barked.

"I'd prefer you didn't mention him coming out when school starts," I said.

Donnie jumped on this right away.

"What's the matter, is Alex upset?"

Knowing this was just what he intended all along, I denied it.

"No, he's just fine," I said and gave Alex the phone.

Donnie talked about the special things Alex had left behind and how Daddy would save them for him until the next time he came out. Then Donnie allowed Patricia to talk.

"Alex, I miss you so very much. All the kids miss you too. We are in our big new house and I wish you were here with us. We'll call you again so all the kids can talk with you."

Alex hung up and was terribly upset. And here I was ready to walk out the door for work. There was no choice but to call my boss and let him know I would be a little late. This was going to take some time to settle him down, yet again. After this call I decided Patricia and her kids did not have a right to talk with Alex. I would not tolerate it going forward.

We had a good Saturday. I devoted all my time to the children, talking, talking, talking. Taking the pediatrician's advice, I planned a special outing for Alex on Sunday. I decided to take him to an amusement park in Omaha. Saturday afternoon I took Jennifer to my folks to spend the night. Once again, my folks doted on the kids. The children enjoyed themselves and it seemed my folks did as well. When we got home Alex and I just sat on the couch together. He seemed to be relaxing a bit.

Sunday, at the park, Alex and I had a wonderful time. We ate whatever Alex wanted to eat and we rode whatever rides he wanted to try. Life seemed to be coming back into his eyes and the smile was returning. It was an ever so slight improvement but, at this point, I would take anything I could get. We picked up Jennifer before heading home. Grandma and Grandpa were a blessing for there was laughter from both kids before we left.

Sunday night the kids were playing outside when Donnie called. Before letting Donnie talk with Alex, I decided to explain how the arrangement was going to go.

"You have every right to talk with Alex, but no one else. Alex won't be talking to Patricia or the kids again."
I knew this would unleash his fury.

"Everyone in my household has a right to talk with him," he shouted.

"No, they don't," I said calmly.

I called Alex to come talk with his dad. He did not want to talk.

"Why do I always have to talk to him?" Alex pleaded.

Coaxing him to the phone, I said, "At least say hello."

Alex did that, but immediately after saying his few words, put the phone on the floor and walked away. Donnie hung up but called back 20 minutes later to chew me out for what I had done. What had I done? Showing love to a child is wrong? Mending their little minds is wrong? I certainly had not brainwashed them like Donnie had. I had not done a thing, but I certainly got blamed for Alex hanging up on his father.

The only thing I knew, for sure, was that it had been a long week since the return of the children.

Sitting on the couch with Alex before bedtime was turning into a bonding experience. Alex started sharing. He mentioned the big gun Daddy had. (Donnie never had a gun before.) He talked more about the rough treatment from the other kids and how he and Jennifer were treated. He shared how Daddy hit the other kids with the big paddle on their heads, arms, and feet. Alex admitted his daddy spanked him awfully hard one day and he did not talk to his daddy for a long time. Alex seemed afraid to say too much about his dad, like he would get into big trouble if his dad found out he told someone. I can understand that fear after living with that man for seven years.

"Mommies do things better than Daddies. I don't want to go back, ever," he said.

Breakthrough! "Hallelujah! Thank you, Jesus!" It had been a long week, but progress had been made! It was not going to be fast, but the shell was cracking. Alex's fears surfaced the most at bedtime and each morning when he awakened. It was going to take time.

The daily harassing phone calls became a big issue. Alex honestly did not want to talk. Donnie accused me of refusing to let Alex talk.

"Why don't you limit the calls to once a week and that way Alex will look forward to them?" I suggested.

Donnie flat out rejected that idea and insisted on talking with Alex.

While talking with Alex, Donnie asked, "Do you want to talk with one of the little girls?"

Immediately I stepped in.

"No! He can only talk with you," I interjected.

That triggered an avalanche of threats I was not prepared to hear.

"You'd better start looking over your shoulder 24 hours a day because some time you're going to go pick up the kids and they won't be there! I can guarantee you one thing, if I had it to do over again, I never would have brought the kids back. You'd have to throw me in jail before you would ever see them again!"

With that, he hung up.

He was NOT joking! I knew this man all too well. These were not just idle threats. I panicked. Donnie knew these kids were my world and through them, he could and would hurt me. Once again, he was controlling my life, and his intent was to win. "Lord, what do You want me to do? I beg for Your protection. I cannot be with these kids 24/7. Donnie could overpower me in a heartbeat. I have not done anything wrong. Please give me guidance."

Panic escalated throughout my bones all night. Questions were swirling. How could I go to work each day worried if my children would be at the sitter when I returned for them? It was not fair to put the sitter in the middle of this situation, but she needed to be aware of the threat. Will anyone believe me regarding the capabilities of this man? It's for sure, no one had believed me up to this point.

I purchased a cassette recorder, tapes, and a listening device so I could start recording the phone calls, because I needed proof. I knew no one would believe me unless they heard him threaten me directly. My intuition was telling me this was going to get ugly.

Donnie continued calling every day. I would hand Alex the phone. Sometimes he would talk, but most of the time he would not. At times he would be in tears trying to get off. Other times, when he refused to talk, I relentlessly heard how it was my fault that Alex did not want to talk. Since Donnie's threat, I was afraid to deny Donnie phone conversations with his son. Alex started begging me to not answer the phone in the evenings. I thought I would give it a try. One Friday night the phone rang eight individual times within an hour, seven to ten rings each time. I refused to answer. Each time it rang, Alex shook with fear. This was not an answer either.

Later, on one of the calls, Alex randomly asked his dad if he was at the airport.

"No, but I'll come to see you very soon. I have a right to see you and Jennifer."

"What's a right, Daddy?" Alex asked.

"It's when I get to see you no matter what anyone says."

"I want you to come but I don't think Mommy does," Alex responded.

"I don't give a damn what Mommy thinks. I'll come when I want." Oh great, what did this mean? Naturally, I did not have the tape recorder set up yet.

Alex must have had the phone conversation on his mind for during breakfast the next morning he asked,

"When will we all go to see Daddy?"

"I don't think that will be happening anytime soon," I replied.

"Maybe, when we get to Daddy's house, Daddy will love you," he said.

This is a complex issue for a four-year-old to sort out. After all, Alex loved both of us, so we should all love each other. Besides, Alex discovered his daddy loved him once he went to daddy's house. If it could only be that simple.

I had not spoken to Carl since the appointment in May where we discussed the duration of the initial visit. He needed to be brought up to date so I made an appointment with him. I filled him in on all the details of the first visit, the physical condition of the children upon their return, Alex's mental state, the constant phone harassment, the phone threat, child support arrearage, and the letter Donnie sent to me regarding a change of custody. I mentioned recording the phone calls. Carl advised they would not be admissible in court and discouraged me from continuing, but, in the back of my mind, I knew I needed to get one recorded to convince Carl of what I was facing. Carl's final advice was to give it more time to see if Donnie would tire of the game he was playing with Alex. To Donnie it might be a game, but there was a four-year-old little boy in the middle of some devastating activity. I did not want to participate in this game, but I knew I had no choice. I had to fight for the children's sake, or I would lose them.

The first part of August I received a letter from Donnie. It was the anticipated child support payment with the following note attached, "Funds are unfortunately short so I am sending you half now and will pay the rest on the 15th. Hope you will understand, and it will not inconvenience you." Inconvenience me? Who did he think he was fooling? He can send whatever amount he wants? What will I do about it? What could I do? I had brought it up to both attorneys but neither one seemed concerned.

I did notice the address on the check. Patricia had told Alex they had moved. Interestingly, there was only a post office box number for the address. The return city was still in Devine, Texas but now I had no idea where they lived in Devine.

August turned out to be another turning point. The children had only been home about twenty days. Jennifer had adjusted well but Alex remained up and down, mostly because of the harassing phone calls. August 3 the phone rang.

"This is a person-to-person call for Alex Schumacher," the voice on the other end said.

Are you kidding me? He has now resorted to calling person-to-person? Alex was not around so that validly ended that call. Has it come to this?

After the kids were in bed, I phoned Donnie to see if we could resolve this phone issue.

"Will you please limit the calls to once a week. That way, Alex will look forward to them rather than dreading them," I asked politely, once again.

This set him off.

"I will not! I am not going to let Alex forget who I am. I can call as often as I want," he declared.

"But we have a life to live as well and I'd like to have a chance to do that," I responded.

With that, the same rant started. It was all my fault, I had shuffled the kids around, my job kept me away from the kids, it was my fault Alex continued to be upset, on, and on, and on. Then he blurted,

"I'm coming to see the kids this weekend!"

"Oh no you're not," I exclaimed. "The kids have only been home three weeks! Besides, visitations have to be agreed upon and I don't agree."

Then the tirade started.

"You bitch! If I had it to do over again, I never would have allowed you custody of the kids in the first place! You're not stable enough to raise children. You're nothing but a stupid fucking idiot trying to get along in life. You can hardly keep your mind from deteriorating daily. Furthermore, I never should have brought them back last month. That will never happen again."

I tried to remain calm but that really was not happening. My insides were turning summersaults. He was pushing me just like he always had.

"I really don't have to take this harassment from you any longer. If you do not stop, I have no other choice but to get an unlisted phone number. Like you have a PO box number for an address," I countered.

"You remember my promise?"

"You mean your threat?" I asked.

"Oh, I guarantee you that was not a threat! That was a promise, and I ALWAYS keep my promises! You'd better start watching your back!"

The tone of his voice was very sarcastic and threatening.

After hanging up I was shaking from head to toe. This call was supposed to be a reconciliation but turned into a bomb throwing incident. But I had recorded it so I could show my attorney how unstable this man was. Rewinding the recorder, I pressed Play, nothing! All you could hear was the tape moving. Damn! DAMN! **DAMN**! It failed. Right back where we were, his word against mine.

The 9th day of August, exactly three weeks since the children had been returned, the phone rang. It was Donnie. I handed the phone to Alex.

"I've tried calling you every day this week, Son, and Mary didn't allow me to talk with you," he spouted.

Donnie could not even start the conversation cordial: not a hello, how are you doing, have you been playing, how's Jennifer?

"I want you to know Daddy is coming to see you next weekend. I can't wait to see you!" Donnie expounded.

Alex did not respond at all. He was done talking. It really was not talking; Alex had just listened. At least this call was recorded. Immediately, Alex became despondent. He went into his quiet place of blank stares and inward, deep thoughts. He would not eat, complained of a stomachache, and had diarrhea. I could not get him to talk. Putting him to bed was an issue. He would cry, I would get him settled, he would call me to make sure I was still there. Multiple times we cycled through the fear.

The next morning, he woke crying and screaming, "Mommy, Mommy, where are you?" It was breaking my heart. He was just coming around and now he was back into the hole. They had to have told him I left him for this to come back to his psyche daily. It was deep!

Monday, August 11, I took Alex to the doctor to see about his ear. I asked the doctor what I could do about Alex's nervousness. Since Saturday's phone call, he had picked his fingernails to the point of bleeding.

"Tell Donnie to leave you alone so the kids can grow up to be stable adults."

The doctor was exasperated like everyone else.

"I know what you are saying but Donnie is not going to leave the children and me alone," I bemoaned.

I just did not know what to do. Everyone knew the answer. Our future depended on one spoiled petulant "adult child" who was not going to be happy until he got his way.

My first call was made to Sam. I explained the situation regarding the harassing phone calls, the threat Donnie made, Donnie's regret of returning the kids in July, and the arrearage of child support. Sam was going to call Donnie's attorney to see if they could resolve some of this.

Next, I called Carl. My recordings had not been successful enough to take into him, but I needed to ask him what to do if Donnie decided to make the trip to Nebraska. As I could have predicted, Carl felt I was overreacting.

"He just returned the children three weeks ago. There is no way he will make a trip from Texas to see them this soon," he said.

It's for sure no one understood this man but me.

This time Sam fulfilled his end of the commitment and called Donnie's attorney, for it became apparent Donnie's attorney had talked with him. Donnie called after the kids were in bed.

"I didn't realize the effect the phone calls had on Alex. I'm only trying to talk with my son," he tried to sound convincing.

He did not realize the effect he had on Alex. Sure, he did! How many times had I asked him to limit his conversations? Donnie knew all along what he was doing. He was extremely calculating and conniving, so I was not buying into his program.

"Going forward I won't call quite as often," he explained.

Not trusting him, I wondered exactly what that meant and where he was going with this.

"I'm in the process of writing down what I will agree to regarding reasonable phone and visitation rights going forward. Obviously, you are too stupid to work with me so I must spell it out for you. Specific rules for YOU to live by," he snarled.

What? I was not working with him. Between the lines, he was telling me that if I did not go along with his visitation guidelines, he would fight me. I knew he was only trying to scare me, but it was working.

He continued. "I thought we'd be able to get along. We always had during the marriage. You have changed. You deceived me. You're nothing but a liar to tell the attorney those things," he accused.

"If what you are saying is that I have stopped doing everything you demand, I guess that's true. But I have never lied or deceived you. I have had enough," I said, "we are done talking," and I ended the call.

This recording was successful.

Wednesday night, August 13, I receive a call from Sherri.

"Have you received a call from Donnie?" she inquired.

"Not yet, what's up?" I asked.

"Well, I just finished speaking with a man that wouldn't identify himself. He asked what church John pastored. (Donnie knew John was my preacher after going with me to pick up the children at the airport but did not know which church he pastored.) I asked him who was speaking, and he said he was John's brother. John does have three brothers, but I know their voices. Besides, they know what church John pastors." Sherri sounded alarmed.

Fear shot through me.

"This doesn't sound good," I said, "I need to make a call."

This upset me to no end. I called Donnie's mother to see if she had heard from Donnie. She had not. She wanted to know what was going on, so I explained the phone call to the preacher's wife. Francis got on the phone.

"You can be thankful, for God is trying to show you that Donnie is planning to come into town and kidnap the children."

"Thank you," I said, "this is exactly what I was thinking. I'm sorry but I have to go now."

"Oh, Dear God, what now?" I was terror stricken. I could not think. Sitting paralyzed, the phone rang again and startled me back into reality. It was Pastor John calling to let me know he had informed the local detective of the situation. I explained the conversation I had just finished with Francis.

"I called Austin to see if they had heard from Donnie. They had not, but based on the call Sherri just received, they were of the strong opinion that Donnie intends to make a trip to Nebraska to kidnap the children."

"I know this sounds trite," Pastor John said, "but try not to worry. I am going to arrange for you and the kids to get out of town for the next several days. Sherri and I need to plan immediately. I do not want you taking the children to your regular sitter tomorrow. Bring the kids over here and Sherri will care for them."

He was not only concerned for the children and me, but for his family as well.

My next call was to Meg where I explained the phone call my pastor's wife received. Even she became concerned. She sounded relieved she was not going to have the children the remainder of the week.

"Please," I begged, "if you see any abnormal activity around your house, call the police. They have your address and are aware of a potential kidnapping. Don't get overly concerned if you see more patrol cars than normal passing by your house."

The following morning, I took the kids to Pastor John's and Sherri's. The children had been to their home several times, so they were comfortable going there for the day. While driving to their home, I was constantly aware of all the cars around and behind me, making sure I was not being followed. My mind was wondering if Donnie would be driving from Texas or flying, whether he was already in town, the details of his plan, attempting to catch me off guard, would he physically hurt me. My mind was racing with the what if's.

Right after work I went to the duplex and packed a suitcase. Fear gripped me as I stepped into the duplex alone, not knowing if Donnie was watching me. I said a quick prayer, "Lord, please protect me and the children." Quickly, I finished packing, and drove to Pastor John's and Sherri's, again being incredibly careful to make sure I was not being followed. Before walking into their home, I had to relax, breathe, and attempt to calm down, for I did not want the children to suspect my anxiety. Sherri explained the kids had a particularly good day, everyone seemed happy and carefree. John and Sherri's girls were playing with the kids, laughing, and carrying on as kids do. If only I felt that way! She had a delightful dinner waiting for us. One would never know there was a potential disaster waiting to happen.

After dinner, the phone rang. Sherri answered.

"Is Cathy home?" a man asked.

"No, you have the wrong number!" After hanging up she said, "That was the same voice as the phone call the night before. I know it was!"

The mood in the household changed abruptly. Everyone got concerned. Pastor John made a quick phone call as we gathered our things to leave immediately.

I put my kids in my car and we followed Pastor John, Sherri, and their girls to our "hide out." I had no idea where we were going or with whom we were staying. All I knew was that we were heading into the country. Pastor John had arranged for another couple from the church to help us. This couple welcomed us with open arms. They were grandparents, so there were plenty of toys for the children to play with.

John and Sherri excused themselves so we could get settled. Once I got the children to bed, Pastor John left instructions for me to call one of the local detectives, regardless of the time. The detective asked if he could come out to our "shelter" to visit with me. He wanted to get information from me directly, as well as he had many questions for me. The detective listened to the last telephone conversation from August 11. In addition, he questioned me about Donnie's appearance, what car he drove, his weapons, his temperament, anything I could tell him about this man.

The next two days Pastor John picked me up from the "hide out" and took me to work, dropping me at the front door. The kids remained sheltered. They were immersed in activities so did not seem to mind a bit. The "hide out" was in the country, so the children loved the freedom to play outside. After work, the detective picked me up at the front door and took me back to our place of refuge. These people were so very gracious to us. Never in my lifetime did I think I would have to hide like a fugitive. I was not the bad guy here, but I needed protection from the real bad guy.

This was one of the first times I was having difficulty concentrating at work. My co-workers knew something was going on. After explaining we were in hiding, my actions made sense to them. Normally, I could compartmentalize, but not under these conditions. Not knowing if Donnie was in town, or not, was playing with my mind. It felt so wrong to leave our duplex and stay with strangers. Sunday, we did not go to church, not knowing if Donnie would attempt a kidnapping there. Pastor John, Sherri, and the detective were all on high alert. This was so unfair to them, their families, their church, and the entire church family. Finally, I called my boss at home and asked for a week off from work. I could not work under this stress.

Sunday afternoon we left our seclusion. I did not feel comfortable taking the kids back to the duplex not knowing if Donnie was still in town. I called my parents and asked if we could spend the week with them. I needed help. My psyche was riddled with panic. It was going to be a challenge getting hold of myself. For the children's sake, I could not show fear. It was relaxing not getting those harassing phone calls every night. Alex seemed to relax as well. Although anytime around dinner time, if the phone rang, he would beg Grandma not to answer it.

During the week I was gone, Donnie called my office twice, asking for me. The second time he asked to speak with my boss. Fortunately, the co-worker who answered my phone, told him my boss was out of the office. That stopped his calls.

The week had passed. Time to return home. How comfortable was I going to be? For the sake of the children, everything had to appear normal. Normal? We had just spent four days in hiding and another week hanging out with Grandma and Grandpa rather than being home and at work. That was not normal. Normal was not looking over your shoulder 24/7. This time, to my knowledge, we had averted a catastrophe. Will there be another attempt? Somehow, I had to find peace regarding sending my children to the sitter and me going to work. "God, you have to return peace to my soul. I can't do this without You."

Just as we walked into the house the phone rang. Even though I was hesitant to answer I knew I must. Thankfully, it was Arlene. She was in Omaha and asked if she could come visit the kids the following week.

"That will be wonderful," I said, "they will be happy to see you!"
Not only the kids, but I would have someone in the house with me.

No more had I hung up and the phone rang again. Hesitantly, I answered.

"Where the hell have you been? I have been trying to reach you for a week! You are a stupid fucking bitch! You've cost me a lot of money!" he kept firing non-stop insults.

"I've been on vacation," I said once he took a breath.

"You're supposed to tell me everywhere you go," he yelled.

"Oh no, I can be away ten days without letting you know," I said calmly.

He finally settled down and asked if he could call the following evening to talk with Alex. I agreed, that would not be a problem.

"Oh, just to let you know your mother is coming to visit us," I shared.

That stopped him cold, he had no comment.

The following day Arlene came. It was refreshing to see her. She enjoyed the children, the kids enjoyed her, and she helped around the house. That night, when Donnie called, Alex asked his dad if he wanted to talk with Grandma.

"No!" he yelled.

He would not so much as talk with his own mother!

Francis phoned a couple days later to talk with Arlene. Francis had just heard from Donnie and felt he needed to share with her that Donnie had been fired from his job. Here he just bought a new house, leased a new Chevrolet Blazer, and had five mouths to feed! Francis explained to Arlene that from what Donnie told him, Donnie hardly went into work during the four weeks the kids were there. Then, the next two weeks, he was busy moving into their new home. He had been warned about his excessive absences but did not heed the warning. This was the third job he had been fired from in the last three years.

When Donnie called again, I asked Arlene to answer the phone because I was busy with the children, which she did with no problem.

"Hello, May I help you?" she asked.

"Let me talk to Alex," Donnie demanded.

"Hi, Son, how are you?"

"I didn't call to talk to you. I called to talk with my son!"

I felt sorry for her for her own son refused to speak to her. I took the phone from her.

"What happened with your work?" I asked.

"I guess they didn't like the way I looked. I'm going to take them to court," he was very cocky.

It became evident he would never accept the fact that his actions caused all his problems. Going forward, this was not going to be easy.

6. Legal Entanglements

~ A noun referring to becoming ensnarled in the legal maze ~

Prior to 1968 children had no rights. Children were considered possessions of their parents, which provided the parent the freedom to do whatever they wanted with, too, and for their children. Following a divorce, it was not uncommon for one or both parents to move out of the state in which the family resided at the time of the divorce. This encouraged child-snatching by the non-custodial parent. The kidnapping parent only had to cross state lines and be fully protected. Parents were exempt from the federal kidnapping law. Therefore, the parent who observed court orders risked ending up the loser. The kidnapping parent generally had little respect for the custody terms and would thumb their nose at court orders.[ii]

In 1968 the Office of Juvenile Justice and Delinquency Prevention in Washington DC recognized a need to protect children of divorced parents. America was becoming a highly mobile society which created a challenging issue regarding which state should exercise jurisdiction over an existing custody order. The Office of Juvenile Justice wrote the Uniform Child Custody Jurisdiction Act (UCCJA). The purpose of this act was to deter interstate child abductions by family members and promote uniform jurisdiction across state lines regarding child custody and visitation matters. The new law became effective ONLY upon adaption by individual State Legislatures. On acceptance, each state could make addendums which ended up defeating the purpose for uniformity.[iii]

Carl was fully aware of the phone harassment, the threat Donnie made to me, the phone calls to my pastor, and the alleged kidnapping attempt the weekend of August 16. Since I was a resident of Nebraska, my question to him was whether Nebraska could protect the kids and me. Carl was fully aware of the UCCJA and explained that this was a perfect example where it could be used. Nebraska had just adapted this law[iv] yet Texas had not,[v] but he did not believe we would experience any difficulties working between the two states.

Carl explained the criteria, under the UCCJA, that would be used to make decisions regarding custody arrangements.

The state making the decision had to be the child's home state for at least six months.

The child must have significant connection with people in the state: teachers, doctors, family, and grandparents.

The child is in the state for safety reasons: abuse, neglect, or abandonment.

There are no custody proceedings concerning the child pending in another state.

This implies that if a state court in one state decides before another court in a different state, the judgment of the first court will be binding.[vi]

After the abduction threat I knew I needed protection from Donnie. Carl had many years in family law and was willing to put this new law to the test. In his estimation, our situation fit the criteria. I had confidence, if anyone could help, it would be Carl. I gave him the approval to proceed. For the well-being of the children I had to try.

The end of August Carl drafted a Petition for Custody Determination, based on the UCCJA. A hearing was set for October 20, 1980. Donnie was personally served a copy of the order the first week in September, providing him plenty of time to retain counsel and prepare for the hearing.

Unbeknown to me, Donnie retained a different Texas attorney and drafted his request for a defined visitation schedule. Sam had received a personal letter from Donnie's attorney and passed it directly along to me mid-September. Sam did not attach an explanation, so it appeared to be a letter between the Texas attorneys. This must have been what Donnie referred to when he threatened that I better accept his offer regarding visitation: two phone calls a week, visitation in Texas every Easter and every July, alternating Christmas and Thanksgiving holidays starting with Christmas '80, Thanksgiving '81, visitation in Nebraska in March, May, and September. Donnie had drawn up this visitation schedule before being fired from his job, but it still sounded like it involved a lot of time off from a job and a lot of traveling. I needed to run this past Carl.

Carl read the letter and agreed Sam should have attached a cover letter indicating how to proceed with the request.

"There is no reason to take this visitation request seriously," he advised. "We have a pending court date set in Nebraska which takes precedence over a written request from an attorney. Besides, Nebraska will take over jurisdiction and sort out the visitation schedule after the court date."

This sounded reasonable to me. I followed his advice.

The end of September Sam sent me a letter requesting that I respond to Donnie's attorney. There were several things here that just did not make sense. First, it was not my position to respond to Donnie's attorney. Second, Sam had not called to discuss Donnie's visitation request. Third, there was no indication anyone had addressed with Donnie the support arrearage. Finally, I was sure Donnie's new attorney had never been informed about Donnie's failure to return the children from the July visit. I finally put a call into Sam and explained Donnie's behavior since returning the children: the threat, the potential abduction, and the upcoming hearing in October to challenge the new UCCJA law. Sam was rather nonchalant about everything I was telling him but wished me luck.

Luck? Was that what it was going to take to get something done? Sam had seemed distant since the July fiasco. Did he believe Donnie's story that I did not seem interested in getting the children back or did he believe me, that Donnie flat out refused to return the children on time? Regardless, Sam seemed to be washing his hands from my case.

My personal life, since the kids return, was nothing short of a disaster. Donnie's harassing calls continued every day, leaving Alex nervous and distraught. Due to the calls, Alex continued having issues each night getting to sleep, bad dreams, and morning anxiety when unable to locate me. Tom was still in the picture. He would drop in every so often just to say hello and play a little with the children. Occasionally I would accept a date with him, but between the kids, Donnie, and work I was not capable of much else. I worried every day I would receive a call from the sitter saying my children had been abducted. I just did not have room for anything else in my life. Since Tom had never been married, I was sure he did not understand why my children came before him, but those were the facts. My plate was full.

The night before the hearing Donnie called.

"With my current situation I'm not planning to come back for the hearing. I'm trusting you will be fair and represent my side as well," he pleaded.

What? Really? That comment did not deserve a response. He really thought I was going to present his wishes. If he wanted representation, he had every chance to retain someone. The conversation was short for I had nothing to say to him.

The day of the hearing rolled around. Carl had prepped me through the questions he was going to ask, so everything was expected to go smoothly.

"All you have to do is tell your story when we get to that point. It will be simple. I'll prompt you through the questions," he said assuredly.

The one unknown factor was whether Donnie would show up at the last minute. Regardless, never experiencing a courtroom environment before, I was petrified.

The hearing took a while to get started as they waited ample time for Donnie or his counsel to show up, which they did not, so we proceeded. After all documents were presented my attorney put me on the witness stand and asked the leading question.

"Tell the Court in your own words what experience you have had with the visitation matters since moving to Nebraska."

With the help of Carl's leading questions, the story was told from the beginning:

Donnie extending the initial visit from fourteen days to nineteen days.

Denying Alex to speak with me until the nineteenth day.

Failure to return the children on the nineteenth day.

Failure to inform me the plane reservations had been cancelled.

How I found out the reservations had been cancelled.

How Donnie claimed a judge had told him he could keep the kids an extra week.

How my Texas attorney finally put pressure on Donnie to return the children.

The children being returned after thirty-one days.

The physical and mental condition of the children when they were returned.

The phone harassment since the kids return and the impact the calls had on Alex.

Donnie's threat that I needed to watch over my shoulder 24/7.

Donnie's comment of his regrets returning the children in the first place.

Donnie telling Alex he was coming to see him the first weekend in August.

The strange phone call to my pastor.

The concern for a possible abduction during that second weekend in August.

Alex's relationship with his father prior to the visit.

It all just rolled out once I got started talking.

One of Carl's final questions was regarding my preferred visitation schedule, since that was the purpose of the hearing: requesting Nebraska protect us by setting a limited visitation timetable until the children were older.

After all the questioning, the judge was interested in knowing more about the physical violence Donnie inflicted on Alex and whether the spankings left any bruises or marks. I explained Alex would get bruises on his arms from Donnie picking him up, but the spankings were mostly on his bottom with the use of a breadboard.

At the end of the testimony the judge said he would take the matter under advisement and get back with my attorney to resolve the issue. But, he continued,

"In the interim, the Respondent (Donnie) in this particular matter is enjoined (prohibited) from removing the children from the State of Nebraska and from Lancaster County therein. That is subject to review by the Court, of course, upon motion at any time by the Respondent or by the Petitioner."

The good news was that, for the time being, the children would not be going out of state or out of the county until this was resolved. On the surface, the judge seemed willing to help. But the bad news was the judge opened the door for Donnie to come in with a motion to reopen the case at any time.

Naturally, Donnie's mother and Francis knew of the court proceedings. They were interested in hearing the outcome so when they called, I shared what the judge proposed. Donnie was going to find out the outcome of the trial anyhow, so it did not matter if I shared with them or not. They must have called Donnie immediately, for he became fully aware of the judge's decision prior to the court sending the ruling to him in the mail.

Thankfully, since Donnie had been fired, the daily phone harassment stopped, but he still called a couple times a week. Anytime he did call, it always left Alex upset.

During one of the calls in Mid-November as Donnie was talking with Alex he blurted, "I'll be coming to get you very soon."

Alex paused. There was a long silence.

"Daddy, please don't lock me in that dark room again," Alex pleaded.

"I won't," Donnie laughed.

Laughed! How could you laugh about this? After he hung up Alex cried. That was the first I had heard that story. It sure explained why Alex got hysterical one day while the kids were playing in the cupboards and Jennifer accidentally shut the door. The day following this call Alex had his fingernails down to the quick and he was very despondent. He fell right back into that dark place.

The next time Donnie called I decided, once again, I needed to talk to him about the calls.

"I'd prefer you not continue to tell Alex you're coming for him. It really upsets him."

Donnie became furious with me.

"You fucking bitch. You are the one upsetting him all the time. He was never upset while he was with me. I am so sick and tired of your crazy games I'm going to take you to court. You'll be sorry you ever messed with me!"

I was sorry for ever marrying him in the first place, but it was too late. For now, I was forced to deal with the monster.

Donnie claimed hardship and went to Legal Services of Nebraska for representation AFTER the initial hearing. Legal Services requested a transcript of the October hearing, and by the end of November filed a motion requesting my testimony be dismissed because Texas maintained jurisdiction over the matter.

Carl reassured me, "This type of nonsense was exactly what the UCCJA was intended to prevent. Just try to relax, I'll take care of everything."

I had to trust him.

Rolling into another year was like riding a roller coaster. The first week in January, I received a call from Arlene.

"I just want to tell you Donnie and Patricia are driving to Nebraska for a hearing. Francis and Cora are taking care of the kids from the 9th through the 13th. I thought you'd want to know."

"Thank you, Arlene, I appreciate the warning," I said.

Then, I panicked.

After hanging up I immediately phoned Carl. As the phone rang my brain was rapidly trying to sort through my panicked thoughts. Hearing? I didn't know anything about a hearing. Carl answered.

"Carl, do you have a hearing scheduled?"

Calmly he said, "Yes, Monday, January 12."

Anger was creeping into my throat.

"You weren't going to tell me?"

"This is nothing to get upset about. This should be a short hearing to determine whether the case is to be reopened for further testimony. There is no need for you to attend. This is strictly between attorneys. Besides, I filed a motion stating this entire dismissal should be thrown out because Donnie had ample time to retain counsel prior to the October hearing."

About this time, I was doing everything I could to keep from screaming.

"You do NOT understand! I just received a call from friends in Texas telling me Donnie and Patricia are driving to Nebraska for the hearing, and they are intending to be here the entire weekend. Donnie didn't tell me he was driving in and neither has he asked for a prearranged visit. Don't you think it a little strange that he just intends to show up? If this man can arrange for an abduction, he will!"

"Like I said, this is between attorneys. Donnie and Patricia have no business attending."

I was getting nowhere; he did not understand the severity of the situation. Or did not want to.

After hanging up I went back through the tapes from the last couple of phone calls Alex had with his father. Just before Christmas Donnie told Alex that he would be coming to see him in a couple… (long hesitation, never finishing his sentence). Donnie knew he'd be coming back but did not want me to know. The last phone call Alex asked his dad why he did not send him any Christmas presents. Donnie told him he had them and would bring them to him. Now it all made sense.

Immediately, I prayed, "Thank you, Lord, for once again showing me Donnie's intentions." I knew I could not stay at the house alone, so I called Barb and arranged to spend a couple nights with her. Early Saturday morning I packed a bag and headed for Omaha. My intention was to return to town Monday morning for work. Barb volunteered to watch the kids on Monday and return them to Lincoln Monday night. Saturday night I called Meg to let her know the children would not be there Monday. I waited until Sunday night to call the nursery schoolteacher to explain the situation and that Alex would not be in school Monday. I also asked her to call me if anything strange occurred.

Monday around 11:30 a.m. my phone rang, and it was the nursery schoolteacher.

"I want you to know I just received a call from a lady identifying herself as Mrs. Weston from the Lancaster County Clerk of Court Office wanting to know if Alex Schumacher was a student here. This lady spoke with an accent, claiming to need information for a court hearing."

"Just as I suspected, it sounds like they are trying to find Alex," I said. "Thank you so much for letting me know."

When would these people stop playing this game? We hung up, but she called again within a couple minutes.

"I called the Clerk of Court's office to see if they had called me requesting information. They told me they had not, so I filed a complaint with them that someone was impersonating them. They appreciated the information and would stay alert if they received another complaint. I just thought you should know."

"Thank you so very, very much. I am sorry you have been put in the middle. I really appreciate this."

No one needed to deal with this sort of deceit.

Around 1:30 in the afternoon I received a call from Donnie.

"Hey, I'm in town and was wondering if I could see the kids."

"So, what are you doing in town?" I asked, not wanting him to know I was aware of his intentions.

Very abruptly he said, "I came in for the hearing."

"Why didn't you call ahead to make arrangements?"

"Oh, I didn't know for sure if I'd be able to make the trip. I didn't want to disappoint Alex."

What an excuse!

"I'll have to check with my attorney since we have a pending court order. Can you call back in a couple hours?" I asked.

Donnie was satisfied with that answer. I immediately called Carl, and he said it would have to be an arrangement worked out between Donnie and me. From the October hearing the judge did not deny visitation, he had ordered there would be no visit outside the state or county. With that, my next call was made to my pastor, who was willing to help. Donnie called again.

"Okay, so when can I see the kids?" he demanded.

"I'm concerned because I haven't had time to prepare Alex," I explained.

With that comment I struck a nerve.

"I don't understand why Alex would need to be prepared. Good God, I am his dad! He should be happy to see me."

Of course, he would not understand, I thought.

"You'll have to call my pastor to make arrangements," I said, and gave him the number at the church.

Pastor John called back to say he had arranged for us to meet at the church at 6:45 that evening, if I agreed to that.

"I agree, with one stipulation, Patricia is not to be there."

"Okay, I'll let him know," Pastor John said.

Barb returned the children early so I would have time to get them dinner, as well as attempt to explain the impromptu visit to Alex.

We met at the church where Pastor John sat quietly in the corner. From my perspective I thought the visit went well. It lasted about an hour. Donnie seemed unusually attentive to Jennifer and ignored Alex. I could see the rejection and disappointment all over Alex's face. Donnie had presents for the kids, which they opened. Just before we left Alex looked at his dad and very emphatically said, "I don't ever want to come out to your house again."

Great! I am sure Donnie thought I had put Alex up to that one. I waited for the pounce.

"Why not, Son? You had such a good time when you were there," Donnie replied.

"I just don't."

With that, Alex was finished talking.

Glancing at Donnie, he was shooting daggers into my heart. If looks could kill, I would have been dead. Alex's comment came out of left field. It had to have been precipitated because Donnie ignored Alex and his feelings were hurt. I knew Donnie would never understand.

The visit impacted Alex immediately. He once again retreated to his dark place. All the same insecurities and symptoms as when he was first returned six months ago. I would give anything if I could erase those bad memories, but it was going to take a lot of time and a lot of prayers to restore his mind.

Like clockwork, Donnie called Friday night, during our dinner time, demanding to talk with Alex. This time I took a stand and refused to let him talk.

"Alex has been upset since the visit on Monday and needs a little time," I explained.

That comment poked the bear.

"I'm so sick and tired of your flimsy excuses. You fucking bitch, you'll be hearing from me because all you do is hassle me every time I call."

He was furious.

I took a deep breath, found some courage, and finally came back at him.

"There have been very few times I have not allowed Alex to talk with you and the times I have refused is because he is still upset from talking with you from the previous call. You have called every week since July. In fact, you called every day for several months or you call and let the phone ring nonstop if we don't answer." About this time, I was starting to raise my voice. This was a huge step for me since I hate confrontation.

"You haven't heard the last from me. You're not fit to be the mother of those kids." Then he threatened, "You just wait to see what's going to happen next."

I looked over and Alex had stopped eating.

"We're done here!" I said.

I hung up the phone.

As soon as I got off the phone, I noticed Alex had wet his pants. He never has accidents. This poor kid. The stress was getting to all of us. This had been one of the first times I stood up to Donnie and it had this effect on Alex. I could not help but ask myself if it was worth the fight.

At 7:03 p.m., same night, the phone rang. This time it was a child saying he was Jimmy Baldwin, a friend of Alex's from school, and wanted to talk with Alex. I had the school roster by the phone. There was no one by that name.

"I'm sorry," I said, "but, I don't see your name on the school list."

They hung up without saying another word.

At 7:33 p.m. the phone rang again. This time the child identified himself as Timmy Johnson, an 'A' student, and a friend of Alex's, wanting to talk with him. Knowing they were having the children call, I became very stern.

"NO one is talking with Alex tonight."

Before I hung up, I heard two phone clicks on the other end. I knew either Donnie or Patricia, or both, had been listening.

The month of February turned out to be a legal disaster. Motions were filed, court dates set, briefs filed, rulings given, more motions. This jurisdiction issue was turning into a legal nightmare!

On February 2, we received the ruling from the January hearing. The judge denied Donnie's request for dismissal of the October testimony and ruled my request for a change of jurisdiction still stood. This was good news for it meant the children were still restricted from leaving the county for visitation until a decision was reached from the initial hearing.

February 17, the doorbell rang. Upon opening the door, I was startled to see a police officer.

"Are you Mary Schumacher?" he asked.

"Yes, I am," I replied.

"I have papers here for you. Please sign acknowledging your acceptance of them."

He handed me a Citation Order, I signed the acknowledgement of receipt, and thanked him.

My hands started shaking as I closed the door and opened the envelope. I was being charged with Contempt of Court for not allowing visitation and ordered to appear in the Texas Court on March 26. What? We still have a pending case here in Nebraska. I really had a hard time understanding this. I was trying to go about this the right way. The Nebraska judge had ruled, no visits outside the county until the jurisdiction issue was resolved. Was I the one really in violation here? I am in violation for not allowing visitation. Donnie just saw the children in January. What about Donnie? There were no legal consequences for keeping the children longer than agreed upon. What about the phone harassment? Donnie's arrearage in child support didn't count either? Donnie's lies were tipping the legal scale very much in his favor.

Great, now I was fighting a legal war on two fronts: Nebraska and Texas. I called Carl to see if he had been informed regarding the contempt of court charge. He had not but asked that I send him a copy. I then asked if I needed to involve Sam since this was going to be in Texas.

"That won't be necessary. I can handle it from here with a letter. Do not worry about it. I do this all the time."
I had to trust him.

About a week had passed after I received the citation, when it dawned on me, we had not received a phone call from Donnie. It was rather pleasant not getting harassed or yelled at, but I could not relax, I knew something was up. Finally, a postcard arrived, Donnie and Patricia had made a trip to Ireland for two weeks. It sure seems funny you can afford a trip to Ireland when you do not have a job and you are behind $2000 in child support. Donnie's priorities made no sense to me.

February 25, the ruling finally came down from the initial October 1980 hearing. My request for change of jurisdiction was denied because I had not proved Texas no longer wanted to maintain jurisdiction. Oh my, that was never the point. We never intended to prove Texas's lack of wanting jurisdiction. The point we were attempting to establish was that jurisdiction should logically be in Nebraska, for the well-being of the children.

If truth be known, I am sure this judge did NOT want to be the first to set a precedence with this new law. In the ruling all the judge's "legal references" were prior to Nebraska adapting the UCCJA. As part of the ruling, the judge granted the opportunity to reopen the case where the evidence, I presented earlier, could be explained once again. Since that door was open, Carl immediately filed the appeal to reopen the case. Here we were four months later, starting all over again with testimony.

Carl responded to the Texas Contempt of Court charge using a Special Appearance letter that explained our outstanding court actions for moving jurisdiction to Nebraska. Even though I kept asking, Carl reassured me we did not need Sam's involvement since the Special Appearance should be recognized automatically. I was nervous because Carl never received a response from the Texas court regarding this motion. It was way too quiet.

April 2, Donnie called and was extremely cocky.

"I'm coming to pick up the kids this Friday, Apr 10, and keeping them for two weeks!"

I fired back, "Wait a minute. No, you're not!"

"By now you've seen the papers and know that I get the kids over Easter," he bellowed.

"What papers? I am sorry, but I have not seen any papers, nor have I heard of any ruling. I'll call my attorney in the morning and see if he has received anything."

"Well, then," he said boastfully, "let me fill you in. The Texas Visitation Order has been ruled on and I get the kids starting this Easter." He was gloating. "And, if you don't comply, I guarantee you there will be an automatic custody hearing," he said jokingly.

This was not a joking matter. I did not sleep all night. Nothing added up. The hearing on March 26 was for contempt, not a visitation ruling.

First thing the next morning I called Carl demanding to talk with him. I wasted no time getting right to the point.

"Have you heard anything from the Texas courts?"

"Oh yeah, I received the ruling earlier this week. Don't get so upset over this, it does not mean a thing because we have filed the appeal here in Nebraska. The upsetting circumstance here is the fact they turned the contempt charge into a ruling on visitation."

"You just don't get it," I said. "Donnie did that on purpose. You nor Sam were notified so he could walk in and say anything he wanted!"

"That never should have happened. We are waiting on the court date here and then we will proceed forward. In the meantime, just try to relax!"

"You have to realize I heard from Donnie last night and he's demanding a visit with the kids over Easter."

"Like I said, we have a pending court date." He sounded confident in what he was saying.

"Would you please send me a copy of the Texas ruling?" I asked.

"Sure, I'll get it in the mail today."

Carl did make a copy of the ruling and sent it to me. Visitation was to be alternate major holidays, Thanksgiving, Christmas, and Easter, beginning Easter 1981. Visitation was granted for six consecutive weeks each summer starting the summer of 1981. Phone calls were scheduled every Monday night. In addition, the judge set child support payments be made through the court starting immediately and would be held until the visitation schedule was complied with. There was NO mention of contempt. So, now the court was going to hold child support payments until I allowed visitation in Texas. Obviously, Donnie told the court that he was current on child support. Unbelievable!

Carl immediately sent a letter to the Texas judge asking three pointed questions: How could a contempt hearing be changed to a modification of decree without notification? How could support obligations be withheld for visitation? Was the judge aware that Donnie had not paid support since August 1980? Much to Carl's surprise, the presiding judge sent Carl a sharp reprimand telling Carl that he would discuss the case with him when Carl was licensed to practice law in Texas. End of discussion! In hindsight, I should have gotten Sam involved.

I was in the middle of a tornado just waiting to be spit out. How could I fight two battles in two different states? Technically, I guess I had already lost the battle in Texas, visitation was set. The one thing I knew, that was ripping at my heart, was the fact that if Donnie got his hands on the children, I would never see them again. How do you convey intuition to a court? I knew this man; he could not be trusted. But he continued to prey on the courts sympathy about being such a caring, loving father while I was a scorned female denying him the right to even have a conversation with his son. How was it okay for Donnie to keep the children beyond the agreed upon visitation dates, continually harass us, and not pay support? I did not understand why I could not get anyone to listen. It seemed so unfair. I felt hopeless.

I requested the afternoon off from work to talk with Pastor John regarding coming up with alternatives for visitation until Nebraska made a final determination. With Carl's blessing Pastor John and I called Donnie. Pastor John extended three different options for Donnie to come back to visit the children. Donnie would not listen to any of it.

"I've been hassled by that woman for a year and I'm done. She left me no choice but to let the courts decide with a custody hearing," he barked and hung up.

After that comment, I knew I would receive a phone call at night. Sure enough, I was ready for my verbal lashing! Before he had a chance to jump down my throat, I decided to ask the first question.

"What is your problem? We offered you several different opportunities to come here to see the kids. I am not denying you visitation. The initial Nebraska ruling said there would not be out of state visitation until this is settled."

"I can't afford to come back," he barked.

"Then why make such a big deal of this?" I questioned.

Donnie provided no response. I knew the answer. He just wanted to get his hands on the children one more time. At least I defused his anger for the time being.

A few days later he called again. I braced myself.

"What would the visitation arrangements be if I come to Nebraska?"

Mercy, has he had a change of heart? He does not sound hostile.

"You're welcome to come to the house and play with the kids."

"But what if I want to take them to the shopping center?" he asked.

"I'll have to see when the time comes," I replied. He sounded rather depressed and just kept talking.

"I didn't get the job I was hoping for. I don't know what I'm going to do now because unemployment has run out and our money is gone."

Trying to sound sympathetic, I said, "I'm sorry to hear that. It can't be easy when you have five children to feed."

After the conversation ended it only confirmed to me his inability to return the children even if he were to get them for a visit.

It was not long before I started receiving phone calls and letters from Donnie's creditors, seventeen of them. He had changed his billing address to my house. These were all the creditors from his San Francisco spending spree in January 1979. Donnie had defaulted on enough payments that the loans/credit cards were about to go to collections. When talking with the creditors they said it was their understanding that I had agreed to take over the payments for Donnie. I explained that Donnie put my name on the account, but I did not sign any application, and he had accepted all debt with the divorce. In many cases I would send them a copy of the Separation Agreement. Some accepted that and others continued to harass. This went on for months.

Every time Donnie called; he asked the same questions.

"When do I get the kids for my six-week visit?"

And I would always give him the same answer.

"We are tied up in the Nebraska court and until that's decided there will be no out of state visitation." I would reiterate and then make the same suggestion, "But, you can make arrangements to visit the children in Nebraska!"

"I can't afford to make the trip!"

"Then why keep asking?"

By mid-summer, the tornado I found myself in just spun faster and faster. Donnie was calling several times a week. Alex refused to talk with him most of the time. Donnie would blow up at me. Alex cried after the calls and asked why he had to talk. Tom wanted a relationship. There were multiple court dates. I had the outstanding contempt of court charge. There were outstanding lawyer bills. Two states were vying to set visitation rights. No one was cooperating. Donnie's creditors were calling. Donnie and Patricia were telling lies. WILL SOMEONE PLEASE LISTEN TO ME? I know everyone thought I was crazy.

Tom enjoyed the kids and they liked him. I liked him also, but I could not keep going. Virtually, I did not have room for him at this point in my life. I finally told Tom I could not even attempt to have a relationship with everything going on. At this point, he was the only one I had a little control over. He was a nice guy and I wanted to remain friends, but he deserved someone without all this baggage. Tom did not take the conversation well, but I could not continue. I had reached my limit.

In August I received a phone call from two of Donnie's former bosses in Omaha. They were friends of mine as well and were seeking me out to come work for them. This was a first for me! Normally, you must seek out new employment. This time, they were pursuing me. They offered a $3,500 increase from my current salary. That was huge. It was really an offer I could not refuse. I did not mind moving to Omaha, as I had plenty of friends there also. Since I had just told Tom

I wanted to be friends, maybe this was the fresh start I needed. I accepted the job offer and in no time, I found a townhouse, a babysitter, moved, and got Alex enrolled into Kindergarten.

About this time Donnie became very pleasant. Initially, he had wanted to visit over Labor Day weekend, but later called asking to push that back to the weekend of September 26 and 27. I agreed. I did not see a problem, but my intuition bell was ringing loudly. I wondered what he was up to.

It did not take long before everything became crystal clear. On the 14th day of September I had a knock at the door.

"Are you Mary Schumacher?" the gentleman asked.

"Yes, I am."

"I have service papers for you to sign," he explained.

Once he left, I looked through the papers. This time, Donnie had charged me with Contempt of Court in Nebraska. The hearing was set for September 24. That was only ten days away! Then I remembered, Donnie asked to see the kids the last week in September. He was coming back for the hearing! I was furious, not only with Donnie but also my attorney. I had been totally caught off guard.

First thing the next morning I put a call into Carl.

"What has been going on?" I asked very pointedly.

"Oh, nothing you should be concerned with," he said very cavalier. I was still pretty upset from being served papers, so I came right back at him.

Very pointedly I responded. "What do you mean, I shouldn't be concerned? Last night I was served with contempt of court charges. I don't take that lightly."

"Well, there have been many letters and orders going back and forth, but you don't need to worry. I'm taking care of them," he said.

"Why don't you get copies of everything that's been going on so I can judge for myself? After I see the papers, I'll give you a call."

"All right, I'll get that out to you today."

"Thank you," I said abruptly and hung up.

The package of papers arrived a couple days later, and I was shocked. I could not believe the stack of paper. This bantering back and forth had been going on between the Nebraska attorneys since

July. There had been a pretrial conference, orders, motions, clarification requests, rulings, appearance requests, motions to strike appearances, motions to reopen, formal notes from the judge, on and on and on. What an idiotic system! It's no wonder the courts are clogged for lawyers seem to be paid large sums of money to generate paper.

There was too much paperwork for me to get a handle on, so I called Tom. I know I had just broken off our relationship, but he was the only one that understood my real intent with this quest. He came right over and providing the support and reassurance I desperately needed while we sorted through all the orders and motions.

The final paper was the Order for Rule to Show Cause: ordering me to show up for court on September 24 to state why I should not be guilty of contempt of court charges. By now, that court date was only a week away.

Since the hearing was rapidly approaching, I needed some information. Once again, I reached out to Tom for assistance.

"Is there any way you can find out if Donnie is coming to Nebraska?" I asked.

By the end of the day he had discovered Donnie and Patricia were arriving on Wednesday, the 23rd, and leaving Sunday night, the 27th.

"You're kidding me," I exclaimed.

"No, I'm not, and I also found out Patricia was flying in under the name of P. Fitzpatrick, presumably her maiden name," Tom explained.

I did not ask from whom or how he acquired this information. It was obvious he pulled some strings somewhere. It did not matter how it was obtained; I was just grateful for the warning. I had to move quickly.

Since Donnie was coming into town for the hearing and staying through the weekend, meant I had to leave. I arranged for the children and myself to stay with friends for five days. After notifying the babysitter, I needed to make an appointment with Alex's teacher since he would be out of school for three days. After I explained the situation, she seemed to understand but looked at me rather perplexed. Since it was Kindergarten, he would not miss anything too critical. She provided me with his worksheets. So, on the 23rd I packed our bags for another adventure.

Carl was too busy to meet with me prior to the hearing. He was not concerned about it in the least. Since he did not want to meet, I wrote him a letter where I explained everything that had transpired the last year regarding Donnie's visits, all the visitation requests he turned down, as well as the harassing phone calls. I also explained that Donnie was now behind $4,500 in support. I felt like I was prepping the witness.

Court date, Thursday, September 24. I was an emotional wreck. The thought of seeing Donnie and Patricia face-to-face was nauseating. Donnie's intimidating power still had control over me. I needed to talk myself into being a fighter and not an innocent lamb being led to the slaughter. I took this very seriously. After all, I was being charged with Contempt of Court, again. By the end of the day, I could be fined, thrown in jail, or both.

Waiting to go into the courtroom was excruciating. Carl meandered in and we walked into the courtroom together. Donnie was already seated next to his Legal Aid counsel. All his charades were sickening. My knees were knocking and my hands shaking but I knew I had to continue; I could not cower now. Thankfully, Patricia was not in the courtroom. The court proceeding started. The attorneys bantered back and forth, seeing who could talk the loudest. No one was making any logical sense. Finally, the presiding judge seemed overwhelmed, and smacked the gavel against the striking base.

"Order in the court!" he yelled.

That certainly got everyone's attention. There was silence.

"I've heard enough for today. The contempt charge against Mary Schumacher will be heard on October 8 with the originating judge from the hearing a year ago. Court is dismissed."

Donnie was furious. He had come all this way to see the contempt case kicked down the road. I am sure he wanted to see me thrown in jail so he could swoop in and immediately take custody of the children, but that was not going to happen, at least not today.

Donnie waited for me outside the courthouse.

"I'm going to be in town through the weekend and I'd like to see the kids," he asked.

I tried to remain calm.

"It will be under my terms."

"Okay, what are they?" he asked.

"You can come to the house and play with the kids there. I don't know if Patricia is with you, but she is not allowed in my home."

I did not want him to know that I knew Patricia had flown in with him.

"Okay, can I see them both days?"

"That should be fine. After all, you have come this far. You can come around 10 o'clock on Saturday morning and I prefer you leave before dinner, which is around 6 o'clock."

I was trying to be accommodating, especially knowing I was going to be back in court in a few weeks.

"That sounds fine. I'll be there about 10 Saturday morning," he said.

"Sounds good, I'll see you then."

Now I had more plans to make. We had the visit arranged for Saturday and Sunday, but that still left Friday for him and Patricia to try to find us, so I was not going back to the house until extremely late Friday night.

Later that afternoon Tom called to see how the hearing went. He was relieved that nothing came from the contempt charge, at least not for now. I explained that Donnie and I had arranged a visit with the children over the weekend. Both of us were uneasy about the children and I being in the house alone with Donnie. Tom wanted to come down and spend the weekend with us, but I did not think that was a good idea. I decided to call Barb, to see if she could help. She knew a lot of people in the city.

I immediately called Barb and explained the situation.

"Give me a couple hours," she explained, "I've got someone in mind."

Barb had the perfect solution. Since Barb worked for a general contracting company, she knew several men. She called back within the hour.

"I have it all worked out. I talked with my friend Dan. He will be available all weekend to help you. Give Dan a call tonight and discuss with him what you want."

She gave me Dan's phone number.

After getting the kids settled, I called Dan. He was more than happy to assist. Barb must have explained the entire story to him. So, basically, I hired a man to sit in my house for two days to be my bodyguard. Dan was a big, strong concrete worker. I explained to him all he had to do was sit and watch tv both Saturday and Sunday. We needed to make it appear as though we were dating so if I touched his arm or had my hand on his shoulder to not get too concerned. He was not to spend the night, just arrive an hour before Donnie and not leave until an hour after Donnie left. Dan was fine with that arrangement. I knew Tom really wanted to spend the weekend and be the bodyguard, but I needed someone big in stature to intimidate Donnie. Barb guaranteed me Dan was a gentle giant.

Dan arrived by 9 Saturday morning, I showed him around the house, gave Dan the remote, and told him to watch whatever he wanted, just make himself look comfortable. Donnie was there by 10 o'clock. Patricia must have dropped him off down the street because I saw Donnie walk up the sidewalk; he did not have a car. He was not happy there was another man in the house, but too bad. Donnie had no idea what our relationship was, neither did he ask. Donnie played most of the time with Alex; he tired of Jennifer quickly. I fixed lunch for everyone. We pretty much stayed in our separate areas, the guys were in the living room while I tried to stay in the kitchen and tend to Jennifer's needs. Donnie left before 6 o'clock, he was tired. Again, he walked down the street. Strange arrangement, but, of course, I was not to know Patricia was in town with him. Dan stayed until 7:00, making sure everything was quiet before he left.

Sunday the arrangement was the same, everyone arrived at the same times. Once again, Donnie walked in from the street. By noon Donnie was bored and even Alex was tired of Donnie, so Dan and Donnie watched football most of the afternoon. After Jennifer's nap Donnie asked if he could take the kids shopping to pick something up for them before he left. I agreed he could, but I was going along. So, we all went shopping, including Dan. After shopping Donnie was more than eager to leave. He told the kids goodbye and walked down the street. The visit went well, just extremely awkward.

The trial was coming up soon and I had not heard from Carl. I called and scheduled a meeting. He was not concerned in the least.

"What about witnesses?" I asked. "All my friends have volunteered to help me. Many know the frustrations I have had with Donnie. Several know what kind of a mother I am and the care I provide for the children. The nursery schoolteacher will testify regarding receiving a call from a woman impersonating the clerk of court office. My pastor will testify about Donnie not returning the kids initially, as well as the multiple offers for visitation here in Nebraska that Donnie refused, and the strange phone calls to his home. My pediatrician will testify about the kid's health upon their return. I have many people to call on."

"Don't get so excited! We do not need witnesses. This is cut and dry. We have been through this once so there will be nothing to it. I am not going to let Donnie, nor his wife testify because they did not bother to show up or have representation at the first hearing. By rights they should not even be there. I am going to try to get them thrown out of the courtroom. You are making a big deal about this," he said in a belittling tone.

"It is a big deal! This is it! From here a decision will be made."
I tried not getting too worked up, for he had to already be thinking I was an irrational female.

"Well, we're not having witnesses. That's that! Maybe I'll contact the pediatrician and take a deposition from him."

"Oh my," I thought. Of all the people I could call upon, the pediatrician is the least important.

We were finished talking, but as I was getting ready to walk out the door, he made one more comment.

"I can guarantee you one thing. After this case I'm never taking another fucking custody case again!"

In my mind I thought, "I hope you do a damn good job then!"

Once I got home, I called Texas to ask Francis, Cora, and Arlene if they would come to Nebraska and testify for me. They all declined.

They did not like the current situation and what Donnie was attempting to do but found themselves unable to assist. Their loyalties were with Donnie.

I was in no state of mind to see Tom the weekend before the hearing. He knew Carl had unnerved me, but he made a trip to Omaha against my wishes. After the children were in bed I broke down. Something was gnawing away in my gut; I did not have a comfortable feeling about this whole thing. My attorney was very nonchalant. The Texas friends had deserted me. It was impossible to get anyone to listen to me. Tom just held me and gave me encouragement while I poured my heart out. At this point, that was all I could do. I felt very hopeless. I silently prayed for the Lord to give me peace and strength to get through this next week.

Three days before the hearing, my attorney did arrange for a deposition from the children's pediatrician. Donnie's attorney was invited. The pediatrician gave his perspective about the effect on a two-year-old and a five-year-old of visitation from the non-custodial parent, especially away from the base home. I was confused, Carl could take the time for a generic deposition but could not see the benefit of witnesses. It did not make any sense to me.

Unable to keep my mind on work, I took the day off before the hearing. Since Donnie was coming to town I, once again, had to abandon the house. I packed suitcases and headed for my parents' house. I took Alex out of school for two days. I could not take a chance.

The dreaded day arrived, October 8, 1981. I met Carl in a side room. You would have thought he was going to church. He did not prep me as to how he was going to proceed or ask any questions of me for clarification. I was not sure he even reviewed for the hearing. My teeth started chattering and my legs were shaking. Meeting in the courtroom you would think Donnie, Patricia, Donnie's attorney, and Carl were old friends. My what pleasantries there were. Patricia was overly gooey to everyone. I sat with a paper and pencil, looking straight ahead.

After the formal introductions, the first order of business from my attorney was to get Donnie and Patricia thrown out of court. After much bantering and posturing between the attorneys, the judge ruled,

"Denied!"

Carl then approached it that they could remain in the courtroom but not testify. Once again, after all the bantering, the judge thought it over and ruled,

"Denied!"

This was NOT off to a good start. I was called to the witness stand.

"Tell the court exactly what you told at the first hearing on October 20, 1980."

I told the story again.

"Tell the court what has transpired since that time."

I explained the harassing phone calls, Alex's behavior whenever the phone rang, the multiple offers for Donnie to see the children in Nebraska, the unusual phone calls my pastor received.

"Objection: Hearsay!" Donnie's attorney interrupted.

"Sustain!" shouted the judge!

I tried to tell the story a different way.

"Objection: Hearsay!" he interrupted again.

"Sustain!" shouted the judge again.

My attorney did not prompt me along a different line of questioning for me to continue the story, I did not know how to proceed, so I dropped it. Then I proceeded to tell the story about the calls to the nursery schoolteacher from the Lancaster County Clerk of Court.

"Objection: Hearsay!"

"Sustain!" shouted the judge.

I tried again.

"Objection: Hearsay!"

"Sustain!"

I looked at my attorney for help. He just stared at me. He offered no advice to direct my answers in an acceptable approach. Once again, I had to give up. I glanced a look at Donnie and Patricia, they were snickering between themselves. Then, Donnie's attorney started on me. By the time he was finished I felt beat up. Carl did not interrupt him once. Questioning was over. Thank, God! I had been on the witness stand three hours. I felt emotionally and mentally spent. We broke for lunch. Carl left me. I needed to talk with someone to reassure me this was going to be okay, so I tried to call Tom. He did not answer. I felt so alone, so hopeless.

After lunch Donnie was called to the witness stand. Every statement from his mouth was a lie. I was busy taking notes to counter each lie. Donnie's attorney asked him about support.

"Have you faithfully been paying child support?"

"Yes, I'm current. Every month I faithfully send her a check for $300."

"Have you paid her extra money for doctor bills and medicine?"

"I've never received a bill for additional expenses to cover medical expenses for the children."

I could not believe his audacity to lie like that. I was ready to jump out of my skin! His lawyer continued with the questions.

"Did you ever make harassing phone calls to Mary's home?"

Donnie looked at me and paused.

"Never! I would call once a week to talk with my son. Several times Mary denied me the privilege of speaking with him, so sometimes it was several weeks before I would get to talk with him. When I would get the chance to talk, she continually interrupted the conversation."

My heart was pounding so hard I was sure everyone could see it pulsate under my shirt. His attorney continued.

"Have you punished the kids?"

"I couldn't punish children. Maybe, I have spanked Alex six times his entire life. I could not hurt him. It would break my heart."

"Have you ever received a payment from your work insurance company for medical expenses for the children?"

"I've never received a payment for Alex or Jennifer."

I had the letters in front of me showing payments sent directly to him. The final question from his attorney made me want to scream.

"Have you ever threatened to kidnap the children?"

Donnie looked right at me, staring a hole through me.

"Never! I would not threaten anyone. I am a kind, loving person. It is just that no one is going to stand between me and my kids. I love them so much and I've been denied the right to see them."

His attorney was finished.

"Thank you, Your Honor, no further questions."

Donnie was on the stand with his attorney about an hour. When my attorney was asked for a cross-examination, I put the papers in front of him where I had highlighted facts.

"No further questions, Your Honor."

What? Did you listen to what he said? I tried to remain calm. Next, Patricia was called to the stand. Why isn't my attorney objecting? This is NOT about her!

Patricia was on the stand about half an hour. She reinforced the same lies spoken by Donnie. She even added a few of her own.

"What about the condition of the children when you saw them during the first visit in June 1980?"

"Alex seemed okay, just very timid, almost backward. I was genuinely concerned about Jennifer. She was extremely underweight and way behind in her speech development. We took her to a doctor, and he was concerned as well. Both children suffered from mental problems, especially attachment difficulties. I have had several foster children before, and we all know foster children have issues. Well, these children were suffering from those same issues."

How can she lie like that? What made her an expert in child psychology? She looked straight at me and smirked. She knew exactly what she was doing. Again, I was taking notes and highlighting facts. When my attorney was asked for a cross-examination I, once again, put the paper in front of him.

"No further questions, Your Honor."

What? Are you kidding me? Did you listen to these people? Did you sleep through the testimony?

The judge gave my attorney a second chance.

"Redirect?"

"No, Your Honor," Carl said.

By this time, the air was completely out of my balloon. The judge gave Donnie's attorney another chance.

"Redirect?"

"No, Your Honor," he said.

Why would he? My attorney had no additional questions and Donnie's attorney certainly would not want to question me again, since Donnie and Patricia had convincingly told their lies. The judge set a date of December 10, 1981, for a Brief to be submitted from both sides and a date of December 18, 1981, for a Counter Brief. The judge cracked the gavel on the strike base. It was deafening to my ears.

"Court is Dismissed."

Great, it was over! It really was ... over. Donnie and Patricia were beaming. They hugged each other. I was shell shocked. I could hardly move away from the table.

As my attorney and I left the courtroom I was unable to open my mouth. In just 90 minutes, Donnie and Patricia had been able to undermine everything I said. They had made a mockery of the judicial system. Carl didn't seem to care. As we were leaving the courthouse Carl made a comment I would not forget.

"I'll be damned if I'm going to do the judge's work for him," he said with great disdain.

At the time, I was not sure what that meant.

Sitting in my car, I was unable to move. I was frozen, in shock. Tom and I had arranged to meet at his house following the hearing. When I got there, he was already waiting for me. I fell into his arms, crying for two hours, unable to get hold of myself. It seemed so surreal. I had been waiting a year for this moment, I had multiple witnesses available to me, everything was in my favor, but Carl let it slip through his fingers.

After I explained to Tom how horrendous the court experience had been, he kicked himself for not being there to provide support. It was after this, I realized how much he really cared for all of us. During the previous months I had always told Tom I could not think about any future, or dragging anyone into my situation, until I had things cleared up in the courts. I knew now that whatever the courts decided, I would have to live within the ruling. I could not fight any longer. The fight was over. I had done all that I could. But I felt truly hopeless.

7. The Eye Of The Storm

*~ The only peaceful part of the hurricane. The point
about which the rest of the storm rotates ~*

Now that the court hearings and contempt of court charges were behind me, I was in a waiting period until the judge rendered his decision. It was time to move forward. My life had been on hold while Donnie continued being the puppeteer, pulling the strings on the puppets.

Tom and I had been dating occasionally since the first night we met, July 7, 1980, the day the children were not returned. He knew the situation with my ex and kids from the very beginning and had a chance to walk away due to the drama, but he did not. Tom was very patient and persistent. In July 1981 I was the one who broke off our relationship, when the pressure of the legal entanglements became overwhelming. Even then, he never totally went away. He would ask to take Alex for ice cream, to a sport event, or just drop in to see how we were doing and play with the children. He even helped me pack and move to Omaha. Tom was not giving up hope. His faith in God gave him strength as he continued to pray for restoration of our relationship. I, on the other hand, was treading water, trying not to drown. At the time I was unable to see his kindness, love, and concern, for Donnie continued to keep my mind clouded.

Being a quiet man, Tom mainly sought the counsel from his mother regarding our relationship. Her advice all along was to be patient, this ordeal with the ex would not last forever. Tom was willing to wait. I knew it was a trying period for him. We would have plans to go out and at the last minute I would have to cancel because one of the children would get sick or the babysitter would back out. When I needed space, he was willing to give it to me.

Tom was devastated when I moved to Omaha but did not show it. He continued to call, checking on the progress of the legal tirades and the phone harassments. Tom knew I was exhausted from the entire ordeal, yet he was the only one, outside of my folks, consistently supporting me. He would make a trip to Omaha every week, just to drop in. When I was in Lincoln, he would watch the kids while I had my appointments with the attorney.

Call it premonition, or listening to God's small voice, I had taken the day off following the Thursday, October 8, hearing. After experiencing the day of testimony, it would have been impossible to concentrate at work. I desperately needed time to process everything that had occurred the day before. The kids and I had planned to stay with my folks through the weekend anyway. Tom asked if we could go for dinner Friday night, which we did.

He wanted to make sure I was okay following the hearing. The last he had seen me I had been crying in his arms for two hours following the testimony. We both shared our feelings over dinner of how unfair this entire ordeal had been. I had followed procedures by the rules of the court and Donnie had played by his own rulebook. Tom agreed with me that my attorney left a lot to be desired regarding fighting on my behalf. It was my belief that Carl had been extremely confident in the beginning to get jurisdiction moved to Nebraska, but he became overly confident when he found he was dealing with a young Legal Aid attorney. Carl insisted it was a slam dunk and found himself unprepared for the events that transpired.

After fully discussing the entire situation, Tom was prepared with his next question.

"Are you ready to move our relationship forward, now that all the legal entanglements are behind you?"

That question caught me off guard. It rather left me speechless since I really had not thought about a future. It was true, I had told him earlier I could not think of any relationship when I was in the middle of the mess.

"I really need some time to get over the disappointment of Thursday's hearing before I can give you an answer."
Tom was satisfied with that response, I had been through a lot the last couple days, and he was going to wait patiently for my response.

I wrestled with that question all night. There was no justifiable reason for Donnie to continue keeping the children and I from moving forward. After all, we deserved to have a life, one not controlled by Donnie. We <u>needed</u> to have a life. I <u>needed</u> to move forward. In all honesty, it was whether I felt I was ready to lower my guard, allowing love to enter again. My first love experience was a disaster. Could I attempt it again? No doubt about it, I was scared, and it was for sure this chapter of my life was not closed, for we were waiting for the court's ruling.

It took me about a month to arrive at the decision. Basically, there was no reason for me to waste my life looking in the rearview mirror. During one of our regular phone calls, I shared with Tom that I was ready to give life another attempt, although I was unable to give him any guarantees. He was extremely excited. We decided to plan something every weekend that would include the children. Tom's parents were excited to meet us. His mother was super with the kids. When in Lincoln, she volunteered to keep them so Tom and I could go out for dinner.

The kids and I were settling into a new normal. Either Tom would come to Omaha for the weekend or the kids and I would go to Lincoln. I felt it important that Tom saw what a daily chaotic routine was like with children before he became too committed. He still had a chance to walk away. The children were becoming pretty attached to Tom and vice versa, which I saw as a positive thing.

Upon finding out Tom was spending the weekends with us; my parents became terribly upset.

"What if Donnie finds out? He'll use it against you," they exclaimed.

"He's used everything he could, as well as lied about many other things. I do not see where he can do any more damage than he has already done. Besides, we are waiting for the final decision," I explained.

It did not make them feel more at ease, but we were 32 years old. What could they say? They had voiced their disapproval and that was that.

Donnie routinely called weekly to talk with Alex. Sometimes Alex would talk, but not always. He would have the phone to his ear but would not say a word. No longer did I see a need to listen in on the calls or attempt to record them. The hearing was over, I was moving on.

Our relationship progressed along quickly. At Thanksgiving I introduced Tom to my family. He seemed to fit in fine. By the end of November Tom asked me to marry him. I emphatically said, "Yes!" The kids were overly excited for Tom asked them if they would be his children. They could not wait to have a dad at home.

The following weekend, we invited both sets of parents over to Tom's house so they could meet, and we could make the announcement. The two dads hit it off from the beginning. The children were keeping both moms occupied with a lot of little chatter. The dads were making enough conversation for everyone. Tom wanted to make the announcement.

"We have some news we want to share with you. Mary and I are getting married."

Silence. You could have heard a pin drop. The room filled with an awkward silence. "Oh dear," I thought, "I can't imagine what they are thinking."

Tom's mom was the first to speak.

"Congratulations, have you set a date?"

"No," Tom said, "we have a lot of details to work out first."

The dads never said a word. Their previously engaging conversation was over. Shortly after breaking the news, both parents excused themselves and went home.

After they left, Tom and I just looked at each other.

"That didn't go as we expected," Tom said.

"No, it didn't. I would guess it has to do with me: the ex, the court hearings, all the above. I've got a lot of baggage."

It took several days of talking with each of our mothers, but we finally reached the reason for each of the father's reaction. Tom's dad was concerned because I was used goods, as he put it. Guess Tom's father was hoping his son would marry someone who had not previously been married or if they had, that there would not be children involved. If the truth were known, Tom's father was always concerned what the town would think; there was always an image he felt he had to uphold. I guess I was not what he imagined for his son.

My dad had his own slant on the situation. He was concerned I would be a two time looser. That comment set me back a bit, but I decided I could not live my life for my folks, I had to live it for myself and the well-being of the children. I never did understand, or find out why, my dad felt the way he did. Guess it was just a feeling he had. If it had been up to my dad, I would have remained single the rest of my life, especially after going through the painful experience I had gone through with Donnie. Through all my pain I had relied on my parents and Dad did not want to see me get hurt again. That, I understood.

Throughout the month of December there were plenty of Christmas parties to attend. These parties gave us an opportunity to meet friends and co-workers from each of our workplaces. Christmas Eve the kids and I were to meet the rest of Tom's family. By the time New Year's Day arrived, we were exhausted but had made the rounds meeting everyone.

This was going to be quite a transition, but I knew we could do it. Rather than Tom coming to Omaha on the weekends, I would pack the children up and head for Lincoln. With the family business we needed to live in Lincoln. Logistically, I could eventually find a carpool and drive to Omaha each day. Since Tom's work was in town, he would be available for the children if any emergency arose. It was imperative for both kids to feel extremely comfortable with Tom and his home. Throwing two small children in with a bachelor was something you must do gradually, for all parties involved. We set the wedding date for June, so we started making plans right after the holidays. By waiting until June, Alex could finish Kindergarten in Omaha.

New Year's Day 1982 was a new beginning. Tom and I were looking forward to what this year held. We continued our distance relationship with phone calls every night and long weekend visits. If the weather were threatening, Tom spared me making the drive to Lincoln with the kids, he would make the trip to Omaha instead.

Sometime after I had moved, Pastor John and Sherri also moved to pastor in another state. Even though I did not know the new pastor well, I still felt that church to be my home church in Lincoln. I wanted to be married there, so Tom and I made an appointment to speak with the new pastor regarding the wedding. After visiting a bit and sharing how much the church meant to me, I asked if he would marry us. He asked me very pointed questions about my past marriage and divorce.

"Did you and your ex have sex before your marriage?"

"Yes," I said cautiously.

"How does that relate to getting married now?" I thought.

"Did you and your ex attend church at the time of your marriage?"

"No, we did not," I replied.

"Did you ever join a church while married to him?"

"No, we did not."

"What was the reason for your divorce?"

"Infidelity on his part," I responded.

He looked directly into my eyes, "Did you have an affair?"

"No, I did not," I replied emphatically.

"Are you members here?" he inquired.

"No, not yet," I replied. "The kids and I attended this church for eighteen months after moving to Lincoln back in 1980."

Again, glaring right at me he asked, "Are you and Tom having sex?"

That question took me back a bit, but I was not going to lie.

"Yes."

Very assertively he said, "The only way I'll marry you is if you promise me that you'll not have sex again until after you are married."

Trying to be very honest, I said, "I'm not sure I can promise you that."

"Then, I won't be able to marry you with a clear conscience," he declared.

"Okay, thank you for your time," I said as we stood up and walked out.

Why was he only concerned about my background? Tom had a history as well. Again, I felt it was my fault for being used goods. We would have to think of something else.

Mid-January I tabulated the medical expenses and past child support for 1981 and sent the itemization to Donnie. As of the end of the year his child support arrearage was $5,500. No one seemed to care. I could not get anyone to pay attention to this. Carl knew about the arrearage in court back in October but never said a word. It seemed I was still the ONLY one in the wrong here.

February 8 Donnie called, only wanting to talk with me.

"Okay, now what are you going to do?" he asked, extremely cocky.

"I don't know what you're referring to," I said.

With a giddy condescending attitude he said, "The judge ruled on the court case and, guess what, you lost!" With that he laughed!

I started shaking. "Let me get back to you tomorrow. I will call my attorney in the morning to see what is going on. Truthfully, I have not heard a word," I said holding back tears.

I was ready to explode!

"Okay, I'll give you that. I'll talk to you tomorrow." He was extremely arrogant and still laughing.

Panic paralyzed me. I could not talk or move; hot tears were streaming down my face and onto my hands. Alex jolted me back into reality.

"Mommy, you okay?"

"Yes, Alex, it'll be fine," I said wiping the tears from my face.

The backside of the storm was about to hit landfall!

After settling the kids into bed, I called Tom. He could not understand what I was saying because I was sobbing so hard. It was too late for him to come to Omaha, but he did his best to console me over the phone. We were trying to figure out what happened. Of course, without the ruling in front of me it was difficult guessing exactly what it said. From Gary's cocky attitude it was obvious Nebraska was not going to fight for jurisdiction.

First thing the next morning I called Carl.

"Good morning, what can I do for you?" Carl said cheerfully.

Very pointedly I started in.

"Sorry, but it's not a good morning. Why did I have to hear from my ex that the judge had ruled on my case?"

"Oh yes, well, I've been busy. I read it and I want you to think about something. I think we should appeal the decision to the

Nebraska Supreme Court. In fact, I have started the paperwork," he said very confidently.

"Why don't you send me a copy of the ruling and I'll decide what I want to do?" I fired back.

"Fair enough, I'll get it in the mail today."

"Thank you," I said and hung up.

Why was that so hard? How long had he been in possession of the ruling? Obviously, Donnie's attorney had received it the same day as Carl. Donnie really didn't say if he had a copy or his attorney had called him with the news. It didn't matter. Later that night I called Donnie and told him I had not seen the order yet. A copy was being sent in the mail, so I would have to get back with him in a couple days. He understood. After all, he got what he wanted, so he was willing to give me a little time.

The envelope arrived in the mail a couple days later, as promised. As I opened it my hands were shaking. I did not have to read past the first paragraph to see the problem. "Having considered the brief and argument submitted by the Respondent (Donnie), none having been submitted by the Petitioner (me)...". I threw the papers across the room! It was a good thing Carl was not in the same room with me. My blood was boiling. He NEVER submitted the brief to the judge. Then I remembered him saying as we left court, "I'll be damned if I'm going to do the judge's work for him." Now I knew what he meant. He had no intention of writing a brief. What a sham! Each side was to submit a brief and the judge gave each attorney a chance for a counter brief. Carl, having several years of experience in family law, had been whipped by a young Legal Aid attorney, all because he was too lazy to have witnesses and too lazy to write a brief. I was furious! My anger upset the kids, I had to calm down for their sake. Previously, through all of this, the children had never been put to bed knowing I was upset. I always saved that for after they were asleep. But tonight, I could not control myself.

Once they were asleep, I continued reading the remainder of the ruling. The reason the judge allowed Donnie to reopen the case in the first place was that Donnie claimed economic hardship and an inability to appear in court because of distance. The brief submitted by

Donnie's attorney included the recent Texas decisions: the Texas ruling setting visitation (the case where notification was never provided to me or either of my attorneys) along with a copy of the Texas contempt citation stating I had failed to provide ANY visitation to Donnie. The judge, once again, sited cases regarding modifying another state's decree prior to the UCCJA ever being accepted in Nebraska. Relevancy? There was none. I questioned how the recent Texas rulings were presented with the brief rather than submitted initially as evidence, but it was irrelevant at this point.

Donnie and Patricia had convinced the judge they were loving parents and their concern for the children's welfare was disconcerting. This statement was priceless, "The Respondent (Donnie) continues to live in Texas and is making his support payments under the jurisdiction of the courts of Texas." No one ever checked! The judge found me guilty of "failure to grant rights of visitation…mittimus (a warrant issued by the court for imprisonment) should be withheld by obeying the order of the Texas court." I could not believe the judge was referencing me, like I was the criminal here. In short, the judge would not put me in jail if I followed the Texas order of visitation.

I was DONE! I was in shock. I did not want to talk to anyone about this. I did not want to talk, period. There were no words to express my feelings regarding the decision or my attorney's actions. In my heart I knew it was Carl's lack of interest in the case that lost it for me. Now, I could only inch my way forward.

I scheduled one last appointment with Carl. Every question I asked, he was armed with excuses.

"Why didn't you file a brief?" I asked.

"Oh, I was tied up on another hearing and ran out of time."

"Our hearing was October 8 and the judge gave you until December 10 to file the brief. That is two months," I fired back.

"I'm sorry, I just ran out of time. Don't worry," he continued, "I have already drafted a notice of appeal to the supreme court, as well as asked for a certified copy of the court transcript. I have this. No need to worry." He sounded so confident.

"NO," I replied emphatically, "I'm DONE! I am NOT appealing. You failed to represent me the first time so why would I trust you to represent me again?" I made it exceptionally clear.

His anger instantly flared.

"You'll regret this if you don't follow through with the appeal," he scorned.

"I'm sorry, but I already regret this. We had everything on our side, but you would not call witnesses. And, on top of that, you did not file the brief. I have no confidence to continue with you."

With that I struck a nerve.

"Then we're finished here," he said profoundly. "You'll be getting my bill."

With that, I left.

I could not determine his real motive. He had to be aware he had screwed up. Was he trying to correct his mistake or was he wanting fame? Either way, I was through. He did a horrible job and now, the children and I, would have to pay a very dear price.

Driving back to Omaha I poured my heart out to God. My mind was rambling. "What have I done wrong? Are you punishing me for something? I am just trying to be a good mother, you know that. Alex and Jennifer are Donnie's children also, but his control and manipulation are not a good influence on them. He will destroy them. I do not understand Patricia's motive. She is a mother herself. Can't she feel the pain she is inflicting on me? If all this is so Donnie does not have to pay child support, then I am willing to drop it. I do not understand. This would not be so bad if Donnie would go by the rules, the same rules that I follow. Donnie has to have it all, or nothing. Lord, help us. I cannot do this without You. I need You!"

Donnie granted me a little space to get my head wrapped around the court's decision. The first scheduled visit, according to the Texas Visitation Rules, allowed Donnie to have the children over Easter weekend, which was April 9 through April 11 this year. Trying to be cooperative, I called Donnie with an alternative.

"Alex has spring break the week before Easter so you can have the children the week of March 27 through April 4."

I was trying to offer a conciliatory arrangement.

I went on to explain, "With the expense of coming to get the kids it would make more sense for you to have them a week rather than the three days over the long weekend of Easter."

"I'll see," he said. The attitude in his voice did not rest easy with me.

I questioned myself, "Why do I keep trying to be nice to this man?"

Rather than just a verbal agreement, I wrote a letter to Donnie, putting in writing, the dates I had agreed to, as well as a noted copy to the judge in Texas that ruled on the initial visitation. In addition to the dates, I expressed my concern that I did not have a specific house address where the children would be staying. I only had a PO box number.

A few days later Donnie's letter was returned "Return to Sender. Not Deliverable as Addressed, Unable to Forward" stamped on the front. That was unsettling. I sent a valentine from the kids. That also was returned as undeliverable. I knew they had moved but knowing the town was small I thought the letter might be delivered. I turned around and sent the letter Certified. That also came back as undeliverable. That unnerved me. What was he up to? Who was he hiding from? How could I send my children to Texas not knowing the address where they would be staying? But it did not seem to bother anyone but me. Besides, I had no one to seek advice. It was for sure I would not be contacting Carl again. Since jurisdiction was remaining in Texas, it was only logical that any legal advice would come from my original attorney, Sam.

Since I was not quite ready to call Sam, I took matters into my own hands. I talked with the Texas State Ombudsman and expressed my concern regarding not knowing the address where the children would be throughout the visit. He suggested I write a letter to the Texas judge stating my concern, but he suggested I do not deny the visit just because I did not know the address of where the children would be staying. I did not tell him I had already sent a letter to the judge. I failed to understand why no one was concerned but me. Here I am, sending my children away for a week to Texas and no one cares where they will be staying? I wanted to ask him if he would do that with his children, but I knew better. Just keep quiet. Follow the rules.

About this same time who shows up in Omaha but Donnie's mother. She asked if she could spend a few days with us so she could see the children. This was the first time our visit seemed strained. By this time, she had to know the outcome of the hearing, although the hearing was never mentioned between us. I was sure Donnie called Francis right away, as he was exploding with joy when he talked with me. Arlene was comfortable with the kids, I tried keeping busy. Prior to her arrival I took off my engagement ring. No reason for her to know any more than necessary. Maybe she had the same premonition as me and wanted to see the kids once again prior to the Texas visit. It was a crazy situation. She and Donnie only lived 90 miles apart, yet they never saw or talked to each other.

Even though the visit to Texas was imminent, life went on. Tom and I continued with the wedding plans. We had visited with the Lutheran minister in Lincoln. He was more than willing to perform the wedding ceremony for us, so we started attending church there with the children. Tom bought a new suit for the wedding and we bought a matching suit for Alex. I had asked Barb to be my maid of honor. She went with me to find a wedding dress. With the help of a friend, we decided to make Barb's dress and a matching dress for Jennifer. We were trying to be very frugal with the plans. I am sure Tom's folks would have preferred a large wedding for Tom, since he had never been married, but I saw no need, especially since most of the costs were going to be at our expense.

When Donnie called to talk with the kids, I asked him about the specific flight schedule. He was very evasive. He said he would call with it next week. Something was up! I felt it brewing in my soul.

Another letter arrives from Carl. Now what? "I sincerely hope you will not regret your decision not to appeal the court's decision. Very truly yours…" Did he think we are best friends here? If he had done his job the first time, I would not be in the position that I am. Enclosed was his itemized statement for his representation for the year, $1,500. And he was too lazy to finish the case. I had already made up my mind that his payments would be slow coming. I was still incredibly angry regarding his lack of representation.

Conversations had to be started with my children about the visit, especially Alex.

"Alex, you know you have spring break coming up at school in another week. That means you have a week away from school and your friends, to be with family. This year your Dad is coming back to pick you and Jennifer up, and fly back to Texas to visit him, Patricia, and the kids."

"I don't want to go, Mommy!" he started crying. "Please don't make me go! Please!" he begged.

"I know, Alex, but we have too. We do not have a choice. I know you do not understand, but it will just be for one-week, seven days. You can count that on your fingers! In seven days, you will be back home ready to go back to school and your friends."

He still did not understand. He just grabbed me around my neck, sobbing, pleading for me not to send him. My heart was breaking. We talked about the visit every day. They had to accept the fact they were going. I had to as well.

Wednesday before the children were to leave, Donnie called me at work.

"I've been to court and they ruled that since I've never been granted visitation, this visit would be extended through Easter, April 11."

He was gloating. I was fuming.

"I haven't heard anything about this. Alex will miss a week of school," I exclaimed, "and it is only a couple days before they are supposed to leave. You haven't supplied me with any plans."

He barked right back, "The order was signed by the judge yesterday, March 23. The judge said that kindergarten is not a required grade, so it doesn't matter if he will miss a week of school. I will arrive in Omaha Saturday the 27 at 1:30 p.m. on United flight 346, turning around to come back to Texas at 2:00 p.m. on flight 215. This will be a quick turn-around so make SURE you are there on time. The return flight is April 11, United flight 742, arriving in Omaha at 6:50 p.m. There it is. I'll see you and the kids in three days."

Donnie was getting really cocky with me. I had nothing to say to him, so I hung up.

I was so upset from Donnie's call; I had to leave work and go home. Once I got hold of myself, I made a couple phone calls. After calling the Omaha school board I found out kindergarten was a required grade in Nebraska. Although, at this point, it really did not matter. Next, I called Sam. He was terribly upset for not being notified of any of the hearings. He wanted to get a confirmation of what just went on and promised to call me back.

As promised, Sam did call back once he obtained a copy of the latest order. Sam said it read exactly as Donnie explained. Since I had agreed Donnie could have the children during the school spring break week the judge extended that to include the Easter week, since Donnie claimed to have been denied any visitation since 1980. Sam said he would get a copy to me, but it would not arrive before the 27th.

"That's okay, just send a copy of the order," I said dejectedly.

"You have every right to fight this since you or myself weren't notified of the hearing, but it would be detrimental to you. Besides, we are running out of time," Sam explained.

"I'm tired of fighting, Sam," I muttered. "I really don't have a choice."

I was defeated. Every avenue I took, there had been no justice of any kind. I was damned everywhere I turned. There was no fight left in me.

"Then go ahead and let Donnie have them, and we will see what he does," Sam recommended.

Being extremely disappointed I said, "I'm afraid I don't have a choice."

We had been down this road before. There again, no one seemed concerned about the past visit, arrearages, or not having an address where my children would be staying, except me. "Lord, this is just so unfair," I prayed.

Two days before the kids were to leave, I had to explain to Alex that he would be staying longer than I had first explained to him. As I expected, he cried, and cried, and begged not to go.

"Don't worry, Alex, I'll be here when you get back. I promise I will pick up your schoolwork and I will help you get caught up once you get home. Your friends will be here when you get back and your teacher will be excited to see you." All he could do was cry. All I wanted to do was cry!

Both kids were well prepared for the trip. They seemed to have a better attitude about it than myself. After lunch on Saturday, Tom and I took the children to the airport. Donnie got off the plane, said a few pleasantries, and was ready to re-board for the return flight. Just as before, Donnie whisked the children away, down the jetway without letting them say goodbye to either Tom or myself. I had the kids prepared so they marched like little robots, but it was more like two little sheep being led to the slaughter; they had no idea what lay ahead of them.

8. The Nightmare

~ A terrifying or very unpleasant experience ~

Even though I had Tom by my side, I was unable to move once the jetway door closed. He put his arm around me and held me tight until the plane pulled away and started taxiing towards the runway. It had been six weeks since the court's decision, when the bottom fell out of my world. This was one of those experiences you cannot prepare for. My heart was so heavy, I could hardly breathe. My body felt like I was wearing a lead X-ray apron. Just putting one foot in front of the other was a chore. My intuition was telling me that I may not see them again, but I could not go down that rabbit hole. I had to maintain positive thoughts regarding this visit. Now that Texas had set the mandate, perhaps Donnie would be more amicable in following the rules. All I could do was pray, "Lord, please make these next two weeks pass quickly, and everything goes according to Your will." This was not going to be an easy two weeks. I knew I would have to keep extremely busy.

Sunday, the 28th, was Jennifer's third birthday. Before she left, I had promised her we would celebrate her birthday when she returned home. Everything got so frantic the week before my kids left, there was no time for a celebration. Besides, I was not in any mood for a party. Jennifer was young enough she did not know the exact date of her birthday. Since the kids had just left the day before, I did not know whether Donnie would allow me to speak to them, but it was Jennifer's birthday. I had nothing to lose so I called. Surprisingly, Donnie answered.

"How is everything?" I asked.

"Couldn't be better," he sounded so chipper.

"Since it's Jennifer's birthday may I speak with her?"

"Sure, not a problem, Alex is here. Do you want to talk with him first?"

I was in shock! He volunteered that I could speak to Alex.

"I sure do. Thank you."

"Hi, Alex, how are you doing?" I inquired.

"Okay. Daddy got me a new puppy and some new clothes," he sounded excited.

"I'm glad to hear that. A puppy will be fun."

"Here's Jennifer, bye," he was in a hurry. I understood.

Very cheerfully I said, "Hello, Jennifer, Happy Birthday, Honey!"

"Hi, Mommy, I got a new kitty and some new clothes."

"That's good, I sure hope you have a nice birthday."

"Yeah, I've gotta go, bye." With that she hung up.

The sound of their upbeat voices made me a little less anxious. But Donnie was using bribery and manipulation by purchasing a puppy and kitten. My intuition alarm was cranked wide open as those were not short-term gifts you give children. He knew it and I knew it. I had to keep telling myself, "Don't go there. Stay busy. Get through the two weeks. Take one day at a time." Those words became my daily mantra.

As with the previous visit in '80 I found it best to keep extremely busy. Work was my escape, I spent long days at the office. I would even take work home, so I did not have time to think. Tom and I would talk each evening on the phone, sharing our days activities. I would work to the point of exhaustion before going to bed. My desire was to collapse into bed and fall right to sleep.

Since we were going to celebrate Jennifer's birthday upon her return, I spent the first weekend shopping for presents. It was a daunting task. Everything I saw reminded me of her sweet little face, I would breakdown and have to leave the store. I had to get hold of myself. Jennifer really would not care what she received as long as she had presents to open. Next, I needed to shop for Easter baskets. I felt it was important for the children to have an Easter basket at home when they arrived Easter night. The Easter bunny could not forget them at their real home.

Wrapping presents became even harder. I knew something was wrong, I could not find peace. Call it mother's intuition or God's small voice. I just knew. And we had a week to go.

Since we were following the Texas visitation schedule, I should have the same phone privileges as Donnie, which was weekly, so I called them on the 5th. Donnie allowed me to talk with both kids. Alex already sounded very distant and depressed, and Jennifer only spoke a few words. This call did not even last a minute. All I could do was tell them I loved them, and I would see them next week. Alex asked me to call again. Kind of a peculiar question when they are to come home in a week. Again, my intuition alarm was ringing. "Don't go there. Stay busy. Get through this last week. Take one day at a time."

Sam called to inquire how the transition of the children had gone. I explained everything was fine, so far, and I had been permitted to speak with the kids. Sam could not understand how Donnie's attorney went into court so quickly. It was obvious to me; they did not want the truth told. By rights, if I had not mentioned Alex's spring break coinciding with Easter weekend, the visit would have only been for three days. In the long run, it would not have mattered. Donnie just wanted his hands on the kids, even if for only a day. His threat rang loud in my ears every day. Sam asked to be brought up to date on what had transpired the past eighteen months. I told him I would be happy to oblige. It was not a quick task because of all the orders that had gone back and forth. Once I completed getting all of copies, I organized them in date sequence and placed the packet in the mail.

Mid-week, just before Easter, I received the Texas court order along with the Recorder's Transcript of the proceedings. Interestingly, it came from Carl. Donnie's attorney had filed an ex parte order (an order considered urgent where you can petition the court without notifying and serving the other party) to get before the judge quickly. Donnie did not want me represented because of the lies he was spinning. Of course, there was no mention regarding the initial visit in 1980. Donnie and his attorney claimed that when I moved to Nebraska I immediately started proceedings to keep Donnie from seeing the children. Donnie's attorney affirmed Donnie had not seen his children since 1979, the day we moved from Texas. In addition, his attorney asserted I was facing a jail sentence in Nebraska for refusing visitation. What a tale! The judge was concerned they had come in ex parte when I had an attorney of record in Texas. Donnie's attorney stated he'd talked with Sam over a year ago, where Sam indicated he was no longer the attorney of record on the case. The judge directed a transcript of the hearing be made, and Donnie's attorney was to send a copy to my attorney.

Donnie's attorney was as deceptive as Donnie. From his perspective my attorney was in Nebraska, so the copy of the transcript and the order was sent to Carl and the Legal Aid attorney that represented Donnie in Nebraska. He never sent the transcript to Sam, nor did he intend to, thus eating up more time.

The Saturday before Easter, April 10, I tried calling Donnie. One of the girls answered, but, of course, my kids were with her parents. They were going to be gone all day. "Okay, I'll try back this evening." I tried to remain calm. It was not this poor girl's fault. When I tried reaching them in the evening, the phone would ring once and then there was a click on the line, like someone picked up the receiver and put it back down. This happened a couple times. It was obvious, they were not going to answer.

Easter Sunday finally arrived, April 11, the day of reckoning. Success or failure would be revealed soon. My gut was in a knot the moment I stepped out of bed. Tom wanted me to call Donnie in the morning, but I could not do it. Since it was Easter, we tried to make the day as normal as possible. The kids were not to arrive until 7 p.m., so we went to church, visited Tom's folks, and my folks before heading to Omaha. First, we stopped at the house where we got the Easter baskets ready, Jennifer's birthday presents accessible, balloons were tied to the chair, and the cake placed on the table. We were ready to celebrate!

Finally, it was time to head for the airport. We were at the gate in plenty of time. The longer we waited, the more nervous I became. Finally, they announced the arrival of flight 742 from San Antonio. My anticipation was mounting as the plane taxied to the jetway. I could not wait to see those smiling faces again! My hands were shaking, my heart pounding, my knees were weak as we watched the travelers disembark from the plane. Finally, the flight attendant emerged from the jetway. I went right up to her.

"Is everyone off?"

"Yes, I was the last person to leave the plane," she replied.

Collapsing into Tom's arms, amid deep sobs, all I could say was, "Please, tell me it isn't so! Please, tell me it isn't so!"

The flight attendant became overly concerned.

"Are you okay?"

"No," I blubbered. "My children were supposed to be on this flight."

"I'm so sorry," she said, "I'm so very sorry."

I was unable to move away from the door. Everyone was staring at me, but I did not care. Tom guided me away to a chair. I could not believe it had happened again, but deep down I knew there was a strong possibility for I had been feeling it every day since the children left. Guess I just did not want to accept it. Then reality slaps you in the face.

It took quite some time for me to pull myself together to get back on my feet. Tom held me up as we walked down the concourse, me still crying. Here I had given it everything I had, petitioning Nebraska to protect the children so this would not happen again, eighteen months of legal entanglements, and this was the net result of that endeavor. Once Nebraska's decision was rendered it took Donnie less than two months to complete the transition of the children.

Once we got downstairs Tom went over to the ticket counter. The ticket agent could see our distress. I was still unable to speak, so Tom explained the situation and asked if there was anyway the reservation could be looked up. He wanted to know when the flight was cancelled. "Sir, those tickets were cancelled about 1:30 this afternoon. I'm so sorry." He thanked her and we made our way to the car.

Walking into the house was dreadful. It was a good thing Tom was with me or I would have thrown everything against the wall. I busied myself putting everything away.

"Can't that wait until morning?" Tom asked.

Spinning around I glared right at him.

"No, it can't!" I snapped.

I had to get everything out of sight. The Easter baskets and cake were thrown in the trash, Jennifer's birthday gifts went to her bedroom, and the balloons were popped. All Tom could do was sit and let me calm down. I wanted to be by myself, so I finally asked him to go back to Lincoln. He did not want to go, but I insisted. I needed my own space and time.

After he left, I was in shock. I felt like I was going to be sick to my stomach, my mind was foggy, my chest was tight, I was shaking all over. I heard a voice inside me ask, "Are you going to fight or roll over and die?" I had fought every way I knew but I was not ready to just let him have those children. I finally sat down and stared off into space. "Lord, what have I done to deserve this? Am I that bad of a person? Am I a terrible mother? These kids are innocent. They do not deserve this. Show me what you want me to do, for right now I can't think."

I knew my folks were expecting a call from me saying the children were home safe and sound. I picked up the phone but dreaded making the call.

"Hi Mom, how are you tonight?" I asked.

"Hello, Mary. How are the kids?"

"They didn't come home."

I could hardly get the words out before we both broke into tears.

"I'm so sorry. What are you going to do?"

"I'll call my attorney in the morning. Right now, there isn't much we can do."

I had to get off the phone for, at this point, I had no answers for anyone.

I eventually tried going to bed but I hardly slept. It was difficult dragging myself out of bed in the morning but getting presentable for work was worse. If I was dressed that was all I cared about. My eyes resembled puffy marshmallows from a night of crying, the dark circles under my eyes looked like deep purple bruises. Since this was a relatively new job, my peers had no idea what I had experienced during the initial visit. I walked to my desk in a trance. People stared but did not say a word.

At the first available opportunity I called Sam. His secretary answered.

"Hello, may I help you?" she was so pleasant.

"This is Mary. I need to speak to Sam immediately."

I was not in the mood for chit chat. Sam took the phone call.

"Mary, what can I do for you?" Sam asked.

"They didn't come home, Sam. He's got the kids and didn't bring them home," I blurted out.

"Let me call Donnie and see if he will explain. I will get back to you as soon as I talk to him. Try to calm down as much as you can," he advised.

Calm down! He had no idea what the last fifteen hours had been like. Fortunately, he did call later in the day.

"I talked with Donnie and he said he'd been into court April 9, with the same judge, and she granted him temporary custody. Again, they went with an ex parte order saying there was not time to notify us as he was supposed to return them in two days. This is what he is saying. I'm going to get right on it to see for myself what's going on."

"That's all I can ask. Thank you. Let me know as soon as you confirm this," I said as tears overflowed from my eyes. I could not stop crying for the grief permeating my body. Unable to control my emotions, I had to leave work.

On my way home I stopped at the elementary school. As soon as the secretary asked if she could help me, I burst into tears. She could see my distress.

"Maybe you should talk with the principal."

It was only a couple minutes before I was ushered into the office.

"I just wanted to tell you I don't know if Alex will be returning to school," I said with tears streaming down my face.

She wanted a few more details, so I told her everything I knew up to that point. She was exceedingly kind and sympathetic.

"Let's just wait and see what happens in the next couple of weeks. From our perspective, everything should be fine. We will deal with his makeup work when he returns. Right now, you try to take care of yourself. Just let us know either way and we'll do what is required at that time."

"Thank you so kindly. I'll be in touch," I answered.

After leaving the school my next stop was the babysitter. This was another conversation I dreaded. As soon as she opened the door and I saw all the little smiling faces I lost it. Attempting to contain myself, I rummaged in my purse for my checkbook.

"The kids were not returned yesterday from their visit. At this point I do not know when the children will return, but I am going to pay you for a couple weeks of sitting. That should help until you can find someone else to take the kids places."

"You don't have to do that."

"Yes, I do. I don't feel right not paying you."

With that I wrote a check for two full weeks of babysitting. Before I left, we were both crying.

"When they come back, give me a call and I'll take them back. They are delightful children. I loved taking care of them," she said.

"That is exceedingly kind of you. Thank you."

Within a couple days, I settled down enough to start burying myself into my work again. That was my only coping skill. I had to or I was going to drive myself crazy. My nights were a mess even though I had Tom to talk with. There was a void in my heart the size of the Grand Canyon. Only my children were going to fill it.

After waiting the entire week for a call from Sam, I finally called his office. He was not in, but the secretary told me what had transpired.

"Sam went to see the judge, but she refused to see him. He has to file a formal motion prior to being allowed into the judge's chambers," she explained.

"Okay, I guess there is nothing we can do until he sees her."

I knew it was a waiting game.

A week had passed before I felt strong enough to attempt to talk to my kids without crying. I knew if I started crying it would only upset them more. I tried on three different occasions throughout the day, no one answered. My heart was feeling the abandonment my children must be feeling. Not knowing if Alex was in school or who was caring for Jennifer was tearing me up.

Because I had become a laughingstock of the judicial system and absolutely no one wanted to help me, I decided to compose a letter that was sent to state and national legislators.

I Plea For Your Help,

I am writing this in hopes you can understand the injustice of a profoundly serious situation ...

I detailed the ages of the children along the history of the case: from the initial visit in 1980, through the court battles, the contempt of court charges, this final visit over spring break and Easter where the children were not returned, and my ex informing my attorney he had been granted temporary custody.

... I trust you can feel just a fraction of the despair, frustration, heartache, and anguish I have been going through. I love my children so very much. I have been trying to raise them in a good Christian home where they know they are loved. I have only been trying to protect them, as any mother would. I feel as though good mothers and innocent children have no rights. The Nebraska courts let me down and the Texas courts are not even following the laws of justice. And, because of this, they have taken my children from me. My ex-husband had threatened to kidnap the children, but I never dreamt he would kidnap the children through the Texas courts.

I am writing this letter to you to point out the atrocity of the court system today when dealing with innocent children's lives, who are continually being torn apart. I feel sorry for so many children today when the courts do not seem to care if children of divorced couples have a stable secure background from which to build their adult lives.
Thank you for your time,

Within the letter I supplied both the Texas and Nebraska case numbers as well as the contact information for both my Texas and Nebraska attorneys. Tom and his father were well connected within the Nebraska political system. Tom sent this letter to each of the Nebraska senators and representatives in Washington DC as well as several state level officials, especially those in the Lincoln congressional district. Basically, enough was enough. Nebraska had adapted the Uniform Child Custody Jurisdiction Act but was afraid to act on it. What a pity that everyone defaults to the same old ways until someone with deep pockets can appeal the case to the Nebraska Supreme Court, letting the higher court decide the first case. In the meantime, children are pawns in this game of life. I had been made out to be the bad parent when I was only trying to protect my innocent children. Now, they had become another "child snatching" statistic.

Sam finally called.

"I've spoken to the judge and there was never an order written April 9 granting Donnie temporary custody. I guess that doesn't surprise you."

I almost laughed for Donnie's charades were unbelievable.

"No, not in the least," I said. "But where do we go from here? How long do we have to wait? This seems so unreasonable. I have legal custody of the children. Why can't they be returned?" I was getting a little testy, but I was extremely short of patience these days.

"It's not that simple. I will draw up a Contempt of Court order and present it before the judge. Right now, that's all we have."

"Okay, I have to rely on your expertise. Please, Sam, try to make this happen soon," I pleaded.

Before he hung up Sam had a suggestion for me.

"As a precautionary measure, I suggest you start thinking of individuals you can rely on to write letters of recommendation on your behalf regarding your work and parenting capabilities."

"Okay, and how would these be used?" I asked.

"In case he files for a change of custody," Sam said.

"Are you kidding me? Should I be concerned?" I asked.

"Right now, I'm not sure what to think. What he has done so far, doesn't make sense."

"Well, during the initial visit in '80 he was trying to find an attorney that would start proceedings to take the kids from me."

"Then we can't be too careful. See what you can do about the letters. I also want to reiterate for you, the wheels of justice move slowly."

"Thanks, Sam. After the Nebraska fiasco I'm quite aware of that."

After I hung up, I felt devastated. I knew I was a good mother, providing for the children despite not receiving support. They were loved, clean, well fed, and happy. What more could I do? Here I was trying to do things the right way through the system and Donnie was lying and doing whatever he needed to get his own way.

Even though I was feeling strong enough to talk with the children, I never got through. I tried different days and different times, but no one would pick up the phone. Donnie harassed us every day and I succumbed to those calls because I was afraid of incurring his wrath. Donnie was not allowing me to speak with the children because he was in control and he knew there was nothing I could do about it. At this point, life seemed so unfair.

April 24, four weeks after my children left, Tom and I had been working at his house all day when I decided to try calling the kids. The last time I spoke with them was three weeks ago. Donnie answered.

"May I talk with Alex?" I asked.

"Sure!"

My hands were shaking with apprehension.

"Hi, Buddy! How are you?"

"Good," Alex said, short and sweet.

"What are you doing?"

"I'm watching tv with the other kids." He sounded detached. "I get to say all kinds of naughty words!"

"Really? Are you going to school?"

"No, I'm going to wait until I get to first grade."

After attempting to talk a bit longer I could tell he was distracted.

"Is Jennifer there?" I asked.

"She's already in bed. She has been crabby all day. She cries a lot."

By this time, I was crying and knew I had to get off the phone before I totally broke down.

"I miss you, Alex, and I love you. Please give Jennifer a big love for me."

"Okay!" Click! Click!

After putting the phone down, I fell apart. Was I better off not talking to them or finding out little things as to what they were doing and how they were being treated? I could not answer that. Right now, I felt terrible.

Work was going well since that was my escape. In fact, I was getting good at it. I would stay at the office after hours and get an immense amount of work completed. Going home, to an empty house, was not something I looked forward to. The weekends were spent completing wedding plans and working at Tom's house. We had plenty of projects and Tom had a lot of sorting to do as he was attempting to make room for us.

I had asked my business associates, friends, and family to write letters of recommendation for me. Even though I asked them to be sent to my attorney, a couple of them gave me copies of the letters. The letter written by my immediate boss brought tears to my eyes.

After talking with Mary, I felt compelled to write hoping I could give you some additional insight to Mary's personal and business life that you may or may not know. If there is nothing new to be gained from this letter, hopefully I can help strengthen your belief in her abilities and her true concern about her children's well-being.

The latest turn of events has left Mary bewildered, confused, and feeling a deep sense of loss. All of us who know Mary, feel the same loss and bewilderment because she is a woman whose every decision is based on what is right for her children.

Mary currently works for me as a Senior Computer Specialist, responsible for the design and implementation of automated business systems. We have, just recently, completed a major system that has been under Mary's direct leadership. The importance of this system, to our company, and the deadline we were under, put a great deal of pressure on all of us. Mary felt this pressure more than any of us. She did a wonderful job for us without neglecting her responsibility as a mother.

When I hired Mary, the only concerns she had in taking the job were directly relating to her children: days off to care for them when ill, must leave the office by 5:00 p.m. to pick up children, no weekend work, special conferences at school, etc. I felt some concern at that time, about her ability to handle a professional career with the challenges we were offering, if she needed this much time off to care for her family.

Our concerns have all been dispelled. She has won the respect of all levels of Management and her professional colleagues, here at the office, and most important she has kept her family together and attended to their every need: physically, educationally, and spiritually.

My family and myself have had several occasions, in the past nine months, to see Mary as the mother. Her children respond very well to her, they know they are loved, they seem to be incredibly happy, well-contented children.

Her current custody problems have caused my family and myself a great deal of concern. Concern about the welfare of two lovely children and concern about Mary's ability to handle the additional, unbearable pressures. To date she has not disappointed us in the least, in her personal or professional life. She is a woman that should be commended not condemned for her tireless effort of playing both roles so successfully.

Hopefully, I have been able to add something positive to your perspective of a good, decent woman who, so desperately needs your every effort and consideration. Our hopes and prayers are with you that justice will prevail in this case and Mary will be reunited, forever, with the only thing that really means anything to her, her children.

If there is anything I can do as her employer and/or her friend, to help in this effort, please do not hesitate to let me know.

Many other friends and family members said they sent letters to my attorney but did not share them with me. "Please, God, I pray I never have to use these letters for a custody determination, but I thank you for these special people in my life to offer up support for us."

Every day I went through the motions of life: get up, bury myself in my job, get home late, fall into bed. There was not much joy to be found. No matter how much I talked with God, I could not understand why this was happening. No human being could reason themselves through this turmoil. My life was in a dense fog where I seemed to be feeling my way along on my hands and knees. The weekends were not much better. Yes, I spent the time with Tom in Lincoln, but I buried myself in remodeling projects. It was a wonderful way to occupy the mind as there remained not one idle second to think. Thinking was extremely dangerous and plummeted me to unhealthy depths of despair.

With all the difficulty I was experiencing, I could only imagine what the children were thinking. I was sure Alex thought I had lied to him since I promised he would only be gone two weeks. Donnie, no doubt, told him again that I had left him and I was not coming back. The betrayal that little boy had to feel broke my heart. Jennifer was old enough now to feel confusion and abandonment. After all, she was now the age of Alex when I sent them on that initial visit. Alex's mental state when they were returned was still etched deep in my soul. Those icy stares continued to pierce my heart.

Sunday, May 2, another week had passed. I tried making my weekly call to Texas. This time I was permitted to speak with the children. Both sounded **very** distant. Alex was excited about new bunkbeds for he and Carlos and new pajamas.

"What do you do all day, Alex, since you're not going to school?"

"We sell fruits and nuts with my Daddy and Mommy."

"That sounds like fun," I answered.

"It's okay but Jennifer cries hard," he added.

"You're the big brother, Alex, so you be sure to give her a hug when she starts crying. Okay?"

Silence. I hoped he was shaking his head yes.

"Can I talk to Jennifer?"

"Sure," he said and passed the phone away before I could tell him I loved him.

"Hello, Jennifer. How are you?"

"Good."

"Are you having fun?"

"No," she responded weakly with a quivering voice. I could tell she was crying.

I was unable to ask her more questions as I started crying. I had to get off the phone.

"I love you, Honey" I replied with a trembling lip and tears running down my cheeks.

185

Silence! Click. Click. She hung up. These phone calls were excruciating, but I had to keep trying.

I had not checked on Arlene for a while, so I called. She said she had tried to talk with the kids a few days earlier but all they'd say is "I don't know," so she didn't talk long. Arlene shared that she had just received a letter from Donnie saying unless she could treat the entire family, all nine, equally including phone calls, birthdays, and holidays she would never have any visiting privileges. Donnie was not joking. He would cut his mother away from his life in a heartbeat, without so much as a guilty conscious.

Arlene continued to share with me that Donnie's only uncle, from Washington, had been in Austin visiting. While there, Ken called Donnie to try reasoning with him regarding the children. Donnie told Ken that he had been laid off from his latest job just the week before. When Ken started to talk to Donnie about the kids, Donnie got angry with him and told him it was none of his business. Ken had intended to visit Donnie's home but could see he had upset Donnie when trying to persuade him to return the children. Donnie told him, "The kids are where they belong!" The conversation was over. No one seemed able to reason with Donnie.

My 'plea for help' letter had made it to the State of Nebraska Department of Justice Assistant Attorney General. His response was classic.

... It would certainly appear that you have spent more than your share of time with lawyers and courts regarding your children. Your frustration is easily understood...My advice would be to continue to pursue your children through the Uniform Child Custody Jurisdiction Act of the Nebraska Code. If you think your attorney has been ineffective, possibly you could seek other counsel.

You really must be kidding me. Are they all drinking the same Kool-Aid? He must not realize no one wants to rule on the UCCJA. The whole system is broken! All they do is shuffle paper. It was going to take years before Nebraska would be ready to step into progressive thinking. How many more children's lives would be in a state of upheaval all because of fear of venturing into a new law. A young, eager attorney might tackle it, but an older, experienced lawyer is too comfortable to have to work that hard. My cynicism regarding the legal profession was still a very raw, festering open sore that would not heal.

Alex's birthday was coming up. JUST in case they would come home Tom and I went shopping for gifts. I had to remain optimistic or I would go crazy. After wrapping his presents, I put them on his bed, as I had Jennifer's a couple months earlier.

Saturday Alex turned six years old. I could not help but think of him all day. What was he up to? Was he having fun? Did he want to come home? My children had now been gone seven weeks and communication with them had been extremely limited. It was heart wrenching. I attempted to call at different times throughout the day but was unsuccessful. Finally, on my last attempt, Patricia answered. It was close to 8 p.m.

"May I talk to Alex, please?"

"No," she replied very snippy, "the kids are all in bed."

"This early?" I questioned. "What time do they normally go to bed?"
I wanted to know for future calls.

"What's it to you?" She was very sarcastic and hung up abruptly.

This was not good. This lady was just as insensitive and cruel as Donnie.

Since I was not successful calling on his birthday, I phoned earlier the following evening. Donnie allowed me to talk.

Trying to sound super excited I said, "Hi Buddy, Happy Birthday!"

"Where are you?" He sounded very depressed.

"I'm home, I've just been working around here. I wanted to see if you had a happy birthday."

"Do you still have my toys?" He sounded very unsure.

"I sure do. They are here waiting for you."

"Why didn't you send me a birthday present?"

"Alex, I have your presents here. I'm saving them for you when you get back."

Silence. I could tell he was confused. Had he been told Mommy did not love him anymore, she did not even send him a birthday present? My eyes had filled with tears and started rolling down my cheeks, I had to get off the phone.

"I'm glad you had a good birthday. Mommy will call you again next week. I love you."

No response, just two clicks from the phone.

Now my thoughts were swirling. Maybe I should have sent a present and a card to him to let him know I cared, but how was I to know if Donnie would even give it to him. I was damned no matter how I worked my way through it. Guilt swept through me. I had no answer, just a feeling of helplessness.

Tom and I were trying to get ready for the wedding. It was not easy, at least, not for me. This was supposed to be a happy occasion, but my thoughts were on the children and all the legal entanglements. I was going through the motions, but my heart was elsewhere.

Tom's mom was taking care of the rehearsal dinner and my mom was helping with the reception plans. Tom and I met with the pastor several times. His concern was whether we should (or could) proceed with the wedding plans under the current circumstances. So far, we were proceeding. I remained hopeful; I knew God could perform a miracle. At the rate progress was being made, it was going to take a miracle.

Since it was getting close to the end of the school year, I made an appointment to see the school principal. I dreaded that meeting.

"Good Morning, Mrs. Schumacher, what can I do for you today?" She was so cheerful.

"I'm here to officially inform you Alex is not returning this school year, so I guess I'm here to pick up his things from the classroom."

This was the first I had uttered those words. It sounded... so final, like I had given up. The words stung my soul and I started crying.

"I'm so sorry," she said empathetically. "I'll go with you and we'll see what the teacher has ready for you."

We walked into the classroom. It broke my heart seeing all the happy children. I kept telling myself, "Don't cry in front of these kids. Don't cry."

"Do you have Alex's things available for Mrs. Schumacher to pick up?" the principal asked the teacher.

"I sure do," she said. "Everything is in his desk. I'm so sorry to hear what you're going through."

"Thank you so much."

That was all I could muster, as tears filled my eyes. I had to get out of the classroom.

As the principal and I walked back down the hall I told her, "I'm moving to Lincoln, so Alex will not be returning in the fall."

"Thank you for letting me know. We were wondering if we should count on him as part of the registry for next year." She walked me to the front door. "I certainly wish you all the best."

"Thank you. I appreciate your patience."

I turned and walked back to the car, crying all the way.

Taking his papers and little things from his desk was gut wrenching. Holding onto his pencils and crayons, pulled at my heart. The teacher had included his last papers. He had drawn a picture of his family, four of us. Not being able to look at them any longer, everything went to his room. Pining for him was not going to get him back.

Then things started getting interesting. More, legal entanglements, only this time from the Texas courts. Sam called to explain the situation.

"I just want you to know that on May 14, Donnie and his attorney went before the judge with a Motion for Change of Custody as well as an Order for a Custody Investigation through the Department of Social Services."

"Please tell me this isn't so, Sam."

"I'm afraid it is. They must have presented a compelling case because the judge signed the Order for Custody Investigation requiring the Social Services report be filed with the court no later than November 2, 1982. The judge set the hearing for Change of Custody for November 18, 1982, following the receipt of the investigative report."

Immediately I prayed, "Lord, can it get much worse? Now I must prepare for an investigation from Social Services. Mentally I am a mess. What if they prove me unfit? What if I fail the test? I feel so helpless!"

"I can't believe this, Sam. This isn't my fault."

"You should get through this with no problem." Sam tried to calm me down as much as possible.

I was **extremely** shook up! Could anyone blame me? I am facing the possibility of an investigation from Social Services to determine if I am "fit" to raise my own children?

"If I'm being investigated can we get a private investigator to look into his situation? I have not done anything wrong. I don't understand why the judge keeps signing these orders despite what Donnie has been doing," I exclaimed.

"I'm sure the judge doesn't realize what he's done. Do not worry, we will get our chance. I am sure the investigation will not start until September, so we have plenty of time. I have filed a couple of orders, so let's see how these play out first. I will send you a copy of these orders. If you have any questions once you receive them, just give me a call."

"Thank you, Sam."

"Wait and see?" It seemed like that was all we had been doing up to this point. I realize the wheels of justice grind slow, but it is because they are so bogged down with motions, counter motions, orders, briefs, counter briefs, rulings, and paper, reams, and reams of paper!

But why had Sam been so slow filing the Contempt of Court charge against Donnie for failure to return the children after Easter. Sam told me the end of April he was going to get the contempt papers started. I tried to justify his delay. Did he forget or was he tied up with other cases? At this point it did not matter, for Donnie and his attorney have jumped ahead of us and painted a bleak picture. Once again, it seemed like the odds just kept stacking up against me.

Sam was terribly upset with Donnie and his attorney on a couple of levels. On several occasions Donnie's attorney had not used the formal channels for filing papers. Orders and hearing notifications were never forwarded to Sam. The copies were sent to Donnie's Nebraska attorney, thereby keeping Sam and Carl out of the loop. Also, waiting until the 11th hour and going before a judge with an ex parte order should only be used in extreme cases. Sam never considered this an extreme situation. In his estimation, no one was being physically harmed. The laws were written such that children belonged to both parents and a parent could do anything they wanted with their children. Therefore, in his estimation, this was not an emergency.

Once I received a copy of Sam's orders everything made sense. After Donnie's attorney had been into court to get the custody investigation approved and the change of custody hearing set, Sam had immediately followed up with the Contempt of Court order against Donnie. A service provider had to personally serve Donnie regarding this charge. According to Sam, it took quite a while to get service on Donnie because the service processor could not locate him or someone at the house always provided an excuse for him not being there. The processor filed a formal complaint with the Devine Sheriff's Office regarding concealment and avoidance. But, along with everything else Donnie did, no one pursued the issue.

In addition to the contempt order, Sam filed an order for The Writ Of Habeas Corpus Complaint. The judge set May 28, 1982, for that complaint to be heard. At the same time, he scheduled a Change of Visitation hearing for July 9, 1982. Of course, all of Sam's motions were filed after Donnie's attorney already did his damage, but Sam intended for everything to be heard prior to the custody investigation by Social Services.

Along with the other orders, Sam had an Order for Judgement drafted to present before the judge as soon as I could send an updated Affidavit showing how much money Donnie was in arrears. It did not take long to complete this task and get the Affidavit off to Sam. Donnie was now $7,000 in arrears. Sam needed this judgement filed with the court so the judge would see it in the file if Donnie and his attorney tried filing additional charges. This was a game I did not enjoy playing, and the future of my children hung in the balance of this game.

Tom and I decided we were going to fly to Texas for the Writ of Habeas Corpus Complaint hearing. Sam said I did not need to attend but Tom and I decided the Texas courts needed to personally see me at these hearings, making it evident I was a concerned parent. If Sam needed me, I would be available for testimony. Nothing could be brushed off as unimportant any longer.

May 27, the children have been gone almost nine weeks. It seemed like an eternity. Tom and I were flying out early in the morning to attend the afternoon hearing. Giving it a long shot, I called to see if I could speak with the children. Donnie answered. For some reason I asked to talk with Jennifer first. He obliged.

"Hi Sweetheart! How are you doing?" I tried to sound very chipper.

"We are moving…" I heard a terrible bang as someone slammed the receiver against the phone. The call ended abruptly.

My heart was in my throat, my stomach turned in a knot, my hands and knees started shaking, I knew something was terribly wrong. I did not realize it at the time, but this was the last I would hear that sweet little girl's voice.

9. The Journey

~ The act of traveling from one place to another ~

Friday, May 28, Tom and I were up early to catch the first flight to San Antonio. We had planned to spend two nights, returning to Lincoln Sunday, May 30. My aunt and uncle lived in San Antonio, so we asked if we could stay with them through the weekend.

Once the plane landed, we got our rental car and headed for the Bexar County Courthouse in San Antonio. We arrived in plenty of time and found ourselves waiting for Sam. Sitting in that courthouse made me feel extremely uncomfortable. The last courtroom experience was a total disaster, I was not looking forward to this one except, this time, Sam would be doing all the talking. When he arrived, we went to a side room where we could talk. I brought him up to date regarding the phone call from the night before.

"The first and only thing Jennifer got out of her mouth was 'We are moving' before someone ended the call. I don't even know the address of the home they currently live in. You don't think…?" I did not want to say it.

"Let's get in to see the judge and explain the truth about what's been going on. She is a reasonable judge. She's going to take this very seriously since Donnie and his attorney have obviously led her down the wrong path."

Sam remained extremely calm. At this point, I needed that reassurance.

Time for the hearing. Basically, the intent of the hearing was to present the facts to the judge that the children, she ordered to spend an extended Easter vacation with their father, were never returned. Sam had no problem convincing the judge the children were now prisoners of their father and were being detained against their will. Although children did not have rights, they were still being held outside of the vacation times ordered by the court, basically from her decision. She wanted to hear from me, so she put me under oath, and she led the questions. Flashbacks raced through my head reminding me of the last time I was on the witness stand. My anxiety level jumped through the roof, I started shaking and my heart was pounding against my chest.

"Mrs. Schumacher, would you please tell me how you and Mr. Schumacher arrived at the dates for visitation starting March 27?"

"I was trying to be conciliatory after losing my court battle in Nebraska. I knew I would have to follow the visitation rules set forth by the Texas Courts. Visitation was to commence Easter 1982. I called Donnie and offered the visit to be during Alex's spring break, March 27 through April 4, since it would allow Donnie a longer time with the children rather than just the long Easter weekend."

"Did you tell Mr. Schumacher he could also have the children the following week leading up to Easter."

"No, that was when he appeared before you to get the time extended."

"What were the dates you agreed upon?"

"Let me put it this way, I really did not agree, but after he went to court, he informed me the arrangement was from March 27 through April 11. The children were to return Easter night."

"And did he return the children?"

"No, Your Honor, we went to the airport, but they were not on the flight."

"Did Mr. Schumacher inform you they were not coming in on that flight?"

"No, Your Honor, but we asked the ticket agent, who informed us the reservations had been cancelled that afternoon."

"Did Mr. Schumacher ever call to explain why he cancelled the tickets?"

"No, communication has been very limited."

"Have you been able to speak with your children?"

"As I said, communication has been extremely limited. I have spoken to them but only for a short period of time. They are only three and five, they really don't like talking on the phone."

"Have you denied visitation from Mr. Schumacher since 1979?"

"No, Your Honor, Donnie and I agreed on a two-week visit in June 1980. When he made the plane reservations, he had extended the visit to nineteen days, without asking. At the end of the nineteen days the children were not returned. With Sam's help, Donnie finally returned them after thirty-one days had elapsed. I started proceedings in Nebraska to see if we could get jurisdiction changed to Nebraska under the UCCJA. This was a long dragged out ordeal that lasted eighteen months. During this time, the judge ruled that visitation would not be outside of my home county until the issue could be resolved. During this time, Donnie was offered, on several different occasions, to come to Nebraska for a visit. In September 1981 Donnie was in Nebraska for one of the hearings and visited with the children on Saturday and Sunday. My pastor attempted, on several occasions, to set up a visitation during the summer of 1981, but Donnie always refused."

"Okay, thank you, Mrs. Schumacher. I am so sorry this has happened to you and your children. You are dismissed."

"Thank you, Your Honor."

Sam took over and explained we had been doing everything imaginable to convince Donnie he should comply and just return the children, but to no avail. He then summed up the facts regarding the first visit and now this last visit, highlighting the legal steps he had gone through. He also outlined the steps Donnie's attorney had gone through, undermining the legal system. She was NOT happy. She knew she had been duped.

The judge had no problem issuing the Writ Of Habeas Corpus immediately, for Sam had supplied "good cause"; substantial reasons to take a certain action. It was noticeably clear, "… Said children are being unlawfully and forcibly detained by the Defendant, Donnie Schumacher…" She ordered, "the Defendant to produce the minor children before this Court on the 1st day of June at 8:00 a.m. at the courthouse to show cause, if he has any, as to why he should so hold said minor children in restraint of their liberty. It is further ordered that the Sheriff shall return said minor children to the custody of the Plaintiff, Mary Schumacher, and use whatever force is necessary."

My heart was skipping! Could this be it? Could we be at the end of this roller coaster ride? I prayed, "Please, Lord, let it be so."

The judge came down from the bench and we all sat casually around a table until the Writ was typed to her satisfaction, signed, and sealed. She looked straight at me.

"I'm so terribly sorry, Mrs. Schumacher. I trust the Writ will be effective."

She was sincerely apologetic. I started tearing up and was unable to say a word. She knew. She looked directly at Tom and I and gave us explicit instructions.

"I'll be calling the Hondo Sheriff's Office to let them know you are on your way with the Writ. Take the Writ to them and then follow the county Sheriff to Devine to pick up the children. It should be that simple. Mr. Schumacher will hand the children over to the Sheriff and the Sheriff will give them to you. Sam, keep me informed. Otherwise, we will see you in court on Tuesday."

I interrupted. "But we don't know the specific house where Donnie lives. I sent the children only knowing a PO box number."

"Don't worry," she said calmly, "the city of Devine is not that large. By the time you get there the sheriff will have the house identified."

"Okay, thank you so much," I said.

As we were walking out the courthouse, Sam wished us luck.

"Let's hope this is the end of it!" he said as he walked away.

Tom and I both agreed with him.

We got into our car. Tom unfolded the map to determine how to get to Hondo. He then grabbed my hand and asked, "Are you ready to pick up the children?"

"I sure am!"

As we drove, I kept looking at the Writ. We finally had the legal piece of paper to make Donnie turn the children over to me. I was almost giddy with excitement. I looked over at Tom and he, too, had a smile on his face.

It took us about 45 minutes to get to the Sheriff's Office in Hondo. Just as she said, an officer was waiting for us. We got out of the car and introduced ourselves. Tom handed the Sheriff the Writ, we got back into our cars, and followed him into Devine, another 30 minutes. When we pulled up to the house a county officer was already parked in front, waiting for us. The Sheriff whom we were following, walked over to our car.

"You wait here. We'll go into the house and get the children."

"Okay."

We were just going to watch and wait. I was so nervous my teeth were chattering. Tom reached over and grabbed my hand to relax me.

They were gone too long. Something was not right. My heart was racing as the Sheriff finally approached the car. He asked that we step outside the car.

"My partner talked with the neighbors prior to us getting here and the neighbors said these people had been moving all day. My partner also said there was a car here just 30 minutes before we arrived. I am sorry, but we have no one at this address to serve the Writ. The house has been vacated. I will call the judge and let her know the situation. Again, I'm sorry."

I fell into Tom's arms, sobbing uncontrollably. Were we really 30 minutes late? I wanted to die I was in so much emotional pain. "Lord, I don't believe this! How can this happen? Here we stand... ready to hold those little babies in my arms and we were 30 minutes late? I need You - NOW!"

My head started pounding! Did Donnie know about the hearing for the request of the Writ? Did he know they had to be gone by the middle of the afternoon? Did he know we were coming? Did we pass them on our way to Devine? I could not think. Getting the Writ signed was the first sign of hope I had in a long time, and now there was no hope, for now there was not even a PO box number.

We could not continue sitting in front of the house. The County Sheriff would not leave until we pulled away. Both of us were in a fog, so we just drove around. Devine was a small town. It could not be more than 4,000 people. Everyone in town had to know the family with seven kids! And I am sure they did.

The first order of business was to make several phone calls. We found a convenience store, for we needed to find a payphone.

In as much as I was still crying, Tom called Sam to explain the situation. Sam was furious.

"Jesus Christ, I don't believe this!"

"No, we can't either," Tom said.

"I guess I'll see you and Mary in court on Tuesday." Sam responded. "You will be there, won't you?"

"Oh, yes," Tom guaranteed him. "We will be there."

Since I was still attempting to get hold of myself, Tom phoned his mother next. There was simply no easy way to tell anyone the outcome of the day. It could not be sugar coated. The day just stunk! Tom's mother felt horrible, but beyond that, there were no words to make anyone feel better.

Thinking I was strong enough to call my mother, I tried. As soon as I heard her voice, I knew I was in trouble, I burst into tears.

"Mary are you okay?" she asked.

"No, Mom, we got the Writ signed by the judge today but by the time we drove to Donnie's house, they were gone! Moved! Vanished!"

"Who was gone?" she asked.

"Donnie, everyone, gone!"

I know I was not making sense, but it was the best I could do.

"Oh, Mary! I'm so sorry!" she muttered for she too was crying by this time.

"We don't know what we're doing yet but when we figure it out, I'll let you know. We have to go back into court on Tuesday so we're not coming home Sunday."

"Okay. That's all I can ask," she responded.

We both had a difficult time saying goodbye.

Since we were dressed up for court, we needed to change clothes. We dug around in our suitcase, found some casual clothes, and went into the convenience store restroom to change. No doubt, they wondered who the strangers were in town, using the payphone and changing clothes in their restroom. Next, we had not eaten since early morning, so we picked up a sandwich from their display case and went back to the car to eat and attempt to think.

We soon discovered we had no paper to write on. We were not prepared for this. Guess we never dreamt there would be a requirement for list making. I went back into the convenience store for paper towels so we could start writing our list: phone calls (work, my aunt), return car, rent another car, change plane tickets. I was not a lot of help, as my head was still going in circles. All I knew was my kids had vanished and we would not be going home on Sunday. And we were… 30 minutes late!

Sitting in a stupor I only had one direction to turn, to My Heavenly Father, where I prayed silently. "Lord, only You know what has happened and why it occurred. Right now, I am calling on You to help me as I ask you to pull me up and help me move forward. Please help me find a way, for right now I see no way." After waiting a little bit, I felt determined I was not going to let Donnie destroy me again. God was clearing my mind and supplying me with some strength. I had to consciously get a grip on myself and keep praying. "Lord, I can't move without You. You know exactly what I am going through. Give me strength in this time of need. Help me rise above this. In Jesus Name, I pray, Amen."

Once I determined I was not going to die, I could feel a little fight come back within me. It was imperative I get hold of myself, for I would be worthless to everyone if I did not. This was exactly what Donnie was counting on: driving me crazy so he could have it all. I had to remain strong for the children's sake.

Tom and I started thinking, maybe, just maybe, they had not gotten everything out of the house. Was there a possibility they would slip back into town and pick something up from the house?

I made a quick call to my aunt to explain a little regarding the highlights of the day. After explaining we were going to spend the night in Devine, I promised to keep her informed as to our plans. Tom positioned the car on a hill where we could observe the house. We basically sat in the car all night, one of us keeping an eye on the house while the other attempted to get a little sleep in the back seat. Needless to say, no one came back to the house Friday night. They were gone.

Saturday morning, we located a private investigator in the Devine area and set up an appointment to meet with him. Not knowing what direction to take, we hired Syd for a few hours to see what details he could find out. Being local to the area he had connections, certainly better than what we were doing, watching an empty house. Not being able to spend another night in the car, we located a small motel near Devine. We both needed a good night's sleep if that were possible.

Sunday, we made a trip to Austin to see Arlene, Francis, and Cora. They did not realize we had come to San Antonio for a hearing, so they were genuinely surprised to see us.

"What brings you to Texas?" Francis questioned.

From the expression on their faces they had no idea what had transpired. It was not an easy story to share with them. They were shocked, for it sounded so unbelievable: a pending investigation from Social Services, a pending custody hearing, and now a true kidnapping. Arlene and I were both crying. There was only one message I had for them.

"If or when you hear from Donnie will you please try to find out where he is and talk him into returning the children," I begged.

They all agreed they would do anything to help for they knew the conditions the kids were living in and it was not good. All three agreed the children needed to be with me. The difficult question needed to be asked.

"If I need you to testify on my behalf for the custody hearing, would you be willing?"

There was a positive "Yes" from all three. I was not sure I could rely on them because I had asked all of them to testify for me back at the hearing on October 8, 1981. At that time, all three refused, stating they could not do that to Donnie. When called upon, I had my doubts regarding getting much help.

Arlene supplied me with the contact information for Donnie's uncle. I requested that she call him, fill him in on the situation, and ask him to call her if he receives word from Donnie. Arlene was going to call as soon as we left. Being too distraught for small talk, we kept our visit short. Truthfully, all I felt like doing was curling up in a fetal position in a corner and shutting the world out, but I knew that was not an option. Not if I wanted to see my children again.

Since our original plan was to return home Sunday, the rental car contract expired Sunday night. So, our next task was to return the car and rent another. It sounded rather foolish, but there was no capability of calling the rental company and extending the contract. We had to physically return the car to the airport and rent another car. I called my aunt, briefly explained what had transpired, and asked if the invitation was still open for us to stay with them the next couple of days. They gladly welcomed us. Even though my heart was breaking I found the commotion of their teenage household distracting, in a good way.

My boss was expecting me back at work the following morning. I called him at home and made him aware of the situation. After explaining what had occurred, he was more than compassionate.

"Take whatever time you need, Mary. Just keep me informed regarding the days you'll be gone."

"All I know at this point is we go back to court Tuesday. I know the earliest I would be back into the office would be Thursday, but I will let you know. Thank you so much for being so understanding."

"It's not a problem, Mary. Take care."

Monday, we drove back to Hondo to speak with the county sheriff's department. We spoke with the same officers we saw Friday along with an officer from the investigative team.

"Is there any information I can give you that might help you?" I pleaded.

"Ma'am, I don't think you understand. There is not a case here. No charges have been filed. There is nothing we can or will do until there is a criminal charge. Our only involvement here was to serve the Writ."

"You mean kidnapping your children is not criminal?" I tried to ask calmly but did not.

"Ma'am, the children are presumably with their father. Right? That does not constitute kidnapping."

I was so exasperated I wanted to scream. Upon seeing my frustration, Tom thanked the officers, got me out of the headquarters, and tried to calm me down.

"You just can't go in there and get upset like that."

"Tom, did you hear what he said? They are not concerned one bit because the kids are with their father, so no harm, no foul. In their eyes, life is copasetic."

"No, it doesn't mean everything is okay. But what he said was true. Their only job was to serve the Writ."

"Then, why did we come here?" I snapped at him.

"I wanted to get their business cards in case we need to contact them in the future."

Since Tom's father owned a business, Tom was familiar with public information recorded at the courthouse. Since Hondo was the county seat of Medina County, we headed to the courthouse to explore what information we could find. We located Donnie's and Patricia's marriage certificate and discovered her maiden name was Maria McCarthy, born in Dublin, Ireland. One can only guess how she became Patricia. The only thing we could find out about the house was that the house was being held as collateral by a financial institution, which implied Donnie used the house to secure a loan. That did not make sense because they had just purchased the house in July 1980. Scanning through reels of microfiche was painstaking, I lacked the patience to sit there, so we headed back to my aunt's house.

Early Tuesday morning we found ourselves back at the San Antonio courthouse for the Writ of Habeas Corpus hearing. The judge had been made aware of the sheriff's office inability to serve the notice. She also knew Donnie and the family had moved. After waiting the allotted time to see if Donnie or his counsel would appear, it took her no time at all to rule, she found Donnie in Contempt of Court for not producing the children. We waited until the order was typed, signed, and sealed. The judge had been trying to do the right thing but, after all this, she knew the truth. She looked me straight in the eye.

"I am so incredibly sorry. If you get any information as to where your children might be, come back and I'll see if I can help you." She knew, as well as I, that she had been tricked!

"Thank you," I said, as tears puddled from my eyes.

As we were leaving the courthouse Sam wanted me to clearly understand what just happened.

"This is a civil contempt of court charge. It is neither a felony nor a misdemeanor, it is just a bench warrant she has issued for Donnie's arrest because he insulted the court. This is not a criminal charge so the police will not perform an investigation. About the only way

Donnie will get caught is if he has a traffic violation, and if he is out of state, nothing will be done."

"Oh?" I said bewildered. "So, you're saying there's nothing we can do?"

"That is correct, I suggest you go back home and see if anything comes up. I'll be in touch."
With that, he walked away.

Looking at Tom I just shrugged my shoulders and shook my head.

"So, basically, we have nothing," I shuttered.

"Looks like it." Tom continued, "Let's go back to your aunt's and uncle's house, make a few phone calls, and process this entire thing. Maybe there is something we have not thought about. Come on, let's get away from here."

"Gladly," I thought, courthouses were making me EXTREMELY uncomfortable.

Sticking around an extra day did not prove fruitful. We made a trip back to Devine, but no one would talk to us. It seemed the people in Hondo and Devine stuck together. You knew they had information, but they would not share a word. Perhaps they had been convinced I was the bad person in this chain of events, looking to kidnap the children or harm Patricia. We headed back to San Antonio, returned the car, and caught our flight. We were heading home, empty handed! I fought tears all the way to Nebraska.

The wedding was now ten days away. Tom and I were strongly considering postponing it until the children could be found. We made an appointment with the pastor hoping he could help us sort through the situation. After a long discussion, we decided it best to go ahead with the ceremony. That way the children would have an established home to return to when they did come back.

My friend that made the dresses for the wedding brought Jennifer's dress to me.

"I can't stand seeing this in my closet any longer. Every time I look at it, I cry. I don't know how you're going to get through this," she explained.

"I'm not sure I will. I am not sure of anything right now. What keeps going through my mind is that we were 30 minutes late. Only 30 minutes! That is all, and now they could be anywhere. At least before, I may not have liked where they were, but I <u>knew</u> where they were. You understand what I am saying? This is an entirely different feeling. It is an emptiness I cannot explain. It runs so deep. It's like a vacuum that is trying to swallow me up from the inside out."

By this time, we were both hugging and in tears. After our visit I, also, had to get the little dress out of my sight. I took it to Jennifer's closet, pushed it against the back corner, closed the doors, and slumped to the floor.

Before I knew it, Friday arrived, and it was time for the rehearsal. Every day since our return had been a blur. Get up, go through the motions, go to bed. When I was at work I could still concentrate, I had to for I had missed a week of work. I did not want to be home, so I would stay at the office until I could not think straight. But here it was Friday and as they say, "The show must go on". It took everything within me to put on a smile and walk into the church.

The wedding party was gathered so we could get our instructions for the following day. The wedding party was small, so it was an easy orchestration. Everyone seemed jovial, but there was an elephant in the room. The pastor gave the instructions for the processional and everyone followed. Next, as Tom and I were facing the pastor you could see there was something on his mind.

"Mary, about this time in the service I would like to say something about the joyous occasion of being together, but there is an emptiness we all feel because of the children not being able to share this event with us. Will you be okay if I say something like that?"

I lost my composure along with everyone in the church. I was not prepared for that. Everyone was crying. No one had tissues. Instantly, I wondered if this was a huge mistake. What if I break down during the service? Who cries at their own wedding? Is this fair to Tom? Are we being selfish to go ahead and marry without the children? All these questions were racing through my mind. I reached out to the only source I had for strength. "Lord, I can't do this alone. Give me an exceptional amount of strength. I hurt all over. I need You."

Immediately the pastor jumped in.

"I can take it out if you prefer," he suggested.

It took me a while before I found my voice.

"I'll be fine. We are having the service recorded so when we share it with them, they will know we acknowledged they were in our thoughts," I muttered.

"Okay then, I'll keep it."

Tom's mom was phenomenal, she hosted the rehearsal dinner at their home. She was a gracious host and did not want Tom or I to worry about a thing. It seemed that once we got past the part about acknowledging the children, everyone relaxed and had a good time.

There was enough excitement and activity the day of the wedding, I did not have time to think about anything else. My father walked me down the aisle. As we were about to start down, I wondered what his thoughts were. I wondered, "Is he still thinking I'll be a two-time loser?" I never wanted to disappoint my dad, but here we were, commitment time. As I got to the front of the church, I looked at Tom's father. I thought, "Is he still condemning me for being used goods?" And the children that authenticated me as used goods were not even here. My mind was a mess. What bride has those thoughts during her wedding?

The pastor started the service. My anticipation spiked as he came to the point of talking about the children. I held my head high as tears streamed down my face. Fortunately, knowing this was coming, I remained as stoic as possible. I could hear sniffles from everywhere behind me. The pastor paused, looking to me for guidance. I closed my eyes, "Oh, Lord, I need your strength! Help me get through this." Tom was prepared to help me, at least he had tissues in his pocket. Once I got hold of myself, I gave the pastor a nod and he proceeded.

The reception was held in the recreation room in our development. It was a labor of love, for all the people helping. There was no way I would ever be able to show everyone my appreciation for all their work to get this accomplished. After everyone left and only family remained, Tom and I helped clean up. The food and gifts were taken to our townhouse. Even though everyone seemed to enjoy themselves, there was unquestionably an emptiness to the day. It was not what Tom and I had envisioned our wedding day to be...without the children.

Sunday afternoon we had family and close friends over for lunch and gift opening. A honeymoon was out of the question. The trip to Texas had cost me well over $2,000 for air fare, car rental, court costs, motel in Devine, and food. Besides, we had been away an additional week from work that we had not planned on. Right now, it would be impossible for me to relax, I needed to go back to work where I could occupy my mind and escape.

Feeling like I had been dropped in the middle of the ocean having only a life jacket, I needed to determine what to do and where to go. The story of Saul came to mind (1 Samuel 9). Saul's father had donkeys that had strayed away. His father told his young son, Saul, to take a servant and go look for his donkeys. Saul had no idea which way to go. These were donkeys after all. They could be anywhere. Do you go north, south, east, or west? Saul did not know, he just started out, trusting God to lead him. Finding some similarity to Saul, I had no idea where to start looking, I just tried to remain calm and as patient as possible. I trusted God had a plan, for I did not know which direction to look; north, south, east, or west.

At this point God was my life jacket. If it had been up to me, I would have begged God to take my life, I was in so much emotional pain and mental anguish, there were no more tears left within me. In fact, there was not much of anything within me, I had become an empty, tired, depressed shell. God had revealed to me back in June '80 the intentions of Donnie's heart: if Donnie ever got his hands on the kids one more time, they would be gone. I had fought so hard for two years, yet no one listened, and, in the end, I was 30 minutes late. I prayed, "Lord, I don't know which way to turn. Please point me in the right direction."

It is funny how life keeps going despite the war going on within you. I was hurting so bad I wanted to give up, but God had other plans for me. Working twelve-hour days to catch up and stay ahead of the work demands was a requirement, work continued to be my escape. Sleep, on the other hand, was nonexistent, two to three hours a night was all I could muster. My brain would not shut down. Bills started coming in from our trip to Texas. The monthly phone bill was staggering, let alone receiving the next attorney's statement. As Tom and I talked I felt the only fair thing to do was for me to absorb all the expenses related to the children. I would help with the normal household expenses when I could. To keep up, I sold all the furniture from my home in Omaha before moving to Lincoln, keeping only the children's things. If I felt they had outgrown anything, that was sold also. By the time I moved to Lincoln, only a small truck was required.

After dinner each night, Tom and I would sit at the table and brainstorm, making notes of leads someone could be following up on. The question was, Who? Tom occasionally made phone calls to the sheriff's office in Hondo and, every so often, we would hear from the Devine private investigator. About the only thing they both knew was the name of the man that had last been seen with Patricia at the house. Of course, his name was for them to know and not us. We soon discovered investigations do not occur without a criminal charge or a court order.

The Devine private investigator was able to uncover a few facts:

He found the name of the leasing agency where Donnie leased a new Chevrolet Blazer.

He had the name of the bank carrying the mortgage on Donnie's house.

Donnie was behind on his house payment.

Donnie had taken out a second mortgage on his house.

Donnie and Patricia owned a company called the Texas Man Fruits and Nuts.

Donnie worked at the local grocery store.

There was not a forwarding address on file with the post office.

The man seen with Patricia at the house the day they moved was seen back in town, but he was not the realtor.

So far, not worth the $500 we paid him.

Depression consumed me for nothing was happening. Weekends, I felt like I was in a trance. Tom suggested little trips to take, concerts to attend, movies to see, anything to get my mind off the situation. My lack of desire to do anything was not fair to Tom. I would attempt to do activities with him, but my heart was not in it. At this point in time, I certainly was not a very loving wife. Just because I was hurting so bad did not mean I had to dig a trench and take up occupancy. But I was there, and it was hard, at this point, even contemplating climbing out to enjoy life.

After the wedding someone in Tom's office remembered an article in the local paper regarding "Custody Child-napping" from April 8, 1982, a syndicated article from the United Press International. Since there were no laws written for children taken by their own parents, the article refused to call it anything other than "Child-napping". The existing kidnapping laws were written for the stealing of children by individuals other than the child's own parents. One interesting tidbit of information was that Senator Malcolm Wallop, a Republican from Wyoming along with Senator Alan Cranston, a Democrat from California had introduced the Parental Kidnaping Prevention Act to congress. "It would establish federal penalties for taking abducted children across state lines, expand the authorized uses of the Federal Parent Locator Service, and require states to follow more uniform custody regulations." Tom and I jumped on this and started a dialogue with these two senators along with seven other senators and representatives. We briefly told our story and requested their support for the bill. We received a ton of information. Talk about justice moving slowly. Senator Wallop introduced the bill January 1979. The bill was meeting resistance because many senators had a difficult time charging a parent with a federal crime, with possible penitentiary time, for taking possession of their own children. Little attention was given to the tremendous heartache and anguish caused from the incidents, let alone the costs involved and mental trauma on the children.

One of the suggestions returned from Senator Wallop in DC was for me to contact the Children's Rights, Inc organization in Washington, DC, a nonprofit organization providing advocacy services to protect abused and neglected kids. I explained my story. Much to my surprise, they responded immediately, providing the name in the DC Passport Office with the instructions to provide names, dates of birth, descriptions of the children and ex-spouse. The passport office would put a notice in the children's names, and I would get notified if applications were made on their behalf. If so, I would have fifteen days to file a restraining order on the Passport Office. Hallelujah, finally, someone helped.

Since I had contacted the Children's Rights, Inc I started receiving their quarterly newsletters. How sad to read the stories others were facing, remarkably similar in nature to mine. Most parents being unsuccessful finding their children, after spending tens of thousands of dollars for the search.

The intent of the newsletter was to share information regarding the progress of the Federal Child-Snatching Bills as well as which states had passed the UCCJA. In one newsletter, they wrote about the long-term effect on the kidnapped children: "the effect of child-snatching is not easily seen, like scars or bruises, but are inside, and difficult to heal." I certainly agreed with that statement. It had taken me nine months to mend Alex from the first emotional visit in '80 and he was only gone thirty-one days. The article went on: "It is common among these children to seek counseling. These children very often have no sense of community because of frequent moves and admonishments and instructions not to talk about their past. They do not trust anybody. These children are usually told: the parent died, the parent is trying to find them to do harm to them, or that parent doesn't love them or want to see them anymore."

Upon reading this, there was only one source for me to turn, I started praying. "Lord, I know these children have been told some terrible things. I commit them to your loving hand and ask for you to protect their little minds."

A pending court date was scheduled for July 9, 1982, for a Change of Visitation hearing. Sam had set this hearing the end of May when he filed for the Writ hearing. At the time this motion was filed, Donnie and his attorney had been notified. Thinking that under the current circumstances this hearing would be cancelled, I called Sam to check on the status.

"Hi, Mary, as far as your question goes, no, I'm not going to cancel the hearing. I realize it seems unnecessary to have a hearing on visitation when we do not know the whereabouts of the children. I want to get before the judge, along with Donnie's attorney, and see what Donnie's attorney has to say."

Hesitantly, I inquired, "Okay, Sam, do I need to attend?"

"Oh no, it will only be the three of us. You don't need to go to that expense right now."

"That's fine, just let me know what happens."

Relief swept over me for I did not want to step foot into a courtroom again.

"I will. Thanks."

"Thank you, Sam."

After the hearing Sam called to inform me of the activities of the day.

"To start things off, Donnie's attorney never showed." Sam almost seemed giddy. "We don't know if he's no longer representing Donnie, but it seemed strange he didn't appear. Perhaps he did not want to get an earful from the judge regarding the shenanigans of his client. Anyway, the judge and I did not talk about visitation, but the judge did write a formal Violation of Custody order against Donnie. In Texas, this is a Class 5 Felony."

Before I got too excited, I asked, "So, what does that mean? We already have the Contempt of Court Charge."

"Again, the contempt charge is civil, and nothing will be done about that. The Violation of Custody is the lowest of felony charges, so realistically, probably nothing will occur, but once it gets on file at the Medina County Sheriff's Office, since that was the origin of the kidnapping, if the detectives want to poke around, they have the legal means to do so."

"That's good, Right?" I asked.

"You have to remember this is a Class 5 Felony. All the other cases take priority over yours."

"At least they can ask questions if they have time. Maybe we will learn something," I was trying to remain optimistic.

After hanging up I had to drive to the library to read about a Violation of Custody Order Class 5 Felony. Basically, the charge is made against the person who takes any child under the age of eighteen from the custody of their parent. This charge fit Donnie. The next question was whether anything would transpire from this.

Because of the family business, Tom had access to information the normal person would not have available. He ordered a credit report on

Donnie which was full of personal information. At the time the report was pulled, Donnie and Patricia owed $27,500. One of the more interesting items was a new loan from Texas Lending, opened March 1982, for $19,000. At the time we did not know what to make of it. There was a note on the account that stated, "payments were slow due to the fact the ex-wife is to pay her share of the joint accounts." How interesting! Not only was I receiving calls from creditors, my aunt and uncle in California were being harassed asking about Donnie's whereabouts, as well as Arlene was fielding all kinds of questions regarding her son. These people were relentless, but I understood they were attempting to recoup their own loss.

Tom and I were both frustrated, but it seemed to be getting to Tom more since he was used to making things happen and fixing problems. What made this so difficult was that we were dealing with another state. Besides, the charges were not severe enough to warrant people spending time on the case. Tom would call the Medina County Sheriff's Office with questions. Then, he would call Sam to see what could be done. I knew they all thought we were crazy. There were times I thought I was losing my mind, but I could not, for my children's sake.

After a couple phone calls to Sam, he asked that I follow up with a letter regarding all the questions we had. I apologized to Sam if we seemed to be unreasonable, but we were extremely frustrated. It had been another six weeks now since Donnie kidnapped the children and as far as Tom and I knew, nothing was being done to locate them. We had several questions.

1) How did he secure the loan from Texas Lending?
2) Do you know of any additional judgements against him?
3) Why didn't my judgement show up?
4) Can't the police talk with Donnie's attorney?
5) Who was the man with Patricia at the house the day we served the writ?
6) Has Donnie's friend been contacted to see when he last talked with Donnie?
7) Since Patricia is originally from Ireland is anyone looking into restricting passports?

8) Is Patricia a citizen?
9) Why can't Patricia be charged as an accessory?
10) Has anyone looked at Donnie's employment/unemployment records?
11) Did they apply for food stamps?
12) Can the kid's school records be gotten?
13) Are they still using their checking account?
14) Does anyone have access to their charge cards?
15) The PO box number has been closed, but there is no forwarding information available. How is their mail being forwarded?
16) Does anyone have access to phone records?
17) Is Donnie maintaining payments on his leased car?
18) Is Patricia's car leased? If so, by whom?

We thought these were good questions that needed to be pursued. The problem was Sam was an attorney and not an investigator. Again, we did not know where to turn.

Even in Lincoln, Tom and I were on our own. Tom's father did not want the story shared with anyone because he did not want the family name/business associated with the "situation". He wanted to protect the family name. Those in Tom's office knew about the kidnapping, but very few of the details were shared. We decided even Tom's family members would be kept at a distance regarding the details. Not wanting to be a family embarrassment, that was the way Tom and I kept it.

Sam was becoming frustrated with us, especially after receiving the letter with the eighteen questions. He did not have time to investigate anything, after all, he was the attorney. From our perspective not nearly enough was happening. Missing now for 2 1/2 months was unnerving me; I needed to know someone was making some progress.

Sam called one afternoon.

"We seem to be running into a situation here. You have more questions for me than I can make inquiries about. I have done some research and talked with some of my colleagues and I am proposing that you hire a full-time private investigator to continue with the investigation. They have ways of getting information that I cannot. I have inquired around and there is a pair of investigators here in San Antonio that come highly recommended by my colleagues. I have been in contact with them and they are expecting your call." He gave me their contact information. "If you decide to seek their assistance let me know."

"I appreciate this Sam. I am sorry if you feel we have been badgering you with questions, but I feel that valuable time is being wasted. I miss my children."

"I know you do. If you decide to hire them, I'll help supply any information I have."

"Fair enough, I'll call and at least get some information. I'll be in touch."

10. Labyrinth

*~A complicated irregular network of paths in which
it is difficult to find one's way~*

That evening, following Sam's phone call, Tom and I discussed hiring the investigators. After discussing the situation, we decided I should call the investigator's office and get some information. It was for sure the local investigator from Devine had not helped in the least, and we did not want to follow that same rabbit trail. Since this firm came highly recommended from Sam's peers, we felt they had to be reputable.

The following afternoon I called.

"Hello, this is Kate, may I help you?"

Her voice was very pleasant, a professional greeting from a young woman.

"Hello, I'm Mary Dietrich, a client of Sam Koffman, who has recommended I call and set up a phone consultation to speak with one of the investigators."

"Sure, can you give me just a little background? Our firm has two investigators. Each of the guys have a little different specialty."

"Sure, my children have been kidnapped by their father. They went for a visit in March over spring break and weren't returned."

"I'm so sorry to hear this. I will pass your information along to Rich. You can expect a call within 24 hours."

"Great."

I thanked her and gave her my contact information.

Early the next morning I received a call from Rich, just as promised.

"Hello, I'm Rich, from Miller and Stone, I understand you called and talked with Kate yesterday," he sounded very personable.

"Yes, I did. My attorney, Sam Koffman, highly recommended your firm to help locate my children."

"That was nice. Can you provide me with a little background?"

I gave him the cliff notes of what had transpired: starting with the divorce in Texas, moving to Nebraska, the initial visit in 1980, the court battle in Nebraska for setting visitation, the contempt of court charge along with the Change of Visitation order in Texas, sending the kids to Texas at Easter, the Writ processed in Devine, and Donnie's disappearance in May before the Writ could be served.

"Wow, I'm sorry you've had to go through all of this!"

"I can't seem to get anyone's attention because the children are with their father and it is not considered kidnapping," I said bemoaning the situation.

"Let me tell you a little bit about our office. I would be more than happy to help but you need to understand how we work. We charge by the hour. Kate, our receptionist, does some of the work for us also, therefore if she is working on your case, her time gets billed out as well. We require a $1000 retainer before we start. That check must clear the bank prior to asking the initial interview questions. Before that money is depleted Kate will call asking for another $1000 payment. I want to be perfectly honest with you. We have never been successful finding missing children. The reason for this is that the client runs out of money long before we ever run out of leads. Do you have any questions?"

"Not really, you've made things perfectly clear. I need to discuss this with my husband, and I'll call you back in the next day or two."

"That sounds great. Let me know what you decide. I look forward to hearing from you."

Rich had presented the cold, hard facts. Retainer of $1000 with additional $1000 increments each request. No children ever found. How long would my money last? Would my money outlast their leads? I had Sam's and Carl's outstanding bills. My head was throbbing.

Tom and I discussed all our options after work. Honestly, we did not think we had a choice, knowing if I did not hire them, I would never see my children again. How long could I write $1000 checks? Or would I be another statistic, like all their other clients and run out of money first. It was for sure we were not making headway continuing the current path. If Tom was willing to maintain all the household expenses, without my input, then I had to try. Tom was willing, so it appeared the discovery would commence soon.

I placed a call to Kate the next morning saying I would like to proceed. I knew what it was going to take to set the wheels into motion. She gave me the mailing address of their office.

"The check will be in the mail today. You should expect it in a couple days."

"Thanks, Mary, I'll be looking for it. Just a reminder, I will deposit the check immediately. As soon as I know the check has cleared, I will call to set up a time when I can start getting some preliminary information. It may be a week before you hear back from me."

"I understand. That will be fine."

A week gave me time to get all the facts together. Kate called exactly as she promised, so the private investigators officially took over on August 16, five months after putting the children on the plane. When Kate called, she totally directed the interview.

My full maiden name, social security number, education level, where born, where currently employed.

Same questions for the father: Donnie Ryan Schumacher, social, education, where born, current employment, unemployed (as far as I knew).

"When were you and Donnie married?" 3/1972

"Where?" Seward, Nebraska

"When were you divorced?" 4/1980

"Where?" San Antonio, Texas

"Is Donnie remarried and to whom?" Yes, Patricia Sanchez 4/1980

I interjected, "Patricia is originally from Ireland. We believe her maiden name is McCarthy, from Dublin, Ireland. We found this information on their marriage certificate at the courthouse with a reference to the name Maria McCarthy. That name we did not understand. She was married to Mateo Sanchez. Mateo is originally from the Dominican Republic. They had five children, three were adopted. She and Mateo were divorced in Phoenix in 1980. She was granted custody of all five children. The kids range in age from 10 - 15, four girls and one boy."

"Donnie's last known address?"

"Their last address was 8225 Kearney Lane. They purchased this home in July 1980. Their first home was 9523 Jasper Lane. It appears to me they owned two homes for a while. Patricia moved in with Donnie in January 1980. They were married in April 1980. Somewhere between those dates, they bought the home on Jasper. It was during the kid's initial visit in 1980, June/July time frame, they decided they needed a larger home, so purchased the house on Kearney Lane. While in Devine, Donnie used two PO box numbers. When I let the children visit this March, I only had a PO box number. We only found out the actual house address the day we were with the Medina County Sheriff to serve the Writ."

"Do you know the vehicle Donnie drives?"

"Yes, he drives a 1980 Chevrolet Blazer. A credit report listed the owner as Century Leasing."

"Do you know the vehicle Patricia drives?"

"No."

"Do you know where the kids were in school?"

"No, but Alex was not put in school so did not complete kindergarten."

"Okay, that should be enough to get us started. Rich will meet with Sam to get caught up on the legal proceedings that have transpired. When I have additional questions or information, I'll call you."

"Thank you, Kate, I appreciate your help. There are a couple more items that may help. First, Tom and I did hire a local investigator in Devine after Donnie fled with the children. His name is Syd Klein. When we hired you, we terminated his endeavors, but we have asked him to cooperate with you. He is a local in Devine, so Tom and I think he knows more than he has been willing to share with us. Hopefully, he will provide some information to you. We also talked with the Sheriff in Hondo. He would not tell us anything because a crime had not been committed at that point. Both the police in Hondo and Syd have pictures of my children. Lastly, since Donnie and Patricia are both on the run, that means Mateo, no doubt, has not heard from his kids either. If we can find him, assuming he is still in Arizona, he may be able to provide information as to Donnie's whereabouts. Mateo must be sending child support to Patricia. It might be a long shot, but you never know."

"Exactly, Mary, the least tidbit of information may be just what is needed. I will pass all this information along to Rich. You'll be hearing from us."

With school getting ready to begin and knowing there were six children to be enrolled, somewhere, I wrote a letter to the Record's Department, at the physician's clinic in Lincoln where my kids doctored. Public schools require new student's immunization records prior to enrollment. I requested that the clinic not release the children's medical records to another state. I explained the situation and even provided the legal felony number for the charge filed against Donnie in Texas, in case they wanted to check the validity of the offense. I pleaded with them to notify me if they received such a request. We knew this was a long shot, but we needed to cover all bases.

Kate called less than two weeks later.

"Hi, Mary, I'm calling to give you an update on our findings."

"Good, I've been wondering if you've been able to find anything."

"Oh, we are off to a good start. Sam has sent copies of all the legal documents. Rich talked with the Sheriff in Hondo as well as Syd. They have conveniently lost the pictures of the children, so if you could send me pictures that would be great."

"Sure, I'll get those right out."

"Rich talked with the postmaster in Devine and was suspicious of some of the answers he received. Do you know of anyone by the name of O'Keefe?"

"No, I'm not familiar with anyone by that name."

"That is okay. For some reason that name keeps coming up. O'Keefe's live in Houston, and there has been some suspicious phone calls we are tracking. We are also trying to locate Patricia's ex-husband. Finding a particular Sanchez in Phoenix has been a challenge."

"I'll bet it has."

"I have several additional questions for you regarding Donnie. We are trying to piece together his personality to know what we are up against."

"That's fine, proceed," I said.
And she did.

What is Donnie's temperament?
How did Donnie treat Alex when he was small?
Could I bring her up to date on Donnie's employment history?
Did I know of any trips Donnie and Patricia may have taken?
What is the current family size?
How does Donnie punish children?
How did Donnie get along with neighbors?
Was I aware of the current living conditions in the house?
Was I aware of all his debts?
Was I responsible for his debts?
What makes him angry?
If in court, what situations would he lie about?
How did he treat his mother?
How did he treat you?

Before hanging up she requested another $1000. That did not take long to go through the first $1000! It appeared they were hitting as many avenues as possible, using all their sources of information to amass facts.

"I'll get it in the mail to you tomorrow. Thanks, Kate, for all your work."

"You're welcome. We're getting a lot of good information," she assured me.

The information she was sharing was somewhat encouraging. "Praise, God!" Someone has finally gotten off the dime. It was promising to hear they had access to phone records. I did not care how they were getting their information, at least they were making progress.

I could feel God put a little strength back into me. The pressure was off Tom and I to attempt to get people to answer our questions. The investigators were doing something. They had uncovered more information in two weeks than we had gotten out of anyone else. Guess that was one way of justifying the first $1000. I could feel myself slowly climbing out of the trench.

Since the investigator was working, Tom poured his energy into Nebraska's Washington DC senators and representatives. Most of the officials we had sent my 'Plea for Help' letter responded by sending their condolences for all the problems we had encountered. Some said they fully supported the bill, and some had doubt regarding the validity of charging a parent with kidnapping. The same old arguments we heard all along.

The weekends were still the hardest for me. Tom was finishing a room in the basement. I was not able to sit still, so I started a project of my own. Tom and I had painted the bedrooms designated as the kid's rooms, but they felt vanilla. Not wanting my children to come home to a generic guest bedroom I decided to make each of the kids a bedspread and matching window treatments. I needed their rooms to feel special. I shopped for material, pulled out my sewing machine, and got busy. It turned out to be very therapeutic. My mind was focused on their return, not their absence.

The following week Kate called again,

"First off, let's get this part out of the way, I need another $1000." This time it had only been a week. I was not making money that fast!

"I have some terrific news though. I was able to locate Mateo in Phoenix."

"That's great!" I said. She was getting me excited.

This could not have been a simple task since, to my knowledge, all she had to work with was telephone books and telephone operators. I was impressed.

"I couldn't get Mateo to answer his phone, so I sent a telegram saying I had important information regarding his children. Upon receiving that, he returned my call and I was able to ask him more questions."

"Did he know where his kids were?"

"He thought they were in Devine. When I told him what happened, and everyone was on the run, he got mad."

"Did he seem concerned to know where they were?" I asked.

"I don't think so, but I really caught him off guard. I gave him our office information and asked that he call if he ever hears from Patricia or one of the kids."

"Did he seem receptive?" I inquired.

"All I can say is that he was upset and wanted to be left alone. I am sure it did not help that he had received our telegram and had been tricked into making the call. I am going to give you his contact information. Let him think about things awhile. Perhaps you can write him a letter explaining how you feel. Coming from you might soften the situation for him."

"Okay, I can do that."

Kate also explained they had gotten hold of Century Leasing company regarding Donnie's Blazer.

"We have confirmed he did lease the Blazer. He is delinquent enough on it now that they have a skip tracer looking for it. This gal works for the leasing company and is a real firecracker. Between this gal and us, I'm sure something is going to break loose."

"That sounds positive."

I felt encouraged something was finally being accomplished.

"I guarantee you, if you think debt collectors are relentless, you don't want a private investigator and a skip tracer on your tail!" Kate laughed. "And, the leasing company has also contacted Mateo, so I'm sure that is another reason he wants to be left alone."

I did not care who found them if someone was successful.

Kate continued sharing details.

"Since Devine is a small community there appears to be some cover up going on. Somehow the realtor found out about the skip tracer through the post office. Someone seems to be going to the post office and cherry-picking certain mail from one of the PO boxes, but the box is technically closed. The other PO box is rented to Nature's Best Products and it is full of mail. It appears that everything, at this point, is stopping with the postmaster. We even had someone go undercover and offered a $100 reward for information, but no one took the bait. We are trying to figure out if the realtor has been set up to extract specific mail from the box and forward it on. We also know there is a connection between the realtor and the O'Keefe's. We just haven't figured it out yet."

"Can there be an investigation into the post office?" I asked.

"That would have to come from the Medina County Sheriff's Office, and I doubt that will happen. Rich talked with the listing realtor and neither she or anyone in the realty office is talking. There must be a person to contact if there is an offer on the house, but no one will say. These people are playing their cards very tight to the chest."

"Oh, I know exactly what you mean. Tom and I kept asking questions and couldn't get a straight answer from anyone."

"The O'Keefe name keeps popping up. They live in Houston so Rich is going to make a trip up there to see what he can find out. We can see from phone records where the O'Keefe's have received collect phone calls, but the calls are originating from a pay phone. There have also been calls between the realty office and the O'Keefe's. There's a connection if we can get someone to talk."

"Why are all of these people protecting them?"

"Donnie and Patricia probably told everyone you were hunting down the kids to kidnap them or cause the family harm."

"I guess that makes sense. No one knows who can be trusted."

Another week passed before I received another call from Kate. Yes, they needed more money. That makes $4,000 in a month. I am understanding the pattern: Kate calls when they need additional funds and that is when I get updates regarding their progress.

"Rich made the trip to Houston to see if he could make any connection with the O'Keefe's. He knows there is something but could not get anyone to provide any information. Rich decided to drop that lead unless the name resurfaces again. Rich also found out foreclosure papers are ready to be filed on the Kearney house. What he found interesting was the second mortgage holder, Texas Lending, was filing the foreclosure. Along with Texas Lending, Starnes Mortgage (the first mortgage holder), Donnie's San Antonio attorney, and yourself were listed as lien holders."

"It's nice to know Sam finally filed my affidavit with the court," I added.

Kate had more to share.

"Rich also found out that Wells Fargo of Texas has written off Donnie's first home in Devine. That would be the Jasper Lane house."

"This is a mess." I exclaimed. "How can anyone do such things?"

"Oh, there's more. Patricia's sister's name in Ireland is Maria McCarthy, we have not discovered Patricia's maiden name yet, but we will. Phone calls have been made to a person named Garcia in California. We do not know who they are yet, but there have been several calls. We will follow up on those. There are two businesses listed for Sanchez. If Mateo cooperates, we will not have to follow up with these. And, lastly, Donnie and Patricia closed their Devine bank accounts mid-July. Since they moved the end of May Rich knew the money had to be sent somewhere, but, again, no one was talking in Devine."

"Wow, you guys have been busy. Something is bound to break pretty soon."

Maybe this wealth of information had cost $4,000 but I spent more than that through the legal system and got nowhere. Before getting back to work, I thanked God for the progress we were making. Hiring the investigators was certainly the right approach to take.

The middle of September I received a certified letter addressed to Donnie at my Omaha address. (Since I was receiving all of Donnie's unwanted collection mail, his letters were being forwarded along with mine.) My curiosity was peaked since I had to sign for the letter. The return address was from the Texas Division of Employment and Training - Investigations. I debated whether to open it but, since I was required to sign for it, I felt responsible. Much to my surprise, Job Services of Texas was looking for Donnie due to an overpayment of unemployment benefits to the amount of $1,227. The letter explained the overpayment was due to the fact Donnie had received unemployment benefits but failed to report he had been working at a job in San Antonio as well as Devine. Basically, he had filed false unemployment claims for a total of eighteen weeks.

After calling Kate to make her aware of this latest event, she immediately called Job Service of Texas to explain why they had not been able to locate Donnie. When Job Service became aware of the kidnapping situation, they told her they were not going to waste any more time, the state would be prosecuting him for theft. Kate could not wait to call me back to share that news. Now we would have one more agency looking for Donnie as well as an outstanding criminal theft charge once it got filed.

About this same time, Sam wrote a letter explaining the situation regarding Donnie's house. The first mortgage had been taken out in May 1980 when Donnie and Patricia bought the home. In March 1982 Donnie did two things. There was a Deed of Trust taken out between the bank and an individual for $14,500. Sam explained this was a personal loan where Donnie gave this personal lender the deed as collateral. About that same time, he took out a second mortgage on the house, withdrawing all the equity in the home. Sam was speculating the loans were taken out to get himself a stash of money that would enable him to get away with the children. There was never a payment made on the second loan. The situation on the house was so bad the second mortgage holder was paying the house payment, preserving their position. It was the second mortgage holder that filed foreclosure to guarantee repayment of their loan. Sam explained these details so I would understand that my judgements, that had been filed with the court, were for naught. Whatever funds were left over after paying off the second mortgage holder would default to the first mortgage holder. The holder of the deed of trust got nothing. Sam did affirm that he had been working with the investigators, sharing information to keep them from duplicating efforts.

Last thing Sam mentioned was that I had not been paying enough of his outstanding bill and I needed to increase the monthly payments to the office. Really? I was ready to pull my hair out the way it was. It was taking more than my salary just to pay the investigators.

This deserved a response, so I wrote a letter.

I apologize for being a little pushy regarding getting liens filed on Donnie's property. If I had known the situation I never would have asked. Your letter explained the foreclosure process and who gets priority ...

Concerning the kidnapping, I wish I could have convinced ANYONE back in '80 about this man's character. He is far better telling lies than I am telling the truth. Everyone believed him, that I was an overprotective, manipulative mother who would not allow this poor father any opportunities to see his children ...

I still question why it took you until May to finally get the Contempt of Court charge filed on Donnie for failure to return my children. Then, who tipped Donnie off that the Writ hearing was scheduled. Was Donnie's attorney notified of this hearing and advised him of his options? Someone must have ...

Now that my children have literally vanished it is easy for everyone to say, "You should have ...". It is not that simple. You told me it was so easy to find anyone today that even if he kidnapped the kids it would not take much to find them. Well, it has now been six months and I am no closer than before. According to the investigators, an exceedingly small percentage of children ever get returned. And now that they are gone, I receive no assistance from officials. The laws make it impossible to be successful...

I am sure you think you are dealing with an irrational female, but I guarantee you that you are not. I have tried to show as much patience as I can possibly find within me. Please realize that since May I have spent $6,800 in out of pocket expenses to find the children. In addition to that, I have paid you $1,100 for your services. I am sorry that in August and September I had to make a minimal payment. I realize, this minimal payment has not covered your monthly expenses, but I am making a legitimate attempt. I guarantee you; you will get paid. Please trust me. I work extremely hard but right now there is just not enough to go around. You know, as well as I, that if we do not pay the investigator I might as well forget that I ever had two children, for they will never be found...

I am not sure you can understand the mental anguish I have gone through. Donnie has been trying to break me every chance he can, from the time we were first married until now. If he could ever prove me incompetent, mentally, or physically, he would have it made. By the Grace of God that will never happen. I will do everything I can to pay each month. I only trust in God that this entire mess is over soon. I want my children back. No man can realize the attachment a mother has for her children after carrying them nine months as they grow within you, bearing them, and then caring for them night and day. By God's Grace I am going to continue looking for my children until there remains no more hope.

The Mama Bear had been provoked one too many times. Sam never again pushed me for additional payments.

I was getting advice from everyone: people at work, family, and friends, offering suggestions as to whether I had tried this approach or that approach. Several times people would give me newspaper articles regarding missing children. One of the suggestions I kept hearing was, "Why don't you just go to a psychic." An acquaintance handed me a news article regarding this psychic in New Jersey that only worked with police in locating missing children. They suggested I go to New Jersey and sit there until she talked with me. I thanked them for the suggestion, but I was not going to New Jersey to sit. To those suggesting I see a psychic, I would explain that my belief was in God and not in psychics. That was a road I was not going to travel. I held firmly to my conviction that it would only be through God directing our path that the children would ever be located. With that response, people would roll their eyes, shrug their shoulders, and walk away.

With all the communication we had with Washington DC I felt compelled to join the Children's Rights, Inc organization. I had attained 450 signatures on a petition for Children's Rights to take to the members of congress to get legislation passed to make the 7-day concealment or 30-day restraint of a child a Federal Offense. The organization sent along a handbook for parents victimized by child-snatching or restraint. Too bad this booklet arrived in September and not March. It contained some good advice.

Keep your job. (Check, did that.)

Get press coverage. (Nope, Tom's dad does not want anyone to know.)

Do not hire a detective unless you feel very sure about where the other parent has gone. Wait to hire the detective in the area once the other parent has been located. (Nope, detective has been hired and we still have no idea where the children are but would not know as much as we do without them.)

Do not give up hope. (Sounds good but it gets so hard.)

As of September 1982, forty-three states had passed the Uniform Child Custody Jurisdiction Act. That was positive information, but there were other items mentioned that were not positive.

UCCJA does not prevent child-snatching.

UCCJA states sometimes only uphold custody decrees from other states which have passed UCCJA.

There is no way for a court to know if there is a pending order from another state.

States are very territorial of their rights when making custody decisions and are reluctant to give up jurisdiction.

Neither the UCCJA nor the courts have the power to locate an abducting parent and child. If your child is gone, it is up to you to find him.

It appeared to me that without enforcement or penalty, the benefits from this law were worthless. Maybe I would not have pursued this avenue in the first place if all of this had been explained to me, but that was two years ago and little to no progress had been made. I felt like we had been used as guinea pigs in testing the validity of the law in Nebraska.

Hiring the private investigators had been one of the best decisions Tom and I made. Yes, we continued to brainstorm each night, attempting to come up with new twists. Every time Kate called, I would take detailed notes and share these conversations with Tom. These discussions would send us down a new way of thinking. If we would come up with something that seemed important, I would share it with Kate. As she said in the beginning, the least tidbit of information is sometimes all it takes.

With some of the pressure off I was able to concentrate more at work. In September, my boss totally surprised me with a promotion, along with a substantial raise. It is for sure the raise came at a good time, for my resources were getting thin. The first thing I thought was to pray, "Thank you, Lord, for allowing me favor with my bosses and the ability to concentrate on my job, in spite of the chaos swirling around me."

One item of business I had not completed for Kate was to write a letter to Mateo. Before September ended, I reached out to him.

We have never formally met but you and I have a lot in common. I am sorry that we had to involve you in this terrible situation, but we were trusting you would be able to help me locate my two children.

The last six months have been the most frightening, heartbreaking months of my life. In March Donnie picked up the children for a visit over spring break. You know the story from there. The entire family has been missing since May 28...

From what I understand you have been denied the right to have your children visit you. I realize Patricia and Donnie have not been fair with you either ...

Mateo, I am hoping that you will cooperate with us. I have had the investigators looking since August. I have spent roughly $10,000 up to this time ...

I understand you would like to have custody of your children as well, and I will do everything I can to help you. If I, or my investigator's, have any information you could use in your pursuit of your children you are welcome to it ...

It has been utterly amazing what they have found out about Donnie and Patricia. None of it has been flattering ...

My two little ones just turned three and six. They have no idea what has happened to them or me ...

Mateo, I will help you in whatever way I can. I ask that you also help me. Maybe together, we can find them. Do you know of any of Patricia's friends that might be covering for her? I am starting to run out of leads, and I cannot give up now. I know if I give up, I will never see the children again. Thank you for returning the call to my investigators. I am sorry they frightened you with the telegram, but I do consider this entire situation extremely dangerous to the well-being of all seven children, yours and mine. Thank you for your help. Please feel free to contact me anytime. Call collect or call the investigators collect. We need to work together.

My letter must have pulled on Mateo's heart because he called the investigator's and provided them with more information:

Work phone.

Home phone and address.

Names and ages of all his children.

Identified which children were his and Patricia's and the ones that had been adopted.

His divorce records.

His and Patricia's social security numbers.

Patricia's maiden name was Fitzpatrick not McCarthy. She was using a false ID. McCarthy is Patricia's sisters married name.

Where he paid child support along with the case number.

Juan and Anna Garcia are mutual friends residing in Escondido, California.

Patricia owes the Garcias $15,000.

Kate shared with him that during the investigation in Devine they discovered that all five children were caught shoplifting in January 1982, Patricia being with them at the time. The Medina County Sheriff's Office had the record on file. That information left him very disturbed.

Once again, Kate not only called to share the information regarding Mateo's cooperation but requested another $1000. At least when she called, she always had more information to share. She was very upbeat regarding the additional leads Mateo supplied.

"We've checked Mateo's child support payments with the Maricopa County Clerk of Court in Phoenix. As with most child support payments, the clerk receives Mateo's check and they reissue a check to Patricia. The address for these checks is being sent to the Devine PO box number. We knew these checks were being pulled from the mail and somehow forwarded to Patricia. What we do not know, is whether the checks are being sent to the O'Keefe's who cash them and then issue another check to Patricia, or if the check itself is being forwarded. Once again, it funnels back to the Devine post office. Rich contacted the Medina County Sheriff's Office to inform them they had a problem there. Now that Rich has given the sheriff more concrete facts, the sheriff has become more interested and said he would pass the information to the fugitive division. Once again, for us, this is as far as this lead has taken us. I'm sorry but it's another dead end."

"You don't have to be sorry, Kate. We have no choice but to follow each path to the end. One of these days you are going to get a breakthrough."

Once Mateo obtained information from Kate regarding his children, he seemed more receptive. One evening the phone rang and it was a collect call from Mateo.

"Yes, I'll accept the call." I was eager to talk with him. "Hello, Mateo, I've been hoping you'd call."

"I'm sorry, Mary, at first I just didn't want to get involved. I had received that alarming telegram about my children being in danger and got overly concerned. It angered me that the investigators used that tactic but the more I thought about it, my kids are in danger. That is when I changed my mind, along with receiving your letter. I could feel your pain, so I called the investigators. Then the more I heard, it made me wonder what my kids have been going through as well. I have not been able to visit my kids since Patricia married Donnie. I miss them so much but haven't spoken with them now since March, about the same time your kids went there for a visit."

"I'm sorry to hear that, Mateo, I know, it's not easy. I am sorry to have to involve you but, in my heart, I feel the only way we will find all the kids is to work together. The investigators were about out of leads, so the real encouragement now is the additional information you provided. I appreciate that. I am begging you, if you think of any additional information or hear from one of your kids, please call Kate at the investigator's office. Any friends or family you can trust, get the word out that you are looking for your children. Anything will help." I was pleading!

"I will, Mary. I can contact the parents of a couple of the kid's friends. I knew them well, although I have not spoken to them for a long time. I'll try."

"That's all any of us can do. I know Kate is following up on all the information you supplied during your last phone call. Thanks, again, Mateo, I appreciate anything you think of."

October started out with a bomb shot from left field! I had come home from work early, feeling drained and depressed. The children had been gone six months and I was running out of energy. The doorbell rang, I shuffled to open the door. Here stood the sheriff.

"Hello, Are you Mary Schumacher Dietrich?"

"Yes, I am." I had no idea what to expect next. Had they found the children dead? My heart was racing.

"I have papers for you. Will you please sign the service notice?"

"Sure."

I signed the forms while my mind was trying to figure out who would serve papers on me. I knew it would not be Donnie looking for me.

"Thank you," he said pleasantly.

I shut the door and opened the envelope. Not being able to believe what I was seeing I slithered down the wall and melted onto the floor, holding my head. About that time, Tom came through the door wondering what was wrong.

"Oh, you're not going to believe this. Carl has filed a Judgment against me for the amount owed to him from April plus interest charges, $1,577. I have twenty days to pay the entire balance."

"Have we even gotten a bill from him since April?" Tom asked.

"No, there has been no correspondence since March when I told him I wasn't going to appeal the case to the Nebraska Supreme Court. Can he do this without so much as a letter?"

"I guess so, because he just did."

This low action by Carl left me inflamed. This was a battle on a whole different front. Truthfully, I had forgotten all about this bill with everything else going on. Carl was so angry the last time I talked with him, I doubted he would work with me to get the billed paid. Oh well, too late now, it had to be dealt with.

To compound the issue, Carl had filed the judgment in such a timely manner that it came out in the free local Saturday paper. Every household in Lincoln and surrounding communities received this paper.

"Carl Smith, no address given, filed a suit Oct 7 seeking $1,577 plus interest and court costs against Mary Lou Dietrich, formerly Mary Lou Schumacher, no address given, alleging the sum is due for services rendered."

Tom's dad was furious! He never once bothered to ask how I was doing regarding the fight for my children. In fact, unless he was talking to Tom directly at work, he never took the time or showed any interest regarding the children's disappearance. He really laid into

Tom regarding embarrassing the family name. Since Tom's dad did not want anyone in town to know about our "situation" I am sure he would spin some tale regarding me and the attorney. Tom would not tell me everything they talked about, but I felt part of it was blaming Tom for marrying someone who was used goods with a truck full of baggage.

After being awake most of the night, I talked with Tom Sunday morning telling him how I was going to solve the problem.

"Since this is my issue, which I incurred before we ever got married, I've decided to sell my car and just pay this off."

"Are you sure?" he asked. "I can find some way to help."

"No, you're not going to pay for my mess. I see no other way. I must retain a little savings for the investigators. I do not have that much left. Since you drive a company truck, we are sitting here with three vehicles. If I can drive your car to meet the carpool we can get by for a while. I am sorry. I don't have many options."

Tom agreed. First thing Monday morning he listed the car in the newspaper, and it sold quickly. Tom was terribly upset the way Carl lost the case for me in the first place. Yes, it was his negligence in the courtroom as well as refusing to write a brief that got us into this situation, but perhaps this was just the road I had to go down, regardless of the court decision. Only God could answer that question someday.

Tom asked me, "Do you mind if I make a few inquiries as to Carl's negligence on your case?"

"I don't care. I still feel the same as I did back in March, I am too tired to fight another legal battle. Nebraska does not want jurisdiction. Neither did Carl want to be the first making a landmark decision. In my opinion, he just wants to coast into retirement."

"I understand how you feel. I just want to know if we have a suit against him for negligence."

"That's fine," I said. "Do what you want. Personally, I would like to go to sleep, wake up, and have this all be just a bad dream, but it's not going to just go away."

Tom took me into his arms, providing comfort to me. The emptiness inside of me just would not go away.

Tom knew the local attorneys would not say anything negative regarding one of their peers, so Tom contacted an attorney in Omaha and set up an initial consultation. At the consultation Tom briefly explained Carl's negligence regarding the court appearance, the net effect of losing the children, and the judgement Carl filed for lack of payment.

After listening to the story, she advised, "Many times you'd rather have a reduced lump sum payment than smaller monthly payments that go on forever. Offer him $1,000 and see if he'll take the offer."

"Sounds like a good idea. We may be calling on you later for additional advice regarding the children," Tom added.

"Not a problem, I'll be glad to help you sort things out," she said.

Tom was excited to share his information with me. At this point I had nothing to lose. I really did not want to talk with Carl again, but knew I had no choice. The following day I got up my courage and called.

"Carl, Mary Dietrich here, I need to bring you up to date about what has happened since we last talked. The Texas courts forced me to send my kids with their father over spring break in March and they have never been returned. Currently, we do not know where they are, but we are still pursuing their return. Because of that, my legal expenses have been astronomical. Would there be a chance you would accept a lump sum payment of $1,000 for my outstanding invoice and we call it even?"

"I didn't know your kids were missing but that's not my concern. No, I am not going to accept a reduced fee. You owe me for the time I put into your case."

He was very cold and emphatic.

"Okay, thank you," I quickly hung up the phone before I said something I would regret.

The next day I paid Carl in full. I had to get that door closed.

After receiving another statement from Sam, I totaled my expenses. At least Sam's charges were subsiding since his involvement was minimal at this point. Most of the recent expenses had been the investigators. My expenses for trying to locate the children since March totaled over $11,000. And that did not include Carl's last expense of $1,577, or what I paid Sam prior to March. It was roughly $14,000. On top of that, what Donnie owed me from 1980 child support, medical bills, and medical insurance was $8,775. All of this just added to my depression.

Rich and Kate had been coming to dead ends with their existing leads, but with all the new information received from Mateo, Kate was reenergized to leap forward. She shared everything she and the skip tracer had discovered. Together they were dynamite.

"Mary, you're never going to believe what we have been able to find out. With Mateo's information we've been able to come at this from a new direction."

"Great," I said, "what do you have?"

"Would you believe Patricia is not a US citizen. Since she is not a citizen, I called Immigration. They said they could help unofficially by tagging the file, but that was all they could do. They had her birthdate and when she came to the United States. The last item they had on file was from 1980 when Patricia and Donnie went to Ireland."

"That is correct, they did go to Ireland. After that trip, I got overly concerned they would take off overseas with the entire family. At that time, I contacted the DC Passport Office and they put a notice on the children's names. I am supposed to get notified if an application is made on their behalf. I'm so thankful I did that based on this information."

"I agree." Kate added. "I've also called the Nature's Best Products company in Utah, a Mormon based company. Donnie was a salesman for them, where he purchased the inventory from them and sold it directly to customers. One of the line items on his credit report was for inventory. They were very sympathetic to my plea for help. Donnie is no longer affiliated with them, but they promised to call if they ever heard from either Donnie or Patricia. When Donnie was selling for them, they only had the PO box number in Devine."

"That confirms what Alex told me that he was with his daddy selling fruits and nuts," I added.

"I've got more," she said. "The Texas Division of Employment and Training - Investigations Department has filed formal charges against Donnie for Fraud, a 5th Degree Felony. The Medina County

District Attorney in Hondo is more receptive to listen to Rich now that there are several things going on here: the formal Felony charge against Donnie from the state for fraud, Century Leasing has filed a charge for theft of the Blazer but we haven't seen it come through yet, all the suspicious activity at the Devine post office, and the children being kidnapped, although it wasn't a criminal charge, everything still occurred in Medina County. And there is still the outstanding Bench Warrant for Donnie's arrest due to the Contempt of Court charge."

All I could do was shake my head. "I'd say Donnie has created more than his share of problems here. And all because he refused to follow a visitation schedule. It still doesn't make sense to me."

"The skip tracer told me the car license for the Blazer was to be renewed in March 1982. Century did not renew the car license themselves, so they do not know if Donnie got it licensed without title, he is driving with an old sticker, or somehow has a stolen license plate. Besides not being licensed, the insurance for the Blazer was held by the State Farm Insurance of Hondo. This coverage was cancelled August 1982, so he may be driving it without being covered by insurance. The leasing contract with Century expires April 1983, so it will be interesting to see where the car is finally located."

"He has been so busy juggling illegal activities and conning people out of money the car is the least of his problems," I responded.

Kate had more. "We've been able to check his bank records. On February 25, a savings account was opened at Hondo Savings under Patricia, Don, or Alex. Back on March 11 a $10,000 deposit was made into Donnie's bank account from an insurance company. In July they closed the checking account, and the savings account was closed in August."

"That's a good sum of money for someone who's not working!" I commented. "When you think about it, someone at the bank has to know where the money was sent, or someone came in to close the accounts on their behalf."

"We realize that," Kate said, "but right now we aren't going to pursue that avenue. We may leave that for the District Attorney. We have discovered Patricia's car, a 1981 Toyota Corolla, was leased through Christopher Crow Toyota. I have found the local pediatrician who saw the children. This showed up on the latest credit report we pulled because they were owed over $500. We'll pursue that lead only if we have to."

"By now I shouldn't be surprised by anything, but it never ceases to amaze me," I exclaimed. "These people are just leaving a path of destruction behind them."

"Aren't they though?" Kate continued, "Mateo provided Patricia's social security number, that has helped both the skip tracer and us. Mateo also explained to us that Garcia's are the children's Godparents, so they must be very good friends. We hired a retired San Antonio cop, currently living in Escondido, California for a few hours to go to the last known address of the Garcias. He found that they had moved. Don't worry though, we will find them also. We discovered the Garcias are being investigated by the San Diego County Sheriff's Office for a suspicious fire at their restaurant. This investigation was triggered by the insurance company."

"This could get really ugly especially since Mateo told you Patricia owes Garcias money and now, they have a suspicious fire? You just can't make this stuff up."

I was beginning to get over being shocked regarding the information Kate shared. Donnie and Patricia's actions were appalling. And when he met her, he claimed God had sent him an angel!

Kate continued, "Mateo confirmed he is going to contact the parents of several of the kid's friends. He is also going to take legal documents to the Phoenix court to see if they will place a hold on Patricia's child support check. He thought this might "smoke her out" since he knew she depended on his check."

"That is a good idea, as long as they go along with that. I hope it doesn't take a court order to get something like that accomplished."

"I hope not either, but he is willing to give it a try. Oh, before I forget it, will you please give me the kids social security numbers. We want to run their numbers also to see what might come up."

"Not a problem," I said, "you never know how deviant these people think."

After she finished sharing all this information, she said they were going to need another $1000.

11. Breakthrough

~ A noun referring to a sudden, dramatic, and important discovery or development~

Wednesday, October 13 was a major turning point. God had shown me the importance of contacting Mateo. For kidnappers it is easy stealing children when they are so young because they do not know how to use the telephone. In this case, it was one of Mateo's children.

Kate called and was bubbling over with excitement.

"We have a big break, Mary!"

"Great! What have you found out?" I could not wait to hear even the least bit of positive news.

"Mateo just called. His friend from Mesa called him to say her son had received a phone call a couple days prior from Brianna, Mateo's fifteen-year-old daughter. Brianna shared with him they were living in Escondido, California, going by the name of Fitzpatrick, and her mom worked at a big hospital. He asked if she liked school and she said they did. She told him they had a little brother and sister, her stepdad's two kids. This is more information than we've had in a long time."

"Yes, it is! My head is exploding with questions," I could hardly talk.

"I know. It's the break we have been waiting for. I must meet with Rich and strategize. I will keep you posted. Right now, I just wanted to share the news with you. I'll call back a little later."

My heart was racing, my hands were shaking. Breathe, Mary, just breathe. This was the best news we had heard in months. I was so excited I could not wait to call Tom to share the information. Naturally, he started asking questions that I could not answer. All I could tell him was that she promised to call back after they have a plan. That satisfied his inquisitiveness. Usually, I was able to compartmentalize and continue to work, but not after this call. I took a long walk outside to have a discussion with God. "Father, I don't know if we will be successful but please watch over everyone involved. Please let the children come home. I cannot do any of this without you. Please let this be the break we have been praying for. We all need to have this over."

After coming back inside, I went into my boss to share the news with him. At this point I did not know whether the information was going to lead to anything or not, but I needed to keep him aware, just in case.

Before the end of the day, Kate called. I had been sitting on pins and needles all afternoon.

"What have you decided?" I asked.

"Rich decided he needs to make a trip to Escondido to see what he can find out. I have made several phone calls and have verified Patricia works at the Palomar Medical Center in the Medical Records Department. She has worked there since the first week of July. Besides the hospital, he is going to check out some of the other addresses we have. We need to make sure you give your consent for him to make the trip since his expenses must be covered."

"Okay, but does he have a plan if he finds Donnie and Patricia?"

"He'll have one by the time he gets there. Oh, and we need another $500 to cover Rich's airline ticket, motel, and car rental in California."

"All right, you'll have it in a couple of days, but I hope you don't need the money before he's able to make the trip."

"No, we know you're good for the expense."

"Is there anything I can do from this end?" I asked.

"If Rich needs something, he'll call me and then I'll contact you. In the meantime, just sit tight." With that, she hung up.

"Sit tight?" There was no way I would be able to "sit tight." I found it hard to sit at all after Kate's very first call in the late morning. Knowing Tom would be eager to hear additional news, I headed straight home after work.

No more had I walked into the house when the phone was ringing. This time it was Mateo. He was so excited about hearing the news!

"I received a call a bit ago telling me your investigator is going to San Diego. I really hope they can find all the children. I'm so eager to talk with my kids again and I know you have to be more than excited to see yours as well."

"I'm excited for both of us, Mateo. It has been such a long time. I am so thankful Brianna was brave enough to call. I feel sorry for her if Donnie ever finds out she was the one that made the call that got us on his trail again."

"He'd better not lay a hand on any of my kids. He'll be sorry!" Mateo was seething with that thought.

"First things first, Mateo, we have to actually get our hands on them."

"The way things look, I imagine you should have your kids Friday or Saturday," Mateo speculated.

"I certainly hope so, Mateo. Thank you so much for all your help. We will continue to be in touch. I promise."

"Thank you, Mary. I may need your help when I try to get the kids from Patricia."

"Anything you need, Mateo. I'll be here for you."

Tom and I did not know if we should celebrate the good news or wait for the other shoe to drop. We knew Escondido was a large area and the investigator was going down to look around. I wanted to be overjoyed, yet I remained tentative. Donnie and Patricia were ruthless. Unless Rich got the police involved, I did not see a clear way through this adventure. Since all the warrants were in Texas, and none of any significance, the police were not going on a hunt for this man. It just seemed like a long shot, but all of us had to remain positive.

The following day I tried with everything within me to keep my mind on work. I was so fidgety you would have thought I had a bad case of ADHD. I stayed by the phone all day, anticipating the call, which came late afternoon.

"Mary, I just received a call from Rich, so I want to bring you up to date."

Rich left for San Diego last night so he'd be there early this morning. He went to the hospital first thing and started asking different personnel and departments if they knew Patricia Fitzpatrick. He decided they must be a tight knit group because before he knew it a security guard accompanied Patricia out to talk with him.

She walked right up to him and said, "I hear you're looking for me?" She was very condescending.

The security guard stood off in a distance while Rich talked with Patricia. She became very belligerent towards him, and her final words were, "I dare you to follow me home."

She spun on her heel and walked off with the security guard. Rich knew then he had to pull back. He left to call the police. He had not been gone long before returning to the hospital where he met a police officer at the front door. Rich explained the situation. Together, they walked up to the front desk.

"Is Patricia Fitzpatrick available? I'd like to speak with her," the police officer said.

The person at the front desk made a phone call.

"I'm sorry but they say she has left the hospital."

"Okay, then let me speak to the security guard," Rich demanded.

The same security guard came to the front desk where the three of them talked.

Kate continued with the story.

"The security guard explained that right after Patricia talked with Rich, he escorted her back to her office, where she asked him to stay. Patricia called Donnie, picked up her purse and a few personal items, and explained to the guard that her life was in danger and her husband was coming to pick her up. The security guard told Patricia to call her husband back to tell him which door she would be waiting for him. The security guard then escorted her to a back obscure door that was an emergency exit. Donnie came to the hospital, to the back entrance, and picked her up."

"You mean to tell me she got away?" I asked.

"Yes, she did."

At this point my emotions exploded and I unleashed my fury on Kate.

"I can't believe Rich blew his cover like that. All this money I've spent, and he blew it!"

"He didn't mean to. He was going to watch and follow her but the people at the hospital were very protective of her."

"I'm sure they were. She is a master fraud. She has everyone convinced I am the bad person here. Everyone protects her. Rich just fell into her snare and got caught. He never should have tried this alone. Here we were so close, and she got away."

I kept ranting. I could not settle down. Kate just let me keep going. I was sure she had experienced this before from other clients, but my frustration and disappointment had gotten the best of me. Once I settled down, she continued.

"Mary, we are all disappointed. Rich feels terrible, although he doesn't think there is anything different he could have done. She has a way of convincing people someone has been looking for her to do her harm."

"Right now, I am a little more than disappointed, I am devastated. I thought for sure I'd have my children this weekend."

"I know. I am so sorry. We cannot give up. We do not know, at this point, if they have left the city. Rich decided to hang around Garcias and see if they show up there. I'll call again in the morning."

I felt as though I had been punched in the gut. I was unable to talk to anyone. My work colleagues knew something had gone terribly wrong since I had raised my voice during the call. They all left me alone. They understood I was on an emotional rollercoaster. Unable to speak, I waited until getting home to break the news to Tom.

"I got a call from Kate late this afternoon." That was as far as I got before breaking down.

Tom took me in his arms and waited a few minutes.

"Okay, what happened?" Tom asked patiently while I got hold of myself.

I gave him all the details that Kate had relayed to me.

"Why did he go in alone?" Tom asked.

"I asked the same thing, except not that nicely. I got pretty upset with Kate, she knew I was terribly upset, everyone in the office knew I was upset."

Tom had multiple questions, but I had no answers. As late as it was, there was no one to call to inquire. Not that it would have done any good, for no one had answers at this point.

"Kate promised she'd call in the morning after talking with Rich. That's all I know."

I had been so upset since Kate's phone call I quickly downed two glasses of wine. Even that did not dull the pain. I had to get hold of myself. Once I knew I could talk without crying, I called my parents to share the news. Just like the rest of us, they found it hard to believe but we were not giving up hope. The rest of the evening was consumed writing questions. We did not want to miss any details when given the next opportunity to speak with the investigators.

Friday was another exceptionally long day, waiting for the phone to ring. Tom called twice to see if I had heard anything, as he was having problems as well. Mid-afternoon Kate called.

"Hello, Mary. I have been concerned about you. How are you today?"

"First, I must apologize to you, Kate. I had no right talking to you the way I did. I was just so upset. Please accept my apology."

"It's okay, Mary, I've talked with you enough to know that was not you, it was your emotions talking. I do not have children so I cannot imagine what you have been going through, but I know enough to realize it has been unbearable at times. And then for Rich to be face-to-face with Patricia, and not able to do a thing about it, must make it even more frustrating. All of us in the office are very discouraged. We have worked so hard trying to locate your children."

"I thought you folks might decide to drop me after the way I talked to you yesterday. You didn't deserve that."

"Oh, you don't have to worry about that. We are going to find your children. Rich talked with Sam several times today. They both feel you need to make a trip to San Diego to assist Rich continue with the investigation. How soon do you think you can get there?"

"I'm not sure. I will call Tom so he can start making reservations while I am driving home. I'll call you in an hour and let you know the arrangements."

"Sounds good."

Kate gave me the address and phone number of the motel where Rich was staying.

"I suggest you see if you can get a room at the same motel. It will make it easier for the three of you to communicate and get around town together."

"Okay. I'll be in touch soon."

Immediately, I phoned Tom to start making reservations for us: the airlines, car, and motel. I checked in with my boss as I headed out the door, telling him I would be in contact with him if I was not back at work on Monday. I prayed all the way home. "Lord, please open a window here. We need your help."

By the time I arrived home, Tom had all the reservations made and was busy packing. We were leaving Omaha at 7:15 p.m. arriving in San Diego by 9:45 p.m. Since I had little time to pack, Tom called Kate to let her know our itinerary.

"No matter what time you arrive, Rich wants to talk with you both. Call his room immediately. He'll be waiting for your call." Kate explained.

"Okay, we will. Tell Rich we should call about 10:30 p.m."
She gave Tom Rich's room number.

Once I was packed, we headed for the airport. Tom had been able to let his dad know our plans. Once we got to the airport, I made a quick call to my folks.

"Hi, Mom, I just want to let you know Tom and I are at the Omaha airport getting ready to head to San Diego."

"Did they find the kids?" She asked with excitement in her voice.

"No, but my attorney and investigator thought it best that we come down to help with the investigation. Maybe we'll stumble across something that would only make sense to me."

"Okay, well, good luck." She was very encouraging.

"It's going to take more than luck, Mom, to find these kids. It's going to take a miracle from God."

"I know, Mary. Just take care and call when you can."

We arrived at the motel by 10:30 p.m. and did as Kate suggested, we called Rich's room. He was waiting for our call.

"Meet me in the lobby in 5 minutes," he said.

We had no idea what Rich looked like, but he did not know us either. We were the only ones in the lobby at the time, when a very tall, thin man came walking up to us.

"You must be Mary."

"Yes, Sir, I am." I replied.

"Hello, Tom, nice meeting both of you. Let's sit down in the corner and I'll go over a few things that I know."

The three of us huddled in the corner as he explained how the Thursday encounter transpired.

"First, I want to apologize for the encounter I had with Patricia. Believe me, that was not what I expected. I understand you were pretty upset when you heard the news, Mary. Again, I'm sorry."

"I'm sorry as well. I have apologized to Kate. She was only doing her job. I am just hurting so bad. Once again, we were so close, and they slipped away. I'm terribly sorry for my tone."

"I understand. It's okay. I have to say, Patricia is good. She knows all the right things to say to get people to buy into her story. Everyone was convinced I was her ex-husband looking to do her harm. Naturally, that is the only story they have been told. She did not hesitate in the least regarding daring me to follow her home. In fact, she was egging me on. I have driven all around the building. The door they must have escorted her out is very obscure. You must know it is there to find it; it is only an exit. I have also driven past Garcia's home. I have not seen any activity there. Sam and I thought it best for you to come down. I only know certain facts and it would take me awhile to piece them together. You, on the other hand, might identify something immediately. Right now, I need your help. I know you must be exhausted after these last couple days. Go back to your room. Get some sleep. Let's meet about 8 o'clock, if that is okay with you?"

"Sounds fine. I doubt that I sleep much anyhow," I added.

With that, we went our separate ways until morning.

What a fitful night's sleep. I would awaken and lay there for the longest time thinking I was once again in the same city the kids had lived, only to have them disappear somewhere quickly, again. With seven people you would not think they could get anywhere fast without help. Were the Garcias helping them? Would someone at the hospital hide them? Who knew, by now they could be traveling across country again! "God, please help me tomorrow so I have a clear mind to catch even the smallest clue you set before me. I'm so tired, I need help!"

Ready or not, the alarm went off, and it was time to face another day. We met Rich in the lobby, got into his car, and he drove us around the immediate area. Driving around the hospital, he showed us the obscure door. He was right, you could hardly see it. Next, we drove around Garcia's neighborhood. It seemed like a typical California neighborhood, every house having a high fence in the backyard. You could not see kids playing if you wanted to. Most of the houses were two stories, good sized. Rich wanted to park the car to observe the neighborhood a bit. I am sure he did the same thing the day before. There was not much activity for a Saturday morning. You did not hear any children playing.

Rich decided to walk both sides of the street, knocking on doors, and asking questions. He wanted to know if I wanted to go along. I declined, but Tom volunteered to go with him. I watched as they would go up to a door, spend a few minutes, then turn around and leave, going to the next. To me, that would look suspicious. The only strangers knocking on your door on a Saturday morning are the Jehovah Witness Lay Missionaries, but you never know, someone might provide some information. When Rich and Tom finished going up and down both sides of the block they came back to the car.

"Did you learn anything?" I asked.

"No," Rich said, "no one is talking. I asked if they heard a lot of kids over in the Garcia's backyard and either they brushed me off as not being able to speak English or I got a quick 'No.' We won't find anything out here. Let's get some breakfast and think about what to do next."

After breakfast we decided to go back to the hospital. Rich thought that perhaps she might have gone back to work. It was Saturday but she had not worked at the hospital that long to have a Monday through Friday workweek. Rich knew what Patricia looked like, I was not sure. I had seen her briefly when she helped Donnie return the children from the 1980 visit, and the courtroom appearance in October 1981. We sauntered around the hallways, trying not to look suspicious. We went to the Medical Records Department. Rich went to the front counter and looked in.

"May I help you?" he was asked, as he scanned each of the desks.

"No, I must be at the wrong place," he said not wanting to arouse anyone's suspicion.

"She doesn't appear to be working today," Rich said. "Let's go back to the motel and see if Sam has any ideas."

"Okay, we're along for the ride," I said.

Returning to the motel we went to Rich's room and re-grouped as best we could. Rich called Sam.

"Good Morning, Sam, sorry to bother you on Saturday, but the Dietrich's have arrived, and I wanted to bring you up to date. We have been around the Garcia's neighborhood. We knocked on the neighbor's doors up and down the block, but no one is cooperating. We stopped at the hospital to see if Patricia was working. She is not. Do you have any suggestions?"

"You have nothing to lose. Go back to the hospital. Talk with as many people around the Medical Records Department as you can. Go for broke. That is what you are down there for," Sam suggested.

"Okay, we will. I'll keep you posted." Hanging up the phone he looked at us and said, "Looks like we're headed back to the hospital."

At the hospital we loitered around the Medical Records Department. Whenever anyone came through the door, Rich would follow them and strike up a conversation. Everyone he talked with; you could see them shaking their heads "No." No one was going to confess to knowing her from that department. We found the personnel office, Rich went in.

"I'm looking for Patricia Fitzpatrick. I'm a friend of hers from out of town and I was told you would know where I might find her."

"I'm sorry but she isn't here today. She had to leave early Thursday due of a family emergency."

"Oh, that's too bad I missed her. Will she be back Monday?"

"No, we're not sure when she'll be expected back."

It was obvious we were not going to get any cooperation from anyone inside the hospital.

"We aren't going to get anywhere here." Rich said. "I've got another idea. Let's go."

Piling into the car, Rich started driving up and down every row of the parking lot.

"What are we looking for?" I asked.

"If Donnie picked Patricia up Thursday, maybe her car is still here in the lot."

"Great idea," Tom said, "do you know what she drives?"

"We are looking for a newer Toyota Corolla Hatchback. I've got the car license number in my notes if we need to confirm the car."

It was a good-sized hospital but there did not appear to be a designated employee parking lot. Fortunately, it was Saturday so there were not as many cars as could have been. We were not having much luck, so he started driving the far edges. There, in the very back corner, all by itself, was a Toyota hatchback. Rich pulled up beside it, grabbed his briefcase, and started looking through his notes for the car license. After finding the note he was searching for, he let out a shout.

"Bingo! This is Patricia's car."

Rich checked the driver's door while Tom checked the passenger side. Dang, both doors were locked. Then Tom checked the hatchback. It opened! Only God could have made that happen for the doors were locked. "Thank you, Lord!" was my thought. With Tom being much smaller than Rich, he got the honors of crawling in through the back to unlock the car doors.

Before we got into the car, Rich gave us specific instructions.

"Go through this car with a fine-tooth comb. Get every piece of paper available. Even if it has chewing gum wadded in it. You just never know if it has a note written on it, letter head, or anything we can use."

The car certainly was dirty. Of course, transporting seven children around, who eat all the time, there was a lot of paper: on the floor, under the front seats, under matts, as well as stuffed behind the seats. We gathered every bit of trash. The only thing Rich left in the glove box was the registration. Once we had the car stripped of evidence Rich opened the hood. Reaching in, he grabbed some part. It looked important to me for it had wires hanging from it.

"Let's go back to the motel and digest all this material," Rich suggested.

As we were driving back to the motel, we were on a road that had a median between the opposite lanes of traffic where the grass was nice and green. Rich made his way to the far left lane, rolled down his window, and hurled the car part into the median. Shocked at what he was doing, I turned around and saw it bouncing along in the grass. I was not quite sure of his motive but knew we would find out.

We went to Rich's room to start digesting what we found. First thing Rich did was call Christopher Crow Toyota, the car dealership leasing Patricia's car.

"Hello, would it be possible to speak with the general manager, please?"

"Hello, this is the manager."

"Good, my name is Rich. I am a private investigator working on a case involving Donnie and Patricia Schumacher. I am aware Patricia leased a 1981 Toyota Corolla Hatchback through your dealership. Our skip tracer has indicated the Schumacher's have not made payment for several months and basically, you've no idea where the car is located. I just want to let you know I have located your car. It is sitting in the Northwest corner of the parking lot at the Palomar Medical Center in Escondido, California. I want you to know you will need to dispatch a wrecker to pick up the car, as the car is not drivable. I removed the distributor cap from the car so the Schumacher's could not come back and drive the car away. I'm sorry for any inconvenience I may have caused you but, at least, you'll get the car back."

"Thank you for the information, I'll check into it."

After hanging up, Rich joined us with the task at hand.

"Okay, one problem solved. What have you identified from these scraps of paper?"

Speaking up first I said, "Here's a pay stub for Don R. Fitzpatrick at Ralph's Grocery Store, so it does confirm the change of names as well as where Donnie worked. Although it doesn't provide the grocery store address."

That part was disappointing, but I knew Kate could find this out.

Tom added, "I have a letterhead for Little Ducklings Daycare in Escondido. Maybe this is where they had Jennifer enrolled."

"We have an address and phone number for Mrs. Garcia," I added.

That was good for we knew they had been in contact with one another. Rich had a library receipt. We knew the kids were by themselves most of the days, so the library had to be within walking or biking distance from their house, providing we could find the house.

I piped up, "I've been studying this deposit slip for Texas Central Bank. These numbers do not add up. They must mean something. Just give me a minute. It was not long before I exclaimed, "I think I've got it."

I rummaged through my notebook for I wanted to confirm what I saw before I said anything.

"Yes, this is Alex's social security number! Let me see that check stub from Ralph's, please."

Rich handed me Donnie's check stub from the grocery store. I started comparing number.

"I've got it. He is using Alex's social for employment and checking account. Great, I wonder how many credit applications have been made using Alex's social?"

I knew that would be a fight for another day.

Tom added, "Here's a check stub from McDonald's. It looks like Patricia is now going by Trish. With no more money than this shows, she had to be working part-time."

"This last piece of paper seems to be a paper carrier's new customer sign-up for delivery. The name written here is Sofia. Is she old enough to deliver papers?" Rich asked.

"Yes," I confirmed, "she should be around fourteen. She's the next to the oldest and, I believe, one of Patricia's and Mateo's adopted children."

For a Saturday we had a productive day, but we were not finished yet. Rich wanted to drive past some of these addresses to see how far apart they were. That might give us some idea as to the vicinity of their home. Our only map was the generic map supplied by the car rental company. There was no such thing as GPS so we had to do the best we could with what we had. This generic map only showed the major streets.

"Mary, will you please mark the significant locations as we get to them? I know it's not the most detailed map, but it'll serve the purpose," Rich asked.

"Sure, no problem," I replied.

Rich wanted to start at the hospital, a known address. Just as we drove into the parking lot a wrecker was leaving with Patricia's car.

"Great," Rich exclaimed, "at least one thing gets returned out of this mess."

From the hospital we went to Little Ducklings Daycare. It was not far from the hospital. Of course, it was closed since it was Saturday. Rich pulled around to the back of the building, stopped the car, and got out. He peered into the garbage bin, reached in, and pulled out a large sack of trash, walked around to the back of the car, opened the hatchback, and threw the trash into the car! Great, day old garbage from a daycare! The rank smell quickly filled the car.

"Monday I'll have Kate call to verify the two kids were here, but in the meantime, maybe we can find something out from the trash. Did you know you can find out a lot of good information from trash?" Rich explained.

"No, I haven't made that a practice," I added, "but, isn't it stealing?"

"No, once it's in the receptacle it's fair game. It no longer belongs to Little Ducklings."

"Um," I thought. This could get interesting.

Finding the nearest grocery store Rich drove to the back of the store, parking next to the trash receptacle. We all started sorting through garbage. Rich admitted it was a long shot since his confrontation with Patricia was Thursday. The school may have thrown some of the kid's things out Thursday or they are waiting to hear the status of the children's return before removing any items. The items in this garbage would have been Friday's waste. His hunch was right, we did not find anything worth keeping. After that experience, we needed to return to the motel to wash up before starting again.

Before the afternoon ended Rich had a couple things he wanted to complete. First, we drove past Garcia's house again. Still no activity. He asked me to mark a proximity on the map. The next location he wanted to find was the library in Escondido for the book receipt we had found in the car. That took several inquiries, but we managed to find it. There, again, he wanted me to mark the approximate location on the map. So far, the map had four marks: the hospital, the daycare,

Garcias, and the library. It was not a big area but, again, this map only had the major streets identified.

"The only other places we haven't found is Ralph's Grocery Store and Texas Central Bank," Rich interjected. "How about we grab dinner and call it a day. Based on the map, I can look up the locations for the grocery store and savings bank and see how close they might be with the map. We can check on them tomorrow or let Kate pursue it Monday."

We grabbed a bite to eat and headed for the motel. Emotional exhaustion had taken over all of us.

"Let's meet for breakfast about 8:30 tomorrow morning," Rich suggested.

"Sounds fine with us," Tom replied.

With that, we headed to the room and collapsed. My body was tired, but my brain continued processing information. This trip seemed déjà vu to our Devine trip, so close but like grabbing a handful of sand, it slips right through your fingers.

Since it was Sunday Tom and I did not know what the day might bring, but after spending the previous day with Rich you did not have to wait long before there was a plan. We met Rich in the motel lobby for breakfast, he already had the day planned out.

"Before striking off for the day, I want to call the newspaper first," Rich suggested.

We went back to his room, where he made the call. It was interesting to hear him work.

"I'm looking for the phone number of Sofia Sanchez, my newspaper delivery person."

"Oh, I'm sorry, she is no longer a carrier for us."

"Really, do you have the name and number of the new carrier?" Rod asked.

"Sure," he said, "not a problem. I'll look it up for you."

They gladly supplied Rich with the new carrier's name and number. Rich called that number.

"Hi," Rich said, "I'm looking for Sofia, my newspaper carrier. I missed her today."

"Sofia had to quit because she's going to a private school and couldn't deliver in the mornings anymore," the kid shared.

These people had no idea how they had been set up.

"That's too bad," Rich said, "I have something for her. Can you tell me where she lives?"

"I don't know for sure. Somewhere between Price and Baseline Drive, but I'm not sure."

"Thank you very much. I'm sure I'll find her."

After completing the call, he was excited.

"We've got all day to drive around," he said, "let's go."

For everyone else this would have been considered a Sunday joyride. For us, we were on a mission. Rich had located the streets on the map. We started at Price and just drove up and down the streets of Escondido. Basically, we were looking for a red Chevrolet Blazer and/or a lot of kids outside playing. My eyes were scanning back and forth, from one side of the street to the other. We were making a weaving pattern traveling up and down the streets. I noticed a U-Haul truck in the upcoming block but did not pay much attention for we were not near the streets the kid had mentioned. It was obvious this family was moving for they had furniture sitting in the front lawn waiting to be loaded. As we drove beside the house something caught my eye.

"Wait, Wait, **Wait** a minute!" I shouted.

"What's wrong?" Rich sounded concerned.

"That's my furniture!"

I was so dumbfounded I could hardly talk.

"Are you sure?" Rich questioned.

"I'm sure. That's the furniture I left behind with Donnie when we separated."

"Okay, you have to be 100% sure. I am going to drive by again and I want you to look closely. I can't be too conspicuous, so I'll just keep driving at our normal pace."

Rich drove back around the block as I paid very close attention. I told him I was sure. The men loading the furniture were Hispanic so that threw us a bit. Rich looked around the area, located a higher area a couple blocks away and headed that direction. He parked the car on the side of the street facing the house. This provided us good visibility of the house, where we could keep everything under surveillance. After watching for several hours, from what we could determine, there were no children and no Blazer. Rich had a small pair of binoculars. Tom and Rich took turns trying to determine if Donnie was assisting with the move. During the timeframe we had been there, only two men were loading the truck and they were both Hispanic. Rich surmised it was perhaps Mr. Garcia and one of his friends. We had watched for hours, knowing that once the truck left it returned anywhere from 45 minutes to an hour later. We needed a break, so we went for coffee.

As we were sitting relaxing, if you could call it that, Rich came up with a plan.

"I think we need to go into the house. It is not going to work unless I have a complete buy-in from both of you because it will take all three of us. I am going to pose as a real estate salesperson looking for a home with you, my clients. Now, the trick is, IF the kids are in the house, we are going to abduct them. Mary, you need to grab Jennifer quickly and run for the car as fast as you can. Tom, I need you to grab Alex and run for the car. I'll run interference and get to the car myself and we'll take off."

Rich fixed a cold stare into my eyes.

"Do you think you are strong enough to do this?" he asked very sternly. "I don't mean physically strong. What I am asking is I cannot have you breakdown in the middle or it is over for all of us. We do not know if there are other people in the house or whether they have a weapon. You cannot stop and think, you must be able to just do! Now, I will ask you again, can you?"

"I can do it." I said boldly, as my knees were already beginning to shake.

"Okay, we'll go back to our surveillance point and when we see the truck leave, I'll pull up close to the house. Let me do all the talking." Once again, he sternly looked into my eyes, "Are you sure you're okay?"

I must have looked distraught. I am sure my face was ashen as I was scared to death. I nodded my head "Yes," for I was petrified.

We did not sit in the car long before the truck headed out.

"Okay, here we go," Rich commanded. "Mary are you still in?" he asked.

"Yes, I'm ready," I had to be. We were moving in.

Rich pulled the car close to the house, facing the corner. He wanted to be able to jump in the car quickly and take off around the corner, if need be. He shut off the car and we got out. My heart was ready to leap out of my chest. We walked casually to the door. There was no sound of children. Rich knocked. A Hispanic lady came to the door. She said something in Spanish.

"You speak English?" Rich asked.
She motioned with her hand, little.

"Hello, I'm a realtor and see that you are moving. My clients need a place to live quickly and we were wondering if you own this house?"

"No, people here had to leave quickly. We only friends helping move."

"Do you know who owns the house?"

"No, but I can ask my friends."

"Okay, I can find that out also. Do you mind if we look around?"

"No," she said, "go ahead. I must keep packing. Much to do."

"I understand, keep packing. We're fine looking around ourselves."

It was obvious there were no children and she was the only one in the house. We all sauntered to one of the back bedrooms.

Rich proceeded with very strict instructions.

"I'm presuming this is Mrs. Garcia. I am going to run interference and keep her occupied. I want the two of you to look everywhere for anything you can get your hands on that proves the kids were here. Stuff your pockets. You must work fast. We can't get any charges on Patricia until we can prove her as an accomplice."
With that, Rich walked back to the kitchen to occupy Mrs. Garcia.

My head was swimming. My blood pressure had to be through the roof. I had just recovered from a mental abduction and now I had to steal. This was not in my DNA!

Tom and I started in the master bedroom going through dresser drawers and nightstands. I looked in jewelry boxes, finding a couple pictures of the kids. Whatever little piece of paper that had any names on, we took. In each of the kid's rooms we did the same thing. Little drawings on the wall, we took. In the kitchen there was a chore list on the refrigerator that had the kid's names on it. Rich asked if the refrigerator stayed. Mrs. Garcia said she thought so, walked over to the refrigerator, took the chore list down, crumpled it up, and threw it on the floor. When Rich had her turned around, I picked it up and stuffed it under my shirt.

"Have you seen enough?" Rich asked us.
We nodded our heads "Yes."

"Okay, thank you so very much for letting us tour the home even though you are working so hard. This is a nice house, I'm sure my clients will love it here!"

We got into the car and drove off. I was a nervous wreck as we headed to the motel to see what we had collected.

It was amazing how much paper we accumulated. Quickly, it became obvious my kids were using their middle names as their first names. Everything for Alex was identified as Matthew and for Jennifer it was Lynn. Patricia's kids were using their real names. I had even managed to get several pictures of my children.

Not even realizing it, we had an Employee Discount receipt from Ralph's, confirming Donnie using Alex's social security number and an employment name for him of Don Fitzpatrick. Rich called Ralph's Grocery Store.

"Hello, is Don there? I am a friend of his from out of town just trying to connect with him. He told me he worked for you," Rich inquired.

"Don usually works Monday, Wednesday, and Friday mornings but he called on Friday morning to say he had an unexpected death in the family and wasn't sure when he'd be back."

"Oh, I'm so sorry to hear that. I'll try to catch him another time."
Interesting!

It was clear we were not going to make it home for work in the morning. I quickly called my boss to let him know I would not be returning as planned. At this point, I did not know when I would be back. I would have to call him later. Tom made a quick call to his dad letting him know the same. Next, I needed to check in with my mom.

Everyone we talked with kept asking questions but all we could say was that it had been a very frustrating trip, but we would have to let them know later, when we got back home.

Once we digested all the information, we got a bite to eat and headed back to our surveillance spot. These people were relentless. It was obvious they were going to keep at this until they finished. All the furniture had been moved during the daylight hours. Now they were loading boxes. The last thing to go out was the trash. They turned out the lights and everyone got in the truck.

"It's too late to unload that truck tonight. I'm sure the truck will be at Garcias overnight."

By this time, it was close to midnight. We had been watching another six hours! My head was still attempting to process all the facts from this unsettling experience. Thursday morning Patricia went to work thinking their tracks had been covered in Texas, only to run into Rich at the hospital. They had to take off again grabbing a few clothes and leaving. But where? How do you explain "running" to teenagers, let alone young children? Now, they were down to one car, unless more friends were helping them. How do you put nine people into one car? You know they left without taking time to think. What clothes would you grab? All their household goods were being stored, somewhere. I felt like I was committing a crime myself as I would have abducted my children had they been at the house. I stole items that did not belong to me. Is this how the world works? I was trying to put it all together. All I knew was that I had to ask forgiveness. "Lord, please forgive me, for I stole things and snooped into private areas. My soul is full of guilt for what I have done, but I had to do it. I trust that you will forgive me for doing what I felt I had to do. I pray that through this, you have given us more clues into finding the children."

We sat in the car longer, watching Donnie's house, making sure Garcias did not return with the truck. Nothing was going on. We were less than two miles from Garcias so Rich drove to their home. We sat on the street a while, waiting to see if anyone was still coming or going from the house. The truck was parked in front of their house. All seemed quiet for the evening.

Rather than go to the motel, Rich drove back to Donnie's house. He turned off the car lights before pulling into the driveway. He pulled extremely close to the garage door and turned off the motor.

"Tom, help me load the garbage into the car."

"Okay."

They both jumped out. Tom opened the hatchback and Rich started throwing in bags. Garbage filled the back. The last bag went to the side of me.

"I wish we could get into the house," Rich stated.

Tom chimed right up, "I'm in construction and I have my Lincoln master key. Let's see if it works."

"Mary, get in the front seat and stay in the car. Tom and I will see if we can get in. If you see a patrol car hit the horn lightly."

How do you hit a horn lightly? Fear started swelling from the tips of my toes to the top of my head. I could feel my heartbeat in my ears!

The guys bounded out of the car. They were on a mission, breaking into a house! Rich had his flashlight and Tom was right behind him. Tom put the key into the lock. It worked! No! You must be kidding me, they are in! I prayed, "God, I am amazed at what you are doing here." I started shaking all over. Now we are breaking and entering! I could see the flashlight bouncing around in the different rooms. Oh, if one of the neighbors see this, we will all end up in jail. A car started coming down the street. Please, Please, Please, do not be a patrol car! I ducked out of sight and held my breath. Whew, once the car got to the streetlight, I could see it was not a police vehicle. Will you guys please hurry? Please, please hurry! There cannot be much left in the house. The stench of garbage had overtaking the car and was permeating my nostrils. Such a rank smell. I thought I was going to be sick.

Good, I could see the flashlight coming to the front of the house. The door opened, Tom locked the door behind them, and they came to the car. What a relief! I could start breathing again. I had never been so scared! Today had stretched me beyond my limits. I never dreamt of doing so many unlawful things, enough wrong today to last a lifetime. This had been a Sunday I would never forget.

The guys had been successful picking up more papers. Our evening was not finished. Rich drove behind a Kroger Supermarket to the trash receptacles in the back of the store. Here it is 12:30 a.m. and we are going to sort trash! Each of us took a bag. Before we opened the first garbage sack Rich gave us orders.

"Just as before, keep anything that has any names on it. Do not take time to read it. I do not care if it has food on it, keep it! We can sort later. We need to get through this quickly. Hopefully, a patrol car won't come through while we're doing this."

I certainly agreed with that statement. Our gleaning of trash went quicker than anticipated. Three giant bags took diligence, especially with the night security lights. Once complete, I did not want to touch a thing! Just get me back to the motel. Rich asked us to keep all the material in our room so we could look it over if we wanted. Rich knew any piece of information would trigger something with me before it would him.

Once into the motel Rich told us he was going to get up early, head for the Garcias, and follow the truck to the storage area. That sounded like a plan. The first thing on my mind was to get in the shower!

Tom and I were too wired to go to sleep, so we started looking at the mound of papers we had confiscated throughout the day. We stayed up until 4:30 a.m. looking through them. It was for sure we had enough evidence to prove the children had been there. Donnie had kidnapped them and was holding them hostage and Patricia was an accessory to the kidnapping.

Even though Tom and I went to bed at 4:30 a.m., for me, getting some sleep after this day proved to be hopeless. While Tom was still sleeping, I snuck out to the lobby for some coffee. Rich came through the front door looking tired and dejected. He came over and sat beside me.

"I got to the Garcias too late, the truck was already gone," he was frustrated.

We were all exhausted after yesterday. He sat beside me and asked if we had gotten some good information. I shared that we had. He wanted to look at it when Tom woke up.

"Today is Monday already, I need to check in with Kate and give her a list of calls to make for me. Let's meet in your room in an hour."

"Sounds good. I'll get Tom up."

Rich came to our room so he could look over the treasure of information. He had talked with Kate and brought her up to date. He had also talked with Sam, asking if he could get a warrant issued for Patricia for aiding and abetting. It would be helpful; in case someone ran into her again.

Monday turned out to be a day for phone calls. Kate worked swiftly from Rich's directions and reported to him all her findings.

"I called Little Ducklings Daycare and they were very cooperative. They told me that during the summer they did have two little kids. Blond hair, blue eyed, Matthew and Lynn Fitzpatrick, ages three and six. Once school started Matthew no longer attended. Last Thursday afternoon Donnie came to the school and took Lynn out of school early. He seemed very agitated. He did not explain why he was taking her out early, and she didn't return to school Friday or today (Monday)."

The next task Rich had given her was to find the U-Haul facility Mr. Garcia used.

"First, I identified all the U-Haul truck rentals within a 20-mile radius from Garcia's home, and started calling each of them to see if a truck had been rented by Mr. Garcia on Sunday. I was successful locating the rental facility they used." She gave Rich the number. He called, impersonating as a police investigator, and talked with them directly.

"I understand you rented a truck to Mr. Garcia yesterday," Rich asked assertively.

"Yes, the truck was rented for a 24-hour period and it was returned with 33 miles on it. Mr. Garcia paid for the truck rental."

"Okay, thank you for your cooperation."

With only 33 miles on it, the storage facility could not be too far. We just were not sure of the number of round trips the truck made. While we were watching them, the truck had moved three times.

One of the papers we had confiscated had a receipt for Shepherd Christian Academy. Kate called and spoke with the principal, impersonating as the police.

"We are attempting to locate Patricia and Donnie Fitzpatrick. I understand you have had six of the Sanchez/Fitzpatrick children enrolled at your school."

"Yes, we do. On Thursday, somewhere between one and two o'clock, Donnie came to the school and removed all the children. All the kids were upset. They did not understand why they had to leave. Donnie was very upset and gave no explanation to the principal, the teacher, or the children."

"Who is listed as the emergency contact number?" Kate asked.

"Anna Garcia."

"What is the monthly tuition for the kids?" Kate asked.

"The tuition is $325 per month for the six children," she volunteered.

"Are they current?"

"Well, they still owe $500 for the initial enrollment for the children."

"Thank you so much. If you hear from them, please give me a call."

Rich called the Garcias. Mr. Garcia answered and said he had no idea where the Fitzpatrick's could be found. Last he knew they were in Escondido. He thought they were having a family issue but was not close enough to them to know the nature of the problem. It was interesting that during this call he spoke exceptionally good English but on Sunday his wife pretended to only speak a little English!

Since we had the savings account number, Kate called Texas Central Bank, posing as Donnie's wife inquiring about the balance of the account.

"I'm sorry but that account was closed last Thursday."

"Okay, thank you for your help."

Rich called the real estate person regarding the rental property where they lived, impersonating as a police investigator.

"Did you rent the property at 8212 del Rio Drive to Don and Patricia Fitzpatrick?"

"Yes, I did, starting in June."

"Was the rent always current?"

"Yes, it was."

"Did Mr. Fitzpatrick pay by check?"
"No, he always paid with cash."
"Do you realize they have abandoned the property?"
"Ah, no, I had no idea."
"You may want to check it out."
"Okay, thank you. I'll get right on that."

By mid-afternoon we decided we had done as much as possible for this trip. Rich had been in contact with Sam regarding the information we had acquired. Sam was trying to get a court date with the presiding judge to see if a warrant could be issued. Rich asked Tom and I to return to San Antonio with him for the court appearance with the judge. Flights were made for the following morning. By the time we checked out of the motel Tuesday morning I paid for two motel rooms, (one for 5 nights, the other for 4 nights), two car rentals, meals for three adults, and now three plane tickets. I did not want to think about it. I could not think about it.

Once back in San Antonio we went our separate ways. Rich said he'd call when he knew the time of the hearing. Exhaustion permeated our bones, plus the disappointment that, once again, we returned empty handed.

My aunt and uncle opened their home up to us once again. It was exhausting just trying to explain some of the things we had been through while in Escondido. I also called mom to let her know the highlights of our adventures. No one needed to know how low we really stooped to get some of this information. Rich called later to say court was set for 10:00 a.m. on Wednesday morning. We were to meet at the courthouse by 9:30 to share our findings with Sam.

Even though I was exhausted, I could not sleep. The kids had to be so close, but we were unsuccessful carrying out the plan to locate them. I had visions of seven children in that small house trying to play, the six kids trying to get themselves to school on three bikes, visions of Donnie storming into the school demanding all the kids leave, packing everyone into one car, drawing out their money from the bank, and heading out of town. Where would they go? They had to have friends helping them. I could not imagine them staying with

Garcias, for they were logistically too close. They had to get out of town, but where?

Bright and early the next morning we arrived at the courthouse. Rich recapped our five days in Escondido with Sam. Once we arrived, we showed Sam some of the more important papers. Sam picked several he wanted Rich to present to the judge. Time for court. Here we go again. This was the same judge that was deceived by Donnie's lies into thinking he was such a concerned father only wanting to see his kids an extra week. This was going to be interesting.

She was furious when she remembered who we were; that we missed the children by 30 minutes when presenting her Writ demanding the children be turned over to the sheriff. Her anger turned into compassion when she heard we had just returned from California empty handed, again.

Rich explained how they slipped away and presented her with the papers and pictures we had confiscated, as well as explained the name changes, and Donnie's use of Alex's social security number. Tom and I did not have to say a word. There was no question in her mind once Rich finished his presentation. She immediately ordered a court document be typed issuing a warrant for Donnie's arrest for kidnapping. With the stroke of the same pen, she terminated Donnie's parental rights until such time he submitted himself before the court to fully explain his actions. "Thank you, Jesus! This is what we'd been waiting for." After two and a half years someone finally saw through the intent of this man's heart besides me!

We left the courthouse with a signed copy of the warrant for Donnie's arrest. The courthouse would send the order to the police station where it would be entered into the NCIC (National Crime Information Center) data base. Now, no matter where Donnie is, he can be arrested and put in jail. Our next stop was the police station. Sam, Rich, Tom, and I spoke directly with the police chief. Sam knew the chief so explained to me that I did not have anything to worry about, the chief would help. Sam explained everything, including our two failed attempts at recovering the children as well as showing him the papers proving a name change and use of Alex's social. Rich explained his encounter with Patricia and how defiant she was to him.

The chief pulled in the state's attorney and they agreed to charge Patricia with a Conspiracy Charge. This way, she would never be able to slip out the back door like she did in Escondido.

Hallelujah, now they both had been charged. Only problem... finding them!

Prior to leaving the police station, Rich thanked us for all our help.

"I couldn't have gotten this far without both of you," he said complimentary. "Together, we made a good team."

Before he went his separate way, he continued.

"I've talked with Kate and these last few days have been awfully expensive. We'll need another $2,000 to continue."

His words from our first conversation screamed in my head, "We've never been successful finding kidnapped kids because the client runs out of money before we run out of leads."

"Rich, I'll write you a check now but please do not cash it until I get home and move some money. I'll call Kate when she can cash it."

"That won't be a problem, Mary, I trust you."

I am sure Sam was wondering about his next payment also. After all, he had just spent his entire morning with us.

Finishing everything possible for the time being, Tom and I caught the first flight home. Arriving home late, the phone rang. It was Mateo.

"Hi, Mary, please tell me the news. Do you have your kids?"

"No, Mateo, I don't." I was very tired and dejected.

"What went wrong?" he questioned. You could hear the disappointment in his voice.

"The investigator's visit at the hospital went terribly wrong and before he knew it a security guard escorted Patricia to him. She was very belligerent, but the investigator had to back off. In the meantime, Donnie swept in and picked her up, took the kids out of school, and disappeared, again. We did locate their house and found Mr. and Mrs. Garcia busy moving everything out."

"Garcias were doing that for them?" he asked.

"Yes, they were doing all the work. I cannot tell you where any of our children are at this point. I would guess Garcias know but they cannot be trusted. If Patricia really owes them $15,000, they will stay on her good side and do whatever she asks of them. It is too bad they are involved in this mess, but they are in deep at this point. I know you think they are your friends also, but I do not believe that. Why would you help a friend disappear? It should make you question what is really going on. Garcias have to know there is something about those two little kids of Donnie's that is upsetting everyone. They should be able to figure out there must be a good reason I'm looking for them."

"I'm sorry, Mary, but now my kids are moving again and out of school."

"Yes, they are, but we did get a lot of good information. I am sure Kate will share the name of the school the kids attended. It was a private church school. I intend to call and talk with the principal once I recover from this ordeal. I feel sorry for all the children. I am sure all of them got questioned as to which one of them said something. I hope the kids' band together for if Donnie discovers which one made the call it will not be pretty. Oh, a couple more things, Mateo, Donnie has changed his name to Don R. Fitzpatrick, and there's a warrant out for his arrest for kidnapping."

"I'm concerned! He better not lay a hand on any of my kids."
I could hear his anger boiling in his throat.

"Donnie has a bad temper and I'm sure they have all seen him in action. I trust they all stick together and protect each other by not saying a word."

"Thanks, Mary. I'll be in touch."

It did not take Mateo long before getting back to me, he called late the following evening.

"Hi, Mateo, what's up?" I asked.

"You're not going to believe this but right after I finished talking with you last night, I started getting harassing phone calls. The phone would ring, I would answer, and no one would be there. If I did not answer, it would ring insistently. Tonight, it started as soon as I got home, only this time I did not recognize the voice, but they were shouting obscenities at me."

"Do you have any idea who's behind it?"

"Sure, I do. And you do as well!"

"I'm sorry, Mateo. They had to figure out you were the one that helped me. If the calls persist you can call the police and notify the phone company," I explained.

"I'm ready to get an unlisted number." He was exasperated.

"Please don't do that yet. We may need to put a tracer on your phone. Start keeping a log of these phone calls. If the phone company needs to track them, they will be more willing if you have a log. The phone company will want to give you a new number but insist on a tracer instead. Besides, you don't want to disconnect your current phone number in case one of your kids tries to contact you."

"You're right. I will just put up with it for a while longer. Maybe they will get tired of this game," Mateo said.

"I certainly hope so. You just don't know who they have working with them."

"I know. That is the bad part. It might end up being people I thought were my friends."

"Exactly, since Donnie had a PO box number, I'm sure Garcias will be picking up the mail for them. We may have to track your child support checks if we can get cooperation through the Arizona system, but we do not have to worry about that just now. Keep me posted as to how it goes, Mateo. Again, I'm so sorry."

After the emotional trip to Escondido I was physically and mentally exhausted, so I stayed home from work the rest of the week. I could not get away from the deluge of questions that raced through my head.

If the warrant is issued in Texas how will the Escondido police find out about it?

What if Patricia issues a stolen vehicle report on her car?

If Donnie is arrested will he be extradited back to Texas for a hearing?

Since this is such a minor offense, will anyone take it seriously?

Have the schools been contacted?

Since Patricia is not a US citizen would they run to Ireland?

Has Texas filed fraud charges against Donnie?

Who has been covering for them?

Who is making the calls to Mateo?

When was the fire at Garcia's business?

Has Century filed a stolen vehicle report?

Can we get hold of Donnie's final telephone bill in Escondido?

All day long, 24/7, this was all I could think about. We were so close, twice! But returned empty handed, once again.

Kate called late Friday afternoon

"I have a little bit of news for you," she said. "I'm still calling storage facilities in Escondido in hopes of finding one rented to Garcia. The best news of all is that I have the number of the warrant that has been issued for Donnie's arrest. Now, it's really official!"

"That is great news, we've needed that to happen for a long time. I've heard from Mateo and he started getting harassing and obscene phone calls yesterday."

"I'm not surprised. Please relay to him not to change his phone number. He has to keep that line open; not only for his friends but also his kids."

"I've already told him that. I know, it is ridiculously hard when your phone keeps ringing constantly. You know who it is and cannot do anything about it. They have several in the family to keep the game going."

"Mary, I also want you to know I've contacted the Christian school the children attended. They will let me know if there are any inquires on behalf of the kids. They know they will not get paid for the delinquent charges so doubted if they will hear from Donnie or Patricia directly. Oh, before I hang up there is one last thing. We need another $1000."

"I'll get it in the mail. You should have it by the first of the week."

Once I hung up it hit me like a freight train. This payment was it. There was nothing left. My savings was gone, my car was gone, my furniture was gone, AND my children were gone! Everything - gone! Despite having a good job, it was not enough, I could not make money as fast as I was writing $1,000 checks. And that did not include five-day trips to cities and attorney fees. If nothing shook loose from this last payment, the investigators would have to put the case aside until I saved enough money for another payment. The facts were stark, the picture was starting to look bleak. Rich's words from our initial conversation continued screaming in my head, "We've never been successful finding kidnapped kids because the client runs out of money before we run out of leads."

Out of the blue Friday night, Arlene calls. I had not heard from her for a long time.

"I haven't talked to you for a long time. How are things going?" she asked.

"I'm fine. Have you heard anything from Donnie?"

"I haven't heard from him for a long time," she said.

I filled her in on the trip to Escondido and that he had changed his name. She grew quiet.

"I just don't understand it," she continued, "he was not raised this way. I do not know where I went wrong. I have been so upset with this entire thing. I know how he acts and how he is when he does not get his way. He can have a terrible temper. I raised him to know right from wrong. He knows God, so he must know right from wrong. I know he did this because he felt threatened, but to do illegal things to get your own way does not make anything right. He has to realize he won't continue to get by with this."

"I'm sorry but I might as well tell you, before we left Texas there is now a warrant out for his arrest."

"Oh, Please! Do not tell me this. Why has it come to this? How could you do that to him?"

That last question set me back. Is this now my fault again? She cannot blame me for Donnie's actions, can she? If I were in her shoes, I know I would feel bad, but I would be looking inwardly as to where I went wrong raising him. We all have free choice, and he chose the wrong path. Perhaps, though, this has been part of the problem for a long time, she thinks her son can do no wrong.

Once I overcame her last startling question I answered, "It came to this because he kidnapped the children. Besides, he never abided by the rules for each of the visits or followed the decree. I beg you, if you ever hear from him try to persuade him to turn himself in and turn the kids over to the authorities. It could be that simple."

"Well, Mary, I'm not going to rest easy until you have those kids back."

"Neither will I," I said.

The feelings of helplessness and hopelessness reigned supreme from the top of my head to the bottom of my feet. The end of the journey was in front of me unless something changed.

It was difficult walking into church Sunday. The pastor knew we had made a trip to California. He did not have to ask. He could discern from the look on my face that we had come home empty handed, again. I was going through the motions of life as though this was normal. Maybe it would become the new normal. At this point I had no idea. It was up to God.

Being so disillusioned after our return, I knew I had to regroup and get myself together before Monday. It was imperative for me to jump right back into my job when I returned. How were my bosses going to handle this? This would make another week I had been absent. Losing my job was out of the question. I prayed, "Lord, I can't do this on my own. Please, pick me up and carry me along until this is over."

Monday, I headed back to work. I attempted to smile as I walked back into my office, but it was difficult, I did not feel it was at all genuine. Co-workers welcomed me back but did not ask many questions. I knew my boss had filled them in when I failed to return after that first weekend. No one had a remote inkling of what I had been through and all the illicit activities I had been an accessory to while in California. No one would believe me even if I told them.

Several days passed without hearing a word from anyone. It was the last week of October. Time was ticking away. Not being overly patient these days, I called Kate, I had several questions.

"Do you have anything new?" I asked.

"No."

"What about Donnie's phone?"

"We haven't tried."

"Did you call the school?"

"No, and we haven't heard from them either."

"Has Rich talked with Garcias again?"

"No."

"Have you contacted the San Antonio District Court?"

"No."

"Do we need to call the Escondido police to let them know Patricia's car was repossessed, just in case they file a stolen vehicle report?"

"No."

"Have you been able to get any of Donnie's phone records?"

"No"

"Did you notify the highway patrol?"

"We did call the State Highway Patrol in San Diego, but an APB for the Blazer won't be out until the middle of next week."

"Will we know if Garcias rent another truck?"

"No."

"Did you talk to anyone at McDonald's?"

"They said they were going to fire her anyway."

"Can your skip tracer find out more from Master Card and Visa?"

"This would have to come through California, and nothing has been filed there yet."

"What about Texas Central?"

"Mary, I'm sorry but we have not found any new information. We have not followed up on any of your questions. These are little side issues that will not assist us in reaching our destination. Having another state involved closes a lot of doors we have available here in San Antonio. We have talked here in the office and if we pursue these little situations it will only eat into your funds quicker and may produce information but not a reliable lead. We know you have spent a lot to get where we are currently. The guys have come up with what you would call a "Hail Mary." This is perhaps our last attempt to locate Donnie. I'm sorry but we have run out of good solid leads."

My heart skipped a beat, for she just acknowledged they were out of leads.

She continued, "Currently, I'm locating all the storage facilities within a ten-mile radius from Donnie's home in Escondido. Once I am sure I have them located, I am going to create a Wanted Bulletin to send to each of the facilities. In addition, we also plan to send the bulletins to any place Donnie and Patricia may have had dealings: the hospital, Ralph's Grocery, Texas Central Bank, the kids school, the U-Haul truck rentals, Hidden Ranch Recreation Center, basically, anywhere we had a place of business identified from the vast amount of paper you guys collected while you were in Escondido. I must ask you now, before we get further down the road with this idea, the bulletin will offer a $1000 reward for information leading to the arrest of Donnie. It will not say anything about returning the children, it is only for Donnie's arrest. Are you willing to pay this?"

"Have you used this tactic before?"

"No, but it's our last shot."

"Okay, then yes, if we get Donnie arrested, we'll surely get my children."

"All right then. We will proceed with our plan. The Wanted Bulletins will be sent out the next day or two, arriving in the Escondido area the first of the month. Don't worry, I'll continue to call and check in if something comes up."

12. 11:59

~ A noun referring to God making you wait until the very last minute before He completes His work ~

After returning from Texas Tom and I were emotionally drained. The last six days had been like riding a terrifying roller coaster; up a steep hill only to plunge into the valley. A lot of positives came from the trip, such as the warrant for Donnie's and Patricia's arrest, but now they had fled once again. Unless something new broke open, the investigators had no more leads.

Disappointment filled every crevice in my body. Every day depression sucked me deeper inward. The feelings of emptiness and hopelessness were consuming me. In my hopelessness, I needed God now more than ever. This I knew! "Lord, let Your peace return once again! I need to feel hope! You know my circumstances are dire. You are my only answer."

I felt like I had two separate minds within me, the one that could function at work and the one that was weak! Thankfully, I was able to jump right back into my job when I returned, head down, never coming up for air. After being gone another week I had so much to catch up on. Sleep was non-existent so I would take work home, starting on it as soon as dinner was finished and working until my eyes would not stay open.

Conversations between Tom and I were strained. For months, our conversations revolved around swapping ideas of leads to follow up on or questions to ask. Now we had no more leads. The trip to San Diego had drained our stamina. At this point in time, we both lacked the drive to persevere. We had turned over every rock we had stumbled upon, only to find a morsel of a crumb leading to the next crumb. Crumbs were not enough sustenance to continue.

I looked at my Bible and knew there were words of comfort within the binding wrapped around the multitude of pages, but I had no idea where to look. I prayed, "God. Are you hearing my prayers? I feel like all I do is cry. Have you left me? I feel so alone! Are you protecting the children?" In my desperation, I opened the Bible about in the middle, looked down and started reading Isaiah 43:1-2.

Do not fear, for I have redeemed you; I have called you by name; you are Mine! When you pass through the waters, I will be with you; And through the rivers, they will not overflow you. When you walk through the fire, you will not be scorched, nor will the flame burn you.

"Thank you, God! Thank you for your answer! I have been through the waters BUT I have NOT drowned. You have led me through the fire BUT I have NOT been burned. I must continue to put my trust in you. Please let Your peace return to my soul. I know Your hand is upon me. You have rekindled my hope!"

Even though all the circumstances around me were telling me otherwise, I held onto these verses. "I'm not going to drown and I'm not going to burn!" Multiple times throughout the day I would repeat these words, for I knew God was working out all things and no harm was going to come to us.

The last Friday of October, mid-afternoon my boss called and wanted me to meet him in the vice president's office. My heart sank. As I left my desk and started walking toward the VP's office, I knew I was going to be fired. My mind was spiraling out of control! I could not understand it because I had met every deadline they had ever given me. I had been back to work a week and I was slowly catching up. I just could not get it all done in just a week. I cried out, "Oh, Lord, help me!"

Walking into the VP's office I encountered three levels of management. I was petrified. My heart was pounding out of my chest. "Please, Lord, don't let them fire me!" All the men were standing but no one was smiling. The Senior VP stepped forward.

"Mary, we know you have been going through an exceedingly difficult time. We want you to know everyone in the company is behind you. We want you to have this."

He handed me an envelope containing two cards. I pulled out the first card and read it. The inside and back were filled with signatures and personal notes from employees in every department. I opened and read the next card. I could not believe all the people who had sent their wishes. Enclosed in the second card was a check for $300. Tears filled my eyes. These were not tears of sadness or distress, but for the outpouring of love and compassion from my colleagues.

"We are so very sorry," the Senior VP said. "We passed around an envelope and everyone contributed to your cause. Please accept this gratitude from us."

By this time, I could not hold the tears back any longer. They each hugged me. I wanted to say more but all I could utter was, "Thank you." My immediate boss offered to stay with me while I got hold of myself. The other two excused themselves for a cup of coffee so I could have a moment to regain my composure. They were all such good people, everyone in the office cared about me and my situation.

Tom was very touched when I got home and showed him the cards and money. This was the first time anyone had done anything like this for us. Although, I had never been through a more desperate situation in my life, it was extremely humbling knowing my friends and co-workers had provided what they could on my behalf.

My depression was impacting my relationship with everyone. My mother called one night. I explained what the people at work had done. I tried to put my emptiness into words. I was crying and she started to cry.

She commented, "I know how you feel."

Hearing those words, I exploded. "No one understands how I feel!" And I hung up on her. From the moment those words leapt out of my mouth, I regretted my actions. She was only trying to help. My pain was so deep there were no comforting words going to reach the depth of my despair.

What bothered me to my core was the way parents treated their children in public: screaming at them, spanking them, grabbing them, calling them names. It made me sick to my stomach. If they acted like that in public, I could only imagine what went on inside their homes. My heart ached for those children. They did not ask to be born. Children are not always going to be perfect, but they all require love. I desperately wanted to go over to the parent and ask them how they would feel if their children were taken from them. But I could not.

The first week in November crept along like pouring dried glue from a container. Seven days seemed more like thirty. I could keep up my work, but while at work I really did not want to converse or socialize with anyone. My immediate boss grew concerned about me personally, for I was not acting normal, as well as being curious regarding the investigation. He called me into his office just to encourage me to share, for he sensed something was terribly wrong. He coaxed me to tell him the latest plan of my investigator.

"You have to realize, there isn't a plan," I explained. "This is it! They have no more leads. There are no more ideas. Nothing! And, on top of that, I have no more money to continue. We are finished!"

"I'm so sorry, Mary. I had no idea it was that critical."

"I don't blame you for asking. You wouldn't have any idea just how dire the situation is at this point."

He was first and foremost concerned about me as a friend, for my demeanor had changed. There were two ways this could go: either I would take off again after another phone call, or I would be settling into a stable working routine. Funny, stable I was not! I could not give him any promises. All I could tell him was that IF Donnie were to get arrested, I would have to leave.

Once I would get home, I was very much into myself, unable to share my feelings or thoughts. Sleep was sporadic at best. The nights were long and filled with memories of my smiling, cheerful, beautiful children laughing, playing, giggling, dancing in my head. Jennifer's laugh was exhilarating. Alex's smile came from deep inside lighting up his blue eyes. Then I would see them walking down the airport ramp. Looking at me with haunting eyes asking, "Why do I have to go?" This recording kept replaying in my head, over and over.

God promised in His word that I was not going to drown or burn, but I had to have a SERIOUS conversation with God. I put it pretty plain, "Lord, the holidays are coming, and I don't see how I'm going to make it through them without my children. At this point, I am giving it to you. We have done all we can. There is nothing left. I would rather know my children are dead than to never know where they are. I am at a point I can accept their death. What I cannot accept is them growing up thinking I deserted them. I am a good mother. My children never deserved this." I did not feel better but through my lips I said it - I would rather know they were dead than to never know where they were. Both options would provide a lifetime of agony, but with the first option there would be closure. And that was what I desperately needed at this point.

Even though I told God I was giving Him the situation, I knew I did not completely turn it over, for as soon as I finished praying, I started worrying again! Yes, as far as the investigation was concerned, we had done all we could. But the images of the children's faces were etched in my brain. As I lay in my bed, after I had prayed this prayer, in my mind I heard very clearly, "*Oh ye of little faith*!" Immediately I found myself praying again, "Lord, please, please forgive me. I am trying so hard to put all my faith in You for the children's return. My faith has never been tested like this before. Please accept my frailty as a human and my love for my children. I just find it hard to let go 100%. I also realize it was not fair of me to put an ultimatum on you. I am so sorry! Help me, Father, for I am a mess! But I do not want to fail you. I'm so weak, I need you!"

Kate had given me the phone number of the Shepherd Christian Academy. I needed to talk with someone regarding the condition of my children, so I made an appointment to speak with the principal Monday, November 8.

"How was Alex, I guess you knew him as Matthew? Was he well? Did he seem adjusted?"

"He seemed okay to us. Incredibly quiet. Very thin. In all honesty, we were all suspicious of this situation. Here you had five older kids, dark skin, different last names, and then you had 'Alex,' blond hair, blue eyes. The whole situation did not fit if you know what I mean. All six kids rode to school on three bikes. The three oldest drove the bikes with the three younger kids on the back. We had a problem with Carlos which required a home visit. It was during that time we found out about a younger sister, also blond hair, blue eyes. At that time, we were told that Matthew, I mean Alex, and Lynn were theirs and the other five were adopted. People just don't do that sort of thing, you know."

"My only concern is that I get my two children returned to me. They have been gone now for seven months. I beg you to please call me if you ever hear from Donnie or Patricia again. If any school asks for their records to be transferred, please let me or the investigator know. This has been a horrific experience for me. I cannot imagine what those kids are going through. Would it be too much to ask to set up a time that I may talk with Alex's teacher?"

"No, let's plan to do it this afternoon after school. Call back at 4:00 p.m. to my office and if she can't be here, I'll let you know."

"That will be great. I have one more question. The investigator has sent a Wanted Bulletin for Donnie's arrest. Have you received it?"

"Yes, I have. I promise I will call you or your investigator if I have any information. They still owe us $500 for the enrollment fees for the six children, so I doubt we hear from them directly. We may get an inquiry from another school and if that happens, I'll get as much information as possible."

"Thank you, that's all I can ask."

As usual, the day inched along but I was able to speak with Alex's teacher after school.

"Alex was doing well, a quiet student but no problems academically. He had very dark circles under his eyes. I did not know if he was sickly or did not eat a healthy diet. Alex made a comment that Daddy reads the Bible to him at night. Of course, we never know if that's the truth or kids have been told to tell us that. There was one thing unusual I noticed about Donnie and Patricia. Of course, I noticed it because I am taking a trip to Egypt next August, so I have been doing a lot of research about the area. Both Donnie and Patricia wore necklaces with a scarab beetle set in gold. That is highly unusual to see anything like that around here."

"I thank you for your time. I do hope you have a wonderful trip."

"It was good talking with you. I trust you locate your children."

Naturally, I immediately had to look up the meaning of a scarab beetle. I discovered the scarab beetle is also known as the dung beetle. In ancient Egyptian religion the scarab was a symbol of immortality, resurrection, transformation, and protection. In more modern times, the bug symbolized the rebirth after death and was used to protect the wearer against evil. That is a far cry from Donnie's religious beliefs while under Francis's teachings. Although their beliefs were a little over the top in some areas at least they believed in God, the creator of all things, and the Bible teachings of His son, Jesus. It sounded, to me, that Donnie had cast those beliefs aside and started worshiping idols.

My cousin, whom I seldom talk with, called to voice her concern regarding the children.

"Have you considered going to a psychic? I have the name of an exceptionally reliable one in Omaha."

"No, I really haven't. I'm not sure I believe in them," I commented.

"I've been to this one a couple times and she seems to know what she is doing. What else do you have going for you? It's for sure you don't have anything to lose."

"Give me the name and phone number and let me think about it."

She gave me the information. I did give it some thought. What did I have to lose? Maybe $100, but with everything I had spent so far this was nothing. We still did not have the children.

After work on Tuesday, November 9, I gave the psychic a call. She inquired as to my intent for an appointment. She explained a little about her charges and I ended up making an appointment for Thursday after work. I kept justifying it internally that it would not hurt anything, I had nothing to lose except a few dollars.

Tuesday night I became so convicted I could not sleep. My stomach churned with the decision I had made. The Bible verse from Isaiah kept coming back to me over and over all night long: you will not drown; you will not burn. Then I heard the message again, very clearly, "***Oh ye, of little faith!***"

Immediately, I asked God to forgive me. Again, I was grasping at straws. Anything and anyone to help find my children. But the one I needed to continue holding onto was God. This was His second warning. I was not going to take a chance of doing it again. My faith was in God, not in a psychic. I prayed to the Lord again for His peace and strength. He was the only one capable of turning my hopelessness into hopefulness.

First thing Wednesday morning, November 10, I called and cancelled the appointment.

"You will regret this. I guarantee you that," the psychic said.

"I'm sorry but my belief in God will not allow me to put my trust in you. If I am ever going to get my children back it will be because of God, not you."

She was not happy and hung up the phone abruptly.

Later that afternoon Kate called with an update. They had talked with the assistant manager at Ralph's Grocery asking how Donnie picked up his last check. Kate was told to call personnel, which she did but they would not talk with her. The same happened when she called McDonald's. No one knew about Patricia's final check and would not cooperate. The telephone had been disconnected with a $72 credit. That check had been mailed to the address in Escondido. Of course, that was the PO box number so Kate knew Garcias were picking up the mail. The director from the Hidden Ranch Recreation Center had called in response to the Wanted Bulletin. He indicated Donnie had tried out for a softball team but lacked skills and was told he would not play much, so he quit. The director also knew they had seven kids, as well as knowing Garcias. He supplied Kate two more names of storage facilities in the area. He volunteered that Donnie did not look like the picture on the bulletin; now he was balder and no beard. He inquired of Kate when he could anticipate receiving the reward money. She told him that the information given must lead to the arrest of Donnie. If his information was successful, then he would receive the reward. Kate said the call seemed like he was seeking some revenge on Donnie. She explained to me that is common when you offer money for information.

Later Wednesday night I called my cousin to say I had cancelled the appointment with the psychic and the reason for the cancellation. She was sorry to hear that.

"I know she could have helped you. You will probably regret this," she said.

Great! This is the second time I have heard this!

"Sorry," I said, "I just can't."

That was all I could say. It did not deserve any further explanation.

HOPE WITH GOD And A MOTHER'S LOVE

Thursday night, November 11, my cousin called again, filled with excitement.

"I went to see the psychic today since you wouldn't. She had so much information. I had been praying about it all day exactly how to tell you. I first called your mother to see if you would be angry at me for going and she said you would not. I just want to share with you what the psychic told me."

You will get the kids back.

Look in the Southeast.

She saw them near water in Columbia, Columbus, or Virginia.

Look at a warehouse. They left something behind.

Look at private or parochial schools.

Jennifer had a bad throat. Look at hospital records.

Donnie is very intelligent but he is desperate for money.

I was extraordinarily strong, but I was in so much hurt and pain she may not have been able to help me. She might not have been able to see past the pain.

My mother would have been a better source.

Give your cousin all the love and support you can. She needs it.

If she isn't pregnant, she soon will be. It will help the pain.

I thanked my cousin for her concern, but I was trusting in God to perform a miracle. I had not seen or heard from my cousin for over a year and I did not expect to hear from her again.

Friday, November 12, we finally received a copy of the Wanted Bulletin from Kate. She had been so busy sending them out, she forgot to send a copy to us. It was dated October 29, so they had been out about two weeks now. I knew I would hate to see a write-up like this appear from someone looking for me!

We are looking for a suspect who has kidnapped his two children from his ex-wife. The suspect uses several different names, Donn Schumacher, Donn Fitzpatrick, and Donn Sanchez. He has since remarried and there is a felony warrant for the arrest of both he and his current wife. His wife's name is Patricia, she speaks with an Irish accent, silver frosted hair, 5'8" average, slender. Schumacher is

5'11" tall, full beard, black hair, receding hairline, and may wear glasses.

Schumacher has been residing in Escondido, California, and we have reason to believe that the suspects have left the Escondido area on October 14, 1982.

A friend of theirs, Juan Garcia may have rented a storage shed on October 17 for their belongings. Please check your records for this name also.

In addition to the two blonde, blue-eyed children that were taken, Schumacher and Patricia have five additional children, all dark complexion.

Schumacher, his wife and the seven children were last known to be traveling in a 1980 Chevrolet Blazer, Autumn Red in color which still may have Texas car license plates.

Should you encounter Donn Schumacher, or his wife Patricia, please contact the San Diego County Sheriff's Department or call us collect at the number listed below.

A $1000 reward is offered for information leading to the arrest of Donn or Patricia Schumacher.

Donn Schumacher a/k/a
Donn Fitzpatrick
5'11"
200 pounds
35 years old

Tom, upon receiving the bulletin, immediately wrote down every alias for both Donnie and Patricia we had seen being used, along with their social security numbers, the social security numbers for Alex and Jennifer, their birth dates, physical descriptions, as well as the charges that were pending against each of them and took this information to the Lincoln Police Department. Tom requested the information be run through the NCIC computer system to see what charges were outstanding on both Donnie and Patricia.

We were assuming they would find a bench warrant for contempt of court, parental kidnapping charge, grand theft motor vehicle charge, and unemployment fraud on Donnie. For Patricia there should have been a conspiracy charge for child stealing. Much to our surprise, the only charge that came up was a Violation of Custody Family Offense on Donnie. That did not sound important enough for any office to waste their time pursuing.

Talk about being disappointed. Were things ever going to turn around? Up to this point, I had paid for the lawyer, the investigator, and all the court appearances only to find nothing. Is the judicial system built to help the criminal or the innocent? Thoughts were swirling through my head that I was being penalized for following the law. How bad does it have to get before anyone takes notice? Anger was spewing from me. Perhaps Donnie was right all along, he knew just how far to go before getting into real trouble, and there was not one thing I could do about it. Coming to my senses, I realized this was nothing more than my depression showing through, my very own pity party, the weariness in my bones was talking. I needed closure, but I **knew** I would not drown nor would I burn. So, I picked myself up believing in God's word. I had to look up and not at my circumstances swirling around me.

Sunday afternoon, November 14, my parents came over for a visit. Mom was concerned about me because I had sounded extremely depressed over the phone. I admitted ... I was. I guess I had every reason to be depressed. I truly felt like I was out on this limb all by myself and it was being sawed off behind me.

When Mom got me aside, she said,

"I've received several calls from friends and relatives asking about the kids and how you were doing. They are hesitant to call and bother you, so they call me instead. Everyone always says to give their best to you, and they are praying for you."

Rather sharply I responded, "Well, that is all appreciated, but from my perspective it looks and feels like no one cares. Tom's folks refuse to talk to me. Maybe Tom keeps them updated at work, but they want to guard the family name. If Tom does not bring it up, I doubt that his dad asks any questions. I can understand why no one wants to talk. It is an ugly situation and there is no guarantee it will change. Everyone moves on with their lives. I feel like I'm stuck in quicksand and being slowly sucked down."

The world seemed to be against me and here I was taking it out on my beautiful mother! I apologized to her for my harsh comments and hanging up on her during our last phone conversation. It was totally wrong of me to take this out on her.

We showed my folks the Wanted Bulletin and brought them up to date. Really, there was not much news to report, we were in a holding pattern. As Dad and Mom were leaving Dad pulled an envelope from his jacket and handed it to me.

"Mom and I want you to have this. We know it has not been easy, but we want to help in some way. We have helped the other two kids at different times when they were struggling so now it's your turn. Don't worry about paying it back, it's a gift for you to use."

Hugging them both, I thanked them and walked them to their car. Once we were back into the house, I opened the envelope. There was a check for $2000! I could not believe it. My dad never lends or gives money to anyone. He toiled, saved, did without all his life to have what little bit they had put away in savings. I was never aware of gifts/loans given to my brother or sister. It never mattered. For Dad and Mom, this was a Big Deal. It was a Big Deal for me as well! Tears streamed from my eyes for I knew my dad, and this was truly a gift of love. He was never one to show affection outwardly, but I knew how much he loved me. I also knew why he gave it to me as they were leaving, otherwise we all would have been in tears. My dad was an immensely proud man, I do not remember ever seeing him breakdown. He knew his limitations.

It took me a couple days to put my thoughts together.

Dear Dad and Mom,
I guess I have been putting this off because I never felt I would be able to come up with the right words to explain how we feel. The money you gave us to help find the children left us in a state of shock. We know how hard one must work to make any money today, we know you worked many hours for it. We just cannot thank you enough for your gift. The Good Lord must have been speaking to you for we need it.

There are times we feel like we are going through this all by ourselves but realize that is not true. Your hearts hurt as bad as ours. Today it is so hard to understand why we must go through this, but I am sure our faith is stronger because of it. I only wish other parents would realize how fortunate they are and would treat their children accordingly. God's precious gift should never be taken for granted.

And another thing that should not be taken for granted are dear and lovely parents, as you. Your sacrifice and caring are something we will always remember. The same gentleness and unconditional love you showed me as a small girl, I still feel as an adult. You have stood by me through every problem I have ever encountered. I love you so for that. You have been such an inspiration to me. I trust I can pass that along to our children. Tom and I are grateful to have such wonderful parents as you. May God richly bless and keep you.

All My Love,
Mary

Tuesday, November 16, Kate called sharing some exciting information with me. She had received a phone call from Larry Dillon, the resident manager of a mini-storage facility in Escondido.

"I'm responding to the Wanted Bulletin. Are you the person I should be talking with?" Larry inquired.

"Yes, I am. Do you have information regarding Donnie Schumacher?" Kate asked.

"Well, not about him directly but a Mr. Garcia did rent two spaces on October 17, one space was 10 X 20 and the other was 5 X 10. The phone number on the application is Garcia but I have already confirmed the address of the nearest relative is fictitious. The monthly payment is $58 per month and Mr. Garcia paid in full through the end of November. The next payment is due December 1. If that payment is not received by December 12, I will put a lock on both spaces. My wife and I reside within the confines of the storage facility, so we have full visibility of these two storage units. The facility is open from 6 a.m. to 7 p.m. seven days a week. The gate is locked at 7 p.m. and no one is allowed in after hours. We will be closed Thanksgiving Day, so no one will have access throughout the entire day."

"That is wonderful information. Thank you so much for calling. I want to reiterate to you that the reward is for information leading to Donnie's arrest. I want you to know this is indeed a legitimate reward offer, so please call again if you notice anything. We don't know if Donnie will return for his possessions or Mr. Garcia, but in either case, please give us a call." Kate stressed this to Larry.

"I will call if I see anything regarding these units," he promised.

"In addition, I want you to be aware that the picture on the bulletin is older and I've been told he currently does not have a beard and he has a more receding hairline," Kate explained.

"I appreciate the update. I will do whatever I can to help. I just can't imagine someone kidnapping two little children," he sympathized.

"Mary, this at least gives us a timeframe to work with," she said. "Think about this. Seven people fled Escondido on October 14 probably with only the clothes on their backs. Today is November 16. Can you imagine? It has been a month without any of their personal items. They had to find a place to live or they are living with someone. They have nothing themselves. I am sure the storage unit was rented for the minimum amount of time required to find a home, and now they will be eager to get their clothes and belongings. I bet we hear something by the end of the month."

"I certainly hope so, Kate."
I know I sounded desperate. I was desperate!

She also shared that she had called the San Diego County Sheriff's Office, in San Diego, that morning. They still had not received any information regarding Patricia, so Kate provided the Texas warrant number for them. Kate told them they should see the warrant come across the NCIC by evening.

Kate had more information to share. Kate said she had sent a Wanted Bulletin to the realtor who had rented the Escondido home to Donnie. Naturally, the realtor was calling to inquire about the reward. The realtor shared that Donnie had called a week or two after they had left and told them his wife's ex-husband had threatened to kill them, so they had to leave immediately. Since they did not have time to clean the house, Donnie told him to keep the $300 deposit. The realtor explained the house was left in a mess.

Kate asked, "Does Donnie owe you anything at this point?"

"No," he replied.

Kate thanked him for the information.

"Mary, do you remember Mateo telling us that Patricia owed Garcias $15,000?"

"Yes, I do. Although I did not think you found it important," I added.

"Well, at the time I didn't because obviously they are friends and lent money to Patricia. What makes all this interesting is the skip tracer has been investigating the Garcias. It seems the Garcias owned a restaurant. There was a fire at the building this spring and the insurance company initially thought it was due to faulty construction, now they are treating the fire as arson. What makes it worse is that a fireman lost his life in this fire. The Garcias may not be squeaky clean here either."

"I really don't understand how these people sleep at night. My mind cannot come up with these things. I guess it takes a criminal to know a criminal. I feel sorry for the fireman's family, especially if the fire was intentionally set."

"That's all we have so far," Kate said, "I'll call in another couple of days."

"Okay, thanks!"

Thursday, November 18, true to her word, Kate calls with another update.

"I've talked with the District Attorney in Hondo. He thought the stolen vehicle charge for the Blazer would be in the NCIC system tomorrow, Friday."

She was happy about that.

"Garcias haven't received any questionable or collect phone calls. The arrest warrant on Patricia, for accessory to child stealing, was on the NCIC system today." She went on to explain, "I called Mrs. Garcia, posing as a UPS delivery person, having a package for Patricia. Mrs. Garcia told me they were just out of town and if it is important, she could get it to them. She had a new phone number for them, so she'd give them a call to see if she needed to pick up the package herself."

This confirmed Garcias knew where Donnie and Patricia were staying. It was pointing to the fact they might still be in California.

She continued, "Rich has talked with the manager of the U-Haul facility where Mr. Garcia had initially rented the truck. Of course, they had received the Wanted Bulletin so were eager to help. They were wanting some of that reward money. The manager and Rich came up with a plan to cover all scenarios. Rich also knew an investigator in San Diego and had inquired to see if he would be available to follow a truck, if need be."

Kate needed to know if I would be willing to pay another investigator.

"Rich worked with this investigator before. He charges $30 per hour and 30 cents per mile."

"Technically, if we get down to that point it means someone is following the truck to the 'lion's den,' so, yes, let's use him if we have to," I agreed.

Another Friday afternoon and I am sitting at my desk, thinking of yet another week gone by. No real breakthroughs had occurred this week, just more information gathering…crumbs Next week would be Thanksgiving, so I presumed not much would transpire.

The phone rings, startling me out of my deep thoughts.

"We've got 'em!"

The person on the phone talked so fast and with such a high pitch voice I could not understand what they said or who it was.

"What?" I asked.

"This is Kate. Donnie and Patricia have just been arrested!"

"You have to be kidding me!"

I shouted loud enough everyone around me turned to stare. God had answered my prayers! "Oh, Thank you, Jesus!" As my eyes welled up with tears, I told Kate, "Please, tell me what happened."

"Mrs. Dillon called to let me know what had transpired. Donnie, Patricia, and one of the girls arrived in a Ryder truck late this morning and started loading the things from the storage sheds. Larry meandered around the area to make sure it was the correct storage numbers and see if he recognized Donnie. Sure enough, it was, so he came back to the house and called the police. Once the police came, Larry went back down to observe what was going on. Donnie and Patricia denied everything, but that did not deter the police. They were both handcuffed and put into separate cars. The police asked the little girl if she needed a ride somewhere and she said, "No," that she could walk. The handcuffs were removed from Donnie and Patricia just long enough for them to put their items back into the shed. Once the truck was empty, the handcuffs went back on, and they were put into separate cars so they could not talk to each other. Larry then put our padlock on the sheds and pulled the truck out of the way. We have the keys for the rental truck secured in the office, so someone will have to come inside before moving the truck. That is what I know for now. I had to call you immediately with the good news!"

Now the tears were in a free fall down my face. "Thank you, Kate. I must get home! I'll call you in an hour to see what you and Rich have planned for the next steps."

"Okay, I'll wait for your call. We'll know more by then."

Before taking off for home, I had to call Tom. My hands were shaking as I dialed the number.

"Donnie and Patricia have been arrested! I'm coming home and will explain when I get there."

He could not believe it either. He started asking questions.

"I don't have time to talk now. I must get home. We'll talk then."

I ran into my boss's office to let him know I was leaving. He already knew something was up as there was a huge commotion on the floor. Everyone was cheering and clapping as I walked up the aisle.

"I don't know when I'll be back." I told him.

"It's okay, Mary, just go get your children. Call me when you can."

All the way home I was crying and thanking God for answering my prayers. It would not be long before I would see my babies again! "Thank you, Lord! Thank you!" I could feel hope firing up within me.

I flew in the door, hugging Tom! I was so excited I could hardly contain myself. We sat at the table and I told him everything Kate had told me.

"What do we do now?"

"I'm not sure. I told Kate I would call as soon as I got home, so I guess I will start there. We need to make a list of people we must call." Tom started making a list and I called Kate.

"Hi, Kate, do you know anymore?"

"No, I don't. You guys need to get to San Diego tonight. First, you must get to the bank, before closing, and get a cashier's check made out to Larry Dillon for $1,000. First thing in the morning, you must go to the storage facility and talk with Larry and his wife. After that you should make a trip to the San Diego County Sheriff's Office. They will give you directions and information from there. Mary, Rich has decided he is not going to make the trip to San Diego this time, so you are on your own. It should be as simple as picking up the children either with police assistance or at CPS (Child Protective Services)."

"Okay, I'll go to the bank while Tom makes flight reservations for us."

"Rich talked with Sam. He should be calling you before the end of the day."

"Since it's Friday, I guess I'm hoping to call you Monday with my children here at home with me."

It sounded too good to be true!

"I hope that for you also, Mary. Keep me posted."

"Oh, I will."

As soon as I got off the phone I rushed to the bank before closing. As I was driving, my thoughts were about my folks, what a blessing it was they gave me money, or I do not know what I would have done. Thus far I had refused to borrow money. My folk's gift would be used to cover the reward. God was supplying my needs! I reached the bank just before the doors closed. Fortunately, I had all the information written down for the check. As the clerk was making out the check, my stomach was in a knot. This check was as promised, for information leading to the arrest of Donnie. He had been arrested, but that was all we knew. "Oh, Lord, I hope and pray this next step is simple." The last $1000 would be allocated for plane fares, car rental, and a couple nights motel costs.

I was a little nervous making this trip on our own, but as Kate said, it should be as simple as picking up the children from the officials. By the time I got home the flight reservations, car rental, and motel reservations had been made. Two days should be ample time for this trip. We did not have much time to catch our flight to San Diego, but it would put us there 9:30 p.m. I threw clothes into my suitcase and packed a change of clothes for each of the children.

Just as we were ready to walk out the door the phone rings. It was Sam.

"Mary, I've talked with the sheriff's office. Both Donnie and Patricia have been booked without bond. That is a good thing."

"What does that mean, Sam?"

"That means they cannot post bond to get out of jail immediately. They must get on the court docket to appear before a judge. Once they appear, the judge will set bail based on the offense and the likelihood of Donnie fleeing again. In this case, that is likely. Once bail is set, Donnie and Patricia will be calling friends and family to find someone to post the bond for them. It is usually not an overnight process. Once I find out the assistant state's attorney assigned to the case, I will call them and provide the background information. Now, you need to take your certified copy of the Separation Agreement, the Divorce Decree, and the Texas Writ. You have to be able to prove you have legal custody of the children."

"Oh, thanks, Sam! I hadn't even thought about that!"

"I've provided the sheriff's office with your investigator's phone number. They will be checking in with Rich for a complete briefing. In addition, I called the Medina County Sheriff in Hondo. They were going to make a call to the San Diego Sheriff. I am giving you my home phone number so you can call if you run into any problems. Now that Donnie and Patricia have been arrested it should be a matter of the police or CPS picking up the children, you prove you have custody, and you all get to come home!"

"Thank you, Sam. I hope it is that simple. We'll be in touch."

My head was trying to absorb everything I had been told the last couple of hours. "Thank you, Lord, that we took that call before leaving. Otherwise, I would not have taken the legal documents required to get my children!" Breathe, Mary, just breathe!

I did not have time to make any additional phone calls before leaving the house, we headed straight for the airport. We arrived at the gate just as the doors to the plane closed. Great! This is not getting off to a good start. Tom was able to rebook the flight, but we were not going to leave Omaha now until 8:30 p.m. and not arrive in San Diego until 1:30 a.m. Now I had a couple hours to make some calls. First call was to my folks.

"Mom, I wanted to let you know Donnie and Patricia have been arrested!"

"Oh, thank you Lord!" she exclaimed.

"Tom and I are on our way to San Diego. I will have to call you later and let you know what is happening. Right now, I don't know much. The investigator is not going with us, so we will be working directly with the police. Keep praying, Mom, it's not over yet!"

"Don't worry, Mary, I will."

Tom had called his mother while I was at the bank. I decided to call Arlene.

"Hi, Mary, how are you?"

"I'm fine. I wanted to let you know Donnie and Patricia have been arrested." There was a gasp on the other end of the line.

"Oh, Dear Jesus, no!" she shrieked and started sobbing.

"Tom and I are on our way to California. I don't know much at this point, but I can call you later when I know something."

"Thanks," she said abruptly and hung up.

Her reaction confused me. Didn't she really want me to find my children? Deep down she had to know this was not going to end well for someone: Donnie, the kids, or myself. There were no winners here. I knew I caught her off guard. Mercy, the news caught me off guard as well.

My stomach was in knots while we waited at the airport. I could picture Donnie sitting in jail with his superior attitude. I am sure he thought he would be able to outsmart everyone and get away with this. It came down to the fact that I had a good job so that gave me financial backing, I had married Tom so he was able to handle the household expenses, and above all else, I had God on my side. I had been holding on to the promise I was not going to drown, and I was not going to get burnt. That was His promise to me. It did not mean I had not been in the fire on several occasions! God was heating me up like gold, purifying me as I went. Each trip to the fire I was getting closer to God. I knew that one of the turning points was when I cancelled the appointment with the psychic. God knew then I put my total trust in Him! I just knew it deep in my soul.

Tom had to call the car rental company and motel to let them know of our late arrival. Tom looked at me and said, "It looks to me like you need a drink!" We found a place where we could relax a little. Time had moved at torpedo speed since the initial call at 1:00 p.m. I felt numb from my head to my feet, not knowing what to think. Naturally, my thoughts turned to my children.

"With Donnie and Patricia in jail, where are the children? I had not thought about that until just now. I'm panicked. There are seven children out there, somewhere. We know one daughter was with Donnie and Patricia at the time of the arrest. Were the other children with Garcias?"

Tom tried to calm me down.

"You know the police have already thought about this. In fact, the kids might already be with CPS tonight. We just do not know, but we cannot worry about that. Sam told the California police about the situation, so we must leave it at that. It wouldn't surprise me that Rich has put a call into them as well."

"You are right. I am concerned because we have been close before and not successful. I know this time it is different; we have the police involved, but I cannot forget the other two times when we were right there, and they slipped away! If they make bail, they'll be gone."

"Look, we'll be there tomorrow. Sam said they will not get on the court docket until tomorrow to even set bail. After that it will take them awhile to actually post bond."

"Even if Patricia gets out first, she'll be gone with the kids," I agonized.

"I know, but let's see what tomorrow brings. That's all we can do."

This was the last flight of the night headed to San Diego. The lights were low and almost everyone slept, except me. My mind kept replaying the nightmare I found myself in since April. After getting the car, we headed for the Escondido area to our motel. We drove past Garcia's before getting to the motel, arriving about 4:00 a.m. Tom crashed, but I tossed and turned. Too many things going through my mind. I just kept praying, "Lord, please let this be the trip to bring the children home. Please make this simple! I heard the Lord say, '**Remain hopeful**!' Yes, Father, with Your strength I will." I knew He had a plan.

Saturday morning Tom called Larry Dillon to see if they were going to be available all morning. Larry said they were, so we left the motel by 10:00 a.m. and headed for the storage facility to meet with the Dillon's. Walking into the office, we asked to speak with Mr. Dillon. Mrs. Dillon, Jeanie, was sitting behind the desk. After telling her who we were, you would have thought we were long lost friends. She ran around the counter and hugged both of us.

"Do you have the children?" She sounded so hopeful.

"No, I replied. We wanted to come here first and then we'll go check with the police department."

"I understand. Let me get my assistant so we can go into the apartment and talk."

Another young man came out from the office to sit at the front desk. Jeanie took us back into their home.

As Jeanie introduced us, Larry's face lit up. He jumped up from his chair and gave us a big hug. Jeanie offered us coffee and cookies, but we had just finished breakfast. Larry wanted to sit next to me on the couch, Tom and Jeanie taking chairs across from us.

"Tell me what happened."

I wanted to hear directly from him what occurred the day before. He told the story exactly as Kate had relayed.

"We were so surprised yesterday when a truck pulled up to those storage sheds. I knew exactly the sheds Mr. Garcia had rented, but I was not sure it was Donnie. That is why I decided to take a casual walk around the facility and strike up a conversation with him. He told me his friends had rented the sheds for him as he had to leave town quickly. He knew the rent was paid until the 1st of the month, but they were eager to have their things by Thanksgiving. I told him to have a good day and came back to the house. I looked at the picture again to make sure it was him. He was thinner, less hair, no beard, and was not wearing glasses but from the story he told me, I knew it was him. Kate had also told me that his appearance had changed since the picture, so I was aware that could be the case. I called the police and there were three squad cars here within minutes. Donnie and Patricia had to unload the truck to put their things back into storage. Even though they locked up the sheds I put my lock on it also. Who knows how long their things will be here now? The police gave me the keys to the truck so I could pull it out of the way. Later yesterday afternoon Mrs. Garcia walked here to pick up the keys. She told Jeanie Mr. Garcia would come after work and move the truck, which they did around 6:30 p.m."

Tom asked, "Do you know where they rented the truck?"

"I didn't study the paperwork all that well, but I thought it said San Bernardino."

"Well, I can't thank you enough for what you have done," I said.

By this time tears were in my eyes. I tried to speak more but my voice left me. Tom also thanked them so I could regain my composure. I reached into my purse and took out the cashier's check for $1,000. I handed it to Larry.

"This is what I promised."

Again, I tried to speak but could not. Larry took over for me.

"Let me share something with you," Larry said. "The first week in November Jeanie and I were sitting here eating lunch. Jeanie had just finished paying the bills for the month. We have four grandchildren ourselves, about the ages of your kids or a little older. Jeanie told me she did not know what we were going to do for Christmas this year because we did not have any extra money for Christmas presents of any kind. I told her we would just have to explain to the kids our situation and make the best of it. We did not have a choice. The Wanted Bulletin came in the mail the following day. It encouraged us to look through our records to see if a Garcia had rented a storage shed on October 17. Knowing the day was a big help. Sure enough, we 'had the goods' so to speak. I hung the Wanted Bulletin by the window so we could observe anything that looked suspicious."

"I guess God has answered both of our prayers. Now you can enjoy Christmas with your family, and I should be able to enjoy Christmas with my children."

By this time, we were all crying. I stood up.

"Thank you for everything you've done." I hugged them both. "May God truly bless you for your help."

As we left, I marveled at how God had blessed them through my circumstances. God had used me to bless them, even though I was hurting so bad. I was having a hard time processing what had just transpired. I guess I could not imagine God using me for anything good at this moment of my life, but He had.

Leaving the Dillon's, we headed for the San Diego County Sheriff's Office. Sam had directed us to ask for the Fugitive Division, where we met Officer Diane Jensen and Officer Bill May. Their desks were one in front of the other. Officer May turned his chair around, they pulled up two additional chairs and invited us to sit down. Officer May started first.

"I was on the scene when they arrested Donnie and Patricia at the storage facility. Both denied having any extra children. They pretended they did not know what we were talking about. I felt it important we keep them separated so they could not talk about a plan, although it seemed to me, they had previously talked about this, in case they ever got caught! I guess I would call it premeditated excuses. When we booked Donnie, he had two outstanding warrants: one for child stealing and the other from Medina County Texas for fraud. He did not have much on him. His driver's license had his name as D. Fitz Patrick, address of 420 Hacienda del Rio Street in San Bernardino. He said he was employed as a car salesman at Hansen Buick in San Bernardino. Outside of a couple necklaces, rings, and a box cutter, that was it. He had no money on him. He had listed the nearest relative as Patricia Schumacher. I performed the initial interview. He would not respond when I asked how he went from Donnie R. Schumacher, to Donnie R. Fitzpatrick, then to Don R. Fitzpatrick, and now D. Fitz Patrick. He did say they just moved to the San Bernardino area last month. They had just come down to San Diego for the day to get their items from storage. When asked how many kids he had, he said five.

Asking where they were, all he would say is 'I don't know.' When asked who is watching your kids, he would answer, 'They are old enough to take care of themselves.' No matter how many times I asked where his kids were, he'd say he didn't know."

Next, it was Officer Jensen's turn.

"Before I had the initial interview with Patricia, I had the opportunity to go through Patricia's purse. I found a treasure trove of information. At Patricia's disposal was six aliases': Patricia Clare Schumacher, Patricia C. Fitzpatrick, Patricia C. Sanchez, Patricia C. Patrick, Trish C. Patrick, and Patricia C. McCarthy. Home address was listed the same as Donnie's. It was interesting that the nearest relative was listed as Donnie Schumacher. I am not sure they knew which name they were supposed to be using. Patricia had received a letter from Mrs. Garcia. It was addressed to a PO box in San Bernardino. I've got the letter here in the file."

She pulled out the letter for us to read.

"It was written by Mrs. Garcia, so it contains several grammatical errors, but it has some interesting things in it."

Escondido 11-7-82

Dear Patricia & Family, we are fine so are the children. They always ask for you and the kids.

We were in San Bernardino last weekend and I stay Monday and Tuesday cleaning our house. They rented the house last Saturday. I went yesterday to Ralph's where you used to work but they did not give the check to me. The manager said that you have to go to San Diego because is already past two weeks.

Juan went to look for the car and look like somebody took it. We didn't call the police to find out what happened. I don't know what you can do about.

The lady who rented your house call me once but didn't send any money. I put the key on the kitchen counter like I told her on the phone.

We rent the truck for one day and took everything to the store place. We have to take 2 storage. One is $59.60 and the other is $23.92. The truck was $52.05. The storage is paid for this month. We have to paid ahead. The storage is located on Broadway and close to our place. Was the only one open that Sunday.

My sister-in-law phone is below. Her name is Teresa. Call her. She will know when we are going again to San Bernardino. I let her know ahead of time please say hello to all and take care.

My neighbor across the street told me that two men went to her house asking about you and the car. We were not home and the way she explains to me are the two men I see at the house the day we were moving the furniture. She said that same night a woman was park across the street for hours just watching who was coming to our house, but they didn't come here. They ask her for our phone and our hour to come home and she said if you want to find out about them go over there and ask them because I don't know anything and I didn't see anybody there. OK. I have nothing also to tell you with respect to those people. Everything is ok here. I hope it will be the same for you over there. My kids have been very nice and not tell anybody anything I explain to them and they are very cooperative.

Write soon, Anna

Officer Jensen continued, "So, from this letter, it is obvious Garcias are covering for Donnie and Patricia. Now they seem to have a relative of Garcias in San Bernardino helping them. Garcias must also be moving the end of the month. Did you go around to the neighbor's asking about the Garcias?"

Tom explained that he and the investigator had knocked on several of the neighbor's doors in October when Donnie fled with the family. As well as we had sat outside their house that Sunday night for a short time to see if there was any activity at the house. Tom also confirmed how we had posed as potential renters to get into the house on the day the Garcias were moving Donnie's things into the storage unit.

"Okay," Officer Jensen said. "Then that all makes sense. Patricia had the Lease Agreement for the Hacienda del Rio address with her, which stated they had three children. Patricia was working on a resume and had an entire list of references. She even had a psychic listed as a reference. It appeared they were both looking for employment. They must have been trying to get a loan from the Garcias. They were going to ask Mr. Garcia to keep Donnie's stereo as collateral for $1350, as well as asking for Juan's social security number. There was a note to set up a change of address card from the Escondido PO box for the Sanchez mail to be sent to Garcias. That way Mrs. Garcia could forward Patricia's child support check. They had inquired into sending the children to a private Christian school. She seemed to be studying psychic crystals and numerology. Those believing in psychic numerology think numbers, dates, and names contains energy, so a number value is assigned each letter and number. Next, a question is written, and under each question, several possible answers are listed. The answer with the highest summed number is the prediction of the question. It is all very strange. She also had a set of tarot cards in her purse. They were even contemplating driving the Blazer across the border and abandoning it for recovery. I had read all of this prior to the initial interview. During that interview Patricia was very uncooperative. She would not acknowledge any question I asked of her, even when asked the whereabouts of the children. She's a pretty tough cookie."

"So, neither one of them are telling where the seven children are?" I asked.

"That's right, we get the same answer from both of them, they don't know."

"So, it appears they're not going to talk and hope they can post bond and get out of jail before my children are located," I said. "Does this make sense to you? We have to find my children first!" I stressed. "I know how they work. If they get out, it is over, I am done, and my children are gone forever."

Officer May said, "One thing to our advantage is they missed the court docket yesterday, but they are on the docket for this afternoon. That has given us time to get facts together for the state's attorney. The judge is not going to look lightly on the fact that neither one of them is talking regarding the whereabouts of the children."

"Okay," I said. "But what if they get out after the hearing?"

"I just don't see that happening," Officer May said. "The warrant is for child stealing and being a fugitive from justice. Donnie may think he can talk his way out of it, but I doubt it."

"It's hard to believe no one can make them talk. We must find my children first. Their silence is not getting us any closer to finding the children. Where do we go from here?" I asked.

"I want you to call Child Protective Services in San Bernardino," Officer May said. "We put a call into them yesterday to go check on the children at the Hacienda del Rio address. They reported back to us that a young lady by the name of Brianna was looking after the kids and everything was fine. They did not get into the house because they did not have any legal papers. Their intent was to check on the welfare of the children."

"You mean CPS can't remove children from a situation without legal papers? You have six children under the care of a 16-year-old, and that is legal?" I did not understand.

"We have reason to believe the children are still in San Bernardino," Diane added. "Let me put another call into the San Bernardino CPS and see if we can get some help. Go back to the motel and wait for our call. There is no need for you to wait around here."

We gave them our phone number at the motel and headed out.

Tom and I understood hanging around the sheriff's office would not accomplish anything, for this case was now totally in the sheriff's control. But, going back to the motel to sit and wait was not resonating with me either. We really did not have a choice. The motel was the only place there was a phone where we could be reached in case anyone needed to get hold of us.

Once back at the motel Tom decided to play investigator. He called Hansen Buick to see if Donnie was there. They had never heard of him. In addition, he got the phone numbers for the Ryder Truck Rental facilities in San Bernardino. Impersonating as Officer May, he started calling each of them, asking if a D. Fitz Patrick had rented a truck the day before. It did not take him long to find the facility. He then asked if a red Chevrolet Blazer was sitting in front and it was! Tom was quite proud of himself. Next, the question was whether there was an APB out for the vehicle. Tom placed a call to Rich, but it was the weekend and the other partner was wearing the pager, and he did not know the facts of our case. Tom had the phone number for Century Leasing so called them to inform them where their car was located. They took our information and said they would call us back. Of course, they wanted to verify the validity of the call.

I decided to call Sam to update him on the events. I told him that Donnie and Patricia were not cooperating with the police regarding the location of the children, we were sitting in the motel waiting for the detectives to call us back, and that Tom was successful finding the location of Donnie's Blazer. At that, he totally blew up at me.

"God Damn it! What are you doing waiting around in a motel? Don't you care about finding your kids or are you only concerned about finding out what happens to Donnie next? Where are your priorities? Just go to a Five and Dime store and buy yourself a fucking toy gun and force your way into the house!"

Did I just hear that right? He wants me to get a toy gun, force myself into someone's house, and kidnap the kids! Whose house did he want us to barge into? Who, in their right mind, would suggest that? I certainly did not want to be put in jail or, worse, get shot myself. The investigating officers told us to go back and wait for a phone call, so that was what we were doing. My emotions got the best of me as I was holding back tears.

"But, Sam, that's the problem we have right now. We don't know where they are!"

"Well, do something!" he barked back and hung up the phone.

I fell apart. This trip should have been easy, but it was turning out to be another nightmare.

The phone rang. It was the state's attorney.

"I just want to let you know how the arraignment went today. They both pleaded not guilty. I told the judge they were not being cooperative in providing the location of the children. The judge asked each of them separately, once again, where the children were and they both said they did not know. Their defense attorney asked if the judge could be lenient on Patricia and let her out on her own recognizance since both parents were being held and one of them needed to be with the children. The judge asked her again where the children were, and she said she did not know. At that, the judge set bail for $11,200 each. I wish it could have been higher but considering the degree of the felony, it is pretty high."

"Thank you for letting us know. I appreciate your help," I said.

With this information we knew it bought us a few more days. Now Donnie and Patricia would be calling friends and relatives to see who would be willing to put money up for their bail.

After receiving the call from the state's attorney, we could focus our attention elsewhere. Sam's last words were to do something, so I called Child Protective Services myself, begging them to help me pick up the children. I shared with them that the sheriff's officers were sure the children were still in San Bernardino.

"Yes, I received a phone call from them this afternoon. Give me your phone number. I need to make a call first."

He called back within the half hour.

"I called our CPS attorney to see if we could help. The attorney said CPS was authorized to help in this situation. His advice is that you get a police officer to go with you to preserve the peace. All you need is the original divorce decree along with the Writ of Habeas Corpus. So, take your papers and go to the San Bernardino County Police Station. I'll give them a call and let them know you are on your way."

I looked at Tom. "Can this be it? After all this time. A police escort to the house and the children come home with us!"

"I don't know," he said. "Let's get going. It's about a 2-hour drive to San Bernardino from here."

It was an incredibly quiet trip to San Bernardino. That part of the country was new to me, so I was trying to enjoy the sights and keep my mind occupied. But, deep down, I just wanted to get my children and head home. I did not care if I ever saw California again!

When we arrived at the San Bernardino County Police Station, we gave them our names. The Fugitive Division officer was expecting us.

"Okay, do you have your papers with you?"

"I sure do," I said with enthusiasm.

"Tell me exactly where the children are supposed to be."

I gave them the Hacienda del Rio address.

"Oh, we can't help you," he said.

My heart sank.

"This address is within the city limits. You're going to have to go to the San Bernardino Police Station."

Breathe, Mary, just breathe, I had to keep telling myself. Tom could see my exasperation. He remained calm and asked for directions to the police station.

I found it difficult getting back into the car.

"Let's just see what happens," Tom kept reassuring me. "There's a difference of jurisdiction between city and county, so we have to comply."

"I know," I said, "it's just that there's a roadblock everywhere we turn."

"I realize that. But every step we take is one step closer!" he sounded optimistic.

By the time we arrived at the police station they were waiting for us. At this point, I had seen enough police stations to last a lifetime. They looked at our papers and gave us directions to a 7-Eleven convenience store at the edge of the county line. They explained that even though the house was up the foothills, there is a little area zoned there as city property. One of the sheriff's officers will meet you at 7-Eleven and take you on up to the residence. Before we left Tom mentioned the APB for Donnie's Blazer.

"Don't worry about it. We saw the APB come across and the Blazer is already in our yard."

We thanked them and left.

Following the directions, was not an easy task. By this time, it was dark and driving up into the foothills was pitch black. You could not see a street sign until it had been passed. Finally, we pulled into the convenience store and saw the sheriff's car sitting in front of the door. Tom parked alongside the car, the officer stepped out of his car, and we did as well. We introduced ourselves and he asked to see our papers. I handed him the documents.

"Okay, everything seems in order. Follow me."

We started further up the hill, around several curves in the road. By this time everything was extremely black. Finally, we turned a corner and you could see a cluster of homes. Anticipation filled my bones. I just knew this was going to be it! We had to be within a block or two of the kids. Then, the sheriff's car pulled off to the side of the road.

We pulled behind him. He got out and walked to our car. Tom rolled down the window.

"I'm sorry. I radioed in my location and my superior officer said we needed California papers before we could execute anything. I am so sorry, but we are going to have to turn around. I do not have authorization to proceed. Please follow me back to one of the main roads and I will direct you back to San Diego from there!"

We had to be within one turn of their home. But there was nothing we could do. The officer returned to his car, turned his car around, and Tom did as well. We followed him back down the hill and to a main road. Once again, he stopped, we did the same. He came back to the car. Tom rolled down his window. He handed Tom our papers, gave Tom directions to get back to I-215, and apologized. We headed back to Escondido…empty handed.

It had been an exceptionally long day. My emotions had been all over the spectrum: from being an answer to Dillon's prayers, being told to buy a toy gun and force my way to a kidnapping, and then to being told the police could not help. I did not know which was worse, being 30 minutes late from serving the Writ in Devine back in June or being within one block of the kids and not being able to pick them up! None of this made sense to me. "Lord, I just don't understand what I'm supposed to do."

13. Complications

*~ A noun referring to a circumstance aggravating
an already difficult situation ~*

Tom and I were exhausted after this day's events: arriving from Nebraska into San Diego at 4 a.m., running around San Diego all day, following up with a round trip to San Bernardino. We had not eaten since breakfast. In fact, I could hardly remember eating for two days now. I laid down but was too exhausted to sleep. In my mind I knew I was within walking distance to the children and could not complete the task. Satan continued to throw roadblocks every step of the way. I did not understand anything. Was there a lesson for me to learn? Was I the obstacle? What had the children done to deserve all the conflict they were forced to endure? What was required of me before God would allow the children to be released from Satan's grip? I was full of questions, but no answers.

Sunday, November 21, turned out to be a slow day for us. I called Arlene in the morning.

"Hi! How are things going?" I asked.

"Not very well, Donnie called last night from jail to talk with Francis to see if he'd be able to help him. I feel so sorry for my Donnie, my poor Donnie. I cannot believe he is sitting in jail. I cannot believe you did this to him! My heart goes out to him."

Did I just hear what I heard? She was so anxious for me to get the kids back, but she did not realize there would be consequences for Donnie in this entire process. Did she not realize who caused all this anguish in the first place? I knew I could not talk with her in this state of mind. It was then that I realized blood was thicker than water, no matter who or what the circumstances.

"May I speak with Francis?"

"Yes," she was glad to get off the phone.

"Hi Francis, so you did hear from Donnie last night?"

"Yes, I did," he explained. "He didn't want to talk with his mother but wanted to talk directly with me. Donnie explained that he and Patricia were in jail and he needed money, quickly. He was crying and begging. Donnie promised to pay back all the money he owed me. He also explained that since one of the warrants was for insurance fraud from the State of Texas, he was facing a possibility of extradition back to Texas to face those charges. Donnie begged me to call his Texas attorney to see if he'd represent him on that case. Do you know what that is all about?"

"Yes, when he was fired from his job in San Antonio, he had filed for unemployment benefits. While receiving those benefits, he did not report his multiple jobs he held during that time. So, he intentionally defrauded the state. That is illegal and they don't take that lightly."

"No, they don't. Donnie also told me he left his attorney owing $800 for the work he'd previously completed, so Donnie begged me to pay this bill for him so he could get representation. He sounded so desperate."

"I'm sure he is desperate. He has taken advantage of everyone he encounters and ends up owing them money."

"Just before Donnie called last night Arlene received a call from Donnie's uncle, Ken, in Washington. Donnie had called him and cried for help. Arlene said Ken told him quite frankly he could not and would not do anything to help him until the kids were returned to me. From the way Arlene explained it, Ken's response really upset Donnie, but it upset Arlene as well."

"I'm sure it did. Donnie has lied and manipulated everyone. Now, he has no one to help him."

"Well, I am unable to help him anymore than I already have. I know he will never repay everything he owes me currently. I don't know what he will do. Arlene is beside herself."

"I can understand that she is, but Donnie has created this entire mess. It never had to be this way. I hope that one day she will understand that."

"I hope so too, but until he gets out of jail, she won't even try."

"Thank you, Francis."

Without Francis or Donnie's uncle, that left Donnie with only the Garcias. And, technically, that was all Patricia had as well.

We drove back downtown to the sheriff's office. Officer Jensen was working through the weekend, Officer May was off for the next couple of days.

"Donnie and Patricia are not able to raise bond," she explained.

"That is good, isn't it? Won't this give us more time to find the children?" I asked.

"Yes, it will. They are standing firm. Even as of today, neither one of them is talking," Officer Jensen said, "so we still have the problem of not knowing where the children are being held."

"That doesn't surprise me. And to think, this could be over so quickly if they would just tell where the children can be found. I don't understand how they think they can continue this charade."

"Well," she said, "they must think one of them will get out of jail, pick up all the kids, and get across the border into Mexico."

"Let's not think along that line right now," I begged.

Officer Jensen had just confirmed the same daunting feeling that I had; if either Donnie or Patricia made it out of jail, I would never see my children again. We discussed with Officer Jensen the details of what occurred the night before during our trip to San Bernardino. Officer Jensen asked me for a description of the children, which I gave her.

"No, sorry, it's not them," she said. "Our department received a call from the San Bernardino CPS last night around 10:45 p.m. regarding two children they had just picked up. I was just wondering if they were your kids."

"Oh, if it could be that simple!" I thought.

Since we had experienced problems in San Bernardino regarding not having California papers, she recommended I talk with Judge Hartmann Monday morning, showing him my documents from Texas, to see if he would issue a California Writ of Habeas Corpus demanding the children be turned over. He was the state's domestic relations judge, so she thought he would be sympathetic. It was worth a try. It was our only hope at this point.

Since we had nothing pressing, we stopped over at the storage facility and talked with the Dillons.

"Do you have the children?" Larry asked so excitedly.

"No, neither Donnie nor Patricia are talking. They will not tell anyone, including the judge, where the kids are being held. I know they are hoping to get released before we find them. If they can, they will be gone again," I said.

Larry explained, "On Saturday afternoon Mrs. Garcia walked to the storage facility, came to the office, and asked for the keys to the Ryder truck. Later, Mr. Garcia came asking for the sheds to be unlocked. Since their name was on the original agreement, I unlocked my padlock from the sheds. Mr. Garcia loaded some things from the smaller shed and drove away. No doubt the truck had been rented for a day and here it was the following day, so someone needed to return the truck."

"I agree with you," I said. "They had to get that truck back to San Bernardino. Since they had one of the girls with them on Friday, my guess is that Mrs. Garcia followed the truck to San Bernardino, unloaded the furniture, and returned the truck for Donnie. Now, what did they do with the kids? That's the million-dollar question!"

They wished us well, one more time, and we were on our way. We had not packed that many clothes, so we had to locate a laundromat before heading back to the motel for the evening.

Bright and early Monday morning we were back at the Sheriff's Office. Tom went to the Fugitive Division to see if anything new had transpired overnight. I headed straight to see the judge. Naturally, Judge Hartmann was not in, but I was able to speak to his bailiff. I explained my situation and he looked at my papers.

"You'll have to have California papers before anything will be done," he explained.

"But California has adapted the Uniform Child Custody Act, and you're saying California won't recognize Texas papers?"

"No, I can tell you that right now, they won't."

"Okay, thank you for the information."

Feeling very dejected, I headed back to the Fugitive Division. I carried on a conversation with myself all the way there. What is the purpose of having a law clarifying that states are to have a reciprocal agreement between themselves when every state in an island unto itself? That was the same problem I had over a year ago in Nebraska. You would think in another year's time things would be different, but they were not!

By this time, we were on a first name basis with the officers. Tom had been sitting with Diane and another officer, Derek, waiting for my return. They were catching Derek up regarding our trip to San Bernardino. Diane was surprised at the response I received from the judge's bailiff. Diane called an attorney they frequently used for legal help.

"Hi Ed, this is Diane Jensen. Do you have time to meet with a couple from Nebraska trying to get her children back? They are running into some roadblocks and I thought you could sort this out."

"Sure, have them come by the office at 1:00 p.m.," he said. "They can bring me up to date and I'll see what we need."

I could not believe you could get into an attorney that fast? Diane gave us the address for Mr. Mason and we were on our way.

When we initially flew into San Diego, Friday, we had rented the car three days. That was because this was supposed to be an easy trip, just pick up the children and return home. We had plenty of time before seeing Mr. Mason so we drove back to the airport to turn in the car and rent another. This was the same situation we ran into in Texas. There was no way to extend the contract, the car had to be physically returned. Being overly optimistic Tom rented this car for one day. After all, we were going to get a California Writ of Habeas Corpus, present it before whomever was holding the children, and be on our way home.

When Mr. Mason returned from lunch, we were waiting for him. I started from the beginning highlighting the story. He had a hard time understanding why the bailiff indicated the judge would not recognize the Texas decree and writ, especially considering the Uniform Child Custody Act being adapted in California. He looked at my papers. I had a certified copy of the Decree and Separation Agreement, but I did not have a certified copy of the Writ.

"We will have to have a certified copy before any judge is even going to look at this," he explained. "I suggest you call your attorney and get copies of all the Texas orders and a certified copy of the Writ. Have him send them Next-Business-Day delivery to me, here at the office. Between San Antonio and San Diego, we should have the papers by 10:00 a.m. I will make sure the judge will be in his chambers in the morning. I should be able to slip in, present the facts, and have him sign a California Writ for us. Be at my office at 10 o'clock in the morning and we'll finish this up."

"Thank you for all your help," I said. "We'll see you in the morning."

I dreaded my next task, calling Sam. The last time I talked with him he told me to buy a toy gun and force my way into a home, some home, didn't matter! I could not wait to hear what he had to say now.

"Sam, I'm sorry to bother you but I need your help," I said, bracing myself.

"Do you have the children?" he asked.

"No, I've been to an attorney here in San Diego because the judge won't recognize the Texas Writ. The attorney is asking for copies of each of the Texas orders. He said he must have a certified copy of the Writ."

"God damn it, they shouldn't need all of this. I thought I told you to take your copy of the Writ with you."

"I did, Sam, but I never received a certified copy from you. He needs these sent out today with a guaranteed Next-Business-Day delivery."

"Jesus Christ, I don't believe this!"

"I'm sorry, Sam. Will you be able to get the copies out tonight?"

"They will be there in the morning!" I immediately heard a click on the line.

At this point everyone was beyond the point of frustration. One could look back at all the people involved and everyone was exasperated to the bone.

Tom and I were extremely disappointed as we headed back to the sheriff's office to talk with Diane. By the time we arrived she was all excited.

"While you were gone, Mrs. Garcia called the police station to say she had the children!"

"Oh, thank you Dear Lord," I thought as I exhaled slowly.

"At least they are back in Escondido! Did she indicate why she was calling you with this information?"

"No, she didn't, but you know Patricia has been in contact with her regarding bail. My guess is that Patricia wants the kids close when she is released from jail so she can pick them up and move quickly. I've got an idea," Diane said. "Let me call CPS to see if they will go with you to pick up the children."

"Great idea," I said, as hope was rising within me again.

Diane called CPS. You could tell by the expression on her face it was not good news. After hanging up she said, "They won't get involved."

"What?" I exclaimed. "Isn't that what they are supposed to do?" I questioned.

"They protect children from abusive environments. They don't deem this as abusive."

My frustration level had reached its peak, I could not hold back the tears any longer. Breathe, Mary, just breathe. My emotions would go up when I thought there was hope and then they would crash, only to start the cycle all over again.

Diane couldn't believe what was happening.

"Let me see what I can do," she said. "I want to see if I can talk with Mrs. Garcia. I will get another deputy to drive me. Tom and Mary, I'll meet you in front of this office and you can follow us to the Garcias."

We did just that. We were a block away when the deputy's car stopped. Tom stopped as well. Diane got out of the car and came to my window. I rolled the window down.

"I want you to stay right here. I don't want you parked in front of their house."

"Okay," Tom agreed.

Now, we really were within a block of the children. I could see the house!

Diane and the deputy drove up to the house, walked up the sidewalk, and knocked on the front door. They were invited in. It was not long before they came out of the house, empty handed. Diane retrieved a paper from the car and returned to the front door. She handed the paper to someone at the door and walked back to the car.

The deputy turned the car around, stopped at our car, Diane got out and walked over to Tom's window. He rolled down the window to speak with her.

"I saw no indication there were any children in the house, let alone blond-haired children. Mrs. Garcia told me that Patricia gave her instructions to pick up the children in San Bernardino but under NO circumstances was she to give the children to anyone. Mrs. Garcia took that very seriously. Mrs. Garcia said she would give up the children if she was forced to let the kids go, otherwise, she was keeping them until Patricia got out of jail. At that, we had to walk away. I did give her a paper of law concerning kidnapping and concealing a child against their will. We will have to see if she reads it. Otherwise, there is nothing further we can do without a signed California Writ. I'm sorry but we'll have to let it go."

"Thank you so much for trying. We'll have to see what tomorrow brings." I said.

At that, Diane got back into her car. They waited for Tom to turn the car around and we followed them out of the neighborhood. After a while we went our separate ways. I could not speak. I was upset and full of disappointment once again. Tom tried asking me questions but all I could do was shake my head. I could not respond. I was coming to an end.

Since it looked like we were going to be here yet another day, we made the trip back to the airport to return this car. Tom rented another car, again for only one day.

We returned to the motel. I was emotionally spent, every bone in my body ached, my arms and legs felt like they had heavy weights attached to them, my head was pounding. Tom made a few phone calls back home. The phone rang, it was Sam. Tom gave me the phone.

"We've spent all afternoon on this God damn request of yours. I consider it a big waste of our time. I cannot believe any of it will make a difference. If you would have just done what I told you in the first place, we wouldn't be doing this now!"

"Thank you, Sam, for doing this for me." I was praying the chastisement would soon be over. I could not tolerate much more of it.

"The packet has been picked up by Fed Ex and it should be in San Diego by 10 o'clock in the morning."

"I really appreciate it, Sam."

"Good luck," he said as he hung up.

I was sure Sam was hoping this would be the last request I would ever ask from him. Then I would be out of his hair. "Hm…he wished me good luck," I thought. I knew there was no luck to this. If God did not perform a miracle, it was not going to happen.

14. 11:59:59

~ The very last second before God completes His work ~

I was unable to sleep all night. These last three days had been an emotional roller coaster: ups, downs, turns, and twists. My entire body felt numb when the alarm went off. We packed up our things and checked out of the motel. Today was going to be the day. Get the California Writ signed and head home with little ones in tow.

Tom and I arrived at Ed Mason's office by 10:00 a.m. The Fed Ex package had already been delivered. Ed was busy reading through it.

"You certainly have had a lot of stumbling blocks along the way, haven't you?" he said rather surprised.

"Oh, you can certainly say that again. More than my share. Donnie basically prayed on the courts sympathy, making me look like the bad guy. He used the courts to kidnap the children."

"I'm so sorry. We have an appointment before the judge at noon. I need to know a few things before I draft the order for the writ."

He needed to know Garcia's name and address. He had gotten mine and Donnie's name from the court documents Sam sent, along with the children's names and birthdates. I asked if he needed to put the alias' for Donnie. He indicated that would not be necessary since the two warrants were issued for Donnie Schumacher. He had his office assistant draft the order. Everything looked ready to go.

Each of us left the office and met at the courthouse by 11:45 a.m. Tom and I sat in the hallway while Ed was called into the judge's chambers. After half an hour he exited, looking disappointed.

"The judge doesn't like the way the order is written. Under the circumstances he thinks it is too specific. I must go back to the office to re-draft it according to his wishes. He wants it written citing Donnie, Mrs. Juan Garcia, or any other person whose identities are unknown at this time, named as accomplices. Get yourselves a bite to eat and meet me back here at 1:30. The judge will look at the order again at that time." Ed looked at me and said, "I'm so sorry."

"Okay, if that's what we have to do. We'll meet you back here at 1:30," Tom agreed.

There was no way I could eat anything. Tom grabbed a bite and we were back at the courthouse early, waiting.

Ed was very punctual and was ready for Round Two. He was called into chambers once again. This time longer. I hoped that would be a good sign. Ed finally came out.

"I have good news and bad news. When I was presenting the facts to the judge, he started getting confused. He finally told me he did not want to make a hasty decision. He needed time to review all the documents in detail. The good news is the judge gave me a Writ for a court hearing, not the Writ itself. The bad news is that he set the court date for November 29, six days from now. Let me get you a copy of the Writ for the hearing before we leave."

I needed fresh air. Everything was closing in around me and turning black. My head was spinning. I thought I was going to faint. We seemed to always end up in this same position, just within arm's reach of the children but not able to close the deal. We had checked out of the motel. The car had to be returned tonight. It looked like it was over.

After getting the copy of the Writ hearing, Tom thanked Ed for us, for I was still unable to speak, and we headed for the sheriff's office. Bill May was back working with Diane. She had filled him in on the events over the weekend. Diane couldn't wait to hear what we had to say.

"Did you get the Writ for us?" she said excitedly.

"No," I said dejectedly. "The judge won't make a decision without time to digest the history of court orders. He wants to hear testimony, so has set Monday, November 29 for a hearing. That is six days from now."

I started crying, not just tears, it was sobs! I was unable to hold it back any longer.

"Our hands are legally tied without a signed order," Diane said sympathetically.

"I understand that. It's just that there is no money left. I cannot afford to stay until Monday. In fact, today is Tuesday and we should have left Sunday. The investigators are out of leads and I am out of money. It is over. I have not slept or been able to eat for days. Donnie wins."

Tears were streaming down my face the entire time I attempted to talk.

"This is all bullshit!" shouted Bill. "Let me see the order that was signed." I handed him the order for the hearing. He looked it over and said, "Let's go get us some kids!"

At that Bill jumped up and put on his suit jacket, Diane took his cue and did the same, and we all headed for the door.

"We'll bring our car around front. You meet us there with your car."

"All right," Tom agreed.

We were parked in front of the sheriff's office when their unmarked car pulled up. We followed them to Garcias. About one and a half blocks from the Garcia's house Bill pulls to the side of the street. Tom pulls in behind him. Bill gets out of the car and comes back to the driver's side window. Tom rolled down the window to get instructions.

"I want you guys to stay here and do not move no matter what you see happen or what you hear. Do you understand? You both have to understand this!"

Bill was profoundly serious and emphatic. He bent down further and glared directly into my eyes.

"Do you understand, Mary?"

"Yes, Sir, I understand," I said.

He got back into the car, proceeded down the street, pulled in front of the Garcia's house, and both he and Diane went inside.

After what seemed like an eternity, Diane came out of the house, walked to the car, retrieved a paper, and went back into the house. No doubt they were going to show Mrs. Garcia the paper for the Writ hearing. It could not have been another five minutes when we saw a black and white patrol car come racing down the street with the lights flashing, but no sirens. He stopped in the middle of the street, jumped out of the car leaving the door open, and ran into Garcia's home, lights still flashing. A couple minutes later, here comes another patrol car from the opposite direction, lights flashing, pulled in front of Bill's car, and that officer ran into the house, also leaving the driver's door open and the lights flashing. I was frantic but continued to pray!

An hour had passed, and we were still waiting. Nothing had moved. The patrol officers were still inside along with Bill and Diane. I was imagining the worst. My prayer to God came back to me, "If I can't get my children back just let me know they are dead." I figured they had found the children dead. I was prepared to accept that if I had to. At least, I think I was prepared to accept it!

The door opened and one of the police officers returned to his squad car. He drove our direction. When he got closer to our car he slowed down, made eye contact with me, and continued to stare until he was past. His facial expression was frozen in a cold stare, no expression whatsoever. "Oh, Lord, please be with everyone in that house!" I really did not know what to expect.

A couple minutes later the other police officer left the house. After getting into his car he turned the car around and drove past us. Just like the first, a cold, icy stare as we locked eyes. My heart was racing. Breathe, Mary, just breathe! You have come this far you can make it the rest of the way.

It was another fifteen minutes. By this time, my hands and legs were shaking like I was standing in the middle of a snowstorm without a jacket. The tips of my fingers had grown numb.

Then, the front door opened. Bill had a suitcase in one hand, and he was holding Alex's hand in the other. Bill walked down the sidewalk and helped Alex into the car!

"Tom!" I shouted, "Tom! Do you see that? They have them! That's Alex! Thank you, Jesus! Oh, God, I don't believe this! Oh God! Oh God! Sweet Jesus, they have them!"

It was only a short time when the front door opened again. This time Diane was holding little Jennifer's hand. Together they walked down the sidewalk and Diane helped her into the car! Tom grabbed my arm. Tom and I looked at each other, tears streaming down our faces!

"They have both of them!" I shouted. "I can't believe this! I can't believe this! After all this time! We have them back!"

Now my heart was pounding out of my chest, I could hardly contain myself. The tears were flowing non-stop from my eyes, only this time they were tears of joy. "Lord, I don't believe it! Thank you, Father. Thank you! Only You, Father, only You! Sweet Jesus!"

It took them a bit to get situated in the car. Bill turned the car around and headed towards us. When he got alongside our car, he did not stop but motioned with his finger for us to follow him. Tom was so nervous he struggled turning on the car key. We got turned around and fell in right behind them. Diane must have told the kids to look out the back window, that Mommy and Tom were behind them. I could see Jennifer turn around. She slowly peaked her head up, just far enough for her eyes to see us behind her. I waved. She immediately ducked back down. "Oh, Tom, she's scared," I said. She probably could not believe what she was seeing. I know for I couldn't believe what I was seeing either! Then, slowly, she peaked again. I waved. She immediately ducked back down. On the third attempt, she got up far enough that I could see her face. I waved again, and she returned a little wave. My heart was aching with joy. I could hardly contain myself in the car. It was such an intense burst of emotion; I felt like running, jumping, and shouting at the top of my lungs, all at the same time! Alex seemed to be having more problems. He was very hesitant to turn around but after Jennifer waved, I saw him turn around. He peeked above the backseat just far enough that I could see his eyes. He ducked back down before I could even wave. He was having difficulty. He tried one more time but was unable to fully comprehend our presence.

Tom continued following Bill. It seemed like we had been driving a long time. Finally, we entered a shopping mall. Bill drove to the back corner of the parking lot where there were no cars. He pulled into a parking stall and Tom pulled in beside him. I bound out of the car almost before Tom got the car turned off. I was at the back of our car when Diane helped Jennifer out of the backseat. I dropped to my knees. Jennifer raced into my outstretched arms and wrapped her arms around my neck.

"I sure did miss you, Mommy."

"Oh, Honey, I've missed you so much!"

Tears were streaming down my face. She would pull away just long enough to look at me and then she would give me another bear hug around the neck.

By this time Alex was standing at the back of Bill's car. He was very hesitant, reluctant. I could see the fear in his eyes. I held out my arms to him. He slowly walked over, and we hugged. I looked into his eyes.

"My little man, I've missed you so much! You've gotten so big!"

He pulled back a little, Jennifer was still wrapped in a bear hug.

He looked straight into my eyes and very deliberately asked, "What took you so long, Mommy?"

I was losing every bit of composure that I had left within me! I was crying so hard I could hardly get the words out, but I knew he needed an answer.

"Oh, Honey, there wasn't a day went by that I didn't look for you!"

"Mommy, I prayed every day that you'd come back!" (I caught what he was inferring by, come back.)

"Alex, I prayed everyday too, and look how Jesus answered our prayers!"

"I prayed to Jesus that I could just go home. All I wanted to do was go home."

"Honey, I kept praying that we'd find you so we could take you home!"

With that, he gave me a big hug. I knew we would be okay!

Tom was thanking Bill and Diane for all they had done. I got up, both kids clinging to my legs, and gave Bill and Diane hugs and thanked them for everything.

"There's no way we'd be standing here if it weren't for the two of you," I said. "I can't thank you enough!" I had to ask, "Why did you call the patrol officers to the house?"

Diane explained, "Mrs. Garcia claimed to not speak enough English to understand what the Writ was about. When she saw her name on the court order, she got frightened. We put out a call to anyone that could speak Spanish to help with the situation. She knew, she just pretended not to."

Bill gave Tom the kid's suitcase and gave us some stern advice.

"I want you to head directly to the airport and catch the first flight out of town. I don't care where you go, just leave as soon as you can!"

"Not a problem!" Tom answered.

"And don't worry, we'll call Ed Mason and let him know you have the children," Diane added.

We said our goodbyes and went our separate ways. I could not keep my eyes off my two beautiful children. There was no life in their eyes, neither one of them had smiled yet, but they had been through so much.

After returning the car we went into the airport to see what flights were available. There were no flights available to Nebraska, but we could get as far as San Antonio, so we booked those four tickets and then the tickets from San Antonio to Omaha the following day.

My kids looked like refugee children: extremely thin, dark circles under their eyes, sunken eyes, faces were drawn, no sparkle to the eyes, matted hair, dirty torn clothes, pants hit above the ankles, shoes were torn and scuffed, faces and hands were dirty. I did not care. They were beautiful to me. They were with me and I was taking them home!

Once the tickets were purchased the kids and I headed for the restroom. I rummaged around in my suitcase and brought out a change of clothes for each of the children. Both were very cooperative. Even the clothes I had for them were a little short. After all, it had been eight months since they left for spring break, but at least the clothes were clean. Throwing the disgusting clothes into the trash, Alex inquired.

"What are you doing throwing our clothes away?"

"You won't need those clothes anymore," I said, "we need to be clean to get on the airplane."

He was satisfied with that. Others in the restroom were giving me questionable looks, but I did not care. I had a job to do and I was on a mission. Next, we cleaned up their hands and faces. I tried to comb their hair but that was going to take a bit. It was obvious their hair had not been washed or combed in an awfully long time for they had food stuck throughout, particularly Jennifer. We did not have that much time. The children walked out of the bathroom looking totally different.

All four of us walked hand in hand to the ticketing gate, and even had time for a soda. The kid's eyes got as big as saucers when they realized they each got a soda. Tom and I had three calls to make.

Tom called his folks while I got the children settled with their drinks. Tom's folks could not believe we had finally gotten the children, thanked Tom for calling with the good news, and said to call them when we got back in town. Then I called my aunt and uncle in San Antonio to see if we could stay with them tonight. I told them it might be a late when we get there, but they did not mind. Their house was open to us no matter what time we arrived; they would be waiting for us.

My last call was to my folks.

"Mom, you aren't going to believe this, but we have the kids!"

"Oh, my, No, I don't believe it! After all this time. Oh, Thank you Jesus!"

"I know Mom, I can't believe it either. I have called Aunt Sharon and we are going to stay with them tonight. We will catch a plane to Omaha about noon tomorrow. I will call you when we get home and you can come over to see the kids. I know they will be eager to see you. They need to reconnect! I love you, Mom!" Mom was crying tears of joy.

While the kids were drinking their soda Tom and I started a running dialogue about the airplane ride, the birthday party we would have when we got home, along with Grandma and Grandpa coming to see them. Both kids seemed to start relaxing a bit.

The plane left over the dinner hour, so we were served dinner on the plane. Jennifer picked at her plate but Alex ate everything in sight. He acted like he had not eaten in months. But then, he looked like he had not eaten much in months. Both kids were terribly thin. The dark circles under their eyes were haunting.

We arrived at Aunt Sharon's and Uncle Jack's late, but they were all up waiting for us. Sharon planned a little last minute party for us. The kids seemed to enjoy that. They were still overwhelmed, no smiles yet. The children did not have pajamas, but Aunt Sharon's girls supplied some big t-shirts that worked fine. I stayed by the kid's side until each of them fell asleep. Alex started talking a little. I refused to ask any questions. If he volunteered anything, then we would talk about it. I just listened.

The following day our plane did not leave until noon, so we said our goodbyes to my aunt and uncle and decided to swing past the investigator's office. Kate was so excited to see us. She said that Rich was away from the office that morning.

"I just want to thank you for all you did to make this possible," I said.

"Mary, without you working along with us, we wouldn't have been successful. You and Tom did an amazing job assisting us!"

"Please give Rich our best and thank him, for us, for all his help. Now, you will be able to say, you have found kidnapped children. Also, I am sure I owe you folks some money. Figure it out and just let me know."

"Mary, that is not our concern right now."

With that we said our goodbyes and headed for the airport.

Tom and I continually kept talking to Alex and Jennifer. Alex was upset that he had missed the wedding. All we could tell him was that we were not sure when they would come home and wanted to be together when that day occurred. So, we talked about their bedrooms and birthday presents that had been waiting for them.

As soon as we arrived in Omaha, I called Mom to say we had made it. I told her we needed to get the kids winter coats, as they had nothing warm. That way, she had an idea about when we would arrive in Lincoln.

As soon as we stepped into the house the kids ran upstairs to their bedrooms. They could not believe they each had a room. Alex found his piggybank first and looked inside.

"We were so poor, Mommy. I'm richer than all of them!"

"I'm glad you are, Alex. Everything will be okay!"

Grandma and Grandpa arrived about fifteen minutes after we did. Oh, what a happy reunion we had! Grandma brought a birthday cake and ice cream. We had the biggest belated birthday party you can imagine! Even if it was only the six of us. The kids opened presents and ate as much cake and ice cream as their little tummies could hold. There were even smiles on their little faces already!

After putting the children to bed I sat a long time just thanking God for the miracle that He had performed. And do you know what day it was? It was the day before Thanksgiving!

EPILOGUE

There is no doubt in my mind, my children's return was a miracle given me from God. The private investigators and I had come to the end of our journey. They were out of leads and I was out of money. It came down to my trust and faith. After every door had been closed to me in California, I was in a deep state of despair. Feeling so hopeless, I did not even know how to pray anymore. But God stayed with me, picked me up into His mighty arms, and carried me along until I was able to walk independently once again. He will do the same for you. As the Bible states, "Don't be afraid. Just stand still and watch the Lord rescue you today." (Exodus 14:13)

The timely return to Nebraska with the children brought about one of the happiest and most joyful Thanksgivings ever celebrated. The Sunday following Thanksgiving my folks held an open house for all the relatives from both sides of the family, church members, and their close friends. It was a houseful of thankful, joyous people. Everyone was smiling and offering congratulations. What I noticed this time was the children adjusted easier to playing with others. It was wonderful to see them smile again. Every so often both kids would locate me and hang on my leg for a bit. I would give them a kiss or pat on the head and they would be off once more. They were just checking to see that I was still there, since for so long, they had been told I had left them.

Was I going to let this experience impact my children? Absolutely not! My only concern was for the children; that they would not be permanently scarred by this experience. Every minute of my attention was directed towards them.

My goal was to never look back but to raise the children in as normal environment as possible. I never spoke of the ordeal with my children or anyone. If the children asked about their father, I could honestly tell them I had no idea where he was. They never questioned it.

As with the initial visit, I never asked questions of them. If they asked a question of me, I did the best I could to answer. Every so often some random thought would come before them and they would share. I was shocked at what I heard, but I could not overreact. All I could do was listen.

Alex was overly concerned regarding what happened to my car. I told him I had to sell it to pay people to help me find him. He wanted to know how much it cost. I explained to him it did not matter, he was my special little boy, and I needed to find him; stressing that he was far more important than any car.

There seems to have been a lot of resentment from Patricia's kids towards Alex and Jennifer. This would only be natural. Patricia's kids kept telling Alex, "We wish both you and Jennifer were back with your mom. All you do is cause trouble at our house." Because of that, my children were picked on. The kids blamed Alex and Jennifer for moving three times in six months. When they disappeared to San Bernardino, the children were whisked off to another city; not even bothering to go back to the house for any personal items for any of the children.

In the beginning, Alex had a hard time showing love and emotion outwardly, especially towards me. One day, out of the blue, he started talking about the day the police took him and Jennifer.

"I wanted to cry when I saw you, Mommy, but I was afraid. I was afraid you would leave us again."

I responded, "It would have been okay for you to cry, Alex. If you remember, I was crying hard enough for both of us! We are together now, and I am not going anywhere. You don't have to be afraid anymore."

He would cry easily when reprimanded, even for the simplest things.

"I know you don't love me. No one loves me!" he'd say.

That would break my heart. I continually reinforced my love for him, for I knew he had been told I did not love him anymore and that is why they were with their father.

When they first moved to California, May 1982, Alex said their last name was Fitzpatrick and they changed their first names to their middle names. Then, when they went to San Bernardino their last name was Patrick. Alex said they went over and over it, again and again, just in case someone asked their name. He told us he was afraid to talk to anyone. No doubt they had all been threatened a major beating if any of them gave away their identity or location. Alex had a hard time answering anyone when asked his name.

Jennifer asked why I made her go to her daddy's house. I told her the courts made me. She told me to just lock her in her room next time; that was what her daddy did to her all the time.

Both children had a long, extensive healing period. There were little things that would come up during the day that I could deal with, but nights were the worst. Both kids did not want me to leave their bedside until they had fallen asleep. Every night one or both would have recurring nightmares. It was pretty much the same dream. Someone or something taking them and once they were away from the house the "thing" always turned into their father. It was exhausting but my heart went out to them having to relive this each night.

As soon as we returned home, I asked to be put on an extended leave of absence from work. The first of the year they wanted me to return in the worse way, but my children were not stable enough for me to leave them. The kids needed to heal and the only way that was going to happen was for me to be around them and provide stability. By the end of February, I wrote my formal resignation letter, terminating my employment. They understood. The offer was left open for me to return whenever I decided to go back to work.

Diane, the San Diego County Fugitive Investigator, would call periodically with updates. Someone paid for an attorney for Patricia. Her bond was reduced to $1100 and she was released from jail on December 6, on her own recognizance. Mateo told me Patricia's sister, from Ireland, had sent the money for bail but it got held up in the Irish Consulate in San Diego. Mateo said Patricia never bothered to tell her sister about being released without paying bail; she just kept the money. Donnie used the same attorney and his bond was lowered to $3,360. Garcias used their travel trailer and Donnie's stereo for collateral. Donnie was released on December 7. Larry Dillon called Kate to say they moved their furniture out of the storage facility December 8.

Mateo made a trip to San Diego December 6 with the intent of picking up his children from Garcias and taking them back to Arizona. His arrival coincided with Patricia's released from jail. He did get to see his kids while he was there, but he was forced to return to Arizona empty handed. This was his first visit with his children since January 1980. One night he took all the kids to dinner. Mateo said the oldest girl was dressed so poorly, he had to take her shopping before they could go eat.

My task in January was to put together a final affidavit for Sam. The figures only included the charges incurred while the children were gone, March 1982 through January 1983. Sam wanted this for his file in case there were any future encounters regarding Donnie Schumacher. It turned out to be rather staggering; a total of $23,446 in fees and expenses.

In February 1983 Patricia filed a $6,000 theft charge on the Garcias for items allegedly missing from their home after the Garcias moved them in October 1982. Donnie and Patricia were like wild animals that turn and bite you after you feed them.

As with everything else Donnie maneuvers, he seems to do whatever it takes to stay out of reach from the legal system's snare. His attorney made a plea bargain with the State of Texas, paying half the amount ($1,300) of unemployment benefits he collected, with the stipulation the other half would be paid in a year. He pleaded no contest to the child stealing charge and was placed on probation for a year. A no contest plea implies he conceded to the guilty charge without admitting guilt. Therefore, he could answer "No" on any employment application regarding prior felony convictions. Once again, he was skating along through the system. The charges against Patricia were dropped.

One question of the law that I never understood was the fact that stealing unemployment benefits from the state of Texas for eighteen weeks had a higher degree of illegitimacy than kidnapping my children for eight months. Donnie and Patricia had spent a total of sixteen days in jail for kidnapping the children. This was their only legal penalty for the kidnapping charge. I am sure, over time, they have paid dearly, for the Bible states clearly, "You will always reap what you sow." (Galatians 6:7)

In March Donnie was fired from his car salesman job when they discovered he was working under an assumed name. In this case he could not collect unemployment benefits. After losing this job, he tried selling real estate and even worked at a restaurant. Donnie had a noble career when I married him, but his lust, greed, selfishness, and deceit destroyed him.

I was extremely concerned about Alex, for he could not get past the recurring nightmares. We were recommended to a very well-known child phycologist in Omaha, where Alex was in counseling for six months. The assessment, at the end of that time, was that Alex was doing remarkably well for what he had been through. Tom and I had to constantly reinforce him that no one was coming to kidnap him. We even took Alex for an evaluation from the Child Guidance Services. At the end of this evaluation the doctor concluded the only way he would find out anything was to really push Alex, and Alex was doing so well he did not want to force him to dredge up the past. I guess I had successfully performed my nurturing job, for we only looked forward.

In July 1983 I found it necessary to go back to work. I could have called my prior employer in Omaha and they would have hired me immediately, but I wanted something closer to the children. I had been home with them seven months. They were still healing and had a long way to go, but it was time for me to help Tom with the household expenses.

In October 1983, I received a call from Donnie's mother. Our communication had been extremely limited since Donnie's arrest. She informed me that Donnie and Patricia had been separated about a month. Donnie gave his mother a sad story about not having any money and having to work two jobs. She felt so sorry for him. She just knew he had turned his life around and did not deserve this hardship. I was not sure why she called me except to convince me that he had turned over a new leaf. I knew better. He was not one to be trusted, nor was he capable of changing. Narcissists spend their lives being calculated, cold schemers.

Right after the first of the year, 1984, while sitting at work, my phone rang. Much to my dismay, it was Donnie. Instantly, my demeanor changed, and I grew extremely anxious. He was whining about going through another divorce. He said he needed my help. My help? How dare he have the audacity to ask me for help? I could not imagine what was coming next. When Patricia filed for divorce, she also filed child molesting charges on him on behalf of the girls. He was pleading with me to be a character witness for him, for he was frightened to go to jail. The net outcome of this charge was that he worked another plea bargain. He pleaded guilty and was put on probation for ten years. This man never quits. He always seemed to circumvent his punishment.

February 1984 Donnie sent a valentine's card to the kids. In the card was a note for me. He urged me to put the past behind me and move forward. He did not admit any guilt or ask my forgiveness for what he had done. The purpose of his request was asking for visitation rights, without going through the court. That was never going to happen. The only way for him to get his parental rights reinstated was to face the Texas judge.

Outside of the initial child support received in 1980 ($2,300), Donnie never paid another dime of support. Calculating support forward until the children became of age Donnie owed over $54,000 in support payments.

In 1994, fourteen years later, I shared my experience during a church service. The entire story had to be condensed into a twenty-minute talk, so only the highlights could be shared. Up to this point, the children had no idea what really happened. All they knew was that they were taken by their father and it took a great deal of effort on my part to find them. My condensed version was the only time I shared my story. All the kids were impacted by the narrative and had questions but did not fully comprehend the severity of the situation.

Once the children were on their own you would have thought this ordeal would have been behind us, but it was not. Alex was in college when he received a letter from JCPenney. He opened it to find his account was being turned over to collections. But he did not own a JCPenney credit card. Calling one of the major credit reporting agencies Alex discovered that JCPenney was only one of several in default. In fact, the creditors had already written off approximately $20,000 of bad debt. Alex told them he had no association with any of the delinquent accounts. Upon further investigation Alex discovered that Donnie, under the name of D. Fitz Patrick, used Alex's social security number to obtain credit. Alex had a mess, which took several months to clean up. He called the other two credit reporting agencies to report fraudulent activity. After that point, he froze his accounts so Donnie could not attempt that trick again.

Just recently, Alex applied for an in-store credit card, but the application was denied. When Alex asked why, he was told it was because he filed for bankruptcy in 1989. "Excuse me, Sir, but in 1989 I was thirteen years old and in the eighth grade." Enough said!

Between being such a naive farm girl when I started my first job, combined with my meek personality, I was easy prey for Donnie. He saw me as weak which set him in a position of power. He was looking for someone he could easily control. Even more enticing was the fact I had the capability of earning a decent salary. Therefore, once I accepted that first date, he became charmingly manipulative, generous, keeping the relationship moving quickly before I recognized the demons that laid deep within his soul. This explains why he turned to ice the first night of our honeymoon.

Being in a relationship like this usually ends with emotional abuse and often, physical abuse. Unfortunately, the emotional abuse has lasted all my life, impacting all my relationships. Fortunately, I never experienced physical abuse. The best thing I did was to muster enough strength to leave, but Donnie continued his control over me for many years because the scars he left within me run very deep.

Did the kidnapping experience influence me? Profoundly! To this day I have a hard time observing children being mistreated by their parents. Hearing an Amber Alert puts a knot in my stomach, and I become extremely anxious. I am unable to watch movies involving child kidnapping. Babies physically abused by a parent, or any adult, to the point of hospitalization or death, brings me to tears. Human trafficking of children and the imagined abuse they suffer provoke nightmares. These feelings never go away.

You may ask why it took so long for me to write this story. I would have to say the timing was not right. I was so busy tending to my children's pain, I never acknowledged my own pain. I buried all my insecurities and negative emotions deep within me, never allowing them to bubble to the surface. My only concern was for the children; that they would not be scarred.

I journaled frequently once the marriage started falling apart. As the legal motions and rulings started coming in, I put everything into a box. I have moved several times in the past forty years and each time I would look at this box wondering if I should dispose of it, but I could not. Since it was nicely packed, it just got thrown in with all the other boxes. But I also could not open it. This box represented fear, anger, hurt, betrayal, and bitterness. I was afraid of "the box" and what it represented. Finally, I felt a nudging from God that the time had come.

With the writing of the book, I was finally able to confess that the religious group Donnie's family was a part of was a cult. Even though I never accepted their beliefs, I was part of it by association. Since Patricia and Donnie were deep into the psychic phenomena, the dung beetle, and the "dark side" of religion, God revealed a curse had been placed on me a long time ago. Finally, I am released from all of this. I have been set free from my bondage. The chains have been broken!

My thanks to Tom for standing by me every step of that journey. During this time, he was my rock in the storm. I am sorry to say our marriage became a casualty due to this experience. From the very first day I met Tom (the day the children were not returned from the initial visit in 1980), Donnie kept me continually upset by causing conflict regarding the children. The first three years of our marriage was totally focused on the children and Donnie, not us. Donnie hovered over our lives, consumed us, and eventually destroyed us. Once again, mending the children's psyche was a full-time job. I eventually had to go back to work. Tom and I had a child. I simply did not have the capacity for everyone's demands. And, as I said, Donnie's mental and emotional abuse ran deep. My low self-esteem and distrust ran to the tips of my toes.

All three of my children are well adjusted adults, with college degrees and good professions. This book will provide my children their first glimpse of the depth of their mother's love to endure frustration and heartache while trying to protect and locate them. I gave everything to locating my children. We must continually remind ourselves, in our daily walk with God, that He gave His only son for us, and Jesus gave His life for our sins. They gave it all for us.

As Nicky Gumbel said, "Many people see only a hopeless end, but with Jesus you can enjoy an endless hope." [vii]

What a wonderful Father we have, knowing we can remain endlessly Hopeful With God.

ENDNOTES

[i] Footprints in The Sand, Mary Stevenson, 1936
[ii] TIME Magazine, "Law: Moving to Stop Child Snatching", February 27, 1978, Vol 111 No. 10
[iii] Patricia M. Hoff, The Uniform Child-Custody Jurisdiction and Enforcement Act, US Department of Justice, Office of Justice Programs, Office of Juvenile Justice and Delinquency Prevention (OJJDP), Juvenile Justice Bulletin, Dec 2001
[iv] Nebraska Child Custody Laws, statelaws.findlaw.com, Nebraska Child Custody Laws, Year Uniform Child Custody Act Adapted
[v] Texas Child Custody Laws, statelaws.findlaw.com, Texas Child Custody Laws, Year Uniform Child Custody Act Adapted
[vi] Interstate Custody Arrangements, family.Findlaw.com , Uniform Child Custody Jurisdiction and Enforcement Act: Basics
[vii] Nicky Gumbel, YouVersion, Bible in One Year, Devotional Day 213

CPSIA information can be obtained
at www.ICGtesting.com
Printed in the USA
LVHW042137131020
668666LV00002B/139

FICTION / CHRISTIAN

In a state of desperation, Mary released her children into God's hands, for she'd rather know they were dead than to never know where they were. She had run out of money and the investigators had run out of leads; all she had left was hope with God to find her missing children.

Following a disparaging marriage, she filed for divorce and relocated with her children from Texas to Nebraska to be close to her family. Shortly after the move, her ex-husband, Donnie, demanded the children return to Texas with him for a two-week visit. The thought of a two-week visit made Mary incredibly anxious given the very young ages of the children coupled with Donnie's erratic behavior towards them. However, Donnie convinced her the children would be just fine, after all, he was their father.

The reluctantly agreed upon 14-day visit turned into a 31-day nightmare. Upon their return, the mental state of her children was haunting: lifeless expressions, fear to be alone at night, nightmares, distant stares, nervous habits and anxieties. The children had clearly suffered trauma at the hands of their father. Because of their changed demeanors, Mary did everything possible to keep from sending her children again. After an 18-month legal battle between Texas and Nebraska, Mary came up short.

Mary had no choice but to follow the Texas-mandated visitation schedule, despite knowing she was sending her children into harm's way. This time, Donnie did everything to keep Mary from ever seeing her children again, including the unthinkable measure of disappearing without a trace.

tjolander.com

Cover image: © lukjonis_AdobeStock.com (storm clouds)